T0312461

Praise for Michael Stewart

'Grips the reader by the hand and refuses to let go' **Essie Fox**

'Visceral, twisting, propulsive – *Black Wood Women* begs to be devoured' **Stacey Halls**

'Complex and heartbreaking . . . an utterly compelling read'
A. G. Slatter

'*Black Wood Women* has the lived-in realism of a great and well-researched historical fiction, and distinguishes itself with its playful, inventive, and occasionally gut-wrenching storytelling'
Nick Cutter

'Modern fiction at its innovative best' **Melvin Burgess**

'Beautifully ammoniacal and intense' **Will Self**

'One of the best novels I have read in years' **David Peace**

'Dark, funny and twisted' **A. L. Kennedy**

'Bleak but wonderful' **Alan Bennett**

'As good as British fiction gets' *Loud and Quiet*

Michael Stewart is the author of three other novels: *King Crow* (winner of the *Guardian's* Not-the-Booker Prize), *Café Assassin* and *Ill Will: The Untold Story of Heathcliff*; two short story collections: *Mr Jolly* and *Four Letter Words*; two poetry collections: *Couples* and *The Dogs*; and a hybrid memoir: *Walking the Invisible: Following in the Brontës' Footsteps*.

He is also the creator of the Brontë Stones project, four monumental stones situated in the landscape between the Brontë sisters' birthplace and the parsonage where they lived, inscribed with poems by Kate Bush, Carol Ann Duffy, Jeanette Winterson and Jackie Kay.

He has written for TV, radio and stage, and is the winner of the BBC Alfred Bradley Bursary Award and the BBC Short Range film competition. His BBC Radio 4 drama *Excluded* was shortlisted for the Imison Award. He was head of Creative Writing at the University of Huddersfield for eighteen years.

Also by Michael Stewart

Walking the Invisible: Following in the Brontës' Footsteps
Ill Will
The Dogs
Four Letter Words
Mr Jolly
Café Assassin
Couples
King Crow

black wood women

MICHAEL STEWART

ONE PLACE. MANY STORIES

HQ
An imprint of HarperCollins*Publishers* Ltd
1 London Bridge Street
London SE1 9GF

www.harpercollins.co.uk

HarperCollins*Publishers*
Macken House, 39/40 Mayor Street Upper,
Dublin 1, D01 C9W8, Ireland
This edition 2024

1
First published in Great Britain by
HQ, an imprint of HarperCollins*Publishers* Ltd 2024

Copyright © Michael Stewart 2024

ISBN: 9780008596132

This book contains FSC™ certified paper and other controlled
sources to ensure responsible forest management.

For more information visit: www.harpercollins.co.uk/green

Typeset in Centaur MT Std by HarperCollins*Publishers* India

Printed and bound in the UK using 100%
Renewable Electricity at CPI Group (UK) Ltd

For Claire O'Callaghan

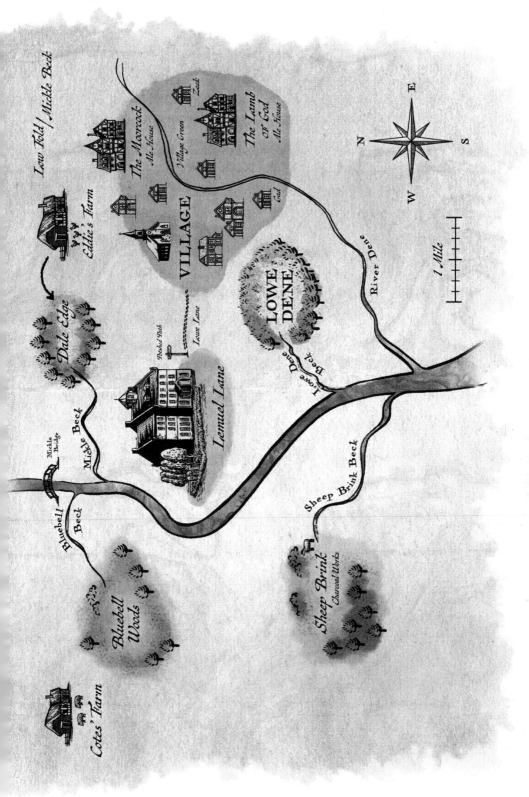

England 1649

1649 was a pivotal year in English and Irish history. On January 4 King Charles I was charged with high treason for pursuing his personal interests rather than the good of England. He was found guilty on the 27th and beheaded outside the Banqueting House in the Palace of Whitehall three days later. A republican government was formed. In March the House of Lords was abolished and in May an act declaring England to be a Commonwealth was passed by the Rump Parliament. With a renewed sense of power, Oliver Cromwell invaded Ireland in August and his conquest began. By September Cromwell had executed the last of the original 2,550 Irish Catholic defenders and their leader. The year ended with Cromwell returning from Ireland having slain fifty thousand innocent men, women and children and deported many more, who were sent as slaves to the West Indies. England was torn in two, with Royalists on one side and Parliamentarians on the other. This division formed the core of our identity: father fought son, daughter fought mother, as they took up arms against each other.

Amidst this turmoil and calamity, radical groups and dissent fomented: the Levellers, the Diggers, the Ranters, the Fifth Monarchists, the Quakers … all proposed new ways to reshape society. Members of the Family of Love believed that Heaven and Hell were to be found on Earth. The established Church was attacked: altars desecrated, rails ripped off, statues destroyed, crosses broken. Patches of England were in a state of chaos, with no firm grip on power. During this time there was a great overturning and questioning of the status quo. Old beliefs and values were challenged. The old world was 'running up like parchment in the fire'. Anything seemed possible, nothing was certain, and the old ways were turned upside down. During this chaos, innocent women were accused of witchcraft, hunted and hanged.

Most lawless of all was the North Country, the darkest corner of the land, where thousands of outlaws lurked: people who were servants to no one. In particular, the Yorkshire Fens, inhabited by water gypsies who were left to fend for themselves and no laws were enforced.

1649 was also a year of disastrous harvests: food prices rose steeply and wages lagged badly behind. People had to choose whether they ate or kept warm. Some starved to death. Roguery and villainy thrived. Many got away with murder. Folk feared to travel because of the threat of robbers. The rich lived in terror in their houses. Servant rose against his master, the tenant against his landlord, and the buyer against the seller.

But this book is not that story. This book is about the last wolf in England: of the men who put a price on its head and the women who tried to save it.

Part One

The Last Wolf

'Thou shalt not suffer a witch to live.'
Exodus 22.18

Blood Wolf Moon

Yorkshire, England: 1649

The sun is retreating from Lowe Dene. Leaves have fallen to the ground and carpet the forest with gold and copper. Through these woods a wolf moves, cat-like. Her steps are slow and silent. She stops to sniff a deer scent. Rich. Musk. Fresh. Maybe an hour old. The smell makes her hungry. She feels sharp juices squirt from the glands behind her teeth with such force that it hurts. She swallows and her gut growls. She is looking for her mate, or indeed any other wolf. She has not seen her mate for many days. And before that, when they were together, they had not seen one of their kind for many more seasons. She cannot believe that he has gone. He must be somewhere. She will find him. Her belly shelters the beginnings of life. The life they have made together. Not old enough yet to move in her womb, but she feels them grow inside her. She will keep on looking for her mate. She does not know that he is dead. There is only her and the unborn pups now. She is the last wolf in England.

She is three years old. The skin on her right hip is scarred from a wild boar gouge. Before she and her pack brought the beast down, it bit deep into her flesh. She has not eaten this day, or the day before. She should stop and rest but she must go on. She must hunt. She must feed. And then she will sleep. After this she will carry on the search for her mate. Her last meal, an emaciated rabbit, sick and lame. More bone than meat. It gave its life easily but it was a bitter breakfast. She

5

ate everything, slurped the warm blood and bile, chewed flesh, guts, sinew and fur, crunched the bones between her back teeth. All she left was the head, perfectly intact. Not a scratch on it. She can smell bittern and woodcock, badger and marten. She can smell hazel and elm, and far off, the stench of the charcoal works, where she knows not to go, for men are to be found there. Men with trap and knife and shot and bow.

Hunting on her own she is not likely to catch large prey and she resigns herself to rabbit, marten, and malkin. Deer, boar, and even sheep are a distant memory. She howls while sitting on her haunches. A single note rising sharply. She does this periodically, through the stillness. She knows her howl will not rouse the pack, but she hopes it will find the ears of her mate. She had watched her pack dwindle, retreating into the woods, away from the world of men. Men who had hunted and murdered her mother. Sometimes when she howls it is simply to cut through the loneliness that seems to seep into her marrow. As she listens to her own mournful voice, the rocks throw it back to her, and she imagines it is the voice of another.

She carries on her way, deeper into the wood. She sniffs fern and grass. Crouches low to ming by a goat willow. She is starving now. The pangs in her gut are constant. They stab and bite. Like the hunger inside her is trying to claw its way out. She has to eat, but she feels weak. And with her weakness she is less able to hunt. The hunger had at first heightened her senses — her sense of smell, the acuity of her vision — but now it dulls them. She is slowing down, becoming less alert. If she could just find some meat. The remains of a hawk kill. The remnants of a fox's supper. Even a rat.

She comes to a clearing in the wood, where the sun pokes over a dark ridge of rock. She sees a raven high up on a beech branch. She stops, watches the bird. She takes pleasure in the company of ravens.

Ravens sometimes follow her to feed on her leftovers. But sometimes they also lead her to prey. They invite her to feast first, so that she will open up the carcass for them. Sometimes they just want to play games. She is not in the mood for games. She hopes the raven senses this. The raven flies down from its perch, so that it is standing a few feet away from her, large and proud. Its slick iridescent feathers gleaming black and blue and green in the sun. It bows and bobs its head and stares, then takes flight again, landing on a lower branch. It opens its huge beak and cronks, a low hoarse rasping sound. It points to the east with its beak and takes flight again. It is beckoning her. She follows it down to a ravine, a steep clough that leads to a stream, past ragged rocks and clumps of gorse, until the raven hovers over a carcass, before landing in a nearby tree. The bird eyes her from its perch, a broad bough, asking her to get to work.

It is a sheep, fallen from the jutting promontory above. It has broken its legs and ribcage. Almost dead. She sniffs the fleece, checking to see if the sheep is diseased. It smells clean. She opens her muzzle wide and locks her jaws around the beast's neck. It flinches but she holds on harder, gripping it tight. She feels its heat and the pulse of its veins in her mouth. She bites down harder, tastes the iron of its blood. The animal gives up the fight, and she feels it soften. Her teeth pierce deep into the flesh and sinew. She rips at the meat muscle, and slurps the soups and juices of its insides. Blood drips from her chin onto her chest, staining the grey red. The flesh is warm, the blood is hot. The need to eat and feast is so strong that she forgets all else and any sense of danger. All there is in the world now is her and the meat of this sheep. She scoffs and gobbles until she is sated.

The raven perches close by, waiting for its turn. It croaks for its mate to join it. The call brings her out of her reverie. She licks her lips and slopes off to the shade beneath a sycamore. She watches as the raven, now joined by another, flies down and starts on her leftovers. The raven's mate dances on the top of the carcass. There's more than enough for them, and they pick and gobble flecks of meat and bits of sinew. She owes these birds her life. She realises now, as she lies close by licking her lips, her stomach full, her hunger replaced with satisfaction, that she was very close to death. She licks blood from her paws.

Fear, Hunger and Wretchedness

The Irish Sea: 1642

We were travelling across the Irish Sea in an open boat that groaned and creaked. It was a journey no one should ever have to make. The sea was choppy and the wind made spikes out of the waves. I stared into the terrible abyss and wondered what sharp-fanged monsters lay beneath. The ocean roared and I was sick over the side, dreadful sick, emptying everything I had into the black depths. But still I heaved, so that I thought I would turn myself inside out. Fear gripped me Somewhere amidst this wretched purging, I was aware of raised voices over the screech of gulls and the relentless screaming of the sea-wind. I knew that there was a fractious air between my kinfolk but I was too young to understand the source of the hostility.

Mammy was telling Daddy that it had been a mistake to leave Ireland and come to the enemy land. Daddy was saying that they had no choice. The man who was pursuing them would not stop until he found them, and he would not think in a million years that they would be bold enough to flee to England. To live amongst their murderers. 'It is out of the frying skittle and into the fires of Hell,' was Mammy's retort. It appeared things had got out of hand. Long-buried hatreds had resurfaced, and Daddy had done a terrible thing. They were arguing about a fella named Phelim. Mammy said he was a viperous man who wanted blood. Daddy was shouting that these things they were saying about this man were not true. As he shouted the waves crashed and the boat rocked. I tried to hide the agonising terror that raced through my veins. It felt like the sea and my kinfolk were part of the same anger.

'For the love of God, man, why did you not get a boat with higher sides?'

'Well, my love, if you remember, there wasn't what you would call a choice.'

'We're almost in the water. I feel like a frog.'

Mammy was trying to make light of it, but I could see the angst in her eyes. For days we had travelled over frozen lands to reach the sea, sleeping under the same blanket in whatever shelter we could find, eating what we could pilfer on the way, stealing the sheep's turnips and the horse's hay. The land was rocks and the air was mist. The thick shroud of milky fog hid us from our enemies, laced us from harm. We slept in beds meant for cattle, waking before dawn to be on the move again, heading east to where the land meets the ocean. We found discarded bones and sucked the marrow. Our cheeks were drawn and haggard from days of hunger. But Daddy had a plan: the man who owed him had land on the other side of this vast water. If we could get to the other side, and find the man's kinfolk, they would repay his debt, and we could start again. We would lose our accents and take on English names. I would no longer answer to Caragh. Instead, I would go by the name Kate. We would concoct a story that would explain our past and sate the curious amongst us. All that mattered was that we stayed together: me, Mammy and Daddy.

As the waves tore against the boat, crashing over and onto the deck, lacerating us like razors, me and Mammy sheltered beneath blanket and tarp, while Daddy tried to keep an even keel. Mammy was kissing my head, 'It will be all right, my baby, it will be all right.' We gripped onto the side, afraid the boat would capsize and we would perish in the cold ocean. Daddy sang us songs and told us stories from his boyhood.

How he had outrun Angus across three fields and eaten more apples than Big-bellied Brennan. Sure, he could swim this sea there and back in one go, so he could. He didn't even need a boat. We had nothing to fear. He knew where he was going all right, so he did. He had the sun and stars to guide him. He'd fished in waters worse than this and steered a boat less seaworthy than this one. He was a good oarsman, and an experienced sailor. We were not to worry. We had God on our side, sure enough. We were travelling away from the troubles and we would find somewhere in the north of the country, where people left you alone.

'They say we tortured women, drowned children, 'tis all nonsense. It is they who are the murtherers. My words are true, so help me God.' And at that Daddy looked up at the heavens to address his creator, pleading with him for justice for us and our people. He went silent for a time but I could tell that he was still agitated. He'd been ranting on and off for weeks. Hours of silence would go by, then he'd start up again, 'The things that liar said about us, so he did, that death was the least punishment we served. That our wanton cruelties could not be satiated. He's a fine one to talk. What that bastard did to our people ...' Mammy would tolerate it for so long then she would interject, 'Will you catch yourself on, in front of the bairn. Don't you think she has upset enough with you not adding to her agitation? And that language, do you wish for damnation? No good will come of it. So cease your tongue. Just get us over this wretched sea in one piece, Conall O'Fealin, that's all I ask.'

As she finished her remonstration I heard thunder crack and the low shoulder of black cloud above us broke. Rain like lead shot fell from the sky. I felt it splat onto my forehead and drip down my nose. Each drop was like an icicle. The rain soaked into my cloak and into the blanket and Mammy pulled the tarp over our heads leaving Daddy to the elements. The rain splashed onto the tarp. It felt like we were being pelted with stones. I heard Mammy mutter Hail Marys and I joined in with her as she gave me some of her rosary to hold. The boat shook, first one way then the other. I heard Daddy curse. I clung to my mother, gripping her by the waist and nuzzling my face into her shawl.

I must have somehow managed to sleep in that state of fear, hunger and wretchedness, though it was a thin and measly sleep and I woke feeling worse than before I had slept. My bones ached and my tongue cleaved to the roof of my mouth. I peeked out from beneath the tarp. There was a light on the eastern horizon, the day was dawning, and the rain had slowed to a fine sea spittle. Mammy asked how I was and stroked my head. Daddy was rowing as best he could, for the water was still very unsettled, the boat bobbing up and down. But I must have got used to it, for the sickness had passed. It had left my tongue furred, my mouth dry, and my insides hollowed.

'That no-good earl and that even less good Lord Whatnot have swindled our people, robbed them of their homes. They stop at nothing to crush us and drive us from our land. What choice did we have? I ask you.' Daddy was ranting again, though his voice was low and weary this time. Mammy let him to it. She held my hand in hers and gave it a squeeze. 'Santry, Clontarf, Bullock, Carrickfergus. Speaking trumpets in their mouths. May God strike them down for what they have done.' From the north there came a mighty wind that knocked Da off his spot. He fell down and gripped the side of the boat, but in so doing, let go of an oar. He tried to grab it but it sank.

'Oh dear God, what are we going to do now?' Mammy looked aghast and Daddy peered into the blackness, trying to discern where the oar had gone. He plunged in his fist but pulled nothing out with it. Mammy crossed herself and muttered a prayer. 'Oh, please God, don't let us die out here.' She was crying now, low and restrained. She tried to hide her sobs beneath her shawl but I could see her eyes well, then tears spilled and rolled down her cheeks. The next thing I was crying too, big gasping sobs, bawling my eyes out. Mammy held me in her arms and we cried together. The wind was getting stronger, rocking the boat one way then the other. Thunder cracked once more and the storm began again, only fiercer than the last one, the winds lancing and the raindrops tearing flesh. Daddy took a length of rope and tied one end through the empty oar loop and the other end he wrapped around all three of us and tied it off with a double knot. We were all praying now and crossing ourselves. But the rain and the wind were unrelenting.

The boat was turned about, then turned about again, tossing us up in the air and throwing us back down. The waves crashed over and the boat filled with water. I could feel the freezing water soak through my boots and through my clothes. It made me gasp. I was blasted by ocean brine and I swallowed some in error, trying to spit it out before it choked me. I clung on to Mammy with all the strength I had as the boat sank. Then we were all in the water, the boat overturned as we clung to it for dear life. The cold numbed my flesh and took my breath away. I could hardly breathe. Daddy was shouting, 'Don't let go, kick with your feet!' I did as Daddy said but it was hopeless – I could feel my legs go numb. We were all going to die out here, halfway between the home that had treated us so cruelly and the place we intended to start again. It was no use. I could feel my body giving up, surrendering to the indifferent forces all around us. I lost all sensation in my body, like I was floating above it, a detached spirit, leaving the flesh behind. *At least the fish will have some food* was my last thought, as everything turned to black.

By some miracle, we did not die, and I came round again maybe an hour or two after I had blacked out. We were all still together, tied to the boat with the rope and clinging to its rim. Daddy had me under one of his vast arms and both Mammy and Daddy were kicking. The storm had gone, the sky was slate-grey clouds in all directions, the sea as calm as I'd ever seen it. I was shivering with such violence, I could feel my bones rattle. I blacked out again. When I came round the second time, we had reached the shore and Daddy was hauling me out. We were now free of the boat, and Mammy was helping Daddy, dragging me through shallow water onto the sands. It didn't feel real somehow, like I wasn't really there. Me on my back, Daddy pressing hard against my chest, turning me on my side, saltwater spewing from my mouth. Somehow I was still alive. God had answered our prayers. God had saved us. I gasped and Mammy collapsed on top of me, kissing me and sobbing her heart out. 'Thank you God, oh, thank you Lord! I thought I'd lost her, so I did.'

The Ballad of the Bad Apple

Yorkshire, England: 21 June 1649

It was the summer solstice and Da had a plan. Da always had a plan. This plan involved the selling of his best sow, and with the money he would get more chickens, some one-a-day layers. We'd have more eggs than we could eat. Whatever we couldn't eat ourselves we could sell in the village or trade for bread, milk, meat and cheese. It would see us through the winter. And if the hens stopped laying, we could eat the hens. He knew a man in another town who would pay a good price for the sow and a farmer who would give us a lift into town. We would make a day out of it. We could go to the fair. Da would buy Ma a new dress and me a new doll. I had just turned thirteen, a little old for toys, but I didn't let on. He would treat us to pie and potatoes. Sink a few jars. It all sounded exciting, but I was sad to see the sow go. Da said you should never give an animal you might eat a name, but I had a secret name for her, Caragh. It was like I was keeping my name safe, or rather that the sow was keeping my name safe, and I was the one who fed her.

Both Ma and Da called me Kate now, even in the privacy of our own home, said it was safer that way. You never knew who was listening. We kept ourselves to ourselves mostly. Ma didn't like me mixing with the village children, so I was happy to have a day out. I could tell Ma was excited as well. She sang a song as she tidied away the breakfast things. I helped her with the chores, while Da cleaned the sow and got her ready for the sale. Seven years had passed since we had landed on the shores of this new world. It had been awful hard at first, starting again, in a foreign place, but we'd managed to settle in quite well. We each now had English names and hid our accents as best we could. I had taken to my new accent the easiest and Ma said I sounded like a native. Da's accent was passable, but there were one or two words he couldn't get right. Ma, even after seven years, struggled to shape her tongue to English sounds and in public she stayed quiet, so as not to give us away. But at home we could be ourselves, celebrate our traditions as best we could. Ma combed my hair a hundred times. I got dressed in my finest frock and Ma tied a ribbon in my hair, the same powder blue as my frock.

'There, you look like a princess.'

'Will I marry a prince, then?' I said.

Ma laughed but I knew that one day I would marry a rich man and live in a big house with servants and a stable full of horses. I didn't remember much about my life before in Ireland but I remembered the hunger and the rags and I was determined to make a better life for myself and my family.

Ma put on her lovely red dress with white frills and picked a white rose from the garden for her hair.

We all walked together, with the sow on a rope, to the farmer's house at the end of the road. There was a fire lit on the hill behind us to welcome the sun. We helped the farmer load his wares for market: boxes of sausages and pies, jars of jams and pickles. We helped the farmer and Da as they lifted the sow onto the back of the cart, then we climbed up with her. I was going to miss her. I gave her the end of a carrot I'd been saving especially. As I waved it in front of her snout she opened her mouth wide and I placed it on her tongue. She had four front teeth in the corners of her mouth that were like tusks, curling out. Two little teeth between at the front top and bottom, like a bairn's teeth. Her snout was grey and pink and wet. She snaffled the carrot then opened her mouth for more, but I didn't have anything else for her. I stroked her head. She was mainly piebald, and she had short stubby black and white hairs, with bald patches on her back where she'd rubbed herself against a tree. It was a fine morning. A clear blue sky with some wisps of white cloud here and there, and the four-hour drive passed quickly. Da told stories from his childhood, and Ma joined in. And when we weren't talking there was plenty to look at on the way. We'd never been to this town before. It was further on than the town we usually went to. It was the farmer who had made the sale. Da said he'd give him something for his troubles.

We rode past a big house with white pillars either side of a great big door, which some men were replacing. The door looked solid enough and I asked Da what the men were doing.

'Fortifications. Them that are rich live in fear of the poor. See that bell there on top of the roof?' Da pointed. 'That's to raise the alarm should they be robbed.'

It was true what Da said: everywhere you looked there were signs of tensions between those with and those without. The day before I had wandered onto the heath above the house, for I liked it up there. I'd watched a merlin perch on a withered bough, plucking feathers from the pipit in its clutches. Something has to die for something else to live. Later that same day, I'd come across a nest of vipers. One of the snakelings was eating the other. I thought back to the land of my birth. Things were just as bad there for folks like us, even worse, but at least there were no snakes in Ireland. St. Patrick had driven the lot into the sea.

After we had travelled in silence for a while, Ma asked me if I'd like to hear a story. I nodded. She wanted to know if I'd heard the story of the bad apple tree, and I shook my head, even though I had heard it.

'Very well then. Here it is … There was once a man and a woman and they had a lovely house with a garden and in the garden was an apple tree. It was wintertime and the woman said, "I can't wait till next autumn and the apples we'll have." And all year they waited. In the summer they started to grow and by autumn they were very large apples but they were misshapen and there were black marks all over them and the woman was very disappointed. The man said, "Maybe if we cut them open they will be delicious inside. They just look bad on the outside." So they plucked the apples from the tree and took them inside. They cut them open but they tasted rancid.'

'What does rancid mean?' I asked.

'Not very nice,' said Ma. 'The man said, "Maybe they are cooking apples and they will only taste good when you have sugared them and baked them." So the woman took all the bad skins off and sliced the apples. She put them in a baking dish and sugared them and cooked them in a pie in the oven. The aroma was tantalising, but when they sliced the pie open it tasted foul. The woman said, "Let's leave the apples that are still on the tree for the birds, maybe they will like them." But the birds didn't eat them, and the apples didn't fall off. Instead, they rotted on the branches, until only one apple was left. One day it snowed and covered everything except the one red apple left. The biggest raven they had ever seen landed on the tree and ate the apple. Then it fell to the ground, dead. The woman and the man went outside to see it. The raven was really a black cloak and underneath it was a woman. The woman in the black cloak stood up and hugged the woman. "Thank you so much. You have freed me. Many years ago, a witch imprisoned me inside a raven's body and I had to eat this bad apple to free myself." Then she reached into her cloak and pulled out a perfect red apple and she said, "Plant this apple and you will never be hungry." So they did, and the apple grew into a tree that bore the most delicious apples they had ever tasted. And they all lived happily ever after ...' Ma smiled. 'Did you like that story?'

I nodded. I had, in fact, heard the story several times before, but I loved it so much I wanted to hear it again. I always liked the bit when the raven turned into the woman.

It was nearly noon when we arrived at the edge of the town, and I could hear the noise of the crowd as we approached the market, past houses and cottages, up a cobbled road, to a square that was surrounded by shops and taverns. There was a church and spire at one end of the square and a town hall at the other. The square was crammed with stalls and full of people gathering round them. I could hear jaunty band music being played in the distance. The farmer pulled up his cart and we climbed off, and we all helped with the sow. She weighed a tonne but didn't mind us lifting her. She groaned a little as we placed her on the ground. It had been my job to feed her and she had got to know me really well, running as fast as her little legs could carry her when she saw me from the top of the field. After I'd fed her I'd always spend some time with her. I'd get the brush and scratch her back for her, which she always liked, and tell her about my day, and what I planned to do later, and she'd listen with a keen ear. I'd tickle the backs of her ears and she would grunt with pleasure. Her eyes were so clear and so human, with long white eyelashes, I felt that she somehow understood me. Still, as Da said, it didn't do to get too fond of something you would be scoffing one day.

I gave her a hug and kissed the top of her head. Then I whispered in her ear, 'Goodbye, Caragh.' Da walked her on the rope to the back of the market, where there were penned animals. He and the farmer got talking to the man they had come to meet. I saw the man counting out some money, handing it to Da, shaking his hand. The farmer stayed chatting to the man, while Da walked back to where we were stood.

'Well, that's that then. We've got most of the day. The farmer said to meet us back here at six o'clock. Gives us seven hours. I've plenty of money in my purse. Let's have some fun.' He grinned at both of us. 'What do you want to do first?'

We wandered round the market. Ma bought soap and ribbons. But we mostly just enjoyed looking at all the pretty stalls and all the nice things on show. We saw a wretched beggar with his only hand held out asking for mercy. Da handed him a penny from his purse. There was a woman selling feast day spiced cakes and biscuits and Ma bought a sugared bun and split it three ways, but Da gave me his third, so that I got to eat most of it. It was so sweet it made my jaw ache. Further on, beyond the square, was an open field and in this field was a fair. A tent was in the centre and around this tent were various stalls and games. There was a tall, skinny man with long scraggy hair who held an enormous mallet in his hand. He approached Da and said, 'You're a big fella now, aren't you? Want to win a shilling?' He showed Da that if he could throw the hammer past a line marked on the field he would give Da a shilling. Was he man enough? Da grabbed hold of the mallet. 'Not so fast, big man, cross my palm with a penny first.'

Da dug into his purse and handed over the coin. Then he swung the hammer with all his might but it only got halfway to its target. The skinny man went to take the mallet off Da. 'Bad luck, not as strong as you thought, eh?' He winked at Da. But Da handed the man another penny, grabbed the hammer tighter and swung it with greater might. This time it landed on the other side of the line. The skinny man seemed surprised but begrudgingly handed over the shilling.

'What did I tell you? Strongest arm is my left one, I was just warming up with my right!'

He laughed as though he'd told a joke. It made my heart glad to see Da so happy. Ma was smiling too. Da gave her a kiss and ruffled my hair.

'You know, we've had some dark days, my love, but I've got a feeling that our luck has turned a corner. From now on the road will rise for us, take my word. There's just some days when everything seems right in the world. The sun shines, the boot fits, the job comes right, even the miserable old cow down the road gives you a smile. It's one of them sort of days, it is.'

We walked further into the fair, past stalls selling jewellery, pewter, bread, seals, farm tools, and rugs. Everyone seemed to be enjoying themselves, smiling and laughing. There was a man doing card tricks. He got Da to pick a card which he somehow magicked into his pocket. We watched a game of find the pea using three cups. It looked easy but we saw half a dozen lose their money thinking they knew which cup the pea was under. We must have wandered round and about for hours, when Da suggested we find a tavern and get some pies and some ale to drink.

There were three taverns positioned around the perimeter of the square, and Da said the second one looked the best as it was the busiest. 'Never argue with the crowd,' he said and he opened the door for us to enter. It was loud and bustling inside, with a thick fug of pipe smoke hanging like a cloud of mist above the people seated at tables and those gathered round the bar. Da ordered pies for each of us, ale for himself, and a glass of brandy each for me and Ma. We sat at the only free table, which was by the window and afforded us a good view of the fair and market.

We took the drink with us and waited for our food. There was a fiddle player by the fireplace belting out a tune and Da tapped his foot to the beat. He held up his ale pot. 'Cheers. To the good health of both of you. The two most important people in my life.' We held up our cups and touched his pot. 'Cheers, Da,' I said, and Ma said, 'Cheers, my love.' I sipped the brandy and it was lovely and sweet. Da supped from his pot then wiped the foam from his mouth with his shirt sleeve and grinned at both of us. 'We've made a pretty penny today. That's a good price we got for the sow, and me winning that shilling is the icing on the cake.'

The barmaid wandered over with our pies and she plonked them on the table in front of us. 'There you go, I hope you enjoy them. My mother made them fresh this morning.'

Da seemed pleased with the pies and he slipped the woman a penny for her trouble. 'Here, keep this, don't give it to the landlord.' He winked. 'It's a fine place you've got here, and that man over there can certainly play the vouyallin.' The word 'violin' was one of those words Da had never managed to say without his accent.

The barmaid put the penny in the pocket of her apron. 'Oh, you're Irish are you?'

Da shook his head. 'No. Certainly not.'

'Well, you could have fooled me. I've been to Ireland. I'd know that accent any place,' said the barmaid before disappearing into the crowd again.

'Oh, my love, please be careful. You almost gave us away there.' Ma gripped Da by the arm.

'I'm sorry, my dear. Just a little slip-up.' He gave a sheepish grin. 'Eat your pie before it goes cold.' He cut a piece from his pie and watched the steam rise. 'Second thoughts, maybe wait for it to cool!'

The pie aroma drifted up and my tummy rumbled in anticipation. I hadn't realised how famished I was. I cut into my pie in order to let it cool, and as I did I saw a big cumbersome fella make his way through the crowd. He was seeing his way over to us. He stood over Da and tapped him on the shoulder, 'My barmaid tells me you're Irish. Well, we don't serve Irish in this tavern.'

Da looked around to see if the rest had heard him. 'Sir, we don't want no trouble. We are just here to sate our bellies and slake our thirst.'

'Did you not hear me?'

'Please, sir, if you will leave us be, we will eat up and go.'

'I'll say it one last time. No Irish in this pub. I want you out of here, NOW!'

Da stood up and said to me and Ma under his breath, 'Come on, let's get out of here.'

Someone shouted, 'Irish scum!' and someone else shouted, 'Murderers! Well, who's got the upper hand now, eh? I hear we're giving your lot what they deserve.' A pot was thrown that just missed Da's head. It broke into pieces on the wall behind us. The violin player had stopped and everyone had ceased talking in their groups. The entire tavern was staring at us with hostile eyes. We tried to leave without a fuss, but a man threw a punch at Da and it hit him on the side of his head just below his ear, knocking him sideways into a table, which turned over, spilling pots of ale. There was shouting and jeering. Da was a fighting man, won many prizes for his fights, but he knew we had to just get out of this place as fast as we could. He grabbed me and Ma protectively and pushed and jostled his way through. Someone booted him in the back and it pushed him forward, dragging us with him. He kept his head down, as he tried to duck boot and fist, getting to the door and pushing us out first before slamming it behind us. We ran away from the tavern and away from the square till we were a safe distance. We stood beneath a tree, Da shaking his head, as Ma tried to nurse his wounds.

'Why is it, when things are going good, trouble has to follow a man? There seems to be no end to it.'

'Well, at least they didn't run after us. I thought they were angry enough to.'

We had done nothing wrong, but the people in that public house had wanted us dead. Their eyes had burned with hate. We sat on a bench beneath a tree waiting for the farmer. As we did we saw a horse and cart drive past with Caragh on the back, tied to a rope. She looked over to where we were sitting and gave me the most mournful look. Those eyes, so human, registered a betrayal. It took me all my strength to not burst out bawling. I swallowed down a lump in my throat and blinked away the tears.

Enemies of God

Yorkshire, England: 1 November 1649

It was the morning of All Saints' Day, in the year of our Lord one thousand six hundred two score and nine. I lay in bed staring at the sky from my window. I'd already opened the shutters and crawled back under the sheets. My breath was mist but it was warm underneath. The clouds were a dull pewter and for once it wasn't raining. It had rained almost non-stop for three weeks and the river had burst its banks and flooded a farm close by. We'd been cut off from the main road into town for two days. I saw Old Connor's field turn into a lake, and watched him opening the gates to let his horses run wild. I saw a pig swim over its sty. Birch and elm had been uprooted and blocked the road that wound south. It took a team of men all day to shift them. Even the parson rolled up the sleeves of his tunic and lent his help.

I'd been awake a while, knowing full well there was work to be done, and that work would be cooking and baking. I hated cooking. I hated baking even more. Sure, I'd rather clean the chickens out, or swill Old Connor's piggery. I had a blackness in my thoughts. Ma had let me stay up late the previous eve, for Da had been out helping to shift the stormfall.

My da had been a sailor for a time in Ireland, but had excelled at farm labour here, with him being so strong. My folk were awful proud of what they had achieved, and grateful for the trouble they had ducked back home. Although it was only a two-room cottage made from simple timbers, to us it was a palace. My ma was awful house-happy, and she kept the place spick and span. Every surface shone and every trinket glistened. My da, too, took great comfort from the beams he'd chopped and ripped and sawed from the trees surrounding our plot six winters ago. He often said that he was the only man of his name to own anything other than the hat on his head, the shirt on his back, and the boots on his feet.

Some mornings I would spring out of bed, but my thoughts lay heavy that morn and although I was not tired, I had no excitement for the day ahead. My mind was still troubled from a dark dream I'd woken from.

My da was calling my name. I let him shout four times before I called back that I was getting up. I said my three Hail Marys and climbed out of bed. I plumped the straw mattress, splashed cold water on my face. I took my blouse off the back of the chair and pulled it over my head. It needed a clean, but it was cleaner than the only other blouse I had. Later, I would go with Ma to the river to wash our laundry. I put on my grey skirts and white apron, the one with pretty flowers that Ma had embroidered in the corners, and I tied my long black hair in a bun. It needed a good brush, to be sure, but I wasn't counting knots.

When I came down into the kitchen, I saw my da was sitting at the table, sharpening his knife on a stone. He was already in his leather jerkin ready for a day of toil, Saints' Day or no, for our Holy Saints we praised in secret. I took after my da with my colouring, although his black hair was like a sheep's fleece, both beard and scalp. There was no contrivance that would pull a comb through it. Da took his knife and tested the bite of the blade on the straw All Saints trinket by his side. A neat little cross. It cut clean. My ma was standing over the stove, cooking oatcakes. Her bonny fair hair was mostly tucked under a cap.

The room was hot and smoky. My mother wiped her hands on her apron as she turned to me. 'Did you have a nice sleep-in?'

'I had a dream.'

'Don't be telling me about your weird dreams, Kate. I'm not interested. What is it with you and dreams anyhow?'

'They say you can tell a lot from dreams.'

'They do say that, love. They do.'

She took the pan off the flames and sat down at the table opposite Da.

'Me and your da have been talking, Kate. Sit down will you.'

Her tone was suddenly ominous. I did as I was instructed and sat at the only other place at the table, between the two.

'What's the matter?' I asked.

'It's not that there's a matter, love. Well, in a way there is, but—'

'What your ma is trying to say, Kate, is that we are going to have to leave this place.'

I didn't understand. We'd all worked so hard to get the house and grounds right, and my parents were so particular about what we'd achieved between us.

'But this is our home.'

'It is, love. It is. But it's not safe.'

I looked around at the heavy beams of wood and the thick wooden door, which we secured at night with a hefty jamb. I thought about where we'd come from, a flimsy hut where we'd shivered round a meagre fire with the wind blowing through the slats.

'That trip we took to town last June,' Da began, '... seems word got out. There's a man lives hereabouts. About twelve miles south-east of here, in the neighbouring parish. He's a bad man, and he wants to harm folk like us, Kate. He's possessed by the devil.'

'Who is this man?'

'He's called Mr Lane. And you remember that name.' Ma was wagging her finger.

'But all the money it's cost us?'

'There's more important things than money, Kate,' Ma said.

'Where will we go?'

'There's a place your da knows about. North-east of here. It's a place where we can be where we won't be persecuted.'

'But ... When will we go?'

'Tomorrow.'

'Tomorrow?'

I looked, first at Da, then at Ma, expecting them to crack a smile and say they were only pulling my leg. But they both nodded gravely. Da told me more about this place, a settlement by the coast, where folk of every creed lived together. A place built on love and trust. Not fear and injustice. There was a movement of people that felt differently, and the movement was growing.

'What about Mary? Will I see her again?' I said.

Mary was the only friend I had. She called me Kate like all the others but I had confided in her, told her of my past – she knew my true name. She was the only one I trusted with the truth.

'You can go over there this afternoon, to say your goodbyes.'

'But ... I don't want to go. Do we have to?'

Ma looked at Da, and turned back to me. 'I'm afraid we do, love. If there was any other way, believe me ... Sometimes in life you have to make hard decisions.' She shook her head.

'Now, don't be upsetting yourself,' Da said. I don't know if his words were addressed to me or Ma, or both of us. Ma lifted a corner of her apron and dabbed at her eyes.

'Listen carefully, Kate,' Da said. 'If anything should happen to us—'

'Like what?'

'Please. Listen. If anything should happen, go east until you get to the sea. It will take you three days to get there at least. When you do, head north for another three days. Eventually you'll arrive at a place—'

'What place?'

'The place your Da knows about,' Ma said.

Da scratched his beard, 'Remember this well, Kate. When you have walked the coast road for three days, heading north, ask for John Beck's Sheep House. Tell the people there you are looking for the safe place. They will be able to help.'

We sat in silence. I didn't know what to say to them. I felt like my world had crumbled in front of my eyes. I looked around again at the four walls and the wooden beams keeping the roof on. I'd watched Da build this home with his bare hands. The walls were without any decoration and the floor was earthen, but it was ours. We owned it, together with the land it was on. We owned this table we were gathered round, and the chairs we were sitting on. We owned the stove and next to that, the cupboard. We owned the plates and cups and bowls and baskets. We owned the knives and forks and spoons. The cansticks and the lanthorns. In the other room, a chest of drawers and two beds, mine and the bigger bed that was my ma and da's. The blankets and the wash basin. It was all ours. For the first time in our lives we owed no one.

Were we going to leave all this behind? All these things we'd worked for? Made or bought, they were our possessions. I remembered my da bartering with the farmer up the road. Him and Ma carrying the chest of drawers over his field, with me walking behind, unsteadily, trying to keep a grip of the three drawers we'd taken out of it.

Ma got to her feet and went over to the stove. She returned the pan to the flame.

'Now these are nearly ready, can you fetch us some eggs? Your father's already let the birds out.'

I looked over to my father, who was now once again absorbed by the task of sharpening his blade. I noticed, only now, as he turned to face the light, a cut above his eye.

'Was that from last night, Da?' I said, pointing to the wound.

'I was hit by a branch. It's just a scratch.'

'Come on, child, will you not get those eggs? Oatcakes on their own are a paltry start to the day.'

I took the basket out from the cupboard and walked into the garden. The sun was rising over Hanging Fall Woods, but a mist clung to the trees like lace. I passed the hawthorn hedge, frosted with webs and red berries. The chicken shed was in the shadow of a sycamore, past a bed of vegetables and a neat stack of chopped wood. The door was unlatched. We kept them locked away at night, safe from Mr Fox. A fox will always kill every chicken there is, if there be a dozen or three score and ten, it's no matter to Reynard, whether he has an appetite for them or not. But it didn't do to keep them locked away once the sun came up, as they'd get all agitated and start pecking at each other. You could hear them inside, making an awful quarrel. Then you'd unlatch the door and let them free and the chickens would march out, clucking and strutting, proud as you like. They always made me smile the way they did that. I walked towards them, swinging my basket. When they spotted me approaching, some of them strutted towards me. Others ignored me, preferring instead to scratch at the earth, and peck about. They liked to turn over bits of wood and stone, in the hope of finding a bug or a grub underneath. They liked worms and slugs, but only the small ones.

Inside the shed, it was cool and dark. The air was damp and tangy. I reached for a sack of corn. I delved in and threw a handful out to the dozen hens that were scratting about.

'There you are now, girls. You have a good feed.'

The corn scattered and they scrabbled around to pick up the

kernels. I reached for the eggs. About half a score, lying on the straw bedding. I held the first in my hand. It was still warm. I loaded the basket with the eggs. The last one was an odd one, very small and misshaped. It wasn't worth the effort to cook it, but I put it in the basket all the same. Ma liked to look at these bad eggs. She put them on the window ledge. Said it was bad luck to get three in a row, and that I was to always bring them to her. She said you were never to smash a bad egg on the first day. She was terrible suspicious. Crossed herself when she saw a lone magpie, and wouldn't settle till she'd found its mate. Fretted if a black cat crossed her trail. If she spilled salt, she'd wait all day for something bad to happen. She said that Judas Iscariot knocked over a salt cellar during the last supper.

Then reality punched me in the chest once more. I'd never see these chickens again. This was the last time I would collect their eggs. Or would there be time for one more collection? I wanted to know what we were going to do with them. Maybe we could give them to Mary and her family. They'd had theirs eaten by the fox in the summer and had never replaced them. My girls were a healthy brood. Good layers, all of them. When I got back I'd ask my ma and da if it would be all right to see if she wanted them when I wandered over to their place later. I threw some more corn out, then shut the shed door. I picked up the basket once more and made my way back to the path.

As I was walking up the path back towards the house I heard first a scream, then a loud gunshot. I knew in that instant, something awful had happened. I put the basket down and, here's the thing, I didn't run. I wanted to, sure, but I just couldn't. My legs were wading through treacle. I walked like one in sleep.

As I entered the house, the first thing I saw was my father's body lying across the earthen floor. His eyes were open, staring up at the ceiling. Blood was puddling around him, oozing from his wounds. He was on his back, his chair tipped up. He was still clutching his knife. I stifled a scream. Then I saw Ma – she was tied to a chair and gagged. Her hands were bound with rope. Seven men with muskets, pistols and knives were standing in the room around her. How odd these men looked crammed into our tiny home and for a horrid moment I wanted to laugh at the absurdity of it. I couldn't take it in.

One man stood apart. He was tallest by far. Taller even than Da. More a bear than a man, with short cropped dark hair, and, like my da, a nose that had clearly been broken at one time in the past. He was dressed in sober clothes. A coarse black suit and a white shirt with a simple frill. I knew that this must be the man Da warned me of: Mr Lane. He turned to me and said, 'I denounce the celebration of Saints' Days.' He picked up the straw trinket from the table and threw it on the floor. 'This is a relic of pagan superstition. Man stands alone before his maker, with nothing but his conscience. No miracle-working effigies, chantries, confessions, or any other pious fraud.' He turned to his men. 'Have nothing but your Bible and your preacher to guide you. No props, no rituals. Make your households like so many little churches.' Then he turned back to address me. 'Caragh, your parents are enemies of God. And as enemies they must pay the price with their lives. Your father is dead. We are going to shoot your mother too.'

I stood there in shock and fear. Ice water ran in my veins. A fist tightened around my heart. Its fingers squeezed hard, blood beating in my brain. My mother was looking over to me with pleading eyes. I couldn't move or speak. My heart was being wrenched from my chest. A terrible sickness. A heaving dread. I couldn't take in the magnitude of it. The room swayed in front of me. I struggled to get my breath. Like my lungs had shrunk. It was all too much. The captain gripped the pistol and raised it to my mother's head.

I could feel something hot and wet on my cheek. I was crying. Tears were rolling down my face and neck. Stinging hot tears. I closed my eyes as the man pulled the trigger. There was a loud bang, a hot spit of blood. I opened my eyes again and saw that my mother was on the floor, blood pouring from a hole in her forehead. I looked down. My grey skirt and white apron were spattered with my mother's blood.

'It's not safe for you here. Go. And tell anyone you see that our enemies will be executed. We mean to rid this land of Papist scum. What your lot did to my kin in Ireland ... my sister almost ready to give birth. They slit her gut and ripped her baby from her womb. We mean to have their blood. We want every Papist's head on a pike. As Catholics, the land of your kin is now our land. Things may have gone all six and seven, but we will right this world again, and heads will roll. I'll be sending some more men later today to secure this place. Make sure you're gone. I can't vouch for your safety if you remain.'

And then they were marching out of the house. As they did, the leader grabbed one of the oatcakes out of the pan and took a bite.

Then it was just me in the kitchen with the bodies of my ma and da. I sat at the table and wept. My parents lay butchered on the floor. Their blood pooled around them. I could still hear the gunshot ringing in my ear, smell the acrid powder in the air, taste it on my tongue. I put my head on the table and closed my eyes. I couldn't think. I could just feel this overwhelming weight crushing me.

I don't know how long I lay there, but eventually I opened my eyes again. The bodies were still there. It wasn't a nightmare. What I'd witnessed was real and I was now an orphan. I had no one in this land to turn to. All my other kin were over the water in Ireland, in Ballina, but I had promised my parents I would never return. We arrived here with nothing. My da had toiled dawn till dusk so that he could provide for us, put a roof over our heads and food on the table. I tried to think prudently. I was alone. I had no one. Pretty soon the men would be back. If they found me they would kill me. All I knew was that I had to get out of there. I must find the safe place Da had told me about. The route took me through Hanging Fall Woods, then east till the coast, where it headed north.

I took a spade from the shed and started to dig a hole beyond the garden fence. The soil was stony and heavy from all the rain. I had to keep stopping to loosen a rock, pull it out of the ground and throw it to the side. I piled the rocks up at one end of the hole and kept on digging. A worm tumbled into the space, wriggling to find a way out. As I dug deeper, the earth became heavier and darker. I could feel its coolness, smell its mustiness. My arms ached with the effort, my palms throbbed, the skin blistering. The muscles in my back were seizing up but I dug on. My whole life gone.

When I could dig no more, I climbed out of the hole and rested. I'd dug down about four feet and my clothes were smeared with soil.

I went into the farmhouse and I took my mother by the hands. They were already cold and lifeless. Hands that had held mine so many times. Those hands would clutch no more. She was heavy, and it was hard work, dragging the body down the garden, to the place where I'd dug the hole. I dragged her to the edge and rolled her into it. Her body made a dull thud as it hit the bottom. I rested, stopping to get my breath again. I stared down at her lifeless body, lying in the black earth, with only worms for company. I thought about how alive she had been just a few hours ago. I saw her over the stove, cooking oatcakes, but now her spirit had left her body. Was she already up there, looking down on me? I tasted a tang in the air.

I went back in and took hold of my father, hugging his cold stiff body. His blood on my apron. I tried not to look at the hole in his

34

chest. Somehow he'd shrunk. I closed the lids of his eyes and kissed the cut above them.

It took me hours to drag him the short distance from the kitchen to the field behind the house, just a few inches at a time. By the halfway mark, my wrists were throbbing with the effort, and every muscle in my arms ached. I stopped for a long rest. Eventually I managed to reach the hole and he joined his wife under the ground. I stared long into that hole, at the two bodies lying side by side, like in life, only limp and cold. I was burying my parents. I was burying everything I'd ever known. There was no going back.

I looked down at my apron, it was smeared with soil, sweat and blood. I wiped my hands on the bits that were still clean, took the spade and scattered a pile of earth over them. Then another. Spade after spade I lifted until at last, the hole was filled. I patted down a mound of earth with the back of the spade. I took two sticks, fastened them with string to form a makeshift crucifix, and stuck the sharp end into the earth at the head of the grave, standing back and muttering a prayer.

'In the name of God the almighty Father, in the name of Jesus Christ, in the name of the Holy Spirit, may you rest in peace, with God in Heaven. Amen.'

I picked some branches from the rowan trees in the garden that were heavy with red berries, tied them in a bouquet, and placed the bouquet at the foot of the grave. I went to the bedchamber and filled a bag with some clothes, took off my dirty apron and changed my outer skirt. I took out my rosary beads with a small crucifix attached from the drawer. They were a gift from my mother – she herself had been given them by her mother. I placed the beads around my throat and wore them as a necklace. In the kitchen, I took the now cold oatcakes out of the pan and wrapped them with a heel of bread and lump of cheese, folding them up in a square cloth. I took some walnuts from an earthen jar and wrapped them in another cloth, placing both bundles into my bag, filled a goatskin flask with water from the jug and corked it firm. Then I walked over to the table where my da's knife gleamed and held it in my hands, felt its weight, sheathed it and placed it under my skirts, tying it to my leg with some cord. I tied a bonnet on my head and wrapped a thick shawl about my shoulders.

I piled the furniture in the middle of the room and took a rag soaked in lamp oil and lit it with a striker. As the flames built, I used it to set fire to the pile of furniture. Watching the fire take, the flames lick the table and the chairs. I wept hot tears.

Outside I went to where the chickens were clucking and scratting, took the first hen and gently tossed her over the fence, so that she was free to wander. I did this with the others, until they were all free. I took the sack of corn and tossed the contents over the fence too. Then I stood a distance away and watched the farmhouse burn to the ground. I saw the roof collapse as the flames engulfed it. Then I tightened the shawl around me, took up my bag, and started to walk away from the dying conflagration. The sky was darkening around me.

I walked through Hanging Fall Wood, following Da's route. The leaves had turned red and gold. They fluttered from the branches onto the forest floor and I mulched them with my boots. The woods were busy with squirrels, caching nuts for the winter, Jays flitted from the branches, the blue bands on their wings flashing. Finch and titmice hopped about. A woodcock furtled in the undergrowth. I thought about Mary and her family, but knew I must do as Da instructed. I must honour his wishes. According to his route, if I kept east I would come to the coast. Three days Da said, and I would reach the sea. I had no home. I had no one. And I was nothing.

Even in my great distress, my instinct to survive must have kicked in, for I found myself a safe spot, a clearing in the wood, and collected up some dry twigs and logs. I used the striker to start a fire and sat on a log and poked at the flames with a stick. Taking out the hoof of bread and the lump of cheese, I took a bite of each, and washed down with water from my flask.

Then I retched. The hot contents of my gut came spilling out and spattered all around me. I sat back down again, clutching my sides. I thought about the chickens. Would the fox already have them? Or would they make it somewhere safe? It was all out of my hands now. Only God knew their fate. As the flames died down into red coals, I wrapped the shawl around me more tightly and curled into a ball. I closed my eyes and thought about the fire I had left behind and of the men that would have found the house now gone. This gave me bitter comfort. Would they try and follow me? Would they track my path? I lay in the dark, shivering, clutching my rosary beads and praying to an indifferent god.

The Quiet Ones

Waking the next day, my mind was a blank. The sun was sifting through the autumn leaves, nuts and berries on the branches of the trees, robin, wren and throstle. I thought how beautiful it all was. Then my heart sagged as I realised who I was and why I was here.

Lying on the forest floor a time, gathering my thoughts, I ached all over – damp and cold. It felt as though the chill had wormed into the marrow of my bones. I wanted the earth to open up and swallow me into its depths. How had I survived and they had died? What had my people done to deserve their graves? I did not want to live. I lay there aching inside and out, cursing the men, and mourning my kin.

Eventually I stood to my feet and brushed off the forest debris. I was shaking. Gathering my things about me and securing them in my bag, I checked that I still had the knife strapped to my leg and recalled Da's route once more, walking towards the sun. There were boar scootling for mushrooms and acorns among the dead leaves and bronzing ferns.

The wooded grundle opened out into a field. I walked along its edge, by the side of a dry-stone wall. It had been ploughed and planted, ready for spring. Crows poked for worms in the dirt, a raven cawed high up in the boughs of an elm, rabbits hopped about, a hedgehog groped for grubs. All about me life was getting ready for winter, stocking up their stores and fattening their bellies. I had enough food for another feed, and even though I felt no hunger, I would need to find some vittles. I stooped down and filled my flask from a stream, then traversed several fields before my path climbed up onto the moors. The heather had bloomed, but there were still a few purple flowers hereabouts.

I kept eastwards as the sun rose in front of me, until it was high above my head. I watched glede and puttock rise in a gyre of midday heat. The path over the moors was hard going, lumpen and uneven, strewn with roots and tussock grass. The winds whipped my bonnet and tangled my shawl. I'd been walking for all of the morn and some of the aft, when I saw in the distance, a spire rise high above a line of trees.

My path dropped back down, through mire and meadow, field and farm, past the stench of a tan house, until I found myself on a country road, approaching a town. I saw people hereabouts. Some on foot, others on horseback. Still others in cart and carriage. I felt a cold finger on my neck, then another on my cheek. I looked up. The clouds had gathered above my head and now they were opening up. Big black drops of rain fell like stones from the clouds. Soon my shawl was soaked. And soon after that, everything else I wore. I was now at the edge of the town. A gibbet cage swung above me, with a partly tarred, half-eaten corpse inside. The eyes had been pecked out of their sockets and a jackdaw poked at the holes with its greasy black beak.

I stopped by the side of the road to rest a while and sat beneath the canopy of a tree that still had some of its leaves, watching people come and go, their mules loaded with bales of wool, earthenware jugs, sacks of turnips and potatoes. After I had rested, I got to my feet again and trudged further down the road. As I did, a man on a grey gelding rode past, so close to me that he nearly knocked me over.

'Out the bloody road!'

I fell to the ground, but then got up and attempted to wipe the mud from my knees. My legs and arms felt heavy, but I carried on along my way. I was now walking through the main street of the town. A cobblers and boot makers. A butchers and a coopers. Stalls lined the way and merchants peddled their wares. My spirit was overcome with weariness. I saw a bench close by and went over to sit on it. The rain had stopped now. A fiddle player was standing outside a hosiers and I listened to his melancholy tune – like I was hearing the sound of my own heart. I thought about those nights when Da had played his fiddle and Ma had jigged to the music. Sometimes he'd bring back other men, itinerant farm labourers, and Ma would fetch out the whisky jar. But this song was not a dancing song. By the side of the fiddle player, a man was fettered by his ankles in a wooden stocks. He stared out miserably, his face and clothes covered in shit and piss and rotten offal. There was another wretch further on, begging for pennies with the one arm he had left. He was still in his Roundhead uniform. I thought about the safe place, and recollected Da's instructions, but I couldn't recall the name. A man's name. But what? *Don't panic*, I thought. *The name will come back once you've rested.*

I watched a well-dressed man weave between the crowd and approach me. He wore an old-fashioned doublet and hose, with stiff ornamental collar. He had shiny silver buckles on his shoes. His hair was neatly shaped beneath a floppy cap. Without asking if I minded his company, he sat down beside me. I was too fatigued to be surprised by this, too weary to have my usual guard up, but as he sat there in silence, quite close to me, I regained my senses. I remembered the knife beneath my skirts.

'Good day to you, madam.'

'And to you, sir.'

He took out a pipe and knocked the bowl on the side of the bench. He started to fill it with tobacco.

'I do like the hubbub of a good market, but the price of everything now! Even a loaf of bread is becoming a luxury for some. It's not the fault of these good market people though, it's the state of this country.'

I nodded half-heartedly.

'Are you new round here?'

'Aye, sir. I'm from the neighbouring parish.'

'Thought so.'

He tamped down the tobacco, put the tin inside a pocket and took out a striker, making several attempts before the tobacco burned and he was blowing out smoke.

He lowered his voice, leant in closer and said, 'Does anyone know you're here?'

I wasn't sure what he meant by that, but I didn't like it. I knew how some parishes refused offcumdens. And I wondered if he simply meant whether I'd sought permission from a parish official.

'I have no one, sir.'

'I see.'

He seemed like a prosperous gentleman. His doublet was elaborately brocaded, so he was not without money or the means of acquiring it, and I thought that, perhaps, he could do me some good. I needed to earn some money if I was to make it all the way to the coast without starving.

'Actually, you may be able to help me.'

'How so?'

I felt nervous of asking, but my ma always said that those who don't ask don't get. So I plucked up the nerve and said, 'I'm looking for work.'

'What manner of work?'

'I can turn my hand to most tasks. I can tend fowl, fetch and carry, patch and mend. I'm a good darner. A neat sewer. I can make butter, oatcakes, cheese. I can clean.'

He finished smoking his pipe and put it in his jerkin pocket.

'I may have some work for you as it happens. Follow me.'

He stood up and offered me his hand.

We walked down the main street, weaving past the mongers and vendors, with their stalls and tables, and turned down a narrow lane.

'I've been looking for a girl like you. The work is well paid.'

We crossed the market square, and down through a flagged ginnel to the side of a public house. By the door, someone had vomited, and a dog was feasting on the remains. The ginnel opened out to a dirt track that went past the backs of houses before we came to a rather dishevelled building at the end of the track. The man approached a door with no number or adornments, and knocked hard, three times. The door opened a fraction. I couldn't see who had opened it – the gap was too narrow. The man leant into the gap and said in a low voice, 'It's only me. Open up.'

The door opened enough for us to enter, and the man led me through the doorway, closing the door behind us. We were in a darkened room. The windows were shuttered. There were tables and chairs and a bar area. The room was lit with lanthorn and candlelight and was full of men and women. The women were scantily clad. I looked around the room. As my eyes adjusted to the dark, I could make them out more fully. Some were in their undergarments, and some had no clothes on at all. It dawned on me where we were. My ma had told me of these places: we were in a bawdy house, and these women were strumpets. I backed away from the man, towards the door.

'Where are you going?'

'I think there has been a misunderstanding.'

'Don't worry, I'll look after you.'

He grabbed my arm firmly and led me through the room.

'Come on. I want to introduce you to someone.'

I tried to shake his grip. But he held me fast.

'Get off me.'

I tried again to free myself. He gripped me harder.

'No need to get shifty.'

His fist was like a vice. He dragged me down a dark corridor, then into another room, where a woman stood in the corner by the fireplace, watching. She wore a gold dress, cut low at the bosom, with her chest pushed up for emphasis. Her lips were rouged, and her cheeks powdered, big garish pearl earrings and matching pearls adorned her neck, hair twisted into ringlets. She looked too old for the clothes she wore. Her upturned nose reminded me of a suckling pig. She smiled, her eyes creasing into crow's feet. Her frog-like chin sagged with spare flesh.

'Afternoon, Annie. Got another for you.'

She walked across to where we were standing and peered at me.

'Give us a smile then.'

I was determined not to be compliant in any way. I pressed my lips together tightly. The man shoved his thumb between my lips and showed her my teeth.

'Got a full set, see.'

The woman circled me, eyeing me up and down.

'You've a nice face. Lovely eyes. Good thick hair. Needs a good brush, mind. Not much tit, but some men like that.'

She had another hard look before turning to the man, 'So where did you find her?'

'On the road, near the market. Says she's got no one.'

They started to chat about where we'd met, and how he'd come to proposition me.

'And she's from another parish you say?'

He nodded.

'Well, I've never set eyes on her.'

'There's not a bairn nor a runt, even, that you don't know about.'

'Happen so.'

She looked me over again, 'She'll need fattening up. No man wants to poke a bag of bones.'

'Whatever you think best, Annie. That's your department.'

'And she'll need a good scrub. Looks like she's been lying with the swine.'

'Whatever you say, dear.'

'Take her up to the storeroom, will you.'

I felt his grip harden as he pushed me forward, down a corridor, up a flight of winding stairs to a plain door with a hasp and padlock. He searched his pockets for a key. As he did, I saw a chance. I slipped his grip, but quick as lightning, he cracked me across the back of my head. I fell to the floor, a shooting hot pain up my spine and neck. He grabbed hold of me again.

'Do that once more, and I'll knock your block off.'

He unlocked the padlock and opened the door, then pushed me into a tiny room that was crammed with casks and barrels, baskets and boxes, with shelves above stocked with bottles and jars. The smell was both rank and sweet, like rotting fruit.

'Annie will see you right, long as you behave yourself.'

He closed the door behind me, fastening it and keying the padlock, then his footsteps faded as he walked back down the stairs. I was in darkness. I tried the door but it wouldn't budge, throwing all my weight at it, but it was no use. I shouldered it harder and heard a bone crack. I winced in pain. Groping around, I found a barrel and perched on top. I sat and waited, and as I did my eyes adjusted to the darkness. There

44

was in fact a fine crack of light around the doorframe, but not enough so that I could make anything out properly. I was just aware that some things were blacker than others and some things were less black.

I don't know how long I waited in that dusty cupboard, my heart's frantic hammer the only company I kept. As I waited my fear grew. Eventually I heard footsteps approach and the door being unfastened once more. It opened and I was first blinded by the rectangle of grey light. I saw the outline of a woman. It was Annie and she held out a tray, entering the room and placing the tray on a barrel top.

'There's meat and cheese and hot broth. You be sure to eat it all up. There's bread and butter pudding if you do.'

I looked down at the tray. There was a plate with a wedge of bread, some slices of ham and a chunk of grey cheese. By the side of this was a bowl of brown liquid, with a spoon poking out of the top.

Annie edged out of the room and closed the door, and I heard her refasten it and her steps fade away on the stairs. I was in darkness again. I groped for the bowl. Finding it, I clutched it to me and rooted for the spoon. Somehow I managed to feed myself without dropping too much of the broth. It was hot, but not scalding. It didn't taste of much but I slurped it all down. When I finished I groped for the plate and ate its contents. Then I waited. I needed to ming. My bladder ached from the pressure. The ache built into a sharp edge, like a razor blade placed between my legs. I sat there in agony, listening for footsteps, holding on as long as I could, but I couldn't keep it in any more. I felt around for the broth bowl, put it beneath me, hitched up my skirts and pissed into the pot. As I did the relief I felt was replaced by a sense of dread. Annie would punish me for this. But worse was what they had in store for me after. I needed to escape. I reached for Da's knife and retrieved it from the bindings round my thigh and clutched it tight. And waited. And waited.

Then I heard Annie's footsteps on the stairs once more. Standing up, clutching the knife behind my back, getting ready to attack, I listened to the key clunk and scrape. The door opened and I leapt forward, lunging at Annie with the knife, but she ducked out of the way and I fell onto the floor, still clutching it. I felt her booted foot stamp hard on my wrist and I screamed out in pain, as she wrestled the knife off me.

'You ungrateful little pickerel! I feed you and look after you and this is how you repay me.'

I felt her boot as she kicked me in the ribs and guts. Over and over.

I must have passed out because when I came round I wasn't in the cupboard any more. I was lying in a bed, as big a bed as I'd ever seen, and the man in the fancy suit who had brought me here was sitting in an armchair at the foot of the bed, smoking his pipe.

'You've been asleep for hours.'

The man stood up and went to the door. He opened it and hollered out of the gap, 'Annie, she's awake.'

He came back into the room and sat down in the chair.

'She's not best pleased with you, I'll tell you that for nothing.'

He puffed his pipe and blew out a cloud of blue-grey smoke. He didn't say anything after that. I lay back on the cushions, my body aching from the kicking. Pretty soon, Annie entered, shutting the door behind her and turning to the man.

'I've been thinking,' she said.

'Steady on,' the man said.

'She needs breaking in. A wild one like that, it's the best cure. I need you to help me strip her and wash her, get her ready for tonight's sport.'

'I'm wanted elsewhere.'

'It won't take long.'

The two of them looked at me like they were staring at a rabid dog. I felt sick with fear.

'I'll get her arms,' Annie said. 'You grab her legs.'

I tried to fight them off, but they were too strong for me. Abject fear gnawed my bones as they half carried, half dragged me, kicking and screaming, out of the room and down another corridor, into a room with a bath in the middle. They stripped me of my clothes and dunked me in the tepid water of the bath.

'You've made a mess of her, Annie. She's not good for renting like this.'

He pointed to the bruises where she'd booted me.

'I've thought about that. We'll offer her up as a cheap one. I've a couple of regular customers who'll be interested.'

'Well, if you're sure they'll be takers.'

'Trust me, I know my customers. Bruises or no, a cherry is a cherry. Such a pity really. If she wasn't so bruised she'd fetch a fortune. You wouldn't have what some men would pay for a strumpet's maidenhead.'

'You should have thought about that before you let your temper fly.'

She approached with a bar of soap in one hand and a scrubbing brush in the other.

'What's this?' she said, putting down the soap and brush and clutching my rosary beads. 'Bloody papist baubles!'

'Please, let me keep them,' I pleaded.

She pulled at the necklace hard, snapping the string. The beads pinged off, scattering, some in the water, some on the floor, rolling in every direction. I couldn't see where the crucifix had fallen.

'What manner of a man would want to look at the Lord Jesus nailed to a cross when he's poking a strumpet?' the woman said.

47

The man laughed. 'A proper testy one.'

'Well, a man like that can find his trifles elsewhere. This is no trugging ken. I keep a respectable house here.'

I tried to stand up. The woman slapped me hard across my face and I winced in pain. The man held my arms behind my back so I couldn't strike either of them. She scrubbed at me roughly. The bristles chafed. She splashed water all over me and scrubbed some more. She rinsed me off with clean water from a jug.

'That'll do it.'

She fetched a towel and the man pulled me out of the water. I stood shivering while she towelled me dry. She took a robe from off a hook behind the door and wrapped it round me. They led me back into the bedroom and over to the bed. The man went to the door.

'Look, Annie, I've got another appointment. Go easy on her will you.'

He closed the door behind him.

'Now, you behave yourself, and you'll have a proper good life here. Plenty of food and drink. A roof over your head. Fine clothes. You'll starve out there on your own. This world, it's no place for a girl like you. All you've got to do is lie on your back and look at the ceiling. Sound as pippin. You'll soon get into the swing of things. Now you rest up and I'll be back in a bit to see how you're getting on.'

And with that she turned to go, shutting the door behind her and locking it. I lay back on the bed. In truth, I was numb. I couldn't comprehend the event that awaited me. All that had happened to me in such a short space of time. I felt raw. The ends of my fingers shook. My bones felt like glass. I was exhausted, had no fight left. I buried my head in the pillow and quietly sobbed, crying until I had no more tears.

I went over to the door and tried the handle. It wouldn't budge. I walked over to the window and pulled back the curtain. The glass was caked in grime. I used the curtain corner to wipe it, just making out the top of a tree and a square of grey sky. I thought about smashing the pane but it was so small that I would barely fit my head through. I was trapped. I had absolutely no way out. I collapsed on the bed once more, staring at the square of light in the wall until it darkened to the colour of spilt ink.

I heard movement outside and the scraping of the key in the lock. Annie walked in holding a lanthorn in one hand and a bag in the other. Locking the door behind her, she put the lanthorn on the table and the bag on the floor. She went back to the bag and began to empty the contents onto the bed.

'I've brought a few different items. All my girls are a good deal bigger than you, so I've had a lot of trouble on to get things that'll fit. Here, try this for size.'

She threw me a light blue frock with white lace trim.

'I'm not putting that on,' I said.

'You'll do as you're bleedin' told. I've had wilful ones before, you know. It's nothing I've not dealt with. Now if you want me to slap you around again I will, it's up to you. Or we can do it the easy way.'

I was still bruised and battered and couldn't face another beating, so I took off the robe and put on the frock.

'Now, that's not too bad. I'm not saying you're fit for high renting yet, but you're fettled for a cheap one. And I know just the man. Lovely chap. He'll be here any time. Regular as clockwork, he is. He's a quick worker too. So it shouldn't be too bad. Be over in no time at all.'

She left the room again, taking the lanthorn with her, locking the door behind. I sat in darkness on the edge of the bed, everything around me a vague grey shape. I was filled with dread for what was to come next. I felt like rats were eating my entrails. I was shaking all over. I thought about screaming but I knew it would only bring me another kicking.

When Annie returned she was not alone. Voices outside the door as she took out her key.

'She's new, like I say. She's been living on the streets. Bit ragged round the edges.'

'And you're sure she's still got her cherry?'

'Oh, she's intact. Don't you worry about that, my dear.'

The door opened and in walked Annie carrying the lanthorn. She placed it on the table at the foot of the bed. The man followed her in. He looked old. Bald head and a grey beard. He wasn't much taller than Annie and slightly built. He walked with a hirple, using a heavy-headed stick to steady his way.

'Evening,' he said, as he caught up with Annie. He smiled weakly, thin lips tightening around a row of yellow teeth.

'Say good evening to this nice gentleman, child. Where's your manners?'

They both stood over me waiting for me to say something. The man placed his stick behind the chair.

'Cat got your tongue?' The man turned to Annie. 'She one of them dumb ones?'

'She's just shy. It's her first time. She'll warm up once you get her going. You'll see.'

The man nodded and unbuttoned his coat. He took it off and draped it over the back of the armchair.

'Right, I'll leave you both to it. See you downstairs in a bit.'

Annie turned around and left the room. My mind was reeling. How was I going to extricate myself? The man started to unlace his shirt, fingers stiff as he fiddled with the strings.

'Don't mind the quiet ones, so don't worry. The wife never shuts up. Nice to get a bit of peace and quiet. You don't have to say nothing.'

He took his shirt off and placed it on top of his coat. Although he was skinny, his flesh sagged and long grey hairs grew from his chest and over the top of his shoulders.

'The kitlings have left home now, so it's just me and her. When they first went, I thought, great. My life can start again now. I had all these things I were going to do. But she had other plans, didn't she? Do this, do that. Gives me a bloody list of jobs every morning. It's like being her personal slave.'

He stopped talking and sat down to take off his boots. I wanted him to keep on talking. At least while he talked I was safe from his clutches. He put his boots under the chair and started to unbutton his breeches.

'Me and her, we've not played any table sport for years. I don't know what it is, but neither of us fancy it. I play with other lasses hereabouts. Just not her. I wish, you know, that things were good between us in that area, do you know what I'm saying? But they're not, and I've given up trying to fix it. It is what it is. It were never right in that department. Of course, you don't know till yer married, then it's too late.'

He was now completely naked. I tried not to look as he approached the bed. All I could see was his wrinkly flesh and his greasy grey hair.

'I mean, a man has needs, dunt he? It's nature, do you know what I'm saying? Even the emmet has appetites.'

The bed creaked as he perched on the edge.

'I hear it's your first time. Don't worry, love. I'll be gentle. So, do you want to take that frock off and we'll get started.'

I couldn't move, frozen in terror. Every muscle in my body was screaming no.

'I'll help you with it if you like.'

He came over to me and started pulling at the frock.

'Come on, don't make it more difficult than it has to be. I'm not getting any younger you know. You'll have to help me.'

He started pulling at the hem, lifting it up. My foot was under his privates and as hard as I could, I kicked him right in the bollocks, as Ma had told me to do should this ever happen to me. He cried out in pain and doubled over. I booted him in the ball sack again, then leapt up from the bed. I grabbed the stick and brought the heavy end down onto the back of his head. He collapsed on the bed. I swung it again and struck the top of his bald pate. He collapsed further into a limp pile, like wet washing.

I ran over to the corner of the room where my shawl was and wrapped it about my shoulders. I looked for my bag, but there was no sign of it. I didn't have time to put my boots on so I grabbed hold of them and carried them instead. I snuck out of the room and along the corridor, then ran down the winding stairs. There were three doors. Which was best? I opened the first one and ran across the room, but as I did the man who had brought me here entered at the other end.

'What's all this commotion? What do you think you're doing?'

I pushed past him and through the door he'd entered. His eyes were wide with surprise. I legged it as fast as I could, running for the next door, opening it and speeding across the bar room. The man was chasing me. 'Someone grab that whore, she's running away.'

The revellers stopped what they were doing and stared at me. One woman, in nought but a necklace, lunged for me, but I dodged her grip. I leaped over the legs of a man who had his whore draped across him. He tried to trip me, but his kick fell short. I upturned a table with glasses of liquor, and heard the glass smash on the stone flags. I heard someone swear. I pushed past a big fat man who was trying to fasten his breeches. He reached for me, but I ducked. The whole place was now in a state of chaos as they stumbled and fumbled and attempted to apprehend me. Amongst the commotion, the man was still pursuing me.

'Stop her! For heaven's sake!' he cried.

I made it to the outside door and gripped the handle. The man was almost upon me as I slammed the door in his face. I sprinted up the lane. He was only a few yards behind and seemed to be gaining on me, but I didn't dare look back. I ran as fast as I could, my heart bursting with the effort. As I did, my shawl fell to the ground, but I had to leave it where it landed. Gradually, the man fell back, and by the time I got to the open street, he'd stopped entirely. I turned back to check. He'd given up, bending down, hands on thighs, panting with the effort. I carried on running.

I got to the main street and ran up its cobbles in the opposite direction to that I had entered the town. I scurried by a set of steps where a legless cripple begged for pennies and a dog sat scratching. There was enough distance between us now and I slowed down. I stopped to put on my boots, then walked out of the village, past pillars and posts, and along a wide potholed road lined with a row of oaks. It had started raining again and I dodged puddles of rainwater. By the time I was a mile or so clear of the town, I was sopping wet once more. I was exhausted. Every step was a drag, my boots getting heavier with each step. I slipped in a patch of mud, and fell backwards onto the ground. My fall was broken by the soft boggy track, and I didn't have the strength to get back up. For a while I lay there in a puddle of mud, shivering all over. I stared up at the coal black sky above and thought about my ma and da, lying side by side in a hole in the ground. I thought about my house burned to ashes and the chickens eaten by foxes. I went to clasp the rosary beads around my throat, but my neck was bare. I no longer had the comfort of them. I lay back and closed my eyes. I would stay there until a cartwheel crushed my skull.

Dirt from a Wheel Rut

As Lemuel Lane dismounted his mare and tethered her to the post by the stables, he thought he saw a shape move in the trees. The shape of a fiend or a demon, and he felt a shiver run down his spine, like a lizard or an aske was crawling across his back. But as he looked more closely he saw that it was just an old rag hanging from a broken bough, forming an almost human shape. He laughed. He was getting soft. Not even pushing forty yet. He wondered whether he should have given more direction to his men, but they knew what they had to do: to return to the O'Fealins' before dusk and secure the property for him. He had the deeds and witnesses. What was a farm labourer doing with his own plot of land in any case? The world had gone mad. The Irish, the Catholics. And what had happened to his family over there, ravaged by a bloody war since the rebellion. Bloody confederates and old English Catholics coming together like that to defeat the Protestant settlers. His people. God's people. He'd served in the parliamentary army against Charles, back in forty-two, forty-three and forty-four. At the time he'd wondered about the wisdom of going to war during harvest. Crops came before kings. But still. He'd lived on a daily ration of a pint of beans, an ounce of butter and a penny loaf. That war had made him tough, made him into the man he was, and for that he was grateful.

He'd fought hard and been rewarded for his courage and his loyalty. He'd been amongst the soldiers who baptised a horse in mockery of the sacrament, joined in as they pissed in the font. They'd shared the same vision: to pull down Babylon. They'd killed the King but what about all the bishops, archbishops and all the rest of them soul-murdering clergy cunts? To cleanse the nation of popery. That's what it was all about. But now it had got personal. Cutting off privy members, ears, fingers, hands, plucking out their eyes, boiling the heads of little children before their mothers' faces. Ripping out their mothers' bowels, stripping women naked, killing children as they were born, ripping up their mothers' bellies, ravishing wives before their husbands and virgins before their parents. And his sister, his youngest, married only two year. It was a bloodbath, make no mistake. Now he was going to feed the soil with their blood. He knew what he was doing was small beer – only a few months since Cromwell had slaughtered thousands in Ireland, cleared all the estates east of the Shannon, and twelve thousand, most of them children, had been transported to the West Indies as slaves – still, he was doing his bit. He would show them that he was capable of even more bloody acts. He was not a gentleman of ancient families and estates, but by good husbandry, clothing, and other thriving arts, he had got himself a great fortune and made himself a man of means. He would spare no pity. They either pledged fealty or they would be slaughtered like dogs.

He let the stable boy liver his horse, and he made his way across the cobbled court to the back door of his manor. Before opening the door he took another look at the estate. There was a good view from this angle, a fine abode, which he'd liberated from his enemies. A three-storey building with a turreted tower at one end. He'd been resident here since forty-five, when he'd returned from battle. The first thing he'd done was to get his servant, Jacob, to remove all the pagan trinkets and pictures, burn the lot in the courtyard. Lemuel and his family had stood and watched them turn to ash. What a stink it had made.

The estate was surrounded by walled gardens, one for flowers and one for vegetables. There was an orchard, and a good-sized stable. A main mistal and a smaller outbuilding that had been a piggery at one time, but where Lemuel now stored his gunpowder. Beyond the gardens, he owned twenty acres of farmland. He grazed beef and milch on the meadows, and grew crops: wheat, corn and barley. Yes, it was a pleasing sight to behold, his domain.

He lifted the latch on the door. He'd had the original flimsy door replaced with this one made of solid oak and studded with square-headed nails. He was taking no chances. A cannon ball would bounce off that bugger! Inside he found his wife and daughters waiting for him at the dining table. His wife, Elizabeth, who was ten years his junior, he'd known since she was just a bairn, and had loved almost as long, and his twin daughters, Catherine and Olivia, now aged fourteen, ready for a husband apiece. He saw it as his duty to find them suitable men. Men with big hearts and strong livers. He already had a few in mind, but wasn't sure yet of their character. He meant to test their mettle. Their social standing was one thing, their wealth was another, but the true measure was how firm their courage stood.

His son, a year younger than the twins, was nowhere to be seen. The boy was a wanderer, a yonderly child his mother called him. Away with the fairies, his grandmother said. But this time it was Lemuel to blame for his absence. The boy had wanted to come with him this morning and he had refused him. As he entered the room, he saw his wife look over and smile. It was a fine thing to come home to, that smile. Like a rainbow at the end of a storm. It never ceased to warm him. Catherine followed suit, but Olivia was sulking about something.

'We've been waiting for you, Lemuel. Olivia's starving. But I've told her she's not to eat before you're at the table. How did it go?' Elizabeth got up to pull his chair out for him. Kissing her on the forehead, he sat down beside her.

'We've got all the paperwork. My men are returning later to secure the timber. It'll make a nice nest for Catherine or Olivia, I've not decided who shall have it yet,' he joked, tucking in his bib.

'I don't want to live in a papist's hut,' Olivia said, without looking up. She was skewering a roll of bread with her fork.

Lemuel laughed. He wouldn't dream of giving her the cast-offs of such a lowly creature. It occurred to him, now that they were fourteen apiece, that they would benefit from some refinement. There was a boarding school for girls about thirty miles west. It was newly opened and boasted that it could provide young gentlewomen with the social graces required to attract a husband. They were also instructed in embroidery, needlework, paper-cutting, japanning, patchwork, shellwork, mosswork, featherwork, and polite conversation. A year at a place like that would do them a world of good. They would both benefit from a more eloquent tongue.

'Stop messing with that. Wait till gracing.'

Elizabeth got up and picked up a cauldron from the middle of the table. She moved over to Lemuel. It occurred to him then, as it had done on other evenings, that they should really hire a maid as well as a cook. A woman who would live with them and be able to help Elizabeth out at all times. They could afford it now. It didn't befit his wife to act as serving wench. He would make the appointment of this maid without delay.

'I saw a mouldwarp this morning, Father,' Catherine said. 'Poking about in the grass. It came up to where I was standing, bold as you like. It looked me in the eye. Like a miniature man.'

The Lord spare him this feminine prattle. He loved his home and family, but sometimes he yearned for the salty banter of the garrison.

'Where's Thomas? Still sulking?' Lemuel said, ignoring his daughter. Perhaps he should have let him come along, he was old enough now.

'He went off fishing. Said you had men enough without him,' Olivia replied.

'He spends too much time fishing.'

She passed him the pan of stew and he reached in with the ladle and served a heap into his bowl.

'You don't complain when it's on your plate.'

Elizabeth was right, the boy needed to learn the business of the estate. 'Perhaps I will take him to Cote's. There's talk of healing and settling. It's a lot of dross and dung.'

'Why can't I learn the business, Father? I can read and write,' Catherine said.

'I can write better than her,' Olivia said.

'He's not a bad lad,' Elizabeth said.

'I'm not saying he's a bad lad. I didn't say that. He's no trouble really.' Lemuel was fond of the boy but worried he was on the soft side. He turned to his girls.

'Which of you will say grace?'

'Me,' they both said at once.

'Catherine, I think it's your turn.'

Catherine gave her sister a look of victory, before pressing her palms together and lowering her head.

'Bless us, oh Lord, and these your gifts, which we are about to receive from your bounty. Through Christ, our Lord. Amen.'

'Amen.'

He blew on the stew to cool it then shovelled it into his mouth. He held a spoon like a gravedigger gripped a spade.

Elizabeth tried again. 'You could do with another pair of hands. It's time he learned the ropes.'

'It's boring being a girl. There's nothing to do. Let me come with you to Cote's Farm,' Olivia said, tearing a chunk of bread.

'I'm oldest. It should be me, not her,' Catherine said, with some justification. But it always made Lemuel smile how she'd play the trump card of being born a few minutes before her sister. And still with the sillyhow over her head. Which some said brought good hap.

'I've seen you with that Levers lad,' Lemuel said.

'They're very fond of each other. That's what I've heard,' Olivia said, still smirking. Lemuel knew that if there was one thing she enjoyed more than a hearty dinner, it was winding up her sister.

'You keep your nose out,' Elizabeth said.

'I'm only saying. They like to touch hands.'

'Well, don't.'

'As long as it's just palm pressing and nowt else?' Lemuel said.

'I swear. Nothing's gone on.'

Lemuel returned to his bowl, spooning it in and slurping it up. He dipped his bread in and chomped down on the softened crust. Joking aside, he didn't want to think of Catherine with that Levers lad. He wasn't good enough for her. He was a well-built lad, and not at all daft, but he had his sights set on someone with a bit more social status. He hadn't climbed this far to let his family slip back down again. He'd come from nothing and look where he was now, in a bloody mansion with a cook and a manservant and a stableboy, waiting on him hand and bloody foot. They'd lick his bloody boots if he asked them. He looked over to his wife who was also getting stuck into the food in front of her. She was a game lass – bagged a good 'un there, make no mistake. She wasn't just pretty to look at – though the comeliness of her body had been noted, and he often caught the lusty eyes of men fixed on her, tracing her form. She was a smart one too. Beneath a cascade of copper curls was a mind both astute and penetrating. But she was no scold. He'd never had to raise his hand to her, although, of course, he approved of a husband's power to discipline an unruly shrew, as long as he did it without excessive noise or brutishness.

He'd worked hard since the war, gaining favour with powerful men and acquiring great wealth, and it was time now to start enjoying it. He wanted more horses, racehorses. Recently he'd made friends with a silk merchant, a man named Mitchell, another keen racer. Mitchell was planning to build a shooting lodge in the neighbouring dene. He wanted it to be a calendar building with twelve bays, fifty-two doors, and three hundred and sixty-five windows. The man wanted Lemuel to invest in the scheme. Something about the audacity of the plan appealed to Lemuel. Elizabeth was not so sure. She said the man was a rake and castigated him for his dissolute ways. But surely a man who had risen from nothing and amassed a great fortune was entitled to put his feet up and enjoy the finer side to life?

His mind drifted back to the morning's work. He didn't like to make more orphans in the world, but something had to be done about these papists. They'd ravished his sister in front of her husband's eyes, then ripped her womb out, ripe with child, cut his privy member from him and fed it to a dog, before bleeding him to death. What sort of depravity sunk to those depths? It had been a mistake for his sister to go to Ireland in the first place. He'd sensed trouble rumbling way before the rebellion. All the signs had been there. But her thick-as-shit husband thought he knew better. Wouldn't listen to Lemuel. By the time he'd got wise it was too late. The King was dead. The lawmakers were fighting each other. The world was upside down. The time was ripe to act without higher dispensation. He, Lemuel Lane, would rid this land of its scourge.

He looked at his daughters. He worried about them, wouldn't ever feel settled until they were both married off. Whereas the absent

Thomas, despite being the more aberrant of his children, worried him the least. It was natural for a boy to wander, go fishing, hunting. The world was there for him to explore and conquer. The natural world was there for him to pursue and capture. One day he would hand everything over to his son. What worried him more than his itinerant spirit, was his quietness. It wasn't good for a young lad not to have friends he could hunt with, mess about with. He remembered his own childhood full of laiking: tree climbing, den building, dam making, rabbit snaring, and a million other healthy pursuits, but always with a handful of friends in tow. He'd take him to the Cotes' after dinner. He'd get his servant, Jacob, to fetch him from whatever beck he was up to his flanks in. There were plenty of trouting becks in the dene.

He supposed he'd been a bit soft with Thomas. Not like his dad, who'd hardened up Lemuel from being a pup. Every night he'd come back from the alehouse cup-shot and give young Lemuel a good hiding. Whether he needed it or not. He'd hated his father for this at the time, but he could see now that it stood him in good stead. Spare the rod and spoil the child. He'd have to toughen up his son.

Elizabeth had wanted to call their boy Lemuel, after his father. But Lemuel had been so named after his father, and he was keen to break the patronymic tradition. He had suggested Henry or James, after the last great kings of England. But Elizabeth didn't like either name. So they had settled on Thomas.

He finished eating and excused himself from the table. He went to find Jacob, who was in the yard, sweeping.

'Jacob, I need you to find the lad.'

'Where is he, sir?'

'If I knew that I wouldn't have to ask you now, would I? He's trouting. So Liz says.'

'Which beck, sir?'

'I don't know. Just bring him to me.'

He went back into the house. His men would be here soon. They were all riding out to the Cotes' Farm. The devil makes work for idle hands and God rewards honest toil. There was a spot of blood on his sleeve, so he went upstairs and changed his shirt. The dirty work was for Ezekiel and Gad. He was now in a position to offer them further responsibility. Ezekiel had been working for him on and off four year, came to him when he'd left the army. Lemuel could hardly turn him down – he owed him one. If it wasn't for Ezekiel, he'd be a dead man. Whereas this Gad chap was new. He'd come with Ezekiel a few months ago when he'd needed extra hands with the harvest, together with recommendations from the yeoman farmers where he'd worked previously. A cousin of sorts. He was always prepared to give a man a fair chance. If he didn't take it, that was his lookout. Never let it be said that Lemuel Lane was an unfair man.

Ezekiel was having a rest between digs. He stroked his ginger beard as he leaned on his spade watching Gad lunge with a mattock. The ground was surprisingly hard, given all the rain they'd had recently. It had rained so much that the only things thriving were green mould and slugs. Digging graves was hard work. He'd done his back in digging graves last year, laid in bed for two days in agony. Poor Kate, his wife, was still giving suck to their daughter, and having to nurse him too. These days he took things a bit easier, besides, Gad was five years younger than him, and a good deal taller. Not broader about the shoulders, but his bones were long and his muscles lean. He was a grafter. Ezekiel stood by his word. It was a sizeable responsibility to recommend someone to Mr Lane. Very much a double-edged sword. If his word was good, Mr Lane would always reward him, he was generous like that, but if his word had been found wanting, then Mr

Lane never forgave. Still, he'd had worse masters. Some that beat you. Some that said they'd pay you but then they'd find a reason not to pay. He was a sawyer by trade, spent many a happy year ripping and sawing timber in the saw-pit, bound by indentures for five years at thirteen that restricted his freedoms and tied him to his master. Despite this, he'd made the best of it. Got on with both freeman and bondman. His father always said, do as you're instructed, keep your head down, and do your time. That was the way to get through life.

He watched Gad drop the mattock and take up his shovel, working his tools with deft skill that only came with strength, graft and practice, his firm boot on the lug, driving the shaft deep. Gad took out heaps of earth and piled with the rest, reaching down and yanking out a large stone, hands black with muck.

He trusted Gad. Gad's sister had delivered his daughter, and Gad was kin of sorts. He was related on his father's side to Ezekiel. Gad's father was his mother's younger sister's husband. No, that wasn't right. His mother's youngest sister's husband, had a sister whose husband was Gad's father. No, that wasn't right either. It was his sister's husband's sister. He tried to work it out but it made his head hurt. He was family. That was enough. Blood was thicker than water, though you wouldn't want to drink it on a hot day.

'Nearly there now. Just another foot,' he said to Gad by way of encouragement. Then he took up his spade and helped Gad dig the last of the hole.

'Right, come on. Let's get the first.'

The two men went back into the house and came out carrying a big fat naked man who had been called, when he was alive an hour or so ago, Mr Cote.

'Jesus. He weighs a tonne.'

As they walked over the uneven land between the garden and the grave they had dug, the corpse slipped out of Ezekiel's hands and the two men dropped him. They agreed to swap ends.

'He keeps slipping through my fingers.'

'Greasy. Like an eel.'

They managed to hold on until the men approached the freshly dug grave, but as they did, they dropped him again.

'Fucking hell. He's such a fat bastard. What do you think he weighs?'

'Probably more than the two of us put together. Let's roll him the rest of the way.'

They bent down low and rolled the corpse a few feet until it rested at the lip of the hole. Then Ezekiel, using the heel of his boot, kicked it over the edge. He stared down into the hole, satisfied with the result. The other two bodies would be light work by comparison. It was always better to do the heavy lifting first. They went back to the house and went inside. When they came out this time they were carrying the corpse of a naked woman. This was Mrs Cote.

'This one's all right.'

'Light as a feather.'

'Like Jack Sprat and his wife.'

'No, that was the other way round. She was fat and he was skinny.'

This time they were able to get to the open grave without dropping the body. They tossed her in easily, where she lay on top of her husband's corpse. They rested for a minute. Ezekiel noticed that Gad had been quieter than usual. He watched him stare into the grave, as if in a daze. But it was too cold to be standing about. Besides, there was still more work to be done.

'You all right?' he said to Gad at last.

Gad nodded.

'You sure?'

Gad nodded again, but Ezekiel wasn't convinced. You had to keep your guard up with work like this. You couldn't think too much about it, or it would lay heavy on your mind. Justice had been done. That was all there was to it. Gad was still young and inexperienced. He had brawn and stamina, but maybe not the mettle needed for a job like this.

'Listen. It gets easier.'

'Can you?' He looked up and over to the house to indicate what he meant. 'I don't think I can.'

'Come on, Gad. Be a man.'

'Just this once. Please.'

Ezekiel's mind went back to the spring of sixteen forty-two, to Hull, where he'd been part of the country's largest arms magazine. King Charles had set up a Royalist court in York where loyalist courtiers with deep pockets had rushed to pledge fealty. And yet Charles' first military strike ended in failure, after he attempted to storm the magazine Ezekiel had been part of, under the command of Lemuel Lane. Thanks in part to their efforts, parliament had control of Hull. It was there he'd made his first kill, slit the throat of a lank-haired fop, watched him try and staunch the flow from the gash, clutching the slit with both hands as the blood gushed out between his fingers like uncorked claret. He remembered how that first time had weighed on his mind. He'd had nightmares about it for weeks. Perhaps he should cut Gad some slack. He and his sister had survived a recent trauma. The plague had taken Gad's parents and all his brothers and sisters except for his one surviving sister. It had practically wiped out the village. They'd been boarded up in their own house, a red cross painted on the door, a miracle to still be alive.

He bade him stay there while he returned for the final corpse. It didn't need two of them in any case. It was only the corpse of a babby.

Could lift it with one hand. He returned with it in his arms, and stood at the opposite side of the hole to Gad. He gave Gad a look before tossing the corpse into the grave. They both stood there in silence for a while, staring into the abyss of the hole they'd dug together.

'Why did we have to do that? He wasn't going to squeal. Poor lickle thing couldn't even talk. Still shitting his pants.'

'Look, the way I see it, it's kinder in the long run. It would have only starved without its mam and dad.'

But Gad did not respond and the two men carried on staring into the hole in silence. At last Ezekiel took up his spade and began to fill it in. Gad joined in and they quickly concealed their work. It was best not to think about it. Physical work could be tough, but work that got into your head, that was a lot tougher. The best thing they could do now was brush off their breeches and go for a beer.

The Lamb of God was a well-frequented alehouse without the tavern pretentions of The Moorcock. Although it was rather dingy and dark inside, Ezekiel liked the atmosphere. The mullion windows were small, so the main source of light came from a large fire that dominated the back wall. Hefty logs burned beneath a thick stone mantel. A stag's antlers jutted out above. There were also several lanthorns and tallows lit on each of the tables. Seating was in the form of unadorned benches. The floor was stone-flagged. There was little else in the way of decoration. No pictures or ornaments. There were only two choices of ale: a dark beer flavoured with mugwort, and a paler beer flavoured with sweet gale.

Both men had sunk two beers apiece and were standing round the bar. Ezekiel took the replenished tankards and ushered Gad over to an empty table. The two men sat down. He handed Gad his tankard.

'There you go. Get that down your neck.'

Gad took hold of it and supped. Ezekiel raised his up. 'All hail the ale!' he said, and clinked Gad's pot. It was still quite early but these late autumn days drew folk to the tavern. It was getting dark by four, so that was when most folk put down their tools and made their way to a drinking hole. Hoary-handed labourers, tradesmen and artisans, with muck on their boots and dirt under their nails. There were groups of farm labourers standing and sitting around. Close by, the village smithy was supping with the miller and the baker. Relaxing for the first time of the day, sinking a few beers, before home to the missus and a meal.

'Told you it would make you feel better. Quick in work and play. That's how it is with me and that's how it is with you. Right?'

'Right.'

'Best beer in the parish this alehouse. They do a decent mutton and potato pie too. If you fancy it?'

'Nah, not hungry.'

'Suit yourself.'

Gad stared into the void of his ale pot.

'I don't think I'm cut out for this.'

'Like I said before, it gets easier.' Ezekiel reached over and patted Gad on the back. 'You'll see.'

'I'm a waller and a delver. I build walls, and dig trenches. Lug lumps of rock around. That's what I do.'

'There's plenty of walls to build, don't you worry about that. Mr Lane plans to enclose all the commons north of the estate ... Look, these are difficult times for everyone. Not just you, you know. We've all got to muck in. Do our bit. Life's like that. Sometimes you have to do things that you don't want to do ... You'll see. You'll be all right.'

Gad nodded. Then he took up his pot and sank the remainder of the ale in one sup. Ezekiel watched him. He could see there was no joy in the action. Poor fellow. Must be hard to lose your family like that, nailed up in your own hovel. All the corpses piled up, and not enough graves to bury them. He'd come round with a few more.

He went back to the bar and ordered another round. No one liked burying bairns, but these were strange times – not even a year had passed since the King had lost his head at Whitehall. Never thought he'd live to see a King with his neck under the axe. The times they lived in had been bent out of shape. One time he believed in the cause, but the Rump Parliament was no better than Charles. All they'd done was swap one tyrant for another.

The two men had meant to report back to Mr Lane, but having supped a gallon each, the thought had been displaced. There were no stars to guide their journey home and no moon either. The night sky was thick with inky clouds. They were walking down a dirt track with two ruts where carts had been. Ezekiel was in front, closely followed by Gad. It was raining and it came down in cold drops, landing on their hats, dripping down their necks, soaking into their clothing. They were drunk and swayed unsteadily as they walked.

'You know you can cure elf-shot with dirt from a wheel rut?'

'Course, I do. What do you take me for? I'm not an idiot. Heard it heals the bite of a shrewmouse too.'

Gad nodded sagely.

'You sure it's all right for me to stay at yours?'

'Said so, didn't I?'

'She won't mind?'

'She'll be asleep.'

Ezekiel didn't let on, but since she'd got with their second child, his wife, Kate, hadn't been so good.

'I can probably find my way back to mine.'

'No need.'

'My sister will wonder where I am.'

'She's not your keeper.'

The two men stumbled on their way. The cold night air had knitted a thick cloak of fog, which hung heavy and clung to every branch and brick. Two blind moles wading through mud, mist and mire. The wheel ruts they had been using to guide their way had run out. Gad stopped and looked around. They were shrouded in a leaden pall.

'Where are we?'

'I don't know.'

'What do you mean, you don't know? Thought you were leading the way?' Gad said.

Ezekiel had now also stopped and was looking around, scratching his head. How could he not find his way home? It was a walk he'd done many times, but as they turned and turned about in the milky mist, it was too dark to see anything. He could just make out the vague shape of trees, a dry-stone wall. Black puddles. Silver rods of rain.

Gad waited for Ezekiel to say something. Eventually Gad said, 'You haven't got a clue where we are, have you?'

Ezekiel laughed. 'Who cares? Who gives a fuck?'

'Listen. I care. We're going to freeze to death out here. We'll catch an ague. Let's go back the way we came. Start again.'

Both men looked around once more. They realised they didn't know which way they had come. They had turned and turned about and now were not sure which direction they faced.

Ezekiel laughed again. 'It dunt matter. It dunt matter.'

Gad was about to say something. He could feel the cold creep under his skin and chill his marrow. He was shivering, but as he opened his mouth to speak, there was a loud howling sound in the near distance that ripped through the blanket of night.

'What was that?'

'It sounded like …'

'Can't be. There aren't any left.'

The two men stood in the middle of the road enveloped in a fleece of fog, listening. But the howl had gone.

'Come on, we need to get back. You must have some idea where we are.'

Ezekiel was suddenly decisive. 'This way.'

They carried on walking down the lane. Then Ezekiel stopped. 'Or is it this way?'

He turned in the opposite direction. He shrugged. Then he started laughing like a maniac.

A Yonderly Child

The dawning sun was shining on two wet, mud-soaked lumps lying in a ditch. Ezekiel opened his eyes first and groaned. Gradually and painfully he got to his feet, aching all over. He cradled his head: a drum was beating inside his skull. He looked over to Gad and gave him a soft kick in the gut.

'Gad. Wake up. It's morning. We need to get to the master's. Come on.'

Opening his eyes, Gad groaned. He looked at Ezekiel.

'Where the hell are we?'

'Looks like we made it to the other side of the village. Somehow. How much did we drink?'

'Don't say that word. I feel like I've had my head kicked in by John the Butcher. Mouth's like the inside of a drover's glove.'

'We need to get cleaned up. He's gonna kill us. We should have reported back to the master last night. Come on. Get up.'

Ezekiel helped Gad to his feet and they made their way along the road to a stream-fed horse trough. Ezekiel took off his coat and shirt. He cupped his hands and drank from the spring, sticking his head underneath and letting the water flow through his hair and over his neck. The cold numbed his neck. He scrubbed the muck off his face and hands and noticed there was a rip on the knee of his breeches. Good job his wife was a fine seamstress, couldn't afford new kecks with the money he was on, must have fallen over last night. Oh, well, no harm done. He nudged Gad. It was his turn.

When they arrived at the master's manor, Ezekiel spoke to the stableboy and the boy went off to fetch the master. The two men waited by the back door.

'He's taking ages.'

'Stop fretting. He'll come.'

The two men stood in silence until they heard the steps of Mr Lane approach. Ezekiel turned to Gad. 'Let me do all the talking.'

The two men stood up straight as the back door opened and Lemuel Lane approached them with a scowl on his face.

'Well?'

'Sir, it's done, sir. Everything you said, sir.'

'When?'

'Last night, sir.'

'Why didn't you come and tell me then?'

'Apologies, sir. It was late. Didn't want to disturb you.'

'Told you to come and tell me, whatever time.'

'Thought you'd be annoyed, master. It was late.'

'So you said. Listen, doesn't matter now. Did it go to plan?'

'Yes, sir.'

'And the bodies?'

'All sorted, sir.'

'You're sure?'

'Absolutely, master.'

Lemuel reached into his jacket and fetched out a purse. He opened it and counted out the money. He handed it to Ezekiel. He explained that Thomas had not arrived home yet, and that he was going out to look for him. He had another job for them while he was away. One Gad seemed more comfortable with. The three of them crossed the yard and walked beyond the field at the back of the house. Lemuel showed them where he wanted them to build a wall. Close by was a pile of stones of different sizes and shapes. He bade the men farewell, and left them to get on with their work.

The two men grafted all morning, shifting through the stones, building up the wall piece by piece. They were both experienced wallers, but you couldn't rush a job like this. It took as long as it took. Although Ezekiel had started his working life in a saw-pit, he'd never returned after the first war, choosing to work for Mr Lane instead. As they grafted the sky cleared and even showed some blue, but the wind picked up towards late morning and by early afternoon the sky had darkened with low-hanging clouds again. Mr Lane had made it clear that the wall must be finished by the end of the day, but the way they were going, there was no chance of this. They were grafters, experienced wallers, but not miracle workers.

'Ever tell you about that time I saw a miracle worker?'

Gad shook his head.

'It was three years ago. An itinerant healer. I'd just left the army. Before I got with Kate. Healed a blind man.'

'How did he do that?'

'He anointed his eyes with mud he'd mixed with his own saliva.'

'Only the son of God can work that miracle.'

'I tell you, I saw it. Just outside York. He wiped the mud off with a cloth, and when the blind man opened his eyes again, he could see.'

Gad wondered about Ezekiel sometimes. Although the older and more experienced of the two, he did think some of what he said stretched credulity. But he kept his mouth shut and looked for an odd-shaped stone to plug a gap. It had started raining and the wind was blowing through the branches of the trees, ripping off what ragged leaves were left. Rooks cawed as they flew overhead.

'How's Kate doing? Must be nearly due now?'

'She's got another month or so.'

'And how's the young 'un?'

'Still colicked. Can't afford the colic water.'

'Tried swaddling her?'

'Aye. Still skrikes all day.'

'My sister says that some bairns are just born that way. She's got some herbs she uses. Think it's caraway. She makes a tincture from the umbels. I'll fetch some if you like?'

Ezekiel nodded as he scurried through a pile of stones, looking for a good one for the wall.

'This stone is shite.'

They stopped for something to eat. Lemuel had instructed Jacob to fetch them bread and cheese, slices of apples and pears, and a flagon of small beer, and they supped and chomped their way through it. They didn't dare stop work long though. It didn't do to dilly-dally. Ezekiel had told Gad about the time he'd watched Mr Lane flog a man for insubordination. Afterwards, the man's back was a lattice of scabs and he hadn't been able to stand up. As soon as the food was done, they carried on building the wall.

'You know as how no month-blood woman is supposed to pickle beef or salt bacon?' Ezekiel asked.

'I've heard it said, aye.'

'Well, how is it with those who are with child?'

'How should I know? I'll ask my sister if you like?'

Ezekiel shrugged. 'Give us a hand with this.'

The two men lifted a huge linking stone and placed it so it connected both sides of the wall. It was important to bridge the gap at intervals, so the wall remained strong.

'Don't want to tempt fate. You know she lost one?'

'Sorry to hear that. Thought you were more bothered about spoiling the beef.'

'Cheeky bugger.'

Both men laughed. Ezekiel would not have taken this from any other man, but he knew that his cousin meant no harm.

It was mid-afternoon when they saw a horse and sat atop the familiar bear shape of Lemuel making his way towards them across the field. They still had an hour of decent light left, but Ezekiel knew that this wasn't enough to get the job done. They would have worked quicker had the quality of the stone been better, some of it was nothing more than shale. So as Lemuel approached, Ezekiel braced himself for a bollocking. He had his excuse lined up. His master looked stern and he feared the worst. But when Lemuel arrived he had nothing to say about the wall or its lack of progress, in fact he didn't even look at the wall.

'I need you to saddle two horses.'

'What for?'

'I've searched every beck for my boy and there's no sign of him. I've got another pair searching Bluebell Clough, and some men at Dale Edge. I want you to ride over to Lowe Dene and search the whole area. Turn every rock, stone and stump. I'm going to take Sheep Brink. Take the palfreys.'

Ezekiel waited for further instruction. None came. He watched his master clench the reins, yanking the strap. Then he turned the horse and galloped back the way he came. The two men downed tools and made their way to the stables.

'He said take the palfreys, right?'

The two men looked at each other. That was what their master had said, but each needed the other to confirm. They saddled the horses and mounted. Ezekiel wondered where the stable lad was. Why have a dog and bark yourself? But he supposed he'd also been recruited to find that foolish boy, Thomas.

'It's no wonder we never get anything finished. Soon as you start something he's got something else for you to do. As if we haven't got enough on our plates without fetching daft lads,' said Ezekiel as he took the reins.

'I've got an idea where he'll be.'

They geed on their horses and rode out of the main gates and south of the estate, across even pasture, where some of Lemuel's young bullocks grazed, before approaching Lowe Dene Wood. It was one of the most compact copses in the region, half the size of Sheep Brink and Long Royd, but big enough to lose your way. It was characterised by a deep gorge where great reaching beech, elm and ash grew. Deer were abundant here, as it was too steep for hunting. The beck below was good clean water and the bed, hard gravel. Best place for trout fishing in that part.

Once they got to the edge of the wood, they dismounted their horses, tied them to a tree, and carried on through the forest on foot, using low boughs to steady their descent. It was mainly beech trees and the floor of the forest was thick with seed casings so that they crunched underfoot.

'I've heard said there was once a white trout down there. No one had ever seen a white trout so they didn't know what to do with it. Then it disappeared. Fairies took it,' Gad said.

'Think you're confusing this wood with Black Clough.'

The water was quite shallow at this part and they walked further on to where it got narrower and deeper.

'Then the next year it came back. Someone caught it, but when he tried to fry it in his pan, it leapt out, screaming like a girl.'

'Stop going on about trout will you. It's Black Clough where the fairies live.'

They followed the bends and undulations in the beck, until they came to the spot that Gad had in mind, where the water ran fast and clear over a bed of hard gravel. They looked for signs of Thomas, but there was nothing. They called out his name, and their call returned as an echo. Searching further up, Gad spotted something resting on top of a dead beech trunk – a bait box. He picked it up and examined it in more detail.

'This must be Master Lane's box. Been using nightcrawlers. That's good bait. Stay on the hook for ages. But do you know what the best bait is?'

Ezekiel was ignoring him as he searched the area for more signs of Thomas.

'Best bait is salmon eggs. If you can get hold of them. Trout love 'em.'

Ezekiel stooped low to the ground. 'Look at this.'

He pointed to something Gad couldn't see. Gad put the bait box down and went over to where Ezekiel was standing.

'What?'

He bent down to get a closer look.

'Blood.'

Ezekiel touched the scarlet patch and moved his finger up to his eye to really scrutinise it, then he offered his finger to Gad.

'That's blood all right.'

Ezekiel wiped the blood on his breeches.

'Look, there's another drop.'

He pointed to a spot further on.

'And another.'

Slowly, they followed the spots of blood as they led them away from the beck, further into the wood until they lost the trail. They decided that Thomas must be around this area and they began to search through bramble and briar with growing trepidation. Ezekiel broke off a beech branch, stripping the smaller twigs from it, making a stick to thrash through the undergrowth. Gad wandered in the opposite direction, found a nice straight length of hazel, where the tree had been coppiced, and he did as Ezekiel, whacking his way through fern and thorn. They cleared the immediate area and began to widen the circle.

'Doesn't look like there's any more,' Gad said. 'Must be rabbit. Or deer?'

Ezekiel hoped Gad was right. For wasn't the blood of any animal similarly constituted? As he searched the area, he reflected on the likeness of all blood. A man's blood was no different from that of a dog or a rat. He'd followed trails of human blood before – an ominous pastime. Men pissing claret from sword, carbine or pistol could bleed for miles. One time a cavalry of cavaliers had ploughed into their troop with fifteen-foot pikes. Those who were left standing had fled the scene leaving blood over everything they'd touched.

'Zeke!'

'What?'

'Look.'

Ezekiel made his way to where Gad was standing. Gad pointed to another patch of blood.

'This way.'

The walked slowly and carefully, backs bent, searching the path for red gouts. Ezekiel hoped it was the blood of any other animal, and even any other human animal, as long as it wasn't the blood of his master's son. They came to a fork in the path. Gad took the first, Ezekiel, the second. Neither man could see any more blood.

'Zeke! Come here.'

'What is it?'

'Come and look.'

Ezekiel put down his stick and ran over to Gad. There in the undergrowth was the mauled and blooded body of Lemuel Lane's only son, Thomas.

'Is he still alive?'

Gad bent down and examined him.

'Just about. He's lost a lot of blood. Here. Give me a hand.'

The two men lifted Thomas above the brambles. They laid him down in a clear spot. Ezekiel tore some cloth from his shirt and wrapped it round the boy's neck close to the wound, making sure not to tie it too tight. He'd had plenty of practice in the field staunching the flow of blood. The war had made butcher-surgeons out of many an untrained swain. The boy was bleeding but the makeshift tourniquet was slowing down the flow. They tried to get him to talk, but he didn't respond.

'He needs a physician.'

'Let's get him back to the house.'

They took an end each and began carrying him back through the wood, towards the tree where they had tethered their horses. Ezekiel offered Thomas words of encouragement, such as, 'Hang on in there, lad' and 'Nearly there now'. They got back to where their horses patiently grazed on meadow grass. Gad mounted his and Ezekiel hitched Master Thomas onto the horse's back, lashing rope round Thomas and Gad so that Thomas wouldn't fall off.

Ezekiel was worried that somehow they would get the blame for this. More often than not the messenger got shot along with the message. In his mind's eye he saw the soldier with his wrists tethered, stripped of his cuirass and shirt, his back latticed with the cut of the whip, Mr Lane sweating from the effort of flogging the man half to death. He remembered the man's eyes, eyes that had once been full of youth and life, full to the brim with fear. The man had died from the wounds the next day.

As they rode back they talked about what kind of animal had done this, but what they were left to conclude after dismissing each suspect in turn, didn't make any sense. As they rode on, the ropes started to loosen and the body sagged down. They stopped to adjust Thomas and retie the ropes. Ezekiel reached for the boy's pulse – faint but it was still beating. They would have to hurry if they were to save his life. What would his master do to him if he returned his son a corpse?

Then, as they rode past the old quarry, Ezekiel saw the creature emerge from gorse and sprint over the hill.

'There!' he shouted.

Gad turned to look.

'See it?'

Gad nodded, 'I don't … It can't be …'

'You saw it as well as I did. A wolf. A bloody wolf! We both saw it, right?'

Gad was dumbstruck. He stared off in the distance, as if he expected the beast to return. He shook his head and muttered under his breath.

Lemuel had word from the others. No one had seen any sign of his boy. There was just Gad and Ezekiel out now, but he held hope that they might have better news. He went into the kitchen, carved a slice of beef and salted it, washing it down with a pot of small beer. He went to look for Elizabeth. She was upstairs sitting by the bay windows that overlooked the orchard. She turned to him expectantly until he shook his head.

'Nothing. I'm waiting on two more men yet.'

'It's just not like him.'

'The boy is just lost. You'll see,' he said with a sureness in his voice that he didn't feel.

'All of yesterday. And now today too.'

'I know, love. I'm doing everything I can.'

'But, I mean, he knows his way.'

'Depends how far he's gone.'

He searched the room for a half-drunk bottle of brandy he knew to be there. He found it on the shelf where his bible was kept. He reached for it.

'Do you think that's a good idea?' Elizabeth said.

He weighed his wife's words. He put the bottle back and sat down beside her, a knot tightening in his chest. He thought the liquor might help, but Elizabeth was right, they had to stay vigilant. He stood up again and paced across to the fireplace, then back to the window. Elizabeth watched him.

'Will you stop doing that. Please.'

He went over to the fire and poked it vigorously, then sat back down at her side. He felt so useless. Perhaps he should take a torch and go out there again? Sitting here was no good. But what could he see in the dark with just a dim light? He looked at his wife. He knew her well enough to know that although outwardly composed, this masked an inner turmoil. He reached for her hand and gave it a squeeze. A gesture he hoped would reassure her. As he did there was a timid knock. It was Jacob.

'Beg pardon, sir. It's your men, sir. I've just seen them come through the gates. And—'

Lemuel didn't wait for his manservant to finish his speech. He pushed past him and raced down the stairs to the hallway and the heavy studded door. As he swung it open, standing in the doorway were Gad and Ezekiel, holding his son in their arms. The boy was limp. The rag around his neck was stained red, as was his collar.

'Sir – he's been attacked.'

'What? Bring him in. Let me have a look,' Lemuel said. It was an effort for him to keep his voice steady.

The men took the boy over to an upholstered bench and laid him down. As Lemuel propped up the boy's head, Elizabeth came running across.

'My boy!' Lemuel cried, incapable of anything more.

'What's happened to him?' Elizabeth said.

'He's lost a lot of blood, sir,' Gad said.

'We found him in Lowe Dene Wood, close to the beck,' Ezekiel said.

Elizabeth turned to Jacob who was standing behind her. 'Fetch the physician,' she yelled.

'Yes, ma'am,' Jacob said, and hurriedly left the room.

'Help me,' Lemuel said, turning to Elizabeth.

Their boy had been bitten and clawed. Blood oozed from a wound on his neck. As they attended to him, they were joined first by Olivia, and then by Catherine. Elizabeth turned to Catherine. 'Fetch a bowl of hot water and a cloth.'

Catherine hurried to the kitchen, as Lemuel told Olivia to find the brandy bottle. Catherine returned with the bowl and Elizabeth loosened Thomas's tunic and washed the wound. The blood loss had drained his complexion of colour.

'Who ... what did this?'

'I can't be sure, madam, but I think it may have been a wolf,' Ezekiel said.

'What are you talking about? There are no more wolves in England!'

'We saw it with our own eyes, sir. Me and Gad, sir. Didn't we, Gad?'

Gad nodded.

'But there are no wolves!'

'You must know the story of the last hunt, it's well told in these parts,' Elizabeth said to Lemuel's men.

'I have, ma'am.'

'And that was years ago. Before my father's time.'

'It was a wolf, ma'am. I'm sure of it.'

'It can't be!' Lemuel said.

'His breathing is weak.'

Olivia arrived with the brandy. Lemuel took it off her, uncorked it, had a swig, then put it to Thomas's lips.

'Here, lad. Have a sip of this.'

But his son was too weak to sip.

'Will he be all right, do you think?' Olivia said.

'He'll pull through, I'm sure,' Lemuel replied, as much to convince himself as his daughter. 'Here, hold this against the wound. Lemuel watched Elizabeth take the cloth to her son's brow. He watched her try to get a response from him, but the boy remained unconscious. He was still breathing – just had to hang on till the physician arrived. Lemuel pressed down on the wound, making sure his son lost no more of his precious blood.

He had seen men and boys bleed aplenty. He had been part of the gun train, firing demi-culverins, pounders and sakers. The leather cuirasses his men wore might well have been musket-proof, but they were no defence against a double or demi. And he'd seen men have their limbs ripped from their bodies, seen them slashed, stabbed, axed, halberded and shot at. He'd seen the poleaxed head of a soldier crack in two like a conker, blood flow like claret. But seeing his own son's blood was a different matter. His son's blood was worth the blood of all those men put together.

He turned to his men. 'You are absolutely sure you saw a wolf? You are certain it wasn't a large dog?'

'Yes, sir, twice the size of any dog, by the old quarry,' said Ezekiel.

Lemuel looked at Gad. 'And you saw it too?'

'Yes, sir, it was a wolf. We both saw it.'

'A wolf. A wolf! My God! How did ...'

But Lemuel didn't finish his sentence. He stared at his son's wound and crossed himself.

The Shadow of Death

I spent another night beneath cold black skies wishing I was in the same hole as Ma and Da, but the next day hunger forced me to go on. I could still not recollect the name of the place, but I carried on eastwards, as my da had instructed, along a winding road under the near-barren branches of elder, alder and elm, until I approached a large farmhouse. I could smell the aroma of fresh-baked bread wafting from the kitchens, which left me salivating like a dog. I walked past piles of stones that had been hunked up by the side of the path and made my way through the gates to the back of the building. There was no one about, so I plucked up the courage and knocked on the door. A maid answered. I told her that I had come seeking alms, that I was lost and hadn't eaten in days. She looked at my filthy attire and the mud on my boots.

'I'm sorry, but I've been given strict instructions from the master of the house. No alms given here.'

'Just a crust of bread. Some curds. A mess of milk. Any morsel would be welcome. I beg you.'

'I'm sorry, child. I've got my instructions.'

Before I had chance to reason with her further, she was closing the door on me. I stood staring at the iron knocker. Furtively, the door opened again, and the maid handed me a moth-eaten shawl.

'Here, have this,' she said, and closed the door once more, before I had chance to thank her. I wrapped the shawl about my shoulders and carried on walking. I followed the contours of the land, letting the shape of the valley determine my journey. Eventually I reached an abandoned barn on the edges of the moor. It was only half-roofed and I coiled up in the driest corner and wrapped the shawl tightly around me. In the gloaming I saw something scurry past me. It was a rat. A big greasy brown rat, with a long tail like a worm. I found a broken broom handle and waited for it to return. Shortly after, it came over to me and sniffed the air. I took a swing at it but it ran off. I groped for my rosary beads, but remembered that I'd lost them. Lord God, Lord Jesus, Mother of God, Mary full of grace, protect me. I crouched, club in hand, until the rat returned, then swung at it. Eventually I convinced myself that I'd seen it off and I lay back down again. The cloak of night had veiled the sky leaving just a few stars and a sliver of moon. I lay there shivering, clinging to the shawl, looking up through the hole in the roof, wishing again I had my rosary beads about me for comfort and protection. I drifted into an uneasy sleep.

The next day I approached a neat stone cottage and peered through the kitchen window where a large pie was cooling on the table. The window was open and the intense aroma drifted over to where I was standing. I yearned for even a small piece of that pie. I knocked on the door and an old lady opened it, but when I asked for alms, she slammed the door shut in my face. I carried on trudging down the lane, overtaking two women carrying wicker bucks. As I walked by them, I brushed the arm of one. I looked up at her. She had a plump red face.

'Look where you're going, won't you?' she said, and tutted.

I don't know why I had walked so close to her, there was plenty of room for me to pass on this road. I stopped and let the women go by. I had the strange urge to hurt this woman, to kick her, or slap her. What I really wanted to do was grab her by her hair and throw her to the ground. I caught up with her again and walked past, turning round and staring at her, but she ignored me, acting as though I didn't exist, and she and her friend chattered together about something or other.

'Well, you know you can cure it with butter from a red cow?'

'I heard it were a white cow?'

'I think either works, as long as the cow is completely red, or completely white.'

I saw that she had some bread in a basket and I yearned for that loaf. I was a fast runner. Maybe I could snatch the loaf before she could stop me. They were both plump lasses and I was sure I could outrun them. Without giving it any more thought, I ran at them, and catching up, reached for the bread. But her reflexes were better than I'd anticipated, and she swung the buck away from me, shouting, 'What are you doing? You thieving little bitch!'

Her chubby friend pushed me, and I staggered, almost falling. I managed to right my balance and ran off up another lane to my left. A big black dog barked at me, and for a moment I thought the girl had set it on me. But then I saw an old man ahead. 'Steady on, boy,' the old man said, and his dog went quiet.

I trudged on, now travelling in a north-easterly direction. I came to a cluster of cottages and a stone trough. Nearby, but set back from the road, was a larger house that looked like it could be part of an estate. It had a square nail-studded black door and fine glazed windows. A girl was cleaning one of the windowpanes. In one hand she held a bucket of water and in the other a wet rag. She wiped the glass half-heartedly, and I could see that she begrudged the task. She wore a scarf of good cloth around her head and looked well fed so I decided I would ask her for some food and beer in exchange for work. I'd happily clean those windows if she would repay me in bread. As I walked towards her, she turned and scowled and I suddenly froze. She had a mean, pinched face, a pointy, upturned nose and thin lips.

I couldn't say the words that I'd prepared. It was like my lips had been sewn together.

At last I stuttered, 'If you like, missus, I'll clean those windows for you.'

She stopped what she was doing, put the bucket down, and crouching over it, wrung out the rag.

'Now, why would you do that?'

'In exchange for some food. I'm hungry, miss.'

She wrung out the rag again, cogitating my offer. Then she picked up the bucket, walked over to me, and handing me first the rag, then the bucket, she said, 'Very well. But be sure to do a good job.'

I thanked her. I could hardly believe my luck. I got to work straight away. The water she had given me was dirty, but I did my best with what I had and scrubbed at the mucky glass. I worked round the house systematically, cleaning one pane at a time, making sure I didn't miss any. With each I started in the top left-hand corner and worked across and then down, so that I made sure all the glass was cleaned. There was a lot of filth on them, and I had to scrub hard. I could feel the girl's eyes on me as I worked. I felt light-headed with the effort, and I realised how badly I needed to eat something. My hunger was affecting my concentration, and I kept having to stop to check I'd done the work properly.

It took me a couple of hours to complete the task, but by the time I'd finished cleaning the last window, I was pleased with my work. All the panes looked much cleaner now, and when they caught the light they shone. I knocked on the door and waited. When the girl answered, I explained that I'd finished. She came out to inspect them, looking at each pane in turn, moving around the house, until she had inspected every one.

'Can I have some food now please?'

She shook her head. 'No, you can't.'

'But … But …' I stammered. 'You said I could.'

'I said you had to do a good job.'

'I have.'

'No you've not. You've left streaks all over. Very shoddy work.'

She pointed to some marks that had been left, not from my neglect, but rather from the muck in the water I'd been given.

'I … I …' I tried to reason with her. 'I did the best I could. The water was dirty.'

'Then you should have asked for fresh, shouldn't you?'

I had no words. The weight of her cruelty was crushing. Hadn't she herself given me the bucket, and hadn't she watched me sweat and toil for hours, knowing I was using the water? I could feel an anger rising and before I even had time to think about it, I'd thrown the bucket of filthy water in her face. She froze in shock. She screamed. The water soaked the scarf around her head and plastered her fringe to her forehead. Grey drops dripped from the end of her pointy upturned nose. I laughed in her face then ran as fast as I could away from her and her house. I stopped about half a mile up the road and collapsed on the ground. My lungs were on fire. I pictured the girl dripping with dirty water, her mouth open and her eyes wide in shock. I wanted to laugh and cry at the same time. Such a peculiar feeling.

As I walked beneath the noonday sun, I came to a field where two boys were playing loggets. One was maybe ten or eleven, the other about twelve or thirteen, and they looked like brothers. The same wavy brown hair and wide nebs. I watched them take it in turns to throw sticks at a stake. When the older boy got his stick to almost touch the stake, he laughed out in joy at his skill or luck. The younger brother seemed impressed. The older boy said something to his brother and they both laughed loud. They must have seen my envy as the older boy nudged his brother and pointed at me, saying something to him I couldn't hear. Both their faces turned mean, and I backed away, turned around and walked on up the road.

As I staggered along, I saw other people whose brows were unfurrowed, swinging their arms like they were about to dance. Not one eye I met showed grief, no shoulders burdened, not a clouded thought in these happy minds. I walked beside them, but I was not of them. I could no longer remember what happiness was, could barely comprehend the injustice I had suffered, the wrong I had been done. The pain in my heart was a gaping wound. I had no one and nothing. Even my god had abandoned me.

Every bit of me ached, inside and out. I walked feebly, hardly even able to stand. I thought about God again. Looking up at the cloudless sky, I shouted, 'Why? Why have you done this to me? And now, why have you abandoned me?' I didn't care who I disturbed. What did it matter how they thought of me? They were nothing to me and I was even less to them.

A little further and I collapsed. I wanted more than anything to weep. But my tears would not come. Did God hate me? Had I done something terrible, and was this now my punishment? I thought back over my life, trying to pinpoint some awful deed. But what had I done? Except to be born and say my prayers and obey my parents and do what they bade me do.

I wracked my brain. I remembered Mary teaching me a swear word and I'd kept it inside all that day yearning to say it. I had waited until we had eaten our evening meal, then gone outside to put the chickens to bed, and when I was a good distance from my home, I shouted it, thrilled to be able to release it from inside me at last. Only my da had followed me out, and hearing me, dragged me inside and gave me a good hiding. Was it for this sin that I was suffering now? But surely I had already taken my punishment?

I tried to recall further trespasses. There was that time Ma caught me stealing a biscuit. She'd rapped my knuckles for that, and together we had knelt and prayed for forgiveness. 'One of the thieves was saved. One of the thieves was saved. One of the thieves was saved,' she muttered under her breath. She fetched her rosary and made me say ten Hail Marys. No matter how hard I searched my mind I could not recall a sin of magnitude.

I felt like Job. No one other than Job would understand what I was going through. For hadn't Job lost everything and then continued to suffer? I wished that I could meet him, here and now along this road, so we could be together in our misery. Share each other's pain. Only Job knew and felt what I knew and felt.

In my mind I went back to my childhood, to the sermons I had listened to at Mass. My God, have you forsaken me? Why are you so far from me? I cry and you hear me not. Our fathers trusted in you, and you did deliver them. Why won't you now deliver me? I am a worm. I am the despised. I am poured out like water. All my bones are out of joint. My heart is like wax. It is melted. My strength is dried up like potsherd. My tongue cleaves to my jaw. You have brought me unto the dust of death. Please God, save me from the lion's mouth.

I lay in the gutter and closed my eyes. Didn't the priest say that the meek would eat? I clasped my hands together and muttered a prayer: The Lord is my shepherd, I shall not want. He maketh me lie down in green pastures. He leadeth me beside still waters. Though I walk through the valley of the shadow of death, I will fear no evil, for thou art with me. O my God, let not mine enemies triumph over me. Remember, O Lord, thy tender mercies, and thy loving kindnesses. Remember me for goodness' sake, O Lord!

But he had forsaken me. I was worse than Job, for God never abandoned him. And at last the tears flowed from my eyes, like rivers of fire and brimstone, bitter and hot.

The Wood that Made the Cross

The next day I woke in the gutter. I got onto all fours like a dog and staggered to my feet. Yesterday I had called to my fellow man for help and I had not received it, prayed to my god and had been ignored. I had only a dirty dress from a whorehouse and a moth-eaten shawl, but I had to go on, for the sake of Ma and Da, I had to. Da had found a place for us, and told me if anything happened I must find it on my own. I must do as Da said and find my way out of this morass somehow. I was raw with grief, scooped out with it, but I had to find food and a life for myself. Somewhere out there, it had to be better. This couldn't be all life had to offer me, could it?

As I walked, I looked not at the road in front of me, but down at my boots, at the worn-out leather and the wrinkles that formed as I lifted my feet and placed them back on the rough surface of the road. There was almost something human about those creases, like the lines that form on the side of a smiling face. As I looked down at my boots, I talked to them.

'Good morrow, how do you do?' I said.

They talked back to me. 'We've been better,' they said in unison. 'Why don't you look after us more? You just don't think about us.'

'I'll get some food. I'll find some work. I'll make some money. Then I'll buy boot polish and a brush. Shine you up good as new. You see if I don't.'

I made promises to them that I didn't know if I could keep.

'I'll buy you nice new laces, and have the cobbler fix you up.'

'You better had do. We won't put up with this.'

'I'm going to a place where boots of any size or description are welcome.'

'Well, we wouldn't take your father's word for it if we were you.'

'My da was a good man.'

'He was a silly Irish peasant.'

'He was strong and faithful. My da was an honourable man.'

'He was a butt-headed bogtrotter with a bashed-in nossle.'

'Have you no respect for those recent passed?'

'We'll say no more about it now, but our opinions on the matter are a fact of public record. You just watch where you're going and mind you don't scuff us up on those stones.'

We talked and bickered like this for some time, I don't know how long, but when I next looked up, I was no longer walking along the road. I was now traipsing on a dirt track that cut across some farmland. I had no idea where it went, only judging by the sun, I was now walking in a due easterly direction. The sun was nearly above me. I guessed it was about eleven o'clock in the morning. In front of me were two gnarly trees, with branches like an old crone's fingers. I amused myself as I looked at them, to think they were a couple who had been together for a very long time, but were now growing apart. I laughed at my own joke. That was the spirit. If I could just keep my chin up, find humour in little things, not let the weight of my situation bear down on me and crush me. I imagined I was with my friend, Mary. We were off on one of our adventures. We had been sent on an errand, or else we were going on a picnic. It was a hot day and we were going to find a cooling pool to swim in. I comforted myself with the thought that one day I would see Mary again, and we could play cherry pit with her young brother, who Mary was often left to look after. I'd have so much to tell her, so many things had happened to me, she'd scarcely believe half of it.

I wondered about the safe place. Once I had eaten and slept properly I would remember the name and I would find good, kind people who loved and judged not. They would make sure no harm would come to me.

There were a few pewter-coloured clouds in the sky now, and the air had turned chilly. I wrapped my shawl tightly around my shoulders as I climbed up, above the farm and past a line of bone-white birch, beneath a canopy of lithe-limbed ash. Trees like wreaths, like animals, like skeletons, like people. The exposed roots reached out like gnarled arms. The bark of a beech had been carved with a heart that had now grown over like a scab. My da had told me all about trees. How to recognise the alder that grows by the water from its racquet-shaped leaves. How the sycamore is the first to emerge in spring, its pale green flowers hanging like grapes. The thick flute of a yew's trunk and its matted canopy providing shelter from the elements. How the blackbird eats its arils in autumn. That the ash is a healing tree and is the last to burst into life. Da had been a barker back in Ballina. He'd worked with tanners, turners and hagmen. He told me about Tom Bell, the wild man that lived in the wood near the iron bloomery. How he made charcoal and sat on a one-legged stool so that he didn't fall asleep during a burn.

Then I felt the shock all over again. Fresh and real: I would never see his face again. I felt pitted out and exhausted with it. There was a hard pain in my chest that wouldn't shift. I couldn't breathe, a tightness around my ribs enveloped me.

The sky darkened and cooled. I looked up and I saw a sparrowhawk above me, watched as it dropped out of the sky and lanced a titmouse. It perched on the corpse of the bird, glaring at me with its gold and black eyes, its yellow legs pinioning its prey. It tore at the flesh with its beak. Its cream chest was striped with brown bars. I climbed further up over moorland. It was peaty and boggy, and I had to tread carefully, so as not to lose my footing. The clag of mud sucked me in. I squelched through stagnant puddles of black water. My feet were freezing. Then they were numb.

'We didn't sign up for this.' My boots were talking to me again.

I convinced myself that I didn't need food at all. I could sustain myself simply by feasting on the air I breathed. Why hadn't it occurred to me before? The air had substance. If it could support the flies and the birds, it could nourish me.

'That's the spirit, Kate.'

It was Mary. She was by my side, trudging through the mud with me.

'Is it really you?' I said.

'Sure as an egg is an egg.'

'I was just thinking about you.'

'Were you now?'

'I was wondering if I'd ever see you again.'

'That's silly talk, Kate. I'm here now, so you can stop that maudlin behaviour. Think of pretty things. Remember that time we found that glade at the other side of Hanging Fall where we saw fox cubs play?'

I recalled the memory. It was an April afternoon and the air was heavy with the scent of meadow sweet, honeysuckle and elderflower. We'd been laiking in the woods when we'd come across a clear green glade all lit up by the sun, and there a fox den with a dog fox and his vixen and four kitlings, all laiking and leaping. We'd crouched by a mulberry bush and watched like the moment wasn't ours and we were stealing it. They were tiny wee things only a few weeks old, tumbling over each other, biting and wrestling. Their parents watching on nonchalantly.

'The cubs seemed so much more alive than their parents,' Mary said.

'Their coats were practically black.'

'Fox cubs are born black and blind. The vixen was a scraggy thing, do you remember?'

I nodded. I could picture her clearly.

'You had that lovely doll with you.'

My da had whittled it from ash for my eighth birthday. Slim and pretty. He'd managed to carve fine features. Good cheekbones and a lovely straight nose. I felt my eyes welling up and I swallowed down the lump in my throat.

'He was so dextrous your da, for such a big lubberly fellow.'

'He thought he'd surprise me with that doll, but I'd spied him a few times, going off into the woods to whittle after work. It took him weeks to complete the carving. Ma made a dress and a shawl and a cap all to match.'

'It was a lovely doll. You brought it to my house. It was prettier than my doll. We played for hours together. It was grand.'

'It was. I loved that house we made for them in the hollow of that tree.'

'We pretended that they lived there as sisters.'

'You said that one day, we'd live together as sisters.'

'I did.'

'Whatever happened to my doll, Mary?' I stopped and looked about. 'Mary? Mary?' I shouted for her but there was no one there. I searched for her – nothing. I was bereft.

The wind was getting stronger, and I wished I still had my bonnet, but at least the wind wasn't rain. I didn't want to get wet again, but just as I had that thought, almost like the clouds had heard me, I felt an icy spot on my cheek, then another on the back of my hand. Now Mary had gone, there was little to keep me company as I walked. I thought about talking to my boots again, but they were too bad-tempered to be companions. I hoped that Mary would come back so we could talk again about those days. The only living souls I came across were two sheep. 'I hope you're not too wet,' I said, but they didn't answer. A crow flew past, then a kestrel. It hovered above me like it was stuck to the sky. The moors were bleak and barren. Scraggy heather and wilted tussock grass. There were lumps of gritstone scattered across the slope, a stunted hawthorn, a withered gorse. It felt like the landscape would swallow me up and I pushed away the crushing feeling. I tried to remember songs my mother had taught me and I sang the verses I knew and la-la-la-ed the words I'd forgotten. I had an awful singing voice, almost as bad as my ma's, but out here it didn't matter, and I sang as loud as I could, bothering no one except the sheep.

The drover's road I was following veered north. It seemed to go nowhere, disappearing on the horizon. I decided I would keep east, travelling as much as I could in the same direction. Somewhere out there was a sanctuary. Get to the coast and then head north. Draw down that thought. It was tough going without a path, and I had to really slow down my pace, so as not to fall or twist my ankle. I could see woodland in the distance and before long, I reached the edges of it. I dropped down from the moor and into a wooded clough. A bostel climbed high above a ravine where a beck ran far below. I found penny buns, the fat brown mushrooms I used to pick with Ma. They were the only mushrooms she'd stomach. We used to slice them and thread them on a line that we'd hang in the kitchen. We'd dry them and use them in stews and soups. I'd never eaten them raw before and their texture was slimy but my hunger overcame my squeamishness and I chewed the stalks and caps and swallowed them. They were maggot-ridden, and I wished I'd kept hold of my da's knife to cut out the bits where the maggots had been before me. I found some withered berries on a bush and gnawed at them. They no longer contained much juice, but they were better than the slimy maggot-pocked mushrooms. I gathered deep red rowan berries and ate them. The taste was sour and with each bite I grimaced. We sometimes kept branches of rowan heavy with berries by the threshold of the door, in order to keep witches at bay. My ma told me that they kept all evil spirits away, not just witches. I had never encountered evil spirits. All the dangers I'd faced so far had come from people, not sprites. So I didn't really fear them, or witches for that matter. My mother always kept a stick of rowan for stirring the milk, so that it didn't sour.

As I ate the rowan berries I became accustomed to their sourness. Me and Ma used to make the berries into jam, but it was only palatable with plenty of sugar added and an apple or two. I liked it best on a slice of bread with a pot of hot beer. I ate the tart fruit and imagined it as sweet jam. An act of transubstantiation. My mind went back to a last autumn afternoon. I was with my ma and da in the garden. Da was chopping wood and I was helping him as the sun shone through patches of white cloud that looked like sheep and a breeze rustled the leaves. Da was stripped to his undershirt. My job was to place each log steady on the block, then shift out of the way as he brought the blade of the axe down to cleave the log in two. 'You stack 'em, I'll crack 'em,' Da said, winking at me. I'd collect this split wood, wherever it fell, fill the wheelbarrow, and then later, stack them in the store. For the bigger ones, we used a splitter, a metal tooth that you first hammered into the centre of the log. I'd have to hold it steady till Da drove it far enough in, then I'd stand back while he wielded the huge hammer, bringing it down hard on the splitter. It was easy work but you had to keep your nerve. I trusted Da. One slip with that hammer and my skull would crack like an egg. Da was getting into the rhythm of it. Beads of sweat prickled his forehead, and wet patches formed under his arms. I'd almost filled my barrow with the split pieces. Ma was walking across with bread and jam and hot beer. We stopped and sat by the log pile, eating the sweet rowan jam and guzzling the ale.

These memories now, recollected in destitution, took on added meaning and fuller emotion. I didn't want to think of my ma and da alive, as it would only lead me to recall their dead bodies lying in a shallow grave of my making. But I didn't *not* want to think of them either. All I had of them were these memories. So I returned to that late September day and the sweet rowan jam, Da slurping his beer and scoffing the bread, wiping his brow with his undershirt. Then watching me stack the wood, as he lay back in the sun, telling me I'd done a good job.

Later that day, I bled for the first time, and Ma told me that I was now a woman. Eve's curse, she called it. She instructed me what to do. As I remembered all this, my eyes started to fill with water. I blinked and wiped at them with my sleeve, pushing the memory out of my mind. I was on my own now. I had no Ma or Da.

I hadn't been eating long when I thought I heard something. I looked up thinking it was a fox or a deer, only to see the head of a girl above the bushes. I thought at first it was Mary, she had come back, the same long straight mousy hair and heart-shaped face, but as she got closer I could see that the girl wasn't as bonny or as tall as Mary, and I realised I was in danger. I ducked down and made myself small. I could hear the girl make her way through bracken and bramble, muttering to herself. Then I heard nothing. I wondered if she'd gone further on, and very carefully, I lifted my head to see. She was standing in front of me. She jumped in shock, as did I.

'What are you doing down there? You gave me a fright!'

I could see her features close now. She would have been pretty if not for her long thin teeth that were too big for her mouth and her pointy ears, that she accentuated by tucking her hair behind.

'What's the matter with you? Can you not speak?'

She couldn't have been much older than me, maybe sixteen, no more. She was shawled but not bonneted. She carried a wicker skep. My da used to say of anyone so out proportioned, that they'd been hit with the ugly stick. But Ma always said that you should never mock the afflicted. I thought at first I might run, but the girl blocked my way. She was no bigger than me, I wagered, and Da had taught me how to fight my own battles. He showed me how to ball my fist, and hide it behind my back, then swing it up when least expected. The one who gets the first punch wins the fight, he told me. The girl came closer still, and I could see now that her feet were bare and black with mud.

'I'm sorry, I didn't mean to startle you.'

'You haven't been eating those have you?' she said, pointing to the rowan berries in my hand. I looked at them also, as if I hadn't seen them before. 'They'll give you belly ache. You need to boil them first. You don't eat them raw, silly.'

'I know,' I said. 'My ma used to make rowan jam. I helped her make it. We mixed the berries with the apples we grew in the garden.'

'Well, if you know that, why are you eating them raw?'

I didn't answer. I just shrugged.

She tilted her head quizzically. 'You must be starving,' she said. 'When did you last eat?'

'Can't remember.'

'Have you eaten today?'

I shrugged.

'Did you eat yesterday?'

I shrugged again.

She walked closer towards me and gave me a hard stare. 'There's nothing of you. You're wasting away, lass.'

She smiled, revealing her long thin teeth again. I was so used to having doors slammed in my face and insults hurled at me, that at first, I wondered if the girl was trying to trick me. Then I thought, is she even here? Have I imagined her? The sun was behind her and she was outlined by a fine halo of golden light. I convinced myself I'd made her up. I must have been staring at her because she laughed out of embarrassment and tucked a loose strand of hair behind her ear.

'What have you got in your basket?' I said by way of distraction. I hadn't meant to make her feel uncomfortable.

She came closer and handed me the basket so I could see inside. There were red and white toadstools. 'Fly mushrooms' Ma called them, and we used them to kill the bluebottles in the kitchen. Ma would break up the flesh in a saucer of milk and leave it on the windowsill. Flies would feast at the dish and die straight after. Ma said flies could get into your head when you were sleeping and make you crazy. I looked at the basket of red and white toadstools. Da called them 'devil's hats'.

'But there aren't any flies,' I said.

'What's that got to do with it?' She gave me another quizzical look.

'Aren't you picking them to kill flies?'

'Why would I want to do that?'

'So why pick them?'

'For Alice.'

'Who's Alice?'

'Well,' she said, thinking about the answer, 'Alice is a person.'

'I didn't think she was a cowbell,' I said.

The girl laughed.

I handed the basket back to her. Although there was something peculiar about this girl, I wasn't frightened. Despite her unconventional attire and strange manner, she had a comely face, and her soft brown eyes were kindly.

'These are the last of the season. The best ones come at the end. Where are you going?'

'I'm just travelling.'

'What for?'

I shrugged.

'You're lost aren't you?'

I shook my head.

'Yes you are.'

She waited for me to respond, but I just looked down and held my tongue.

'You must be on your way to some place?'

I shrugged.

'Or else, coming from somewhere?'

I shrugged again.

'Very well, have it your way. You don't have to tell me your business. You're wise to mind people what you tell them. There's some ronkers out there.'

She stood and scrutinised me, tilting her head the way a bird does. As she did, my belly made a loud rumble. The girl laughed.

'Sounds like you're in want of a good meal. Alice says we should look after those like ourselves. She also says we should be careful of strangers. But I can see you're a poor thing. You're just rag and bone.'

I sensed she was making fun of me now. 'Well, it was nice meeting you, but I must be on my way,' I said.

'On your way where? We've still not established where you're going.'

'I'm travelling east,' I said. I felt even that was too much information.

'Same way as I'm heading. Why don't we walk together? You can keep me company.'

'I don't know.'

'Listen, have you walked through these woods before?'

I shrugged.

'Well then, let me tell you this, there is great danger ahead of you.'

'How do you mean?'

'These woods. It can be perilous here for those who don't know the way through. There are swamps that suck you in and swallow you. And that's your end. Gone!'

She seemed to take pleasure from this warning. I didn't know whether she was pulling my leg or whether to heed her advice. I thought about it. What harm could there be walking with her a spell? I was a fast runner. Hadn't I run away from trouble plenty already? I shrugged.

'That's settled then. Come on. It's this way.'

She pointed towards a meandering path that was more a rabbit run. I followed her, part of me still wondering whether she was a thing made out of my head. She hardly seemed real at all. She walked with a bounce in her stride, and she tossed her hair over her shoulders. It went halfway down her back.

'My name's Jenny.' She turned, stopped and offered me her left hand to shake. I shook it awkwardly with my right.

'We always shake with our left hand. Alice says.'

My stomach rumbled once more.

'My, my. I've never heard such belly-fretting. We've got some good broth at home. And there's bread and butter and jam and biscuits and havercakes.'

At the mention of food, I felt a pain in my mouth above my back teeth. I swallowed saliva. I tried to calculate when I'd last had a proper meal. I yearned for something to eat. Sweet or sour, hot or cold. I imagined a steaming bowl of hot broth with a side plate stacked with buttered bread, spread thick like Ma always did. I imagined folding a slice and dipping it into the bowl. That feeling in the mouth as the hot broth and the soft bread reached the tongue. The salted butter melting.

'You've got jam and biscuits?'

'Alice knows a place. Listen, why don't you come back with me and have something to eat. Alice might be a bit funny, but leave that to me. I can talk her round. If you don't eat soon, you'll die. You're on death's door, can you not see that, lass?'

Accepting invitations from strangers hadn't worked out for me so far, but what choice did I have? I was in the middle of a wood. I hadn't eaten for days and she was right, I was close to starvation. I nodded my head. She led the way through the heart of the wood, beneath lime and willow, yew and spruce. I tried to keep a track of the way in case I'd have to double back. Past a patch of shrogg, a treecreeper crawled in a spiral up a stately horse chestnut, its huge leaves a rich orange. I made a mental note of a curious mossy bowl of rock, balanced on its side.

'So, where is it we're going, anyway?'

'It's not that far. Alice found it. I've been there over a year now. One of the longest. We made the huts ourselves. Alice has axes and saws. She can get anything.'

She explained that there were seven of them but one had been thrown out. Ivy, Holly, Thorn and Heather. And Alice of course, and herself. I commented on their names, they struck me as funny. They didn't sound like girls' names, more like the names you'd give to a pet. She explained that they were given these names by Alice.

'She might give you a name too. Wait and see.'

But I didn't want to be given a name. I was happy with the name my ma and da had given me.

'I got mine because when I met her there was a spinning jenny in my hair. Alice plucked it out and said that was to be my name: Jenny. Alice has it all sorted. We take it in turns to cook and forage. There's other work too. Sometimes we have to fix things or make things. But it's not like work. Sometimes we argue but Alice sets things right again. We're all runaways. Even Alice.'

'How do you mean?'

'Well, I ran away from my village the summer before last.'

'Why did you run away?'

'Because I was accused. That's why.'

'Accused? Of what?'

'Witchcraft.'

I'd heard of people being accused of sorcery. Ma had told me of a case thirty year or more, in the neighbouring county, where eleven were accused. Ten were found guilty and hanged, but I'd never encountered it for myself, and I was intrigued.

'Why were you accused?'

'All of my brothers and sisters are dead. I am the last of my kin. I am the seventh child of a seventh child. Some say that makes me a witch.'

'And that was why they accused you?'

'My father won favour with the yeoman who employed him. So much so that he left him three acres of land. But during Lammas night we had a gathering on the land. We brought the wheat in. Folk brought loaves to church then we made merry on our farm. There was a farmer there who asked me to help him tend his cows. Thinking it would bring more money in, I agreed. But we quarrelled and two months after that two of his cows died.'

'And that's why he called you witch?'

'All the village got behind him. He was an important man.

Employed a lot of the folk around there. What he said went. He told folk he'd heard me speak the paternoster backwards.'

'Did you?'

'No. I can't even speak it forwards.'

She told me how they'd swimmed her. Nearly drowned her, in the river. How they'd stripped her and shaved off all her hair looking for the devil's mark. How they'd probed her private places. How she'd managed to trick her jailer and run away. She'd kept running. I wondered why she was telling me all of this. Both Ma and Da had always told me to keep my cards close to my chest. 'Don't be telling nothing to no one, child, it's nought to do with them,' Da'd say if he thought my tongue was too loose. As we talked we walked further into the woods. The path we were walking along was so faint that it was hardly there at all. If it wasn't for Jenny leading the way, I wouldn't have been able to make it out. I was still trying to make a mental note of the route but it was getting more difficult.

As we went further into the woods, everything around glowed green. The trees that do not shed their leaves: pine, yew and spruce. Despite the time of the year, and the bare branches on some of the trees we had passed, here it was a verdant forest, made up of huge luscious holly, thick vines of ivy that snaked along the trunks and up the branches. The bark of these trees was covered in a rich green wool made by the thick moss growing all over it. We walked along a beautiful carpet of orange-yellow larch needles. I'd never seen a forest so green at this time of year. I'd never seen holly trees so tall and thick, or ivy so lustrous. In some places the ivy vines were thicker than the trunks of the trees. The holly bushes hung with bright red berries that the sun made even brighter, like there were lanthorns dangling from the end of the branches. Spruce formed dense cloaks of impenetrable forest. The effect of this was to turn an autumn woodland into something closer to summer in full bloom. It was hard to imagine, close by, that everything was withered and dead. The whole place was teeming with life. Birds flitted from the branches and clambered up trunks. Creeper, nuthatch, green and red pecker, jay, throstle, and red-breasted dob. Goldfinch, bullfinch, blue and great titmouse. There were flashes of gold, pink, red, yellow and blue, and, in fact, every colour of the rainbow.

'Look at me, I'm forgetting my manners. I haven't even asked your name.'

Without even thinking, I said, 'My name is Caragh.' I had let my guard down. Somehow it didn't feel right to lie to this girl who had entrusted me with her secrets.

As we walked still further, we had to negotiate thick black pools and mires. The pools became so vast, that there was hardly a path between them, and I watched where Jenny placed her feet, with great care and attention, placing mine in the exact same position. As I did, the sun turned the black pools into sparkling mirrors, reflecting all the colours, but especially the verdant green. I noted the red buds of a birch whose outstretched arms resembled a stag's antlers. A twisted wych elm. Da said wych elms were good for nought but gates and coffins. All the time we walked I was listening to Jenny tell me about her life here, thinking that what she said sounded crazy. But if what she said was true then there was a meal in it for me. In truth, it was the need to eat that was driving me, making me be careless with this strange girl. I was darkly interested by the eccentricity of her tale. I tried not to focus on the knot of trepidation building in my gut, because I wanted to see this place in the woods where they all lived for myself. I wanted to meet the others she had talked of with the queer names. More than anything, I wanted to meet this Alice woman that Jenny seemed so in awe of.

'Men don't come this far,' Jenny said.

'Why's that then?'

'Too dangerous. Lots of men have died. Sucked into the mire. You start by getting your feet stuck, before you know it, you're up to your middle. Then it's impossible to get out. Even if you grab on to a branch. The force of the suction is too strong, and you sink slowly into the swamp until there's no trace of you. No one owns this part of the woods, and no magistrate will take responsibility. So technically there are no laws here. We're free of the courts and assizes. The only laws we obey are the ones we make ourselves.'

We ventured deeper into the forest, where the thick green moss clung to every surface. The path was so precarious, but it was clear that Jenny knew her way through the mire and I followed her lead. I was yet even more careful to stand exactly where she had just stood. We walked at a snail's pace.

'Then there are the people who refuse to come here because they think it's cursed.'

'How do you mean?'

'They say there are bad spirits in these woods, that lure you into the swamps. And horned beasts that walk on two legs like men. But are twice their size.'

'And is that true?'

'We don't see it like that.'

We walked further on, where the fen was deep either side of us, and I had to concentrate not to slip down into its oil-black waters. If I had been on my own I would have turned back. But then it occurred to me that I wouldn't find my way. I was too deep in and there was no way I would remember how to return to where I was. The bones and feathers of a dead heron. I felt a growing sense of dread. I needed to eat. If I didn't it would be the end of me. The way looked impassable, but Jenny navigated the patches of dry land, and we wended our way around the dark muddy pools and deep impenetrable ponds. Trees had become unrooted and had fallen across our way. We had to clamber over them.

We came to an area of the woodland fen, that was less water than land, and then the pools started to shrink in size and there were fewer of them. Jenny explained that we'd passed through the danger zone. The rest of the way was much easier, though I was still careful to follow her lead. She told me that it was precisely for the reason that men shunned it, that Alice had chosen where they lived. If you knew your way through, the fens would protect you.

'So what happened to you?' she said.

'Ah, it's a long story,' I replied.

'Come on now. I've told you mine. It's only fair.'

I thought about my kinfolk. I heard Da's words again: *say nothing to no one, child. Keep your cards back.* But this girl had trusted me with her story. Told me her intimate secrets. Why, I didn't yet know, but somehow it gave me the liberty to share more than I would ordinarily. Maybe it was the effects of the hunger. I felt light-headed. Part of me wondered whether she was real at all, if any of it was, and I opened up. I started talking and I couldn't stop.

I told her about the men who had shot my da and ma. I told her about the grave I dug and the fire I built. I told her about the man in doublet and hose, and Annie, the brothel keeper. I told her about my failed attempt to find food and work. She listened attentively.

'We're all runaways one way or another. We know what it's like to have no one.'

Eventually the wood cleared and we entered a green glade. I saw in the distance three huts made of branches. They looked like they'd been thrown together, hig, hag, hog. Not a true line or square angle in sight. They were assembled round a firepit: an oval hole with rocks and stones piled along the edge. I saw wet clothes hanging from the branches of the trees. Perched over the middle of the fire were chitty irons, and hanging from the chain a steaming pot. Standing back from all this, on a raised area, was a larger hut. It was painted bright green and red and decorated with curling golden symbols. A little yellow ladder led to a red and green door. Outside was a blue wooden rocking chair with a red cushion on the seat. It was like something out of one of Da's stories, about the little people. Stories he'd brought with him from Ballina. I'd heard somewhere that extreme hunger can play tricks on one's mind, making things appear that then vanish in thin air. I wondered if this vision was one such trick.

There was a woman with a long spoon stirring the pot. As we got closer, I could see that she was about Jenny's age, maybe a year older. Big-boned with short dark hair and eyes too small for her head. She looked like she'd cut her hair with sheep shears. She saw us approaching. As we got closer, the girl said, 'Who's this?'

'Look at these,' Jenny said, tipping her basket so the girl could see inside.

'Jenny. Who've you brought back? You know what Alice said.'

'This is Caragh. Don't worry about Alice. I'll speak to her.'

'And who's Caragh?'

'I found her in the woods. The poor thing is half-starved.'

'But—'

'Leave it.' She nodded. Then she turned to me, 'Caragh, this is Ivy. Take no notice of her, she's just a bit tetchy.' I saw Ivy give Jenny a dark look, and I wondered what I'd got myself into.

'Where are the others?' Jenny asked.

Looking over to me warily all the time she talked, she explained to Jenny that the other girls were still out foraging.

'And Alice?'

'She's not gone far.'

Ivy continued to eye me with suspicion as she recommenced stirring. How odd all this was, to find this aberrant enclave in the depths of seemingly impassable fen and forest. I couldn't fathom how I felt about it. I wondered what sort of person this Alice could be, that they would all want to stay here, following her orders. The only time I'd observed people obeying in this way before were children with their parents, or folk obeying those who had legal authority over them, such as the alderman, the constable, or the beadle. They were not obeyed naturally.

A few minutes later the door of the raised hut opened, and out walked a woman who I could see, even from this distance, was a good deal older than us, maybe two score. Possibly even older. She was dressed in a plain red frock, with no shoes or stockings. She had long black hair that she wore lose like Jenny and Ivy. It was grizzled with silver. Her skin was very dark, like the bark of an oak.

As she entered our circle, I could see that she clutched in one hand a clay pipe, which she now drew from, blowing smoke out in a blue-white dragon. She had a deep scar around her neck. Alice walked up to me and cast her eye over. She turned to Jenny. 'Well?'

'This is Caragh. I found her in the woods near where I was foraging. She was so hungry she was eating raw rowan berries. The poor lass hasn't eaten for days. I know what you said, but I couldn't leave her. I thought you might let her have something from the pot.'

'And you brought her here? Without asking?'

'I couldn't see what else to do. She was in the same state I was when you found me.'

Alice scrutinised me again. I cringed with discomfort. I was struck by how green her eyes were. Like a cat's.

'The men came for her. They killed her family.'

'We'll talk later,' Alice said. Then she turned to me, wiped her left hand on her frock and, like Jenny had done, offered it.

'A pleasure to make your acquaintance.'

Again, I wasn't sure to offer my left, as she had done, or my right, as was customary. I hesitated briefly, before offering my sinister hand. We shook.

'She's got no other family.'

'We don't welcome strangers, but you can stay for tonight, Caragh. And you're free to eat with us. You can share Jenny's bed if you like. But tomorrow you will have to be on your way. Jenny will take you back to the place you met. You'll not find it on your own.'

I was grateful for the offer of food and shelter. Something in my belly and a place to lay my head was all I could fixate on. Alice gave me the spoon and instructed me to stir the pot. She took the basket over to the largest hut and disappeared inside.

'She likes you,' Jenny said.

'Really? I was just thinking the opposite.'

'If she didn't like you, you'd know about it.'

We hung around the pot, taking it in turns to stir. As I stirred, the smell of the broth strengthened, and all I could think about was food. I felt like I could eat the whole pot on my own. I saw Alice walk out of the hut and over to Jenny. She nodded and the two of them went over to Alice's and disappeared inside. I could see that my presence had caused some tension, so I tried to strike up a conversation with Ivy. She was also dressed in a simple frock, hers was a tawny colour and badly stained. Her bare feet were also caked in mud, her nails were bitten to the quick and there were faint scratches on the backs of her hands, the kind you get picking imbers.

'I don't expect you get many visitors,' I said.

'I can't say we do.'

'Have you been here as long as Jenny?'

'Not so much.'

'How long?'

'You'll have to stir harder than that or the bottom will stick.'

I did as I was told.

'End of last winter,' she said, once she was satisfied with my stirring.

'When will it be ready?' I said, nodding to the pot.

'It has to thicken yet.'

I asked her what was in it, and she listed off the ingredients.

'Wood blewits, sorrel, chanterelle, bittercress, oak moss, waxcap, yarrow.'

I didn't know what all these things were, but the smell was rich and savoury, like the Sunday gravy Ma used to make.

'Here, let me show you.'

She took the spoon back off me and recommenced stirring, putting her weight behind it.

'Give the fire a poke,' she said.

I found a stick close by with a burnt end. I pushed the logs closer and poked the ashes. Motes of orange fire dust rose. We stood in silence for a time, then she said, 'Sorry to hear about your family. How did it happen?'

I got tearful as I told her the details and afterwards we were quiet again. I took my turn with the spoon and said, 'How about you? Do you still have family?'

'Don't know. Don't care.'

She brought some logs over from a pile close by and placed them on the flames under the pot. She started to tell me how she had come to be here. How she was chased out of town.

'I went to the bedmaker's to beg a mess of milk. And I was refused.

I was angry because I knew they had plenty and me and my mother had none. I wanted to say something to the bedmaker, but I didn't, I just scowled and left. I was told that shortly after that the bedmaker had an ache in his ankle. But I didn't know that then. I went after to the ostler, and asked him for a mess of milk, and he said he had no alms to give me. I was told that shortly after the ostler reported a stabbing pain in his lower back. It wouldn't go away, so he went to a wise man who told him that he'd been bewitched. That night in the tavern, he told the bedmaker, who still had an ache in his ankle, and he decided that he too had been bewitched.'

'And that's how you were chased out of town?'

'They said they saw me feed my cat with milk, mingled with my own blood.'

'Did you?'

'No, of course not. Why would I do that?' She laughed bitterly. 'Some men came to the house and told my mother and father that they thought I was a witch. They said that they had been instructed to take a tile from over that part of the roof where I took my lodging. One of them climbed up and removed the tile. Then they built a fire and laid the tile in it. The tile sparkled, and they said this must mean that I was in league with the devil.'

I had never heard anything so stupid. I thought Ma believed in some foolish notions, but nought as daft as this, but Ivy explained that it was not a joke. The men were deadly serious. She knew if she were to stay then she would die at their hands. I watched her as she told her tale, looked into her small brown eyes – her words were true.

'And what about your near of kin?'

'Don't care.' She kicked a log. Red sparks flew. 'They took their side.'

I supposed, like me, she'd lost her kin as well, only they were lying in a grave in her mind, not a hole she'd dug herself. I watched her tend to the fire, moving lumps of timber, stoking up the flames. I stirred the pot. My wrist still ached from the digging I'd done. My kin were gone. I'd never watch Ma cook oatcakes again, or Da sharpen his blade. Once again the agony of loss shot through my veins and my bones, leaving me weak and jittered.

Another girl joined us, short-necked with little arms and she walked with a funny shuffle. She brought bread and potatoes and put the plate down on a table, placing the potatoes in the ashes.

'These is cooked, need heating up. Alice said. Who's this?' She eyed me warily and pointed.

'This is Caragh. Caragh, this is Heather.'

We waited for Heather to offer her hand. She didn't.

'She's spending the night with us.'

'Do *she* know?'

Ivy gave Heather a look that said, what do you take me for?

'Jenny brought her back. She's not eaten.'

'Me can see,' she said, looking at me now with less suspicion. 'If Alice say, is good.'

'I was just telling Caragh about my kin,' she said to Heather, before turning to me. 'Heather shares my cynical view of family.'

Heather was maybe another year older than Ivy. She wore grey skirts with a pleated blouse, which was frayed at the cuffs. Her long blonde hair looked like it hadn't been brushed for months.

'This me family now. Me have two families. Me born with and me choose,' Heather said.

'Caragh's family are dead,' Ivy said.

'Me sorry. Me speak out of turn.'

'What happened to Heather left a bitter feeling. A very sour taste. Didn't it Heather?'

'Me father and mother chuck me out.'

'Why would they do that?' I asked.

'Me not want to say.'

'It's all right. Let it out. We're here for you.'

'Farm boys ...'

Heather's bottom lip quivered and her eyes filled with water. Ivy put her arm around her. 'Now there. It's not good to be upsetting yourself.'

'They pay for what they do. They be long time in hell.'

'They will. Satan's got a special place for them.'

She seemed to recover as quickly as she'd upset and she offered me the same sinister greeting. She sat close to the fire fiddling with her tangled tresses. I could see the poor girl was what Da called gorked. Shortly afterwards another girl joined us. This was Thorn. Like the others, she viewed me with suspicion to begin with, until Ivy offered reassurances.

Thorn was older, in her early twenties, with curly, flame-coloured hair. She had a black shawl about her shoulders. When Ivy finished her summary, Thorn seemed more eased at my company.

'Well, as long as Alice says it's all right.'

Ivy turned to me. 'It's not that we are naturally hostile, Caragh, you understand. It's just experience that has made us careful.'

'We not bad, we need be sure,' Heather said.

'I understand,' I said. I could hardly blame them, given what they had been through, what we had all gone through. We were like strange cats circling each other first, fur raised, before settling down. We talked about this and that, and I could see Thorn relax even more. Eventually she told me how she had left home.

'Gave birth to a bairn had six fingers. Words were said. Mum said Hag-Seed had six fingers. Another woman sez mi child is a changeling. Mi childer. Mi lovely baby girl.'

'What happened to her?'

Ivy answered. 'We don't talk about that, Caragh.'

'Sorry. I shouldn't have asked.'

'You weren't to know.'

Thorn carried on. 'Some men came. Found a mammet under mi bed. Made it for mi bairn to play with. They said it were a thing o' sorcery.' She shook her head, unable to finish her story.

As the sky darkened we put some more logs on the fire and crept closer to the flames. A bat flitted through the trees. The haunting chirr of a nightjar. Da told me that they could steal milk from goats. Eventually the whole group had gathered: Ivy, Jenny, Holly, Thorn and Heather. Alice walked across with bowls and spoons, and she served out the food. There was plenty in the pot and she was generous with the ladle. I was as hungry as I'd ever been in my life, but tried not to seem too eager. I dipped my spoon into the bowl and brought the broth to my lips. It was hot and I blew on it first before eating it. I poured the thick sauce into my mouth and tasted the salt and the herbs and the earthy chunks of mushroom. The sensation was overpowering. I chewed and swallowed. I was overcome by the richness of the flavours. For a moment everything in those woods went out of focus – there was just me and the bowl of broth. The broth was all that mattered in the world. I paid no one any mind and ate it without looking up. When I eventually came out of my reverie and looked at the others, I could see that they were all staring at me. I must have looked shocked because the six women burst into laughter. My cheeks burned.

'Well, well, I'm glad you appreciate our cooking,' Alice said. 'There's more if you want it?' She didn't wait for my answer. She took my bowl and replenished it.

'Reminds me of you, Jenny, when I first fed you. But even you paused for breath.' She handed me the bowl. She took a potato from the side of the fire, cut it in half, smothered it with butter and put it on a plate. She placed the plate close to where I was sitting.

'That's for you, when you finish.'

I quickly emptied the second bowl and went to work on the potato.

'Slow down, Caragh. When you've not eaten for a long time, your stomach shrinks. It can make you feel poorly.'

More slowly now, I spooned soft hot buttery chunks of potato. When I had finished, I wiped my mouth with the hem of my dress.

'Thank you,' I said to Alice and the others. I had never been so grateful for a meal. The others were still eating as Alice addressed the group.

'I want you all to welcome Caragh to our circle.' Her voice was deep and resonant, soothing to the ear. She had a strange accent I couldn't place. I couldn't tell if it was northern or southern, or from another quarter. It wasn't common like mine. She was careful with her words, enunciating slowly and clearly. Although the girls had already been introduced to me, they all turned and looked in my direction. Alice continued, 'Like us, she has come from a perilous place, to one of safety. Here, in these woods, beyond the fens, we are left alone by men. We reject their world. We reject their violence. We reject their tyranny of evil. We live off the land and worship the world that provides for us. This is where the chamber opens up. These woods are our hearth. She who teaches from the book and not from the anointing is no true minister. God speaks in stones and trees. The bones of things.'

She bade we praise the food in our bowls even though mine was empty.

The other girls nodded, as though this pagan prayer were something normal. I didn't know what to make of Alice, or the other girls. I thought about what my mother would think – that they were the devil's minions. She would be horrified by their attire, let alone the way they lived and even worse, the way they spoke and thought. But Ma was no longer here, and though I wanted to respect her wishes, I now had to find my own way in this world. A world that had murdered both my parents. A world that had tried to make me a strumpet. A world that had rejected my pleas for help. The world I knew had been turned upside down and I had to balance all this up with Ma's voice inside my head saying these women were against God. Because if they were against God, they were still offering me something that I had found in short supply lately: kindness. I looked around the camp, at the makeshift digs, at the warming fire, and at the girls gathered about. They all looked so peaceful and at ease in their own skin. They were far away from men who judged and punished and from a world that meted out cruelty and suffering.

I thought about my da and what he would say. He was a man who often spared his words, but his way of thinking was a simple one. He always said, give people a chance, no matter how different they are to you. A coat is made of many threads.

I looked at the girl named Holly. Wrapped in a thin shawl, she had arrived last at the meeting and had spoken the least. She kept her head down a lot but when she looked up I saw that she was squint-eyed. I wanted to know more of her story. While the other girls were chatting, I put some more stew in my bowl, using this as an excuse to get closer to her.

'I'm sorry if you thought I was staring at you,' I said.

She just shrugged.

'I didn't mean to stare. My ma always said it was rude to stare.'

She shrugged again.

'It's just. I . . .' I realised I was stuck for words, now I'd initiated the conversation.

'Used to it,' she said, looking down at her feet and not making eye contact.

'I was just wondering what your story was. You know, how you came to be in these woods? I've heard from all the others.'

She looked down at her feet, but I persisted.

'Come on, now. I've told you my story. That only seems fair,' I said, repeating Jenny's words to me earlier.

She eyed me properly for the first time, and I smiled at her. She smiled back. Just a little smile that hardly creased her face, but a smile, nonetheless.

'Sure, you've a lovely smile when you can be bothered to crease your face,' I said, my Ma's words, I realised as I spoke them.

She laughed.

'So how long have you been here?'

'Not long. It was Ivy brought me here, back end of summer.'

'Are you a runaway too?'

'Sort of.'

It was hard to prise her story from her, but Ma always said that I was like a dog with a bone once I got it into me, and I persisted. Eventually she yielded. She told me how she had been viewed with suspicion all her life, due to how she looked.

'Some called me a Devil childer, even from the day I was born. Mi Mam said. I was picked on by the other girls, even by my sisters. It was only mi oldest brother, Tom, who stuck up for me. And he died of fever when I were thirteen. I were called names, spat on, beaten and stoned.'

She stared at her feet. I thought she was done talking, but she recommenced.

'When I were sixteen, I met this man. He were a minstrel, who travelled the country singing songs for money. He couldn't half play the lute. He could make it sing like a nightingale. The thing was, I'd always been able to carry a tune. Mi Mam said I couldn't be a devil childer, 'cos I had the voice of an angel. The man heard me sing one day when I were down by the beck doing some laundry. He asked me if I'd join him that night. Said he had a song we could sing together. We practised it and that evening we sang and people came to listen. We got them right there.'

She hit her chest with her fist.

'After, they clapped like thunder. He passed his hat and it were soon stuffed with coins. I were at the centre of everyone's attention but this time I liked it. It were good attention. We sang together again the next night and the night after that. We practised some more songs. One evening, after we'd shared some brandy, he leant in and kissed me. And I didn't try and stop him.'

She looked yonderly for a moment then continued. 'He told me he had to go, move on to the next town. He said he wanted me to come with him. I thought he were joking at first but he kept saying it. The thing is, I'd never felt welcome in that village. I wanted a chance of a new start. So the next day, I packed a bag with a few things, and without a word to mi family, me and him, we left. We roamed from town to town, and village to village, drawing crowds everywhere we went. What had marked me out in my home village and made me a target for name-calling and worse, were now an advantage on the road. People were curious about the way I looked, and they wanted to hear mi song. I'd never been so happy.'

'What was he called, this minstrel?'

'He were called Carlow.' She stared into the fire. 'He weren't like other men.'

'How so?'

'He dint believe in marriage, or churches, or any of the conventions

I were brought up with. He loved the fact I were so different to other lasses.'

'So why aren't you with him now?'

'In the late spring, he died. I woke up one morning, and there he were, lying by my side as usual. Only he weren't breathing and his flesh were cold.'

She stopped talking again and stared deeper into the flames. I felt like I'd pried too far into her life. Her tragedy was none of my business.

'I'm sorry,' I said at last. 'I shouldn't have asked you.'

'I knew what people would say. That they'd blame me, because there weren't a mark on him. And I thought, maybe they're right. Maybe I am cursed. Even mi own sisters thought so. He were young. He were healthy. There were no reason for him to sicken and die.'

'So what did you do?'

'I knew they'd fault me. I left his body in the bed we had shared and I took to the road.'

'And Ivy found you?'

'Weeks after. I were a vagrant. She saw me stealing eggs from a farm and told me how she had been refused alms and how she'd been accused of sorcery. She brought me here.'

I waited for her to say something else, but she was silent.

Jenny came over to where we were sitting. She seemed on edge about something.

'I've been speaking with Alice,' she said.

'Is everything all right?'

'Alice has good reason to be wary of strangers.'

I nodded. I shared Alice's suspicions of others, but somehow these girls, this camp, this place in the forest. The trees. They were like one of my weird dreams that so vexed Ma.

'Alice thinks you should join us tonight, in our ceremony.'

'What sort of ceremony?'

'Those toadstools I picked. Alice makes a special potion. She says you can have some.'

'Will you have some?'

'Yes.'

'Will the others?'

'Yes.'

'Does it hurt?'

'No. Not at all. We all take it because it connects us. Alice will be able to tell if she can trust you.'

I was puzzled by what she meant, and a little scared at the idea of taking a strange potion.

'Does everyone take it?'

Jenny nodded. 'But don't join us if you don't want to. No one will mind. But Alice thinks it will help.'

I decided I would watch and see how the others were affected.

It wasn't long afterwards, that Alice disappeared into her hut again and returned with a griddle pan. She set the griddle pan over the fire. I saw that it was full of the toadstools that Jenny had picked, only sliced finely and lined up, side by side. The heat from the fire made them sweat and soon the juice from the fruit was dripping and collecting in the gutters of the griddle. Alice drained this liquid into a cup and I could see in the bright firelight that the juice was blood red. She took the griddle off the fire. She supped from the cup then passed it to Ivy. Ivy supped and passed it to Heather. And so it went round till it came to me.

Jenny said, 'Caragh is going to stand out this time.'

But instead, I took the cup and supped the juice back. Alice didn't say anything, just nodded sagely, then she passed around the dried slices, which were now like biscuits, and we each ate them. Alice banged on a tabor and the others sang. After a while, Alice said, 'If you want to cast, you can cast. The potion will purify you.' And I hadn't felt sick at all, but as soon as she suggested it we squatted on all fours and vomited the poison out. A poison that I hadn't even been aware was inside me. 'This is the original form of sacred communion,' Alice said. 'You have drunk the blood and eaten the flesh of the spirit of the woods.'

She drummed a beat that matched the rhythm of my heart. I vomited. But when I got up I felt excited. I felt renewed. I was energised. As I stared into the fire I had a feeling of timelessness. I felt like a Viking attending a funeral pyre. I had the feeling that this fire was not only every fire I had ever stood by, it was actually any fire that anyone had ever stood by. Ever. The overwhelming knowledge came into me that this fire was one of the things that was unchanged since the start of human life. Standing round the fire we were all communing with everyone that had ever lived on this Earth. I had a strong feeling of fearlessness. I felt like a statue, solid and immoveable. Or like a tree with my roots deep in the ground. And as I thought that, I was suddenly fifty foot high. As tall as the tallest tree. I could see as though it were daylight. Then I was just five inches. No bigger than a sparrow. I saw the smallest things. The beech casings were like saddlebags. Acorns were the size of ale barrels. Then I was my size again. And I just thought, here I am. As I looked at the mug, I saw it as the mud and clay that it was made of. And I could see the maker of the mug. I was standing on the doorstep of a massive truth. Alice passed more of the juice and we supped once more from the cup.

She stopped beating the tabor and turned to me.

'What I have to say to you, Caragh, is what everyone here already knows. Everything you have been told so far is a lie. Know this. There is no original sin.' The girls nodded in agreement. 'The serpent did not poison. The serpent brought truth. The garden was a prison. Eve's eyes were opened. Nothing you do, if it is true, is a sin. The only sin is to deny your true self. Mary Magdalene was not a whore.' Again, the girls nodded in unison. 'She was a priestess. She anointed the head of Jesus with nard oil. This is a symbol of the sacred marriage. A ceremony performed by a temple priestess. Jesus called her the "woman who knows all". She was the bride of Christ and bore his child ...'

As I listened to Alice, I became enraptured, first by her voice, then by her words. Her voice seemed to emanate from the trees and the earth. She spoke slowly and carefully. Her words had colour and form. I could see them leave her body and dance over the flames of the fire like moths.

Alice turned to me. 'What do you know, Caragh? What can you tell us?'

What could I say? But then the words spoke themselves. 'I know about trees,' I said.

'Trees?'

'What my da taught me.'

'And what did he teach you?'

'I know that the hazel is a magical tree, whose fruits are the nuts of knowledge. I know the alder bleeds when it's cut because it was the wood that made the cross that Jesus was nailed to. I know that elm is the best wood for a chopping block. And spruce wood makes the sweetest-sounding fiddle.'

Alice nodded sagely. 'Trees are lungs,' she said.

I started to laugh. Something was being released from me. All the fear and grief I had been carrying inside rose up and evaporated. Alice laughed also. Her laugh was warm and soft. It enfolded me. I looked around. We were all now laughing. We were one person, laughing together. We were the ferns, we were the birds, we were the trees. Laughing out of pure joy, complete delight, in the knowledge that we were free.

Eyes as Black as Gun Holes

Lane's men finally returned to the O'Fealins' after the physician had arrived only to find ash, rubble and charred timbers. Now they were following her trail, travelling through Hanging Fall woods on horseback, dismounting where the trees were densest, and leading their beasts by the reins. She would be punished for burning Mr Lane's property.

The men were Neb, Meth and Gibbs. Neb and Meth were twins, alike as two peas, and although Lemuel couldn't tell either of them apart and frequently called Neb, Meth, and Meth, Neb, he trusted them. When he'd first come across them, they were working for the Lord and Lady he'd executed and whose manor he had taken for his own and he had thought that he would have to kill the twins as well, until he found out that they were secretly supporters of the Republic. The twins had convinced him. Gibbs was more cut-throat. But you needed men like that also. He was easy to recognise in a crowd as he had several distinguishing features: his ears had been cropped, and he wore two branded letters on his cheeks – an S and an L. The combined effect of these features was generally to unnerve the onlooker.

They came to the first town Caragh had rested.

'What makes you sure she went this way?' asked one of the twins.

'Stands to reason,' said the other twin. 'If she came out of the woods in this direction, she would have headed for this town. Closest place. She'd be looking for food and shelter. Maybe even work.'

'I say we ask around,' said Neb. 'See if anyone has spotted her.'

They searched the market streets, and asked barrow and stall holders. They went into the hosiery, the butcher's, the rope-maker, the smithy, the cobbler and bootmaker's. Nothing. They found a tavern and rested their horses.

'I'm parched,' said Gibbs. For Gibbs, drinking was a vocation.

They agreed that they should drink some ale to replenish their strength.

'Let's get something to eat. My belly thinks my throat's been slit.'

The ostler helped them tether their horses but eyed the men nervously. The twins were thickset, but it wasn't their formidable height or broadness that disconcerted the ostler. Nor was it their prominent brows or mean-looking mouths. It was their eyes, as black as gun holes. Gibbs unsettled him in a different way. As well as having his ears cropped and his cheeks branded, he was wiry with arms too long for his body, and his eyes were as crazy as a snake's.

Inside the men bought an ale apiece, ordered mutton pie and ox tripe. Gibbs finished his food and drink quickly, licking gravy spatters from his knuckles, and seeing the brothers still sitting behind a pile of grub, he said that he was going to search on and would return shortly. The brothers nodded and went back to their plates and pots.

After they had finished they looked around the room. There were the usual sorts, farm labourers most of them. Work at this time of year was thin on the ground, and the days were short. There were coopers and smiths, botchers and carpenters, sawyers and millers. If you wanted a tradesman to do a job, you could always find one in a tavern in the afternoon.

Gibbs returned an hour later with no news. The brothers wondered if he hadn't merely found another alehouse but they said nothing. They bought more drinks and decided to rest up for the night. They made enquiries and were told that there were spare rooms.

The next day they asked about the town. No one seemed to be able to give them any information, until they questioned a monger who thought he'd seen a man accompany a girl by this description. They discovered that the man worked for the bawdy-house keeper. He was away for the day but would be back that evening.

Gibbs persuaded them to take refreshment while they waited. When evening set in, Gibbs returned to the bawdy house, leaving the brothers in the tavern. After a while, Gibbs came back with a smartly attired gentleman who wore an old-fashioned doublet and hose, with a stiff ornamental collar.

'This man may be able to help us.'

'Good afternoon, gentleman. For a penny I may remember.'

'Let me have it. If I like it, I'll throw you a penny,' Neb said.

The gentlemen eyed the twins warily. 'Your friend here was telling me you were looking for a girl, about thirteen or fourteen? Dark curly hair. Dark eyes. Someone without a family who might be looking for work. Might even be a bit desperate?'

'That's the one. Have you seen her? Her name is Caragh, but she goes by the name of Kate.'

'Yes, as a matter of fact I have.'

'Well?'

'Like I say, memory is a funny old thing. A penny might help me recollect. A groat would be rosemary.'

Neb put his hand around the man's throat and squeezed.

'It is coming back to me as it happens.'

Loosening his grip, he asked, 'So what do you know?'

'Like you thought, she was looking for work so I offered her some. Good work too. Not just cleaning and scrubbing work. All she had to do was lie on her back and count the wooden beams.' He laughed heartily at his own joke.

'So what happened?'

'Seems she didn't like that kind of work. Injured one of our most loyal customers. I don't think he'll ever be the same. It's like he's cupshot. Slurring his words and staggering about. No gratitude some folk. She ran off. I tried to keep up with her. Fast as a fox.'

'Which way did she go?'

'She was going east, out towards Trout Beck. If you come with me, I can point you in the right direction.'

The men followed him outside. He pointed past the cobbler's and the butcher's, in the direction Caragh had run. He shook the men's hands and bade them farewell.

It wasn't much of a lead. Maybe they should spend another night at the inn, Gibbs suggested. He wasn't in the mood for a goose chase. He'd eyed a bottle of brandy behind the bar, with his name on. The brothers shook their heads. 'Plenty of time for supping once we've caught our goose.'

A Marten's Remains

The wolf was digging for worms and the ground was cold and hard. Her legs were weak. She was using her front paws to scrape through the frozen crust of leaf mulch and topsoil. The dark earth was white with frost. As she dug down, the earth softened, becoming damp and claggy, and then hardened again. A small worm was wriggling its tail, trying to drive itself to a place of safety. It used the point of its nose like a claw to shift granules of soil and grit. As it did, she bit the pink flesh, gripping its fat muscular body between her front teeth, just enough to drag the worm out of its hole. It stretched out long and thin before pinging out of the hole and into her mouth. She used her back teeth to chew the worm before swallowing. It tasted of soil and mizzle.

There was nothing else in her gut. Beneath, the womb growing with life. The days had got cold. The nights colder. Food was scarce. She smelled for a crow's cache. It had already been plundered by rats. She dug by a tree root and found a small heap of nuts and acorns. A squirrel's larder. She chewed what she could and swallowed.

It was then that she saw in the frost, a grease-clogged chain. A ring and a heavy snap. In the jaws of the trap the remains of a marten. A fox had eaten the meat most likely. But there were some dried remnants clinging to the bones. She nibbled them free, then bit into the bones, crunching them to fragments. She sucked on the skull, crushing it between her huge back molars. She spat out the marten's teeth. The trap was a wolf trap. The marten had not been its intended quarry. But because it was, she would live for another day. They had swapped life for life.

As Dark As A Tanner's Hands

The funeral party was small, just his wife, two daughters, his manservant and two of his men: Gad and Ezekiel. And of course, the village curate. They had done everything they could to save Thomas, Lemuel's only son. They had managed to staunch the blood that was flowing, but by the time Doctor Stoker had arrived, Lemuel could see that his son was slipping fast. Stoker had tried to revive him. At first he had perked up, opening his eyes and drinking a cup of sack. Then he'd taken a turn for the worse. Stoker had used every medicine and every treatment there was, but it was no good. Thomas had died in Lemuel's arms. He'd held his body as it went limp. He'd fought back the tears so that his daughters and his wife would not see his weakness, and now he was stood over the hole where they were lowering his coffin. It took everything he had to hold himself up, to keep himself together. The Lord did indeed work in mysterious ways. And try as he might, he could never fathom God's plan. He tried to cling on to the faith that God saw the bigger picture, and that they would be united once more in heaven, but he could not get a grip on it. Not see nor grapple with it.

He also wondered whether he had driven the boy away. If he had not been so forceful, perhaps Thomas would have accompanied him and not instead taken himself off trouting. God had made a covenant with Abraham and spared him his son. Was this a test of his faith?

He remembered his boy that morning. He had looked in on him

as he had slept, how peaceful he had looked, how innocent, flesh smooth and uncorrupted, flesh of his flesh, blood of his blood. He had watched him sleep before gently shaking him awake. And now he watched as the casket was lowered into the hole. He looked down at the wooden top. He clenched the muscles around his eyes to dam the tears that were lining up to show his frailty. He swallowed back the lump in his gullet and bit his balled fist. His son would wake no more.

He'd told the curate that he would say a few words, but now, standing over the hole, his wife crying beside him, his two girls close by cloaked in grief, he couldn't find any words, and he nodded to the curate for him to have the last word. A man who barely knew his son.

One thing he knew, if there was a wolf out there and that wolf was the culprit, then he would hunt that wolf down and see justice done. He had thought all wolves gone – they had all thought this. But the woods and cloughs were good hiding places. He would put a price on that wolf's head that would bring the best bounty hunters in the land to his door. They would scour every fen and forest. Every moor and mire. Every clough and dene. He would have that wolf strung up. He would make a hat from its head and a cloak from its coat. He would have its teeth made into a necklace.

In the main dining room he uncorked a bottle of brandy and poured them all drinks. Jacob fetched his fiddle and played a melancholy tune. Lemuel sat on his own, away from the others, watching them talk, drink and laugh. What did they have to laugh about? His son was dead. His boy. They shouldn't be sitting here, they should be out there, hunting down the wolf.

He had heard of wolf hunts in Scotland and Wales. Over in Ireland too. In other parts of Europa, the wolf hunt was part and parcel of rural life. He'd heard about wolf pits concealed with foliage, and traps in the woods. Men who tracked the wolf over many miles. Why wait for permission from those above him? Who even were those people now the King had lost his head? And the lord of this land dead by his own hands. Should he go to Cromwell and kneel? Why seek blessing from a bastard council? He did not need consent to hunt man's sworn enemy. Did men ask approval to kill a rat or a rook? He would clutch the skull of his son's killer. He would clean and bleach it, mount it on his wall, next to the boar and bear skulls in his hallway.

When the guests had gone, and his wife and daughters had retired to bed, he turned to Jacob, who was tidying away the remnants of the funeral meal.

'Tomorrow, I want to hold a meeting first thing. I'm putting a bounty on that wolf's head.'

'Sir, beg pardon. Is it wise, sir, to act with haste? Should you not, first, speak to—'

'There is no one to speak to! It's all sixes and sevens. And I hear wolves can roam many miles.'

'Yes, I've heard this too, sir.'

'So we shouldn't dilly-dally.'

'It is said, sir, that December and January are the wolf months.'

'And why is that said, then?'

'Because, sir, when wolves ran freely in these lands, people were always in more danger of being devoured at that time of year. Through the extremities of cold and snow, those ravenous beasts cannot find other creatures sufficient to feast on.'

'That animal has met his match, Jacob. I'll have his skull on that wall by the end of November. Before the wolf months.'

They discussed all the arrangements. Lemuel drained his glass and he left Jacob to clear up. He went down into the kitchens and took another bottle of brandy and uncorked it. He went out into the courtyard. Inky clouds covered the moon and most of the stars, and it took a while for his eyes to adjust. The night was cold but the bottle had numbed his senses. He made his way across the yard, through the gardens and into the orchard. He sat down on a bench and slugged the brandy. He was tired but he knew that sleep wouldn't visit him until he'd got to the end of the bottle. He wondered if Elizabeth was asleep or whether she was waiting up for him, as she often did. There were apples in the grass by his feet. Some pockmarked and half eaten by bugs and birds. Some were perfectly smooth and round. A sweet-rank smell of rotting fruit. He looked up, trying to find the North Star. Any star. A cloud cleared, and he could just make out the tail of the Great Bear. He'd sat with Thomas in the summer and pointed out the constellations. It had been a beautiful clear night, the stars like jewels pinned to the ink-blue curtain of sky. Then they'd seen it, a shooting star, travelling west to east, lancing the skin of night before burning itself out. It glowed white and gold, red and green and blue. They'd watched its path, neither speaking. Silently sharing the moment. Lemuel had pointed out other constellations: the Herdsman, the Lion, the Serpent. Just as his father had done when he was Thomas's age. He glugged from the bottle. The liquor burned his gullet. He'd never seen so many apples on the ground before. They'd need collecting soon. It was Thomas who went out in autumn, skep in hand, to fetch the fruit. Not this year. Not any year. The thought stabbed him hard. Speared his heart. He got to his feet and stumbled out of the orchard.

He made it to the furthest north of the estate. To the high wall, and to the wooden door. He unfastened the latches and traipsed across the first field, over to the meadow, until he got to the banks of Mickle Beck. He could just make out the sway of the reeds. He sat down on the damp grass and guzzled the brandy. His gullet was numb now and the bottle nearly empty.

Something moved to his left. He couldn't see it clearly. In the water. A creature rising out of its blackness, crawling up the adjacent bank. A fox? A dog? It lowered its haunches, stretched its entire body, then stood and shook its fur. It looked over to Lemuel. Their eyes locked. He recognised it for what it was. That was no dog or fox. Far too big a beast. It was his wolf. His wolf. There.

For a moment the two of them remained with eyes locked. In that frozen moment Lemuel could see the beast's soul, as cold and as ancient as time. He jumped up. The wolf ran into the trees. Lemuel threw the brandy bottle at its vanishing shape. It landed short of its target, hitting the black waters. He leapt into the beck, up to his knees, then up to his middle. The ice water took his breath away. He made it to the other side, clambered up the bank. He ran after his animal. As he did, he slipped, and fell into the mud. He must have been drunker than he realised, and he struggled to stand, fighting with the claggy banks of the beck, grappling for reed and alder root. He grasped a limb, then another, pulling himself upright. He ran towards the line of trees where the beast had loped. He looked around. He could see nothing. The clouds had thickened above him, veiling the night even further. The wolf had gone. Gone. Gone. Gone.

When he woke the next day with a sore head, his tongue stuck to the roof of his mouth, a dryness in this throat, his first thought: wolf. He'd met his enemy. He was at home, in bed. Somehow he'd made it back. He was still dressed, wet and covered in mud. His wife was sleeping beside him, only she was under the covers. He got up, careful not to wake her, and stripped off his shirt and breeches. He washed in the other room and found some dry clothes. As he was fastening his buttons, Elizabeth entered.

'I looked for you last night,' she said. 'I was worried.'

'I'm sorry. I just needed some time on my own. I saw it, love. Last night, by the beck.'

'What did you see?'

'Our son's killer. The wolf. It was climbing out of the water. It saw me. It looked me in the eye. It was like some beast from hell. I ran after it but it got away.'

'Why didn't you wake me?'

'It was too late. There was nothing we could do, but it won't get away for long. I'm calling a meeting. You'll see, love. We'll get our killer. I promise.'

He kissed her on the forehead. She put her arms around him and they stood like that, clinging on to one another, neither wanting to be the first to break the bond.

A few hours later the men assembled for the meeting he'd called. His men, and a few town officials. Lemuel would look as if he were going through the official motions. Some of them at least. The beadle, the bellman, and the constable. What was left of officiation. For the year they had witnessed with the death of the King and the dissolution of what had been the state had left the world upturned and unfixed. Gad and Ezekiel were there, as were the men who he had sent off to fetch Caragh, once he'd learned that she had burned her house down. His house down. The deeds he held in his safe were worthless now. All that was left of his property were smoking embers. He spoke to Neb.

'What do you mean you lost her?'

'We know which way she's heading, sir, but we had to get back.'

'I tell you when you call it off.'

'Apologies, sir. We can set off again, today, sir. The weather is better and we'll soon catch up to her on horseback, my men know the area well. If she's headed the way she was heading, she might have made it to the fens. If she has, she'll not see the other side.'

'The swamps will eat her or worse.'

'We could hire a guide to show us a way through.'

'Look, it doesn't matter now. My priorities have changed.'

Lemuel called all the men to the table. 'Please, gentlemen, be seated.' He gave them chance to settle. 'As you all know, yesterday I buried my son. No man should have to bury his own son. It's against nature. A son should outlive his father and carry his name. But that's not—'

Lemuel was suddenly choked. He stopped and took a sip of the good claret that he'd laid out for the party. It wouldn't do for these men to see him get upset and he swallowed back the lump in his throat.

'We thought there were no more wolves. Alas, it looks like we made a mistake. For it was a wolf that murdered my son.'

'Forgive me, sir,' the constable said. 'But how can you be sure?'

'These two men here have seen it.' He pointed first to Ezekiel then to Gad. 'And I've seen it with my own eyes. That's how I can be sure.' He told them of his midnight encounter. 'And I am determined to catch that wolf and make it pay, tooth for tooth, eye for eye, life for life. I am putting a price of a hundred pound on that wolf's head.'

Lemuel paused to let the gravity of the offer sink in.

'Hundred pound? For a wolf?' the landlord of The Moorcock said. 'Are you sure you've thought this through, sir?'

'My son. My boy. What price do you put on the cost of a man's son?'

He stared at the landlord with such cold determination that the landlord looked down at the table and mumbled an apology.

'One hundred pound for anyone who can bring me the wolf intact. I want the full carcass – skull undamaged. I've a special place for it on my wall, between boar and bear.'

'What about lead shot? How can we be sure it won't pepper its skull?' said Gibbs.

'How you do it is up to you. But I don't want a mark on that head bone. I want the message to be clear, the graveness to be acknowledged, and I want to attract the best bounty hunters in the land.'

'But, sir, you'll bring in offcumdens from across the borders. There will be gangs everywhere. It will be carnage,' the beadle said. The constable nodded in agreement.

'We'll need to speak with the alderman and the sheriff.'

'Aye, you speak to the alderman if you like. And the sheriff. Speak to old Ironside himself if you want. I don't care, as long as I get my corpse.'

There were more questions but Lemuel cut through them with the wave of his arm. He walked away from the table and stood by the window looking out over his estate. He stared at the tops of the trees and further on, the fields that until a few weeks ago had been planted with grain. He'd walked the fields with Thomas, explaining how the harvest worked. When to plough, when to sow, when to reap. He saw one of his cats slinking across to the hedgerow where some finches were flitting. She was a sneaky one, that cat. Brought him a gift every morning: a shrewmouse today, a warbler the day before. A fine animal.

'Sir ... Master ...' It was Ezekiel.

'What is it?'

'Me and Gad, we can show you where we saw it.'

Gad gave Ezekiel a look. He'd spoken too loudly. The other men were listening to what Ezekiel was saying. Should have kept the knowledge to themselves. It might have given them a head start.

'Me and these two men will start our search straight away. The rest of you, I want you to put the word out. You—' he pointed to the bellman '—I want you to draw up some posters. Position them in all the main places. Outside the church, in the main street, by the two alehouses.' Then he turned to his servant. 'Jacob, get the stableboy to saddle three horses.'

'Which ones, sir?'

'Which ones? The fastest! Now go! Get them ready! Godspeed!'

His servant sped out of the room.

To Gad and Ezekiel: 'Come with me, both of you.'

He led them to the store cupboard where he kept his German matchlock musket. He put some musket balls in a bag along with a quantity of powder.'

'Sir?'

'What is it? What now?'

'Sorry, sir, it's just I thought you wanted the skull intact?' Ezekiel almost whispered.

He stopped what he was doing. He wasn't thinking straight. He put the bag and the musket back.

'That's right. Not a mark.'

He reached, instead, for his crossbow and bag of bolts. The three men put on their cloaks and went outside to wait for the horses. Jacob walked across the court with the saddled beasts. The men took each a piece and mounted them.

'Let's head to where you found my son first,' Lemuel said. Didn't a criminal always return to the scene of the crime?

They rode out of Lemuel's estate, travelling east, along Lowe Lane, across a potsherd path, then dropping down into Lowe Dene, tethering the horses where the russeting fern and bronzing bramble prohibited hooves. They clambered through the undergrowth, along the ragged edge of the beck, to the clearing where his men had found his son. Ezekiel and Gad showed Lemuel the spot, they looked for fresh tracks, but there was no sign of the wolf. They rode north along the river, across the bridge, then beside Mickle Beck, where Lemuel had locked eyes with his enemy the night before.

'It was here,' he said. 'You can see where I fought with the bank.'

The edge was still churned up with boot and fist marks. The brandy bottle bobbed in the water, caught by a fallen beech. Lemuel dismounted and bent low.

'See! Wolf prints.'

They followed the prints some way, beneath an imposing crag and through a lumb of frail birch, bark like parchment. Ash saplings. They clambered over a snedded oak, where the path got rougher and rockier and the prints ran out.

'What now?' Lemuel said. 'The bastard must be somewhere!'

Ezekiel led the way to the place they'd seen the wolf.

'It was here, by this stoop.' He pointed to a large tooth-shaped stone that jutted out of the field near a blackthorn hedge.

'By that copse,' said Gad, pointing to a clump of trees at Dale Edge.

Lemuel looked around. It was an exposed spot. Apart from the wooded copse it was all fields and meadows. What would a wolf be doing roaming these parts, unless it was desperate? Together they rode over to the copse and tied their horses to a tree. They explored the area. There was a clump of trees that grew round a steep clough. It was clear that the farmer had only left them because the ground was too steep for his plough. They searched through the undergrowth and disturbed a pheasant as they did. It gave a warning rattle before flying up to roost in the branches of a wych elm. They looked for wolf prints. Nothing. In the middle of the copse there was a clearing and evidence of a fire. A few stones had been placed to form a circle, and there were clumps of charcoal in the middle.

'Just kids, probably.'

'Or poachers?'

'What's to poach round here, apart from a pheasant or two?'

'Sir, I know plenty men who'd be happy with a brace of birds. It's a good supper.'

'It's Eddie's land, this. Might be worth asking him if he's seen any sign of it?'

Lemuel ordered his men to go up to Eddie's farmhouse and make enquiries. There were clearly no signs of the wolf now, better for them to form two parties. He'd search further on.

'Here, take this.' He handed Ezekiel his crossbow. 'Don't lose it. I'll head back. Get another. Search over yonder.' He pointed in the opposite direction to Eddie's farmhouse.

He didn't like Eddie and would rather not deal with him. Tried to buy his land off him a few years ago, when he came back from battle hungry to expand his estate, but he was one of those men you couldn't do a deal with and he had no time for men like that. More importantly, the three of them were wasting time. Wolves moved fast. He'd seen for himself, last night, the beast's speed and stealth.

As he rode back he noticed something to the side of the potsherd path and he whoa'd his horse to stop. He dismounted and went over, bending down to examine the object that had caught his attention. He picked it up by one of its ears – a rabbit's head. No body or bones or any other sign of the animal, just the head, perfectly intact. A raven or a rook would have pecked its eyes out, picked out the brain beneath. A fox would have left its spine. He supposed it could be the work of a large dog, but more likely, given what he now knew, this was the work of the wolf. He took it back to his horse and placed it in the saddle bag.

He thought about the different ways he could kill the wolf. If they knew what wood it was in, he could get his men to surround it, then slowly move in. But it was more likely that it would be harder to pin down. The last wolf killed in this Riding had been a century ago. He'd travelled widely, but never beyond the shores of his country. Never killed a wolf, or even seen one until last night. He'd killed foxes, plenty of them. He once killed a dog-fox that was easily as big as a mastiff. But that was hardly much comparison. Like the wolf, the fox was sly, that was true enough. And stupid creatures, not even as bright as a farm dog. But a fox had never killed a human child, to his knowledge. He'd caught that dog-fox when it had got its back leg gripped in an iron trap. It had stood on three legs, staring straight at him. He'd always thought foxes craven animals but this one looked deep into his eyes. No fear.

He had stood over the beast, the hot stink of it, placed the muzzle of his pistol between the animal's eyes and the beast hadn't flinched. Amber eyes kohled with black. Wet black nose. Black whiskers and ears. Red-orange fur. White cheeks and chin. A sadness in those amber eyes, and a defiance. He'd pulled the trigger, the powder had exploded, and the fox's skull had shattered into pieces. He had felt almost a respect for the animal then. He had felt small in its presence, and that killing it was a weak and petty thing to do. Although the fox was dead, the fox had beaten him. The fox was more than him. He might call himself the lord of this land but compared to that fox, he was a pauper and the fox was a King. And he'd hated that fox for how he had shrunk in his presence. He had wiped the hot blood from his hands and pushed the thought away, saying, 'Don't be daft, man, a fox is a venal and cowering animal. A lily-livered caitiff.' Man was beneath God but above the beast – that was just the natural order of things.

As he approached the village, he saw a bill notice fastened to a post outside the church. It said:

WANTED

WOLF

£100 REWARD

His men hadn't wasted any time. He knew that few men would be able to read it, but that those men who could would spread the word among those who could not.

Gad and Ezekiel took the packhorse trail over Low Fold, crossing Mickle Beck where it was broadest and most shallow. Even here, though, they were deeper than the horses liked, on account of the perpetual downpour they'd suffered. Ezekiel was relieved the floods had abated. At one point he feared that the burst bank water would reach his cottage. Lemuel was a decent landlord, and had rented him the place with furniture, but still, there would be flood damage whether he owned it or not. The wind, blowing from the north, almost plucked their broad-brimmed hats from their heads. They dropped down under gnarled ash, over scrubland, to Eddie's farmhouse. As they rode to the yard at the back, they saw Meg, Eddie's wife, pegging out the washing. She was heavy built, with a big bosom, curly russet hair and legs like butchers' knives. Two dogs were lying down close by, both lurchers, one dun, the other brinded. It was forbidden in these parts for ordinary folk to keep sighthounds. Any commoner found with a sighthound would have the feet of that hound chopped off, but most got round this by having sight and scent crossed. Meg saw them approaching, put down the basket of washing, and waddled over. The dogs sprang up and ran at them, barking.

Gad pulled his mare back. 'Hold your dogs, will you.'

He didn't like any type of hound, especially not big angry ones.

'They'll not hurt you, 'less they lick you to death. Bark's worse than their bite,' she said, turning to the dogs and scowling. Both dogs cowered. 'Shush, the pair of you,' she said to them before turning to the men. 'What do you two want?'

'Well, that's not quite the welcome we were expecting, ma'am,' Ezekiel said, tipping his hat sarcastically.

'You've not come for a social visit. I know that. Your lord and master sent you, has he?'

How did she always know what was what? That's what Ezekiel wanted to know.

'We are wanting a word with your husband. We'll not take up too much of his time.'

'Wait here.'

She walked over to the farmhouse and went through the back door.

'Let me do the talking,' Ezekiel said.

'I always do,' Gad said.

When she returned she was joined by Eddie. A big bald man in a coarse cloth and a pair of saggy slops.

'What do you two want?'

'Pair of charmers,' Ezekiel said, under his breath. 'Look, I suppose you've heard about Mr Lane's son?'

Eddie nodded. 'Terrible business. Only a year older than my lad. Thought we'd rid this land of wolves yonks ago. I can hardly believe it's true!'

'Me and Gad, the other night. We heard it howling from the copse just behind your farmhouse. Then we saw it later, when we were bringing the lad back to the estate.'

He pointed to the clump of trees they had just explored.

'Oh, aye. What time was this then?'

'It were late when we heard it, chucking-out time. When we saw it the day after it were gloaming.'

'Nothing wakes me up, does it, love?' Eddie said, turning to his wife.

'Sleeps like the dead,' she said, tutting. 'Wish I could sleep like that.'

'So did you hear anything then, missus?'

'No, can't say I did.'

Ezekiel nodded. 'And you've not seen no sign of it? Not troubled yer fowl, or any of yer animals?'

'Keep 'em locked away at night. Dogs would see it off in any case.'

'You let 'em have the run of the place do you?'

'Can't take any chances with fox round here.'

'What about pheasants?'

'What about them?'

'Not come across any that have been mauled, or any other signs of a wolf?'

'A wolf won't harm a pheasant. Not unless there's nothing else to eat.'

Ezekiel thanked them for their time and the two men rode off in the same direction, travelling up above the farmhouse towards the nearest woods.

'Do you believe them?' Gad asked, once they'd made some distance.

'No.'

'I mean, £100. They'll want it for themselves. And you can't blame them.'

'You do realise what this means, don't you?' Ezekiel said.

'What?'

146

'From now on, we can't trust any cunt.'

Money like that turned them all against each other. From this day on they'd have to be sneaky. As sly as foxes and as cunning as hedge weasels. As they rode over to the wood, he thought about how he would spend a hundred pound. It was life-changing, a sum like that. He'd never really thought big before. Men like him, it didn't pay to think big. The trick was to stay grounded. Be happy with what God had given you, and not envy those who had more, or get puffed up with ambition. But a hundred pound. It could really make a difference for him and the wife and the bairns. He could buy Kate all the fine frocks and bonnets in the land. They could have their own horses. Maybe rent a bigger place now another bairn was on its way. But that wouldn't even put a dent in it. What did he really want? But what? He didn't know where to start thinking.

'What would you do with it?' he said at last to Gad.

'Eh?'

'A hundred pound.'

'Dunno.'

'You must have some ideas.'

They rode on in silence, although Ezekiel could almost hear the cogs and wheels of Gad's brain turning over.

'Come on, think.'

'It's a lot of money.'

'Yep.'

'Dunno.'

'Come on, man, think harder.'

'I'd go to the pub. Buy everyone a round.'

'Then what?'

Gad scratched his head and thought. At last he said, 'I'd get myself the best three whores in Christendom.'

'And that's it?'

'What do you mean? I'm talking three really top-flower whores. The sort that will do whatever you ask them.'

'They all do that.'

Gad shrugged. 'But a hundred pound will get you anything.'

'I dunno. I just dunno.'

They had reached the edge of Hazel Hirst Wood. They dismounted and tied the horses to a fence post and looked around for wolf prints. They found deer and fox and hog, but no wolf. The ground was still damp and held the print of the beasts almost like a clay cast. They saw some prints that could be wolf, could be dog. It was hard to tell.

'If them are wolf prints, we'll need to dig a trap.'

'Yeah.'

'But guess what?'

'Eh?'

'Not brought any spades.'

Ezekiel was irritated with himself for not thinking about it earlier. Didn't Kate always say that he was too rash in his thinking? He was also annoyed that it hadn't occurred to Gad either. He had to do the thinking for both of them. Well, the dozy bugger could wait here. His own fault.

'Hang on, I'm just going to ride back for some spades.'

Gad watched Ezekiel get back, untether his horse, remount it and ride off. He wondered, too late, whether he should have gone with him. He waited. It was chilly when you weren't moving around and he pulled the collar of his gabardine tighter around him. Ezekiel must have been gone nearly an hour, and Gad was sitting against a tree chewing a blade of grass when he saw his friend on the horizon. He watched him ride across the field until he reached the spot where Gad's horse was tethered. He got off his horse and tied it with Gad's, then took two spades from the bundle he'd tied to his saddle and reached for the bag he'd packed with two dead rabbits.

The wood was shaped like an arrowhead, thick and broad to the east, but tapering up as it went west, so that it came to a sharp point. They started at this point, at first sticking to the path, but then veering off, following deer and rabbit runs. It was damp and musty beneath the canopy of half-bare trees. Sometimes their feet crunched on old hazelnuts, and other times they squelched in the layer of leaf mould that lined the forest floor. As they tromped through the undergrowth, they saw titmouse and warbler flit from branch to branch. Culver and ousel gave alarm calls. Half a dozen deer scampered into a denser patch of wood. They walked past a badger's sett. The main entrance was vast, and they could see other ways in and out all around. Must be an old sett, Ezekiel thought. Taken years of industry to get it this big. They carried on walking through fern and bramble until they came to a beck. It had been dammed by a fallen tree, and they could see, despite it being autumn, that some life was still thriving in the slow-flowing water. Ezekiel stopped and looked around. Nothing.

They walked further up by the bank of the river, then followed the path as it moved back into the woods, where moss grew around the trunks and branches of the trees, and a creeper pecked at the crevices in the gnarled bark of an elm.

'See here.'

Ezekiel bent down and examined a footprint. Gad crouched over him.

'Maybe that's a wolf's paw print?'

'How do you know it's not one of Eddie's dogs?'

'Too big.'

He looked around for another print mark. Seeing another, and then another, he followed it, until the ground was rocky and he couldn't see the print marks any more. He walked back to where they stood before, where the ground was soft.

'Here's a good spot.'

'You reckon?'

Plenty of deer and badger about. Rabbit, fitchew, marten. If I was a wolf, I'd have plenty to pick at. It's been here once before. Good chance it'll come again. Maybe at gloaming. The prints are fresh.'

Ezekiel knew very little about wolves, save the stories he'd been told as a child, but he wanted his cousin to think highly of him.

He took the spades and gave one to Gad. He thrust his own into the loamy soil and started to dig. The two of them worked on, until they had a pit that was a good six foot in diameter and nearly five foot in depth.

'That should do it.'

They helped each other climb out of the hole then stood back and admired their work. The sides were good and steep and smooth, too steep for a man or beast to scramble up. If a wolf fell in, it wouldn't get out again, but just to make sure, they cut some willow lengths that were thick and straight, and hammered them in with a boulder. Then they sharpened the protruding ends with their knives until they were all well pointed. They climbed back out of the pit and admired their labour.

'Nice little trap that.'

'Anything falls into that, it's a goner.'

They snapped off some still-leafy branches and covered the pit over. Then they took heaps of mulch and scattered it on top. Finally, Gad took one of the dead rabbits from out of the sack, and using a broken off branch, positioned it carefully so that it lay in the middle of the pit roof.

'Let's dig one at the other side of the wood, too.'

Gad nodded. The men hacked their way through the brambles with branches they'd picked for the purpose, until they made it to some sort of path again. They trudged through the forest until they reached its base, where it was widest. The trees here, mostly alder, were close together and this had caused them to reach tall and thin, as they outdid each other to find the best light. There were no low branches and this made it easy to wend between trunks, traipsing through a carpet of woody cones and nutlets.

'I think we should have two more here. One that end, and one there,' Ezekiel said, pointing out the two spots he'd chosen.

'But we've only got one more rabbit,' Gad said.

'Fair point.' Ezekiel nodded, and the two men took up their spades once more.

'Do we need to leave a mark?'

'How do you mean?'

'If we're digging all these pits everywhere, how are we going to remember where they are?'

'We could tie some coloured ribbon, close by.'

'Too expensive.'

'Rope?'

'Have you got some?'

Ezekiel shook his head.

'Well, in that case, we can't can we?'

After riding back to the village, they called into the haberdasher's and bought a bag of red rags. They decided to stop for a drink and tethered their horses outside The Moorcock Tavern and went in. Ezekiel ordered two ales.

'I'm only having a couple. I'm fucking knackered. Want to get back. It'll be dark soon. And the wife will wonder where I've gone.'

Ezekiel didn't want to let on that he was worried about the missus. She was off her food and complaining about aches and pains. He didn't want to think about it but this is how she was last time, when she'd lost the son she was carrying. His son. His daughter was only two year old. A lot of work for an ailing woman.

'Just thinking. What if we trap one of Eddie's dogs?' Gad said.

'Eddie's dogs shouldn't be in there. That wood isn't Eddie's wood. The copse below is his, but his land stops at the boundary fence. We'll check them traps first thing tomorrow. Don't tell anyone where they are will you?'

'I'm not daft. Course I won't.'

Ezekiel nodded, eyeing the other customers suspiciously. He recognised most of them, but there was a group of three men in the far corner he hadn't seen before, and he was convinced they had come to their village because of the bounty on the wolf. Why else would they be there? Word had got out fast. There was no time for them to be hanging around taverns. There would be plenty of time to sup ale once they'd claimed their reward. He nudged Gad and nodded to where the men were sitting.

'See them there?'

Gad looked over, trying not to be conspicuous, 'What about them?'

'Do you think they could be bounty hunters?'

'Don't be daft. The posters have only just gone up. They'll be the new hires. I heard the tan house were taking on some more men. Look at their hands.'

Ezekiel looked at the men's hands. They were stained with the dark markings characteristic of tanners. Gad was right. Still, it wouldn't be long before the strangers came to their village in droves. They would have to be wick.

Cream Instead of Milk

I was drowning in a thick black bog, trying not to swallow mud, gasping for air as it poured into my mouth and down my throat. I was choking. Sinking. There was no way out. I couldn't lift my arms. I tried to scream for help but I could make no sound. Then a beast that was neither man nor woman and was entirely white, appeared above me. I knew the beast meant me harm but I couldn't move. The beast placed its red-hot hand on my head and pushed me under.

Then I was lying on a bed of straw, dried moss and cotton grass. I'd been having a nightmare. I looked over to where Jenny slumbered, her mouse-brown hair poking above the blankets she was sleeping beneath. Just a nightmare, I thought. I wasn't in a swamp, but a bed that was more like a throstle's nest. I thought back to last night and the powerful brew Alice had served out. The words that she had uttered that had seemed so much more than words. It hardly felt real, like I had dreamed the whole thing. I pulled back the blankets and saw the dress Annie had made me wear, but my boots were close to the doorway. I walked over to them and put them on, tying the laces.

The sun was rising and shafts of green light filtered through the moss-covered trees, verdant ivy, and holly bushes. A russet-coloured squirrel flitted, climbing high before jumping across to another branch. A nuthatch scurried along the smooth grey bark of a goat willow, stopping at a patch that had been deer-nibbled to probe for creepy-crawlies. Bugs were sluggish this time of year, some reaching the end of their life cycle, a few others finding a place to sleep out the winter. A jay picked a berry from a bush and flew off with the bright red prize in its bill. The still water of the fen reflected back the green canopy and the golden sun. The whole scene seemed enchanted and I felt for a moment like a character in one of the stories Da used to spin. As I thought of him, the loss was fresh again, and I clung to the trunk of a tree. He was strong in my mind's eye and it stung and bruised all over.

I walked to the still-smouldering firepit and poked it with a stick, revealing the dull embers underneath. They glowed orange as the morning breeze travelled across them. I placed some smallish logs on top. Last night, after the effects of the toadstools had worn off, we drank birch wine that Alice and the others had made earlier in the year. They told me how in March, when the sap was rising, they would tap the birch and collect the juice. It was strong and sweet and we laughed and chatted. Alice brought her fiddle over and some sang and danced a jig. The evening had been one of bliss and I reflected that I hadn't laughed like that, or, in fact, laughed at all since the fateful morning when the men had murdered my ma and da. For a moment, the enchanted scene and the blissful feeling were threatened by an all-engulfing wave of guilt, but I pushed this away. As I stood over the remnants of the fire, continuing to poke the embers with a stick, I closed my eyes and tried to picture each man who had been party to the slaughter of my kinfolk. My dear, sweet ma, and my big, kind da. I started with the leader, Lemuel Lane, a bear of a man with dark, short-cropped hair and a bashed-in nose, then I worked my way through the rest. Some of them were sketchy, but I could remember most. A stocky man with a ginger beard. Twins with coal-black eyes. Then there was the man with his ears cut off and letters burned into his face. Not easy to forget someone marked in such a way.

'You been up long?'

I looked up. Jenny was standing close by.

'I was thinking about last night,' I said.

'Alice says the ceremony helps us connect with the spirits of the forest. She's got other potions too.'

'What for?'

She raised her eyebrows and smiled. 'Give me a hand getting this fire going again.'

We went over to the woodpile and gathered more logs. We used some kindling first, to coax the flames, then added some of the smaller logs, before placing the biggest ones on top: oak, ash, birch. The flames licked between the chucks, lapping up the bark first before blackening the heartwood.

'What do you do if the fire goes out?' I asked.

'We never let the fire die. We keep it burning,' she said.

I thought about Tom Bell again, sitting on his one-legged stool. His fingers black with charcoal. We watched the flames rise like orange tongues. The only sound, the hiss and crackle of the fire. A throstle plucked a holly berry, then took flight.

Jenny went into one of the huts that was used as a storeroom. Inside there were jars, and casks, baskets and barrels. She reached for two large jars. She brought them to the table and put them on top. Then she searched around for some wooden bowls. She tipped a mixture of dried fruit and nuts into each bowl, then passed me one of them. It was a wonky shape but functioned all the same. I thought about Da and the finery of his whittling.

'Nuts and seeds and fruit. Alice says that they're the forest's bounty. We just help ourselves at breakfast, as we all wake up at different times. I'm normally the first one up. Alice is normally the last. She stays up later than the rest of us.'

'She can play that fiddle,' I said as I chewed some of the fruit. Although my da was the better player, I thought.

'She writes her own songs.'

I thought her songs had gone on too long and they lacked melody – my da's songs always made you tap your feet – but I didn't say anything.

I nodded. I ate some more fruit.

'What you told me yesterday, about how you came to be here. When was that?'

'When did I run away? It would have been early autumn. Just over a year since.'

'How did you find this place?'

'When I ran, I didn't know where I was going. I walked for days before I came across a town to the south of my village. I tried to find work, but there was nothing for me. I slept in an old outhouse that had no door. I went to the church and asked the curate if he had any alms. He gave me porridge with sour milk and stale cake. He found a blanket for me and he said a prayer, asking God to come to my aid. I went round all the shops and farms and asked if there was any work for me. I approached the mongers at the market too. There wasn't any. After a few days, I was desperate. I hadn't eaten anything other than what the curate had given me. I sat down on the cobbles of the main street and held my hand out, begging for pennies. For hours I sat there. For my rewards I earned two ha'pennies. Eventually I begged enough for an apple from the shop. It was bruised and marked, but I ate it all the same. The woman who worked there felt sorry for me and she gave me a broken biscuit. I lived like that for over a month. Begging for pennies during the day, sleeping in a building that was falling down around me at night. One afternoon, this black-haired woman came up to me and started talking to me. She was interested in me. Asked me what my name was, where I was from, how I'd come to be there.'

'Alice?'

Jenny nodded. 'She took me to a pie shop and bought me an egg and onion tart and a cup of burdock cordial. It was the first substantial meal I'd had in days and I gobbled it down. She told me that she was a runaway too, and that she had a place I could live where I'd be safe.'

'And she brought you here?'

'There were only four of us then. Me, Alice, Holly and Thorn. Holly has been with her the longest, she got together with her the autumn two year since. There was another, but she had to leave.'

'Why was that?'

'Alice said.'

We ate in silence. I thought about my own destitution and how close I had come to starvation.

I saw Ivy approaching, wishing us good morning.

'Here, have this,' Jenny said, and gave Ivy her empty bowl. Ivy tipped some of the fruit and the nuts into it and sat down beside us.

'Do you think Alice will let me stay?' I said to Jenny.

Jenny shrugged. 'Hard to say.' She turned to Ivy. 'I was telling Caragh about when I got here. You came in the spring didn't you?'

'You were picking hearlick from the forest floor. Huge baskets full of it. I remember the forest full of its scent.'

'Alice says it strengthens the blood.'

As we sat and ate the rest of the breakfast, I had two voices in my head. My ma's voice, saying that these women were heathens and were against the Christian God, and my own voice that said no matter how strange all this was, it was better than what I'd experienced so far. For the first time since I'd run away, my belly was full. I had nowhere else to go. I tried once more to remember the name of the safe place but I had to accept that it had fallen out of my head. I would try and stay here with these wild women in their fenny wood where no man ventured.

'When nothing else grows, there's sorrel and yarrow and bittercress. Alice knows where the edible roots are. She marks them in spring so she can find them in winter.'

It was a strange kind of freedom these girls had, I thought. They were free to do as they pleased, as long as Alice gave them permission. My ma's voice in my head, spoke up once more. *You can't trust these people. They're in league with the devil, sure as oats is oats.* But I reasoned that they were all carrying out Alice's orders willingly. She wasn't enforcing any of this, from what I could see, and there didn't seem to be any form of punishment meted for those who disobeyed. *You wouldn't know, Caragh. You haven't seen anyone disobey yet, you silly child.* My ma's voice again. I emptied it out of my head. As if I didn't have enough going on without her constant contumely.

'Last winter we had a hard spell, when the ground was frozen. All the fens were iced over. Frozen snow coated all the boughs of the trees. We went into town with Alice. She sang and played, Holly joined in, and a crowd gathered around them in the market square. Alice put her hat down and we had enough money by the end of the day to feed us for the rest of the week. We bought plenty of food from the market and brought it back with us.'

As we talked we were joined first by Holly and then by Thorn. And eventually everyone was gathered round the fire except for Alice. I wondered if they ever woke her up or whether they left her to wake of her own accord. We talked some more about how their family functioned. We kept the fire going as Jenny took an axe and started on the woodpile. I helped out, in the same way I used to help Da, setting up the bigger pieces, moving and stacking. Jenny explained that there was a lot of dead wood in the forest, because of all the beavers.

'Alice says that the beavers are the bailiffs of the forest.'

I shrugged. I didn't understand what she meant.

'Life thrives in slow-moving water. Beavers slow the river down. Plants can grow, bugs lay eggs, fish eat the plants and bugs. If it wasn't for the beaver, the river would be a barren place. This is the only forest left where beavers still live.'

I was confused. My da said the beaver was no more. They were hunted to extinction before he was a boy. He said his da used to collect their pelts and eat their meat and told me how their scent glands were once used in perfume.

'But I thought there were no more beavers?'

'Alice brought some back with her.'

'Where from?'

'She never says.'

'Alice finds things.'

'Their importance to us is not in what their corpses give up, but the life they can bring through their damming of the river. That's what Alice says.'

'Alice knows.'

As we talked I saw the door of Alice's hut open and she appeared in the doorway, stretching and yawning like a cat. I watched her take her red shawl and wrap it round her shoulders. She walked towards us, stopping by the fire to warm her hands.

'Morning, everyone.' We all said good morning to her. She rubbed her hands together and wrapped her shawl tighter. 'We have two fires we must feed. The fire that warms us and the fire that drives us.'

They all nodded sagely.

'We must make the most of this dry weather. It won't last. It will rain tomorrow. And the next day. I want Heather and Holly to fetch more wood. Jenny, can you take Caragh with you and bring in the autumn harvest. Gather all there is.'

Jenny nodded.

'Ivy, Thorn, you will work with me today.'

Again, it occurred to me that they all seemed happy to be ordered about in this fashion, but I wondered what would happen if they refused to do as Alice said. The devil in me wanted to test this. But the pragmatist inside said leave it. *You are safe here, you are fed here, what matter if it requires your subordination? Didn't you happily follow the wishes of your parents without quarrel?*

Once we'd finished chopping our pile of wood, I followed Jenny over to her hut, and we fetched two baskets.

'We'll have to go further afield,' she said. 'We've picked the woods round here clean.'

We walked up through the fens and along the beck until we came to a flattish clearing that was cluttered with dried leaves. We shifted through them until we found the yellow-white caps of the chanterelle. We saw from the base of a beech tree a mushroom that Jenny called plums and custard. Yet despite this appetising name, Jenny explained that it wasn't edible. We found some oyster mushrooms growing from a dead tree trunk. We plucked their caps and left the root in the bark. We found some grey, gnarly mushrooms growing from some grassy tufts, and Jenny explained that despite their unappetising appearance, these were saffron milk caps, and very good to eat.

'Alice says not to pick everything. Always leave the little ones for the wood folk.'

'Who are the wood folk?'

'They're all around us. Only we can't see them.'

'How do you know?'

'Alice gives us something that lets us see.'

I wondered what she meant, and whether Alice would give me the same thing. And if she did, whether I would take it. I thought about my da and his tales of the fairy folk back over in Ballina.

'Look at this.'

Jenny went over to a clearing above some standing water, where two dead trees lay. Near to these, she crouched down and with her knife she sliced a big fat mushroom at the base of its stem.

'Ceps. The forest's true prize.'

There were half a dozen, clustered quite close to each other. These were what I called penny buns. What I'd been eating when she found me at the point of near starvation. I helped her pick them and clean them, before transferring them to the basket. Their stems were fat and milk-white. The caps were toffee-coloured. Instead of gills they had a yellowy sponge beneath the caps. They were fresher than the ones I'd found the day before. Not as grub-holed. I'd picked them before this. Da liked a few in his malkin stew, although Ma was suspicious of any mushrooms. Said they were charmed and not to be trusted.

'What are we going to do with all these?'

'When we get back, we'll slice them and thread them. Hang them out to dry.'

I pulled back a curtain of bracken. A massive cep was standing in the middle, its base even fatter than its fat cap.

'That's a big one!' said Jenny. 'You've got a real eye for them.'

I cleaned the stem with the knife she had given me and put it in the basket with the others. We walked up into a denser part of the wood and came across some hedgehog mushrooms. Jenny showed me the underside of the caps, which were not gilled or sponged, but spiked, like the jacket of the animal that gave them their name.

'These are good eating ones too,' she said.

We must have been picking for less than an hour, but already we had two baskets full of food.

'Thought Alice said they were thin on the ground?'

'They were. You must have a good eye, like I said.'

We found a clearing where sorrel grew and picked a few leaves.

'You have to be careful not to confuse this,' Jenny said.

'Why's that?'

'It looks like lords-and-ladies. Lords-and-ladies is deadly poisonous. But look.'

She held up the leaf for me to see.

'Both have backward-pointing lobes. But with lords-and-ladies the point of the lobe is rounded, whereas with this sorrel the lobe is sharp. See? Or is it the other way round?'

I must have looked worried because Jenny said, 'Take no notice of me, I'm only teasing.'

She picked up some more leaves and put them in the basket.

We'd been foraging for hours and were heading back when we heard some voices in the distance. Jenny ducked behind a gorse bush and I followed her lead.

'What are we hiding for?' I whispered.

'Some men try and stop us from living here.'

We waited in silence. The men got closer, and we could hear their conversation.

'I've lost its trail now. The path is too dry here.'

'Wait, what's that?'

The men came closer. I could see now that one wore black boots and a tall black hat. The other two wore rough cloth and farm labourers' caps.

'That's a wolf's footprint, no mistake.'

There were three men and they had stopped to examine the mark.

'Let's dig a place for it. Good a spot as any.'

The men took spades and started to dig. Jenny put her finger over her lips to indicate that we needed to stay silent. Through the gorse bush we watched the men dig a hole.

'How many others do you think are after that hundred pound?'

'Don't know, but word's out there, that's for sure. So we need to catch that fucking wolf before anyone else does.'

'Hundred quid. What's that split three ways?'

'It dunt split.'

'What do you mean, it dunt split?'

'Not even.'

'There's thirty-three pound for two of us and thirty four for t'other.'

'So who gets the thirty-four? It's not fair.'

'We'll toss for it.'

'Wait a minute. It does split. Thirty-three pound six shillings and eight pence each, yer cheating bastard!'

'Stop arguing. We'll have a party, and the drinks will be on us.'

'Money we'll have, we can have parties till this time next year and still not eat into it.'

'Ale, steak and strumpets.'

They carried on digging their hole in silence. I wondered how long we'd have to wait until it was safe. Crouched behind the bush, my legs were starting to ache.

'They say the brains of a wolf decrease and increase with the moon. If the neck of a wolf is short, then it has a treacherous nature.'

'All wolves have treacherous natures, you daft cunt.'

'If a travelling man or a labouring man wears the skin of a wolf about his feet, his shoes shall never pain him.'

'I heard that on Hook's Farm. Back in the day, they caught a wolf by taking the farmer's border bitch on heat and staking it to a post. The bitch lured the wolf. And when they copulated they couldn't break apart, so the farmer and his mate clubbed the fucker to death.'

'That's the way to go!'

The men laughed.

'That should do it.'

'Dunt need to be deep. Just enough to cover.'

'Have you got the irons?'

'This is the last one now. Let's call it a day.'

'You're kidding. It's not even midday. We'll go back and get some more.'

There was some shuffling around and then the men put their spades back in the sack.

'I'm not carrying them this time.'

'Not my turn neither.'

'You moan like fucking girls. I'll take 'em. Hang on. Need to ming.'

The black-hatted man walked over to where we were crouched. We curled up even further, trying to make ourselves smaller. I could just see from a gap in the gorse, the man's pink fleshy member and an arc of amber liquid, which hit the ground near my feet. The arc dried up and the man shook the drips from the end and buttoned himself back.

'Where next then?'

'We don't want to go any further that way. It's all fenland.'

'They say them fens are cursed. I've heard there are woodland sprites that try and drown you. Men have died trying to get through them.'

'I wouldn't risk it.'

'Besides, wolves don't like water. It won't have gone any further east. Come on then, let's go this way next.'

The three men made their way out of the woods the way they came.

'They've come for the wolf. We need to get back to tell Alice.'

My head was reeling. First beavers, now wolves. Animals I thought were no more. I remember Da telling me of wolves over in Ireland. He'd been part of a group who'd caught and killed one. He told me how Ma had said, 'Well good riddance to that then'. She'd brought out the jug of whisky from the pantry and poured them a dram. Ma and Da knocking them back, saying, 'To the wolf's end'.

Jenny went over to where the men had buried the trap beneath twigs and leaves and dug the shallow pit. She took hold of the trap and placed a stick in its mouth to set off the jaws. The jaws bit hard into the wood. It splintered and split in the angry black teeth of the contraption. Jenny slung the spent trap into her bag and we made our way back to camp.

'What did you mean back there, when you said they'd come for the wolf? There are no wolves.'

Jenny shrugged. We ducked under the low bough of a goat willow.

'Those men must be mistaken,' I said. 'Perhaps it's a dog. A rabid dog can be awful fierce.'

'It's not a dog.'

'How do you know?'

'Just do.'

I'd heard the last wolf was caught over at Wraysholm, back in the time of Edward's reign. The King had put a price on its head and there had been a hunting party. A chase with lords and bloodhounds to keep the scent, and wolfhounds to pursue the wolf. Jenny just said, 'It's like Alice says. Everything you think you know you don't.' She looked at me and raised her eyebrows.

When we got back to camp it was mid-after. There was just Ivy by the fire.

We put the baskets on the table and Jenny went over to her. 'Where's Alice?'

'She went up to the north side of the wood, stripping fireweed.'

We found her by a massive colony that was growing above the beck. The seed capsules had split and the heads of the flower were white and fluffy like duck down. Alice was stripping the plants with her hands, then using a knife, slicing the stems and scooping out the pale green pith. As she did, she spotted us walking across.

'You know, you can use every part of this plant. The leaves, the flowers, the seed pods. If you know where to look you will find God in all things.'

She passed me some of the pith.

'Try it, it's a bit like cucumber.'

I reached for the curl of pith on the palm of her hand and placed it on my tongue. I tentatively chewed it. I nodded. I had never tasted cucumber.

'We make tea from the leaves.'

She reached for her basket and started to place the pith she'd already gathered into it.

'In the spring, we collect the young fireweed. You can eat the whole thing raw. But the best bit is the tap root. They have massive tap roots. You only need a few to fill you up.'

She stripped some more of the pith. She collected the cottony seed heads in a sack.

'How did you fare?'

Jenny explained that we had filled two baskets with good mushrooms.

'The thing is, as we were heading back, we came across a party of men.' She reached into the bag and pulled out the trap. She handed it to Alice. 'Three of them.'

'Hunters?'

'They know about our wolf.'

'How?' Alice examined the trap. 'You sure they weren't catching deer?'

'We heard them, didn't we, Caragh?'

I nodded.

'They were talking about a bounty. There's a hundred pound on the wolf's head.'

Alice didn't say anything. She nodded slowly, deep in thought.

'They said it would split three ways, thirty-three pound six shillings and eight pence each.'

'Who would put that kind of money down on a wolf's head?'

'I don't know, but you know if they're asking for that much, there will be strife.'

Alice examined the trap again. She turned it round in her hands.

'Did you recognise these men?'

'No.'

Alice gathered up her equipment and we walked back together. When we returned, Ivy had been joined by Thorn. They were cooking potatoes, moving the cinders around them. Alice fetched some dried beans and added them to a steaming pot of stock. She took a handful of dried leaves from a bag and dropped them into the pot, giving it a stir, then passed me the wooden spoon.

'Here, you keep stirring that.'

She checked on the potatoes by prodding them with a thin metal spike, then addressed the group.

'I expect that you've heard from Jenny and Caragh about this.'

She picked up the irons and placed them on the table for all to see.

'Seems there's a bounty on our she-wolf. A big 'un too. And you know what that means?'

She looked around for a response.

'Men.'

'Hunters.'

'Yes, men will come looking for the wolf, and if they catch her and kill her, something in this wood dies. If they kill her something in us will die. The force that keeps these woods alive is strongest in her blood and in her bones. It is our duty to this forest to protect her from these men. We need to stop them any way we can. That means spoiling their traps, filling in their pits, putting them off the scent, and doing anything we have to.'

Alice went into her hut and came out with a black crown and mantle. She pulled up a stool and sat by the fire. The other girls carried their stools and formed a circle around her. Except Jenny. I couldn't see any sign of her. Alice placed the mantle round her shoulders and tied it at the neck. She put the crown on her head and I could see it was made of feathers. She plucked one of the feathers and held it to her mouth, breathing over the feather, running it between her lips. Then she began to whisper something through its barbs. She placed the feather on the fire, and we watched as the flames consumed it. Then Jenny appeared holding a cup. Alice took out a pouch. She poured some grey-brown flakes into the cup and Jenny ladled some of the broth and swilled it around. Alice blew on the broth to cool it, then sipped. She did this until she had emptied the vessel, then she started to mumble something. The others joined in. Jenny sat down beside me.

'What's she doing?' I said.

'She has a familiar.'

I must have looked puzzled because she added, 'It's a raven. She can enter its body. She can fly where she wants.'

I'd heard the word 'familiar' before. Ma said it was what witches had and was a sure sign, along with the mark. When I'd asked her about this mark she'd said, 'The devil baptises the witch with blood from the mark he makes when he bites her flesh. The Lord protect us from witches and long-nebbed things.'

'She can see through the raven's eyes.'

I'd never heard anything like this. Ma never mentioned that witches could enter the body of a beast and see through its eyes, and I wondered for a moment if Jenny was pulling my leg. The longer I stayed with these women, the weirder their world seemed to be. But somehow, there was something in me that just accepted this, went along with it, even though Ma's voice was screaming 'witch!' I could hear her voice in my head quoting from Exodus. *Thou shalt not suffer a witch to live.*

The girls were chanting now, but what I couldn't tell. It could have been another language or just gibberish. I wondered if they had taken leave of their senses. The chanting got louder until it simplified into one low note. They sustained the note for several minutes. Somehow this drone soothed. It seemed to reverberate with the forest. Alice raised her arms slowly above her head, her palms spread. As she raised her arms, the note the girls harmonised gained volume. Then she lowered them, and the sound faded away. She placed her hands on her knees and closed her eyes. Nothing. Silence. I looked around. The girls were sitting like Alice, with their hands on their knees. Only their eyes were open and they were watching Alice attentively. Still nothing. I heard the wind wiffle through the branches, rustling those still with leaves. Debris from the wych elm floated down. A leaf flitted to and fro as it spiralled through the air. Still nothing. I sat and I waited. What for, I did not know. This was insanity, surely. I was a guest at a madwoman's tryst. Minutes went by, still nothing. A woodcock zigzagged between wicken and withen. I wanted to say something, anything, just to break the silence. I wanted to ask how long we were to sit like this. Then the sky darkened and cooled and something moved above me.

I looked up and saw a large black bird fly across, landing in a tree close by. It was a raven. It perched on a bare branch and scrutinised Alice. It bowed its glossy black head towards her, opened its massive bill and croaked. Alice opened her eyes and looked directly at the bird. She held out her arm, and the bird flew across and landed on it. It bowed its head again and croaked longer. Alice bowed her head and hunched up her shoulders. She closed her eyes and made a raven-like croak. Nothing. Then the bird flew off and Alice collapsed on the ground, like she had fainted. What on earth was going on?

'Is she all right?' I asked Jenny, trying to keep my voice steady.

'That's not her. That's just her body. Alice is now in the body of the raven.'

The bird flew up over the trees and disappeared.

Again, my mind was struggling to process what I'd seen. People couldn't really enter the body of another animal, could they? But if not, what had I just witnessed? We waited by the fire for the bird to return. Jenny and Holly talked about how they'd first learned about the wolf through Alice's possession of the raven. How the raven and the wolf had formed a bond. They talked about the bounty on the wolf. Men would come. Hunters. They'd bring iron traps, crossbows, pistols and muskets. They would dig wolf pits and lay poisoned meat trails.

As we talked about the wolf, I noticed the sky darken, and the raven return once more. It landed close to where Alice's body lay and bobbed its head three times, croaked and then it flew off as quickly as it came. We went over to Alice's body. Holly took hold of one of her hands and squeezed it.

'Alice, are you there? Alice?'

At first the body didn't move. Then the hand stirred and the head turned. Alice opened her eyes and looked up at Holly. She allowed Holly to help her to her feet and guide her to the stool. She helped her wrap her red shawl around her. Jenny fetched a bowl of broth and gave it to Alice, who smiled and thanked her. She blew on it before bringing the lip of the bowl to her mouth. She supped the broth.

'Did you find the wolf?' Holly asked.

Alice nodded.

'Is she in danger?' Jenny asked.

'The wolf is the monarch of the forest. Without the wolf, roe, red and fallow will take over. The tender stems of the trees will be eaten before they've had chance to grow, and life on the land will be reduced. Once men and women lived alongside the wolf, but when they changed their way of life to that of farmers, the wolf was no longer an ally. The wolf was seen as a threat. Once man caged his food, the wolf was man's enemy. For hundreds of years man has hunted the wolf. Before man caged his food he lived with the green world. Now he has set himself apart. There is a price to pay.'

'Me give you all me money,' Heather said.

I wanted to laugh, but none of the others were laughing.

'We must protect the wolf.'

'How do we do that?' Thorn asked.

'We will eat. Then I will tell you how.'

She took hold of the irons and held them up. 'I want you to bring me as many of these as you can find. We will heat them in our crucible and hammer them into spades. Look out for pits and where you find them, fill them in. Watch for poisoned bait and bring it back here so we can burn it in the flames.'

I stirred the stew as Jenny chucked in clover leaves and flower heads. She took burdock roots and peeled the outer skin off with her knife, chopping them into small chunks, throwing them into the pot. As I stirred the pot my mind returned to what I had just witnessed. What had I seen? Alice. The raven. The wolf. Was this witchcraft? When the liquid thickened Jenny ladled out the broth. We each took a bowl and ate the stew and drank pine-needle tea. Holly fetched a carboy of birch wine. She drank from it and then passed it around. We all took a good sup of the sweet liquor.

Alice spoke: 'I'm old enough to remember a different time. I speak of a time before any of you here now lived. My mother and my father were part of a sect. How would you call it? Let's say, a religiously unorthodox group. There was an agreement between freeholders and copyholders to enclose and divide a common. My mother and father were part of a congregation that opposed the enclosure. Fifty charges were drawn up against my kin. My parents believed that heaven and hell were not worlds beyond ours, but rather, they were placed here in this world. They denied the significance of ordination and put the spirit above the word. My father preached that God was in man and in nature and located heaven and hell in the heart of men. He taught me that miracles have not ceased, rather our eyes are now blinded and it is we who cannot see them. He said that prayers were petitions for lickspittles. We stood on the other side of the room to Job's comforters. We, like the wolf, are the despised of the world. We, like the wolf, are hunted by men. We are one flesh, one matter.'

I looked around at the other girls. They seemed enraptured by Alice's words, as though spellbound. I too felt their power, the truth of her words, even though I knew them to be irreligious. Blasphemous. Was I now in the company of witches? Were we in fact a coven? And if so, what did that make me? *Thou shalt not suffer a witch to live.* Ma's voice in my head.

'God is in everyone and every living thing: man and beast, fish and fowl, and every creeping thing, and every green thing, from the highest cedar to the ivy on the wall. He is me. I am him. The day of judgement is a bugbear to keep men in awe. There is no life after death. Even as a stream from the ocean is distinct in itself while it is a stream, when it returns to the ocean it is swallowed and becomes one with the ocean. So the spirit in you, whilst in your body, is distinct from God, but when death comes your spirit will return to God, and so become one with God, yea God itself. The spirit of the wolf is God. And more so, this spirit has a special place in our world. Our duty is to protect this spirit and deliver this wolf from the avarice of evil men. Tonight, when I go to sleep, my mind will turn over and over the best way to protect the wolf and honour her spirit and the spirit of this forest, and every green thing.'

The girls cheered Alice, and I joined in with them. 'Together we are strong. The more of us the stronger.' Alice turned to me and said, 'If you will stay with us, we would like you to join us.'

I looked at Alice and then at the others. They were urging me to accept. I felt a strange feeling of desire and horror mingled, my heart entire tearing itself away from the world I had known. I nodded, and they gathered around me, placing their hands on my shoulders. They began to chant again in a language I did not understand. They circled me seven times, before Alice brought the ritual to a halt.

'Caragh, you are now one of us.'

The carboy was passed around once more. I was honoured. I was told how important I was to them now. I felt true acceptance for the first time. I was them. They were me. I wondered, when Alice had been so hostile to the idea of me staying with them, why she had now accepted me. What had changed? I pushed the thought out. Alice gave me a name. I was baptised again. My name was given to me because I had been eating the berries when Jenny found me. I was no longer Caragh. I was no longer Kate. My name was Rowan.

Alice splashed birch wine on my crown and the girls chanted my new name.

The howlets and the nightjars flashed as the forest grew dark. Alice turned to Jenny and asked her if she wanted to stay the night with her. I saw them both walk hand in hand to Alice's hut.

I wondered why she would rather sleep with Alice than in her own hut, but perhaps Alice's hut was cosier. I shrugged. It only meant that I would have more room to spread in Jenny's hut. It didn't matter to me who slept where, I had been accepted into the group. I was one of them. I watched as Alice and Jenny reached the door. Jenny turned to look at Ivy. Not at me. It was a look I'd not seen before. Except on a cat that was given cream instead of milk. Alice opened the green and red painted door, then they climbed the yellow steps. Alice placed her arm around Jenny's neck and the two of them went inside. Ivy stared after them. She bit her lip and poked the fire with a stick.

'Pass me the carboy,' she said.

Wolves' Tongues

Ezekiel loved spiders, the way they looked, the fact that they gave some people the jibber-jobs, and it tended to be people that he had little or no respect for in the first place. So the way they reacted to spiders just confirmed his gut reaction. Then there was the fact that they made webs. He'd idled many an hour watching a house spider spin its silk and cast the fine threads across a chasm, making an intricately layered maze to ensnare its prey. He'd watched them dance lightly over the fine lines they'd made, then sit back in a hidden place, resting one leg on the hotline, waiting like a fisherman waits with his line in still water. Minutes, sometimes hours, before the quarry would take the bait. He loved the fact they ate flies. And not even immediately. The way they wrapped them up like a Michaelmas goose and saved them till later. The way they sucked the insides out of them, leaving the husk, a ghost of a fly, as a totem of their strength and power. He loved the fact they were silent. They didn't buzz around you or fly into your soup. They didn't drown in your beer in the summer or get stuck in the jam.

He'd once seen a wasp and a spider fighting. The wasp was easily twice as big and had landed slap bang in the middle of the spider's web. He'd watched it struggle to free itself. Its frenetic dance had alerted the spider, who, being clever, didn't rush over all at once. No, what the spider did, was simply stay where it was, eyeing the wasp greedily. It knew the value of patience. It let the wasp spend itself, using all its energy trying to escape the silken ropes the spider had spun so craftily. Then, when the wasp had no more fight left, the spider nonchalantly trotted across and wrapped it up, twisting and turning it, as though it were a mere bauble, completely encasing it in its trap.

He was thinking about all this as he watched a spider work on some repairs to a web it had woven on the outside of his window. He was waiting for Gad to knock so they could check on the traps. They had been hunting the wolf for over a week now but they were no nearer their prize. Men had arrived from out of town, offcumdens with only one thing on their minds – the bounty on a certain elusive beast. As he waited and watched the spider at work, he thought about what they could learn from it. They had their quarry to catch all right, a big bloody wolf. But what about the men who had come into town? Then there were all the men in the village, the sawyers, the delvers, coopers, tanners, smithies and farm labourers, who would all be starting to feel the pinch. Who all had families and hungry mouths to feed. Who had all been affected by recent flooding. Had bags of grain spoilt, and other foodstuffs. Who were all worried about the oncoming winter. It got tough. December was just about bearable as long as you'd stored up enough, but by January, things were getting hard. And by February, the hardship really kicked in. You couldn't always expect to eat every day and what you did eat might be a meagre supper. This was when the scant rations he received in the army seemed plentiful. When he yearned for a penny loaf, an ounce of butter and a pint of beans a day. Hard times like that bred hard men. If he and Gad were going to stand a chance of bagging that bounty for themselves, they were going to have to act like the spider. Know when to pounce and when to sit tight.

He stared at the spider as it put the finishing touches to its web. Spiders made good mothers. Didn't leave their bairns to cope with life on their own, carried them about and made sure they were safe.

As his mother had done. And how Kate, his dear wife, did with their daughter. Not like flies, who abandoned their young in the rivers and lakes, or in the carcasses of dead beasts, or worse still, in the shit of those same beasts, to be eaten by birds and fish and other predators. That was no way to bring up a bairn. He thought about Kate, still sickly but stoic, made of tough stuff. That morning he'd found her by the midden, gripping her middle and wincing. He thought she was worse than she was letting on.

He spotted Gad approaching the house, got to his feet and opened the door.

'You're late,' he said.

'We didn't say a time.'

'Come in. We need to chat first.'

'I wouldn't mind a cuppa if there's one going?'

'There's some barley tea in the pot.'

Ezekiel poured them both a cup and they sat at the table.

'So what do you want to talk about?' Gad said.

'I've had it confirmed.'

'Eh?'

'Offcumdens. Here for the bounty. Kate told me. She finds out all kinds of things, doing other folks' laundry.'

'Thought as much. Better get going then, hadn't we?'

'Here's the thing, what do you think they'll all be doing?'

'To catch the wolf? They'll be setting traps, putting poison down.'

'Right. And how will they know where to put the traps, or leave the poison?'

'They'll look for wolf prints.'

'Right again. So if those wolf prints didn't lead them to a wolf, but to something else—'

'I don't follow you.'

'I've had an idea.'

'Go on.'

'We make some dummy wolf prints. We lead false trails. And we cover the real trails up. As long as we know where its tracks go and other men don't, we've got the upper hand.'

Gad thought about this as he sipped barley tea. It was a tad bitter. He reached over to a bowl in the middle of the table, scooped out some honey with a spoon, and dunked it in his cup. He stirred the honey round, the hot tea dissolving it, and tasted the brew once more. That was better. When they had their money, he would sweeten everything with honey.

'It's a good idea. How are we going to make the dummies?'

'Drink up.'

Ezekiel led them to the shed at the back of the house, where he kept his tools and the lathe that he'd made himself, three summers ago, when he and Kate had got married at the chapel in town and moved in together. He showed him a toy that he'd made for his daughter. A little cloth pig that he'd constructed by sewing two cut-outs of cloth together and filling them with sand. He explained how they could adapt this method, fill calf-skin sacks with sand, sew them together so they resembled the paw pads of the wolf, and how they could carve wooden shapes that looked like wolf claws. Attach it all together on the underside of a wooden board. Then fix a handle to this board.

They worked all morning on the device, then took it outside to test it along a boggy part of the path. They stood back.

Ezekiel grinned. 'You'd never know the difference.'

'It's perfect.'

Just then, Kate came back from the miller's house with a wooden buck of laundry. Ever since his missus had died unexpectedly last fall, she'd been doing his laundry. It didn't pay much but when times were hard, it all helped. She botched his garments too, darning his socks and sewing buttons on his jerkins. As well as money, the miller gave her bags of flour: rye, wheat and corn. As much as she wanted. Ezekiel watched her struggle with the buck and took hold of it, placing it on the table.

'You don't need to be doing that. Rest up.'

'I'm all right.'

He could see how flushed she was.

'Listen, when I've got this fifty quid there'll be no more laundry for you.'

Kate nodded. 'If you get it.'

'Don't worry, I've had an idea.'

Ezekiel showed her the device and Kate examined it.

'You've done a decent job of that but aren't you forgetting something?'

Ezekiel looked over to Gad. Gad shrugged. 'What?'

'You need a left and right, not just a right, you bloody clod-pated clowns.'

Ezekiel went red in the face. Why hadn't this occurred to him? He looked over to Gad again, who shook his head, ready now to side with Kate.

'Yeah, well we were going to do another. We were just checking it worked,' he lied.

They went back inside, working quicker this time. When they were finished, they loaded up their bags and saddled up the horses, then took the iron traps that Gad had bought from the smith. The blacksmith told them they'd have to wait if they wanted any more – orders in now for the next two months. All the smithies in the Riding were working overtime to cope with demand. Gad and Ezekiel loaded up some rabbit bait and two graving spades. They went back to where they'd dug the wolf pits the day before. The first was still undisturbed and they decided to leave this. When they got to the second though, they saw that the rabbit was gone and the roof of the pit had been disturbed. They moved closer tentatively, with Ezekiel wielding his axe. But when they peered into the pit, they saw, not a wolf impaled on the spikes, but a fox. It was in a bad way, hardly able to move. A wooden pike poked through its side. Blood stained its white underbelly. Must have been there some hours. It bared its teeth and gave them a fierce look but they both knew there was little it could do to defend itself. Ezekiel took his axe and finished it off. They removed its corpse and repaired the trap. They used the fox corpse as bait, carefully laying it over the top.

'Fox corpse, good food for a starving wolf.'

They broke off some pine branches and used them as brooms to sweep any sign of wolf prints away. Then Ezekiel took the dummy device and laid a false trail in the opposite direction to the pit.

'The thing about the wolf, it's not like us. Hasn't got the brains for starters, but it relies on its friends and family for survival. This is the last wolf in the Ridings, could be the last wolf in England for all we know, and that makes it vulnerable. Do you see what I mean?'

Gad nodded.

'They say the wolf takes no pleasure in life. Like it's angry all the time and wants to get even. I've known some men like that. And I've heard wolves don't like foxes, so our wolf will like the idea of eating one of its enemies.' He was rambling now in his attempt to sound knowledgeable about wolves.

'What now?'

'Let's see if we can track it further on and use some of these irons.'

They walked out of the wood and got back onto Lemuel's horses, rode half a mile or so to the next patch of woodland: bare boughs of birch and the lithe limbs of ash. They trudged through black puddles and rotting leaf mould, kicking the sludge off their boots, searched around but couldn't find any trace of the wolf.

'Let's wander a bit deeper. Chances are, it's been here. A wolf on the run will see a place like this as a refuge.'

They walked beyond the path, following a deer run, using sticks to hack back the brambles and bracken that grew across the run. Eventually they came to a clearer part of the path. Ezekiel bent down.

'See, them's wolf.'

He pointed to some prints that were too large for a dog. Gad took one of the iron traps and they dug a shallow pit for it to sit in so that its jaws were flush with the forest floor. They set it so that it could spring shut, then covered it up with leaves and bracken. Gad took out a rabbit corpse, and using Gad's axe, he chopped a hind leg off, placing the hacked leg close to the trap.

'No point wasting a whole rabbit. We need to ration ourselves or we'll end up running out of rabbits if we're not careful.'

Ezekiel took hold of the dummy and assiduously laid a false trail. Gad took out a red rag and tied it round a trunk of a neighbouring tree, low down where it wouldn't be spotted by men who didn't know to look for it. While he did this, Ezekiel moved further into the woods, searching for more signs of the wolf. They found another set of prints, and set a trap close by, baiting it with the spare hind leg of the rabbit.

'I tell you what else has occurred to me,' Ezekiel said, as they stood back to check the iron jaws were well concealed.

'What's that?'

'Mr Lane's boy.'

'What about him?'

'Well, I mean, why was he even fishing in the first place? Think about it. He was supposed to be working with us. Imagine if that was me or you, and instead of turning up for work, you went to catch trout instead?'

Gad shrugged. 'Mr Lane didn't want him on the job, is what I heard. Anyway, it's different when it's a father and his son.'

'Well, I tell you this, when my lad gets to that age, he'll be working with me. I'm not going to let him swan around like he's lord of the bleedin' manor. Honour thy father. Int that what the good book says?'

They scouted further into the forest but decided it would be best to ride up to Long Royd to set the other traps. It didn't do to put all your traps in one forest. Instead, they made a circuitous route back to where they'd tethered the nags. Ezekiel pulled out a cloth wrap from his saddlebag and unwrapped a thick slice of havercake. He broke it in two and gave a piece to Gad.

'You know what, it's only a matter of time now before we catch this wolf and claim the reward.'

Gad scratched his stubble. Ezekiel could tell that he wasn't convinced.

'No, think about it. A thousand years ago, there were wolves running around everywhere, stealing sheep, eating farrow and the like, even killing human bairns. A wolf will kill anything. But we are smarter than the wolf. You don't see all those wolves now, do you, because we've killed them all. Look around you, what do you see?'

Gad shrugged.

'Fences, houses, ploughed fields, walls. Signs of human life. Not wolf life.'

'I dunno. I've heard that wolves can be really smart. Smarter than a dog or a fox.'

'Listen, when a wolf can get up in the morning, go to work, do a day's graft, earn a groat, go to the alehouse at night, then you can tell me a wolf is a smart animal.'

Gad scratched his chin.

'We're the top dog. The wolf is beneath us. God gave all the animals to us. It's our job to husband them and to cull them. We are carrying out God's work.'

'The thing is, in them days, we didn't have guns, or arrows, or iron traps. We would have had to work in large groups, not just me and you, to get really close to the animal to stab it.'

'Exactly, so you see, we've learned haven't we, improved our methods over time. Invented guns and powder. But the wolf hasn't learned. The wolf still goes about its business same as it always has.'

'And that's why there are no wolves left?'

'Well, after we've culled this one, touch wood.'

Ezekiel looked around for a tree to tap.

'The wolf has always been our enemy. He doesn't think anything, except for killing and eating. Them's his only thoughts. That's all the wolf is, a killing machine.'

'Not for much longer, right?' They both laughed.

'I tell you what, when we get this money, I'm going straight to The Moorcock and I'm going to order us both a dram of that special whisky the drawer keeps on the top shelf. Always wondered what a shot of that tasted like.'

'Fuck that. I'll buy the bottle.'

They finished the havercake and got back onto their nags. They rode across the fields owned by High Cragg farm and through some meadowland that had until recently been a common. They rode beneath the ridge of Broad Head Moor, until they saw Long Royd's wood in the distance. They got to the edge of the wood, where the trees were spread out and they were able to ride through. The oaks on the outskirts of the forest had stretched their boughs wide, leaving plenty of open space. The men tethered their nags and continued on foot, pushing through browning bracken. As they did they disturbed a weasel and they watched its little body dart across their path and under bramble, wick as water. There was a rough track that had been made by deer, or rabbit, or even man, and they stuck along this path for a while, until they came to a fork.

'Left or right?'

'Dunt matter.'

'Let's take the left one and do a big loop, coming back on this one.'

'How do you know it loops back?'

'How do you know it doesn't?'

The ground was soft underfoot and the air was thick with the damp musty smell of leaf mould. Gradually the path became boggier, and the effort of trudging through the mud slowed them down. The path opened out a bit and then led down to a beck. A flash of yaffle. The waters trickled over green-grey boulders and ran in rivulets through beck pebbles. Ezekiel took out his flask and uncorked it. He placed the mouth of the flask beneath a flurry of water and filled it to the top, tipping the lid to his lips and guzzling the cold water.

'Want some?'

He handed the flask to Gad, who was looking over to his right and not paying attention to Ezekiel.

'Do you want some or not? Good clean water?'

Gad stared hard at something Ezekiel hadn't spotted.

'What is it?'

'See that there?' He pointed to a part of the forest floor that was spread even with fern leaves, and at this angle of light, they could both see that the forest floor had sunk ever so slightly in an even rectangular dip.

'Looks like a trap.'

Both men went over to the clearing. Gad took his staff and poked through the ferns. He disturbed them and they could both see that the ferns sat on top of some branches. The two men cleared more of the ferns to reveal an iron trap.

'Looks like someone has beaten us to it.'

They talked about whether it was better to spoil the trap or sit it out and see if the trap would entice the wolf.

'Thing is, wolves have a great sense of smell,' Ezekiel lied. He had no idea really about a wolf's olfactory ability. He was recalling a childhood story, of a wolf sniffing out a baby from a well. 'If we hide here, even if we cover ourselves in fox shit, the wolf will sniff us out.'

'So what then?'

'Let's take the trap and use it somewhere else, that way we spoil the trap for the men who laid it and we get a free trap to use in some other part of the wood they don't know about. We get to keep our cake and we get to eat it too.'

Gad nodded. 'Good idea.'

Very carefully, Gad used his staff to probe the iron jaws of the trap until the stick set off the spring and the iron jaws bit into the end of his staff. He took hold of the trap and released it, putting it in his bag. They covered the area over again with fern leaves.

'But, hang on, then they'll know that we've taken their trap and they'll come looking for us.'

Gad had a point for once. Ezekiel thought about it. What was the best thing to do, to keep hidden from the others, and that way retain the advantage of surprise, or reveal that they were onto them but stay one step ahead? The thing to do was to catch that wolf as quickly as possible.

'Right, here's what we do. We put this iron back, and disturb the covering, so that the trap can't catch anything and if the men who set it come across it, they'll think that an animal has set it off and managed to escape its grips. Then we set a false trail, so the men follow it. Only when they get to the end of the trail we set another type of trap for them.'

'How do you mean?'

'A man trap. Stop them in their tracks.'

'But we'll swing for that.'

'Not if we don't get caught we won't. And we won't get caught.'

'How do you know that?'

'Trust me. I know what I'm doing.' He lied again.

The two men placed the now spent trap back where they had found it and disturbed the scene sufficiently so that it looked like an animal had been. Then Ezekiel, using the left paw print, and Gad using the right paw print, laid a trail some distance away. Then took their spades and dug through the mulch of leaf mould, then the soft loam of soil, before reaching the compacted earth beneath. Ezekiel caught a worm with the blade of his spade, slicing it in two. He watched as the two ends of the worm wriggled and writhed.

'You ever tasted a worm?'

'Eh?'

'They taste of slime and soil. Sort of musty. It varies with the seasons. And depends where they live. Some taste of pig shit. Others have a leathery taste.'

'How come you know so much about eating worms?'

'Needs must. We ate them out of desperation. Been marching days without any food. The group bringing our rations had been ambushed by Royalists. Middle of the arse end of nowhere. Good food if you can stomach them. Takes a bit of getting used to. The first bite is the worst. It gets easier after that.'

'Here, give us a hand with this.'

Gad had hit a rock. He dug around it and scraped the top layer of earth so that the wet grey slate of its surface was exposed. He reached in and grabbed one side underneath, waggling to loosen it. Ezekiel used his spade at the other end to lever it out.

'It's coming. Pull harder.'

Eventually they loosened the rock sufficiently to be able to pull it from the ground. It was jagged and shaped like a lead weight. The two of them lifted it clear.

'After me, one, two, three.'

They swung the stone like they were rocking a cot, with both men either end. Then, when the swing was wide enough, they let go and watched it hurtle into the bracken a few feet away.

'Big bugger, that. Shame to waste it.'

'I'm not carrying it back with us. Must weigh two quarters.'

'Shame though. Could use a stone like that.'

They dug further down, where the earth was cool and smelled of iron and clay, and their spades squelched as they cut into the ground. Eventually they had dug a hole about six feet deep, long enough to lay end to end in and wide enough to go shoulder to shoulder. They fashioned poles from hazel shoots and planted them solidly in the ground, sharpening the ends into good keen pikes. As they worked, Ezekiel was starting to regret the suggestion. Even if they did catch one of their competition in this pit, there would be others. And if they killed them, still more men would come. The men would keep coming as long as there was a price on that wolf's head. Still, it was too late now to back down. Leaders didn't go back on their word. He'd never known Mr Lane to back down. Once Mr Lane had made a decision, that was the be all and end of it. Perhaps, if he acted like his master, one day he could be as rich as him. Though beyond aping Mr Lane's actions, he had no further plan. How men made money, after that paid at the end of the week, was a mystery to Ezekiel.

They rode beneath High Cragg and along the river, crossing it at Mickle Bridge. The bridge was huge chucks of stone cobs, built to carry coffins from the neighbouring village, where there were no rights of burial. By the river, alder grew, their roots extending into the brown water. Their dried cones and catkins covered the stone way. The men rode over to Dale Edge. The first clump of the wood was dominated by mature oak with bark like a hag's knee. There were a few of Eddie's pigs shuffling acorns – he had pannage rights hereabouts – then over to Hazel Hirst where some of the trees had recently been coppiced and the nuts collected, those cut back offering their stumps like amputees.

'I've ordered some poison,' Ezekiel said.

'Oh, yeah?'

'All the smithies are booked up. Forget iron traps. We won't see another before Michaelmas.'

'We can dig pits still.'

'We've got to think about efficiency. Digging pits takes time. If we get good poison, we can lace as much meat as we like.'

'But that will cost.'

'See it as an investment. You have to fork out if you want what's owed. Don't you think that's what the rest will be doing? And if not now, soon enough? You have to stay ahead of the game. Besides, we know some have already started on poison trails. When we're sat in The Moorcock, drinking the drawer's good stuff, you'll think it was worth it.'

In fact, the poison had been Kate's idea, but he didn't tell Gad that. He thought about Kate. She wasn't getting any better. He'd ride back home once they'd finished, forgo the alehouse.

He got back that evening to find his wife on the bed, still fully dressed. The room was dark, but he could see, even in the weak light of the

tallow, that her skin was glistening with a silver sheen. He felt her brow
– she was burning up. Mother Hunt's herbs had not worked.

'Bloody hell, lass, you're as sick as a lepered sow.' He tried to keep
the fear out of his voice.

'It's not as bad as all that.'

'I'll get the physician.'

'It's fine. It'll pass.'

He loosened her clothes and fetched cold water and a flannel to
cool her brow.

'Have you had anything to drink?'

She shook her head. He went into the kitchen and found some
barley water, poured it into a cup and came back into the bedroom.
He carefully poured some of the water onto her lips.

'Here. Drink this.'

She attempted to swallow some of the liquid. He caught the
spillage with the flannel.

'I'm going to go for him.'

'At this time of night?'

'I'll be as quick as I can.'

'We can't afford it, Zeke.'

She was right. Money was tight. And the doctor charged a fortune
for his services and didn't always care what ailed even after that. Still,
if they got that fifty pound he'd pay him soon enough. He gave her
some more of the water, then placed the cup on the table by the side
of the bed. Fastening up his gabardine, he rode Lemuel's mare over to
the physician's house.

As he rode, something was bothering him besides the worry he had
about his wife's health. It was the man trap they'd set. Gad was right.
It was obvious what their intention was from the size and the shape
of it. The beadle was a shrewd man. The constable was even shrewder.

Any magistrate would find them guilty. And that meant a swinging. He had no desire to wear a hemp necklace or do the last drop dance. He didn't have the protection Mr Lane had, or the clout. It was true that since the King had been dispatched the ordinary laws did not always apply, and some folk took advantage of that, but for lowly folk like him not that much was different. Just how did Mr Lane get away with murder? Ezekiel suspected that he had certain men on his payroll. He knew that he invited the constable and the beadle for supper once a week, and other men of influence. The invitation had never been extended to him or Gad, or any man of toil. He doubled back for a spade, then made a detour to Long Royd's Wood. He found the man trap and filled in enough of it, so that they couldn't be accused of any fell purpose.

He rode back towards the village and over to the physician's cottage, which was positioned on the northern outskirts, behind the church and the graveyard. As he rode, he tried not to think of Kate's ailment and instead turned his thinking to the wolf. Just how were they going to catch the bastard? It had been days of work so far for nothing. And then there was the expense of it all. Iron traps weren't cheap. Poison was expensive. Lemuel had stood them some money to tide them over, but it wasn't a full wage. And now the place was crawling with other men hunting the same bounty. The truth was, he just didn't have the know-how to catch this wolf. Stupid and craven, yet able to outsmart him. He would have to sit down with Gad tomorrow and work out what was best. One thing he knew, their strategy wasn't working. If someone else beat them to it he'd never pay the physic bill.

As he rode his thoughts were disturbed by a night howlet. Its call was a keening whistle. Oh to be that bird, with nothing on its mind except catching a shrew-mouse. He was grateful for the work Lemuel gave him, knew that he'd kept him in employment oftentimes when there was no real labour, finding knacks for him, trifles that didn't really need doing, out of a sense of gratitude. But he wished for a simpler life. Being in the army was a daily grind, forever chasing a hunger that a cup of beans could never sate, but at least you knew who your enemy was: a poncy-haired fop. And he knew how to kill that enemy: you stuck them like a pig. He'd been happy being a pikeman, a pilcher dangling from his girdle. Life now was one of uncertainty, always worried about what tomorrow would bring for him and Kate and for their daughter and his unborn bairn.

He thought back to the battles they'd had against the Royalists. He'd joined in when the rest of his pals had sung songs about Royalist scum. But in fact, he had no strong feeling at all about the King. This new Rump Parliament was no better nor worse than life under Charles. What he cared about was Kate and his bairns. What matter who wore the crown or sat in the throne?

As he rode past the church towards the physician's house, the howlet flew low over his head, flashing its white belly, looking for all the world like a ghostly spirit. Its flight was completely silent, and something about the snow-white bird in the darkness, moving so quietly, put an ice-cold chill down his spine.

The physician was a man by the name of Stoker and he made the skin on Ezekiel's neck tighten. He tried to avoid the man wherever possible. It was Stoker who had come to the aid of Master Thomas. Who had poked and prodded him and put God only knows what down the poor boy's throat. When he and Gad had delivered Thomas to Lemuel and his family on that November night the boy was still breathing. When Jacob fetched Stoker from The Lamb of God shortly afterwards, the man was clearly cup-shot. He actually fell up the stairs. Ezekiel had seen a man fall down a set of stairs before, but never up them. Less than twenty-four hours later, Thomas was as dead as a doornail and the Lanes were presented with an extortionate bill. But Kate was running a fever.

Stoker's wife didn't even invite him in. Instead, she bade him wait there in the cold November air while she fetched him. Ezekiel stood outside the man's house holding his horse's reins, close to a lanthorn, and blew out white smoke from his lungs. It was a well-appointed property, nothing on the scale or grandeur of Lemuel's estate, but sizeable in comparison with his own meagre cottage. There was a bite in the night's veil. He could see the frail light of the moon, frost beginning to creep along the bare boughs of the trees. It was already whitening the windowpanes. Above him he could see the bright guards of the Little Bear, next in brightness to the Pole Star. But everything else was cloaked in a velvety darkness.

Stoker appeared at the door, already coated, carrying a leather case. Ezekiel could see from the man's eyes he'd been hitting the bottle. They were wet like a bloodhound's, the bags beneath drooping, revealing red crescents.

'Hold this, will you, while I fetch my nag.'

He handed his bag to Ezekiel and disappeared round the back of the house. Ezekiel waited. He rubbed his hands together. He cupped them and blew hot breath into the hollow. He watched the air turn white. Stoker reappeared on horseback. Ezekiel handed him the case and mounted his own beast. Together they rode back to Ezekiel's house.

'And you say Mother Hunt has been attending to her?'

'That's right, sir. She's tried everything.'

'With herbs you mean?'

'Aye, sir.'

'Look, man, all illnesses spring from an imbalance of the four humours. You know what those are, don't you?'

'No, sir.'

'Blood, phlegm, yellow bile and black bile. The best cure for fever is bloodletting.'

Ezekiel didn't know anything about the four humours. The only humour he knew was that he received at The Moorcock or The Lamb over a few ales. But he did know that Mother Hunt had cured their daughter Rose's colic by placing a hare foot round her neck. He also knew that she'd cured his father's jaundice with yellow blossom.

'Apoplexy, strangury, fever, common ague ... you can only cure these ailments if you understand the science behind them. Mark my words. I've cured tumours, ulcers, fractures and venereal diseases, not through herbs, grace-wife potions, or silly superstitions, but through the application of science. Once you understand how the four humours work, that's when you really begin to get to grips with cures. Do you see?'

Ezekiel didn't see. Nor did he like the man's superior tone. He had heard that Stoker had drilled a hole in the ostler's head to rid him of a migraine, and the ostler said the pain had gone away, but the ostler had also been treated by Mother Hunt, with goose fat and bishop's wort.

'Take plague, for example. I hear they killed all the cats and dogs in the village where your cousin Gad is from?'

'That's right, sir.'

'See, this is simply ignorance. Did it cure the plague?'

'No, sir.'

'No, it did not. And if I'm right, it made it worse, did it not? What science teaches the learned man is that plague is caused by a combination of noxious vapours in the air and corrupt humours in the body. Arsenic, quicksilver, dried toads. All nonsense, of course.'

'Are you licensed then, sir? I heard the Royal College only lets in a small number.'

'Licensed? What the devil are you talking about? Of course not. You'll not find a physician outside of London with a licence. It's a lot of ninnyhammer. I don't need a piece of paper to prove my expertise. Years of experience.'

Ezekiel didn't care too much about licences either. Just as long as this man had physic to cure poor Kate, that wouldn't put them in penury.

'So then, tell me, what has old Mother Hunt been using to treat your wife's fever?'

'A tincture of willow bark, sir.'

Stoker laughed bitterly. 'Willow bark indeed. I've heard it all now. Only last week, I found out that woman had been using foxglove to treat the blacksmith for dropsy. Do you know how poisonous that plant is? It's lethal.'

Ezekiel just nodded. The smithy's dropsy had been a lot better since. They pulled up outside Ezekiel's cottage, dismounted and tethered their animals.

Inside, Ezekiel lit a few more tallows, and led the way to where Kate lay, glowing with fever. Stoker examined her. Poked her, prodded her. Hummed and hawed. He opened up his case and took out some cups.

'Something to warm the cockles wouldn't go amiss.'

Ezekiel fetched the only liquor they had in the house. A jar of kill-priest. He poured the doctor a generous measure, making sure to keep hold of the jar himself.

'You can wait in the other room. I'll come and get you when I'm done.'

He dismissed Ezekiel with the wave of an arm. Ezekiel went into the other room and stood by the hearth. He put a lump of peat on the fire and reached for the jar of kill-priest, glugging it back. He watched the brick of black peat take flame. He moved it further back with iron tongs and settled in the chair, nursing his pot of liquor. The brick was burned down to a thin wedge before Stoker reappeared.

'She needs resting now. And don't be downing that all yourself. You'll need it for your wife as well. Give her a cup with two drops of this, twice a day, until the fever lifts.'

He handed Ezekiel a small pothecary jar.

'Thank you, sir. How much do I owe you?'

'Now, let's see, with the visit, the consultation, the treatment and the medicine, let's call it five shillings.'

'Five shilling?'

'Now listen here. I charged Mr Lane a pound a day for my medical attention.'

'But I don't have five shilling.'

'How much have you got?'

Ezekiel went over to the drawer, took out a box and counted his coins.

'Two shilling and three halfpence.'

Stoker took hold of the coins and secreted them.

'You owe me two shillings and ten pence. I'll let you off the half.'

He put on his hat and fastened his cloak. Ezekiel saw him out.

When the physician had gone, Ezekiel took the jar and the cup into the bedchamber. He checked on Rose who was asleep in her cot. Kate was propped up in bed, attempting a smile. He poured her a drink.

'Here, have this.'

She was too weak to drink the liquor unaided so he fed her three or four sips, then wiped her brow again with the cool cloth. He kissed her clammy forehead. It was still hot. She lay back and closed her eyes. He sat beside her, watching her sleep. He would stay by her side until she woke. At least she didn't know that Stoker had wiped them out. They had not even a halfpenny to their names and it would take some graft to raise what he owed.

Once he was satisfied that she was in a deep sleep, he knelt by the foot of the bed and prayed. 'Please, God, spare her. Don't take her from me. I'll do anything you ask. But please have mercy. We are good people that observe your ways, and this is a good woman. Make her fever go away and I promise I'll rid this land of the wolf. For I know it is Satan's dog. And when this land is free again from that hellhound, I promise to serve you all my days. I'll never miss another day at chapel. Just please, bring Kate back to me, and the baby she carries.'

He looked up at the ceiling. Was God there? Could he see him? Was he listening to him? He couldn't be sure, but he thought he felt God's eye upon him.

Strange Beasts

It rained the next day and the day after, just as Alice had predicted. It rained so hard that it found its way through our densely thatched roof and I woke up in an icy puddle. We stayed close to camp and Jenny and I worked on the roof of the hut, weaving in holly, myrtle and mountain laurel. We patched the gaps with moss, hanging out our bedding to dry on the branches above.

Ivy approached as we were adding the finishing touches and explained that Alice wanted to talk to me. I left them to prepare some food while I went over to Alice's hut, knocking on the door. It opened and Alice ushered me in.

'Ivy said you wanted to see me.'

'Sit down. Please.'

There was only a bed and a stool. Alice sat on the bed and I took the stool, sitting by the fire. She took out her pipe and packed it with tobacco. The walls were painted dark blue and there was a picture of a strange creature I'd never seen before in a frame above the bed. The bed was covered in a brightly coloured patchwork quilt.

Alice nodded. She went over to the little potbellied stove, opened the door and lit a still. She used this to fire her pipe.

'I thought now would be a good time for you and I to conversate. And, well, get to know each other a little better. I'm much older than you and I remember the world before it all went top-over-terve. When the laws of this land were intractable and the King ruled over every aspect of our lives. Though some say there were always two laws: those for the poor and those for the rich. This land has changed so much in the past few years that it's hard to keep on top of it. But for you, and the others, it's much easier. This world is all you have known. But let me tell you, things maybe in turmoil right now, with no one knowing whether they are coming or going, not knowing who to trust, or what to think, but it was no better before. Certainty and stability didn't bring social change. It didn't ring in opportunity, not for people like us. For people like us, the old world was rigged. At least now we have a chance of real and lasting change. People are questioning the old ways. They are willing to think differently and try different ways of living. And maybe out of this willingness, we can make a better world. So yes, the things that were fixed are now broken. The Church, the state, the rule of law. None of these may exist in the future. This is an exciting time to be alive. I can see it for what it is: a chance to remake the world so that it favours people like us. Do you agree, Rowan?'

I nodded my head. I wasn't sure what to think any more.

'Good. You're Irish aren't you?'

I shrugged.

'But you've lived in England for at least a few years? Long enough to lose your accent.'

How did she know so much about me?

'Don't worry. It's all right. I'm not prying, I'm just interested. I said I wanted to get to know you a little better, and that's all we are doing. What part of Ireland are you from?'

'West coast.'

'And when did you come to England?'

'It was the winter of forty-two.'

'So, just after the Irish rebellion then. Were your folks running from trouble?'

I nodded. There seemed no point in denying it. It was clear she had discerned much of my past already.

'And they thought fleeing to the North of England was a good idea? Interesting. Well, I know a little about the situation over there at that time. But tell me your story, Rowan. What happened to your family?'

'My da was a sailor. When he met my ma he gave up his sea legs, worked as a barker. He wasn't political and he never went looking for trouble. But Ma said, "Sometimes trouble follows a man whether he is looking for it or not." There were a lot of English settlers near where we lived, Protestants. Some had been in Ireland for generations, others were newcomers. It started with thieving mostly, and name-calling. Somehow it escalated pretty quickly. Men died. Some were murdered. Some were stripped of their clothes and died in that terrible winter of forty-one. Protestants were tortured and drowned. Da would have nothing to do with it. Some men wanted him to fight for them, but he said he wasn't a soldier. He'd only fight a man one on one, who had agreed to fight him. He wouldn't be any man's dog. Da had a friend who just happened to be the son of English settlers. The two of them went back a long way and when some men attacked Da's friend, Da stood up to them. Fought three men on his own. Things turned nasty, got out of hand. One of the men died. Da didn't kill him, least, he hadn't meant to. Da saved his friend's life, but in so doing, he endangered his own, and his family's. As a thank you, the man gave Da a half-acre of land in Yorkshire. Gave him some money to escape.'

'And that's how you ended up here?'

'Things were good at first. We fitted in well, worked hard, made a life for ourselves. Only Ma said, "Sometimes a man's past catches up with him." And that's what happened to us.'

'And the man who killed your parents?'

'His name is Mr Lane. Some of his family settled in our village back in Ireland. I don't know the details. The man who died, who they claim my father killed, was Mr Lane's brother-in-law. He blamed my father for his death, and for his sister's death. I don't know why – my father was an innocent man. He would have come for us anyway. He hates our people. He'll not rest until we are wiped off the face of the Earth.'

'I know, child. I understand. Now, listen to me. You have lost your family and I'm deeply sorry for your loss. I know the pain well. I still feel it, even though I lost mine many years ago. But you have gained a new family. We are your family now. You are one of us, Rowan, you will be free. You will be strong. You will be true. We live to show the world what it means to be liberated from dogma. From man's poison. I have been called an enchanter, a pestilent pythonist, a figure caster, and much worse. But my vocation is to serve.'

She blew out a thick white cloud of smoke that filled the small room.

'You are part of this family now.'

She held my gaze and I nodded, trying to take comfort from this thought. I looked over to the picture and thought I saw one of the strange beasts wink at me.

Part Two

The Hour of the Wolf

'The wolf doth grin before he barketh.'
Venus & Adonis, William Shakespeare

The Man From Gothenburg

1 December 1649

As Lemuel straightened his jabot in the hallway mirror, he stared back at his reflection. It was a good face. A lived-in face. Only his nose was crooked. It had once been straight but a scrap with a Royalist popinjay in Derby had seen to that. Still, he'd got the better of the man, strung out his guts for cross-gartering. He ran his fingers through his short-cropped hair. Above his ears, the edges were grizzled. He fiddled with the jabot, tugging it this way then the other, trying to get the collar even on both sides. What did it matter? He wasn't a vain man, and cared little about his attire or his appearance. He had a good tailor and trusted the man's judgement. As long as his hair was combed and there wasn't any food on his face, or any of his garments, that was all that mattered. He realised, as he tugged at the lace, that he was nervous. He was getting ready to meet the man from Gothenburg, a man who, he hoped, would solve his problem once and for all. At last he was satisfied that the jabot was straight. He called in to see the girls on the way to the main dining chamber. They were quarrelling as usual. What about, he did not know or care.

'He's going to be here soon. So no funny business.'

'Can't we come and see him?'

'I want to meet him.'

'You can say your greetings, but no more. We've got a lot to talk about, and I don't want to be disturbed.'

He closed the door behind him before they could protest further and continued down the corridor, past mounted heads of ounce and fox, deer and badger. Animals he had killed himself. But he realised now that there was a limit to his hunting prowess.

According to the word of men Lemuel trusted, the man from Gothenburg was not just an expert, he was the best, and he wanted to impress him. There was no one in North Europa who was better skilled or provisioned. The man had travelled through Sweden, Norway, Denmark, Saxony and Bohemia, where wolves were still commonplace, and earned a certain reputation as the greatest wolf killer in the land. He was now something of a legend, talked about in hushed tones, revered in all corners of the northern world. The man's name was Johan Hellström and Lemuel had first heard of him when he was garrisoned at York, in sixteen hundred and forty-three, but had never met him in the flesh. Tales of Hellström had travelled across oceans. Hellström could track a wolf from its scent. Hellström had killed a wolf with his bare hands. Hellström had butchered over five hundred wolves. Or so they said.

Elizabeth was laying out an ample supper of heathen cakes and roast potatoes. On the table she had already placed plates of beef, capons, veal, stockfish and ox-tripe. There was also a large flagon of Lemuel's best claret. He wanted to set the right impression. Lemuel wasn't an impatient man, but he liked to get a job done. And despite a gaggle of bounty hunters about the town, causing mayhem in the alehouses, taverns and trugging kens, there had been hardly even any news of a wolf being seen, let alone captured and killed.

He had Ezekiel report to him every morning now. He knew how hard he and Gad were working, how many traps there were in Lowe Dene, Sheep Brink, Dale Edge, Low Fold, Bluebell Woods and Long Royd. The village was crawling with hungry young men, desperate to claim their bounty. They were drinking the inns dry, throwing money at tray-tip and ring-the-bull. The Moorcock had banned a gang of offcumdens when a fight had broken out over something no one could remember any more. The Lamb of God had soon followed suit when a young tyke had called the ostler's wife a strumpet maid and the ostler had given the lad a good braying, only to have three of the lad's mates jump him on the way home. Lusty young men with beer in their bellies and vexation simmering in their loins. They were fired up. Tetchy as two sticks. It felt like the whole place was a powder keg about to blow, and meanwhile, that wolf was swanning around like lord of the bloody manor. Every day it lived and breathed it was mocking Lemuel. Every day it stalked the woods and cloughs that surrounded his estate, it was sticking two fingers up at him, Lemuel Lane. That wolf was taunting him. Tainting his reputation. Long weeks had passed since his son had been savaged by the black beast. It was time for him, Lemuel Lane, to escalate the situation.

'Thought he'd be here by now,' Elizabeth said as she set the table.

'It's this weather.' The rain was lashing the window. 'It slows down a nag.'

Elizabeth shook her head. 'They say he leaves lots of death in his wake.'

'I don't care, love, as long as I get my wolf.'

He helped himself to a roast potato. It was still hot and he had to blow before biting into it. Crispy on the outside, but soft and fluffy on the inside. Roasted in goose fat. Just how he liked them. His father had forbidden his family from eating potatoes, refused to eat them on the grounds that potatoes were not mentioned in the Bible. He said they were food for Catholics and other God-hating folk. But Lemuel viewed this as a silly superstition. As long as you planted them on St George's Day, Palm Sunday or Good Friday, God would make sure you came to no harm. He poured himself a goblet of claret and took a sip. He was no connoisseur, but he knew a decent tipple when it passed his lips, and this was a decent tipple. He'd supped with Fairfax and Valentine, Crawford and Baillie. Men who knew their lap from their lush. To his regret he had never supped with the man himself. 'Ironside' they called him. But nevertheless, he would have laid his life down for such a valiant fellow.

'Don't be eating them till he gets here.' Elizabeth gave him a gentle slap and smiled.

He thought again that there really should be a daily maid to carry out these tasks. One that was there at Elizabeth's beck and call, night and day, instead of one that was dismissed after the evening meal was prepared. When all this was over, he would see to it.

'Will you keep the girls with you? I don't mind them saying their greetings, but we've got business to discuss and I'd rather they weren't privy to it.'

'Don't worry about the girls. I'll take care of the girls. You just worry about this Hellström fellow.'

Lemuel went over to the window again. The light was already dimming. They called it daylight gate round here. Rooks were flitting and croaking around the largest of the beech trees, going through their quotidian ritual before settling down for the night. Lemuel paced the room. He went over to the fire and gave it a poke. He watched the sparks fly up, then chucked on a couple more logs – birch and oak from last year's coppicing.

'Do you want some more wood fetching?'

'Don't trouble yourself, love.'

'I wasn't. I was going to ask Jacob.' She smiled. It was good to see her smile. Neither of them had smiled much lately. Grief cloaked them like a leaden pall. They would both go days without barely speaking to each other, silently bonded by their bereavement. Waking up was the hardest thing. He'd open his eyes, and for a moment he'd have no recollection of his situation. The sun would pour through a gap in the wooden shutters, lighting up the face of the woman he loved, sleeping beside him. Then he'd remember that his son was dead and the wolf was free. Like a ship's ballast was fixed on his chest, he would feel the enormous weight of that realization and it would nail him to the spot. Unable to move, hardly able to breathe, he'd lie there, wishing there were a loaded matchlock on the table so he could rest the barrel against his temple and pull the trigger. There was a black place deep inside his heart and he dared not venture there. Instead he would circumnavigate it, redirect his thoughts. He knew that his Elizabeth had the same black place at the centre of her heart too.

'We're all right for now. I'll have him fetch some later.'

'I hope this Hellström is as good a man as they say.' She was fussing with the plates, moving them this way and that.

Lemuel nodded, distracted by his thoughts. He knew his wife was concerned about the effect of so many bounty hunters, which was another reason to bring matters to a swift close. It was getting out of hand. Drunkenness, debauchery, criminal damage. Flatting, dicing, ballocking and lugging. The beadle had expressed his grievances. So had the constable. This anarchy that had been let loose was down to Lemuel and no one else. And now it was down to him, Lemuel Lane, to put a stop to it. He answered to no one, not even the sheriff. The world was bent out of shape and he would take full advantage.

There was a knock on the door and Jacob entered. 'He's here, sir.'

Lemuel hesitated for a moment. 'Show him in then.'

As Jacob left the room, Elizabeth started fussing with the plates again.

'Leave them. They're fine as they are. Please.' He fiddled with his jabot and brushed some dust from his breeches.

The two of them watched the door. What was keeping them? Lemuel wondered. Then he heard footsteps in the hall, Jacob's familiar shuffle behind more strident steps. He saw first the man's long legs, then his long arms, enter the room, before the tall gaunt body of a man accompanied it, like a giant spider or a vulture unfolding its wings. The creature before him was improbably tall and thin. He was in his mid-forties but had an ageless quality. His short golden hair and straw-coloured beard seemed somehow illuminated. He had sunken cheekbones and bright grey piercing eyes. Lemuel had been expecting a man well-clad, but Hellström was very ordinary apparelled. A dull sea-gown and a plain cloth suit, which seemed to have been made by an ill country tailor. The linen was plain and not very clean. As he walked into the room, Lemuel noticed that he had a slight stoop to his gait. His wide-brimmed hat was without a hatband. His sword stuck close to his side. And yet, he wore these rags like a prince in exile. Lemuel got to his feet, lost for words for a moment. The man from Gothenburg towered over him. Lemuel was used to towering over other men, but now he felt like he was in the shadow of a greater man.

'Mr Hellström, please, come in and join us. We were just about to have some supper. I trust your journey has worked up an appetite?'

Hellström removed his hat and sea-gown and handed them to Jacob, who took hold of them respectfully, and left the room. Hellström didn't answer. Instead he looked first at Lemuel, then at Elizabeth, like an eagle eyeing up its quarry. Elizabeth stood up and made a step towards him.

'Mr Lane, and your good wife, Mrs Lane. It is an honour.'

He spoke slowly, with a thick accent. He took another step towards them and peered around the room. He looked over to the logs burning in the fire, then the food laid out on the table, the flagon of claret, the view from the window. He took another step forward and offered Lemuel his hand. For a moment Lemuel just stared at it. The man's hand was deformed, misshapen and scarred. More than half of the hand was missing, including three fingers. There was just a thumb and index finger. It looked like a crab's pincers. Where the skin was damaged it was ridged with a livid pink seam. Lemuel became conscious that he was staring at the man's hand, and his cheeks coloured. He held out his own hand and the two men shook awkwardly.

'An honour to meet you too, Mr Hellström. I've heard so many stories.'

Hellström nodded. Elizabeth came forward and offered her hand. The two shook a little less cumbrously.

'May I welcome you, sir, into our home. Would you like some wine?' Elizabeth said.

She went to the table and took up the flagon, pouring wine into pewter goblets. Hellström took hold of the goblet with his good hand.

'Now, if you will excuse me.' She curtsied and left the room.

Hellström drank greedily from the goblet. A red rivulet ran down his neck, staining the lace of his collar.

'Have you travelled far?'

'I have business in Lancaster yesterday. Before that, I am visiting a friend in Huntingdon. It is my first time back in England for two years. I have business in Scotland last winter.'

'I hear they still have problems with wolves up there.'

'I hear you still have problem too.' He grinned, revealing a row of narrow, pointy teeth, like a jack pike's.

'Come, let's sit at the table and eat. All that travel must have surely worked up an appetite?' Lemuel felt stupid repeating himself.

The two men sat at opposing chairs and helped themselves to the heathen cakes and roast potatoes, veal and capons.

'We've had bad floods hereabouts. The whole village was cut off for days about six weeks since.'

'I hear that you are having floods across the land. Nine rivers are bursting their banks. The Ouse, the Severn, the Aire, the Calder, the Avon, the Trent, Thames, Exe, and Derwent.'

'Sir, you are well informed. We've had our share of trouble that way.'

'It is in the Bible, no?' Hellström laughed. 'There are some who blame the weather on recent events. They say the killing of a King angers God. The floods are his retribution.'

'And what do you say, Mr Hellström? Are you for King or for Parliament?'

'You expect me to choose between two fools? The question is beneath me.'

The man from Gothenburg held Lemuel's gaze like he was fixing him to the spot. Lemuel had heard how some snakes could hold their prey firm with just a look.

'I say the King is of the other party, and if the floods are any retribution, is the devil who sent them.' The man from Gothenburg grinned.

'Then we agree,' said Lemuel, relieved to have this man release him from his ocular grip. He tried to regain his composure. 'My only regret, Mr Hellström, is that I didn't see his head part company with his neck myself.'

The two men laughed.

'I hear they call him Charlie Two Shirts.'

'I do not hear this. Why is this name?'

'He insisted on wearing two shirts for his execution, so he wouldn't

shiver in front of the crowd, and his chill mistaken for cowardice.'
Lemuel relaxed a little and stuffed a large slice of veal into his mouth.
He talked with his mouth full. 'I fought for the Parliamentary Army
in forty-two, forty-three and forty-four. At first I was a pikeman, but I
soon after became a musketeer. Later I was made a captain. And men
served under me. Killed a lot of the King's men and saw a lot of my
men stain. Saw a man lose his hucklebone from a cannon shot just a
few yards from where I stood. Shot a hole right through him. That
iron ball had my name on it.'

'The Earth is fed by the blood of fell men and good men both.'

'Many a man passed over Whinny Moor. One time we were charged
both front and flank. We stood at sword's point, hacking each other.
But, so it pleased God, we broke through. Scattered them like dust.'

'In Sweden, we have war also. We only now are finishing. You have
heard?'

'Aye, the thirty-year war. Your people are to be congratulated on
your victory over those Catholic bastards.'

'After this war, many war veterans become wolf hunters.'

'And this is how you got started?'

'I hunt wolf before this. I was born hunting the wolf. And even
before I was born. In the ancient law of my land it says, all who live
must build a wolf pen. One should also possess a wolf drum, wolf
tongs, spear, gun and *lapptyg*.'

'Lap-what?'

'*Lapptyg*. It is rope with bunting and small flags.'

'What do you use that for?'

'We use this to scare the animal so that it goes towards the trap.
Is especially good if having picture of little devil.' Hellström laughed.
'In my land there is bounty: two *daler* for adult wolf. One *daler* for cub.'

Lemuel had no idea how much a *daler* was worth. He assumed from the widening of the man's eyes that it was a great sum but he didn't ask, as his question would reveal his ignorance.

They talked more about the long war that had ravaged the man's homeland, but Hellström did not seem concerned at the great losses his kin had suffered.

'Mr Lane, war is God. Do you see?'

Lemuel nodded, caught in the man's raptor eyes again.

'There is no start and there is no end. Before there is man there is war. Before there is wolf there is war. War is waiting for man to be born. Is game? A man takes another man's life. It is good game.' The man from Gothenburg grinned.

Lemuel had thought this man was in his forties but now he wondered if he was as old as the Earth. As old as time.

They talked more about the political upheaval in both their countries. Hellström elaborated further the ancient laws in Sweden, before turning to the business of the wolf.

'The wolf is a social animal. He depends on cooperation for his survival. Same as me and you, Mr Lane. The mistake man has made is to underestimate the wolf, to see him as just another animal, and not his equal. But if you want to catch your wolf, you need to know the measure of him. Now, you say as far as you know, this is the last wolf left in this land?'

'Yes, I believe so.'

'But you believe the one before that was the last one, no?' Hellström grinned and bit into a slice of ox-tripe.

Lemuel shrugged. He didn't like being wrong about anything.

'Very well, let us assume you are right then. A lone wolf is a desperate wolf. Is he not? And this is both to our advantage and our disadvantage.'

'How so?'

'Well, Mr Lane, to our advantage because, as I say, the wolf is needing other wolves for his strength. Our disadvantage because desperation is making the wolf fiercer. He has nothing left to lose, and this is making him fearless.'

Lemuel couldn't stop looking at Hellström's right hand, at the missing fingers and at the livid pink flesh. The wound was a ragged ridge of skin. It looked like a badly darned sock. Hellström caught Lemuel eyeing it and smiled. Lemuel looked away, embarrassed.

'It is natural to look. A wolf wound. I am lucky he does not have my whole hand.'

'What happened?'

'Ah, my own fault. I underestimate his power. Never underestimate the wolf. I have this wolf trapped and tethered. He is bleeding to death, and yet he is still finding the strength to give me a little kiss.'

Hellström held up his crab hand and pinched his fingers together like a crab's pincers. He laughed, flashing his pike teeth again.

'So, now, tell me what you know of your wolf.'

Lemuel felt oppressed by the man's presence. It was like he had some hold on him that he couldn't slacken. He got to his feet, refilled their goblets, and stood by the fire. He leaned down and threw on another log, sending red cinder dust up into the air.

'I don't know much. Only that a few weeks ago, it attacked my only son, Thomas, when he was out fishing for trout in Lowe Dene. My men brought him back. We called for the physician. He tried everything but the next day he died in my arms.'

He should have insisted that day that Thomas accompany him and his men to the O'Fealins'. He should not have been so lax as to let the boy go trouting. His son had wanted to join the men and he had denied him. It was his fault that his son was dead. Lemuel could feel himself sink into the black chasm deep inside himself. He kicked back as hard as he could. He glugged at the claret.

'We thought we'd rid this land of wolves. Thought we'd killed the last one many years since.'

'And this wolf, is a he or a she?'

'I don't know.'

'You don't know?'

Lemuel shook his head, suddenly shamed by his ignorance.

'You do not know much about your wolf, do you, Mr Lane?'

'There's been sightings of it. Saw it myself, crawling out of the beck like a swamp fiend. It's a loathsome creature. And big. Haunches like hams. Some have come forward to say they've lost their beasts. A sheep, some geese. I thought a hundred pound would be enough to entice an army of wolf-killers. Wherever it's hiding out, it can't be that far, going off the attacks that have been reported. But despite all these hungry young bucks rampaging about town, so far, nothing.'

'Do they *rovdjursskall*?'

'Eh?'

'It is done in my land. Farmers must form a chain. Sometimes a thousand men. They walk through the forest. They drive out the wolf.'

'Er, no.'

'These men who come, they are not killers of the wolf. They do not have the experience or the expertise. However much you offer them they will blunder on, like blind mice, never catching this wolf.'

'I'm also arriving at that conclusion. Which is why I am hoping to hire you, Mr Hellström.'

'Very well, we turn to business. I can catch your wolf for you. But there will be a price.'

'Just name it. How much?'

'I am not talking about money, Mr Lane. We will get to this. I am talking about a price above money.'

'I don't follow.'

'You allow me full rein of this land to come and go as I please?'

'Yes, of course.'

'And all landowners in this area, they agree?'

'We can come to some arrangement, I'm sure.'

'The wolf is a hunter. There is order in his world. But many things the wolf is doing are inexplicable to us. I have seen the wolf start to chase an animal then, for no reason, turn and walk away. I have seen the wolf glance at a set of elk tracks, no more than a minute old, sniff and go on ignoring them. A wolf, before he kills, has a conversation of death with his prey. I have seen this. Our domestic beasts have this conversation bred out of them. They no longer understand the language of the wolf.'

Lemuel didn't intend to show on his face the confusion he felt inside, but he must have done, because Hellström shuck his head. 'I give you example. A horse is a large animal, is he not?'

Lemuel nodded.

'Yes, good. He is large animal, as capable as a moose of cracking the wolf's ribs and splitting his head open with a kick. But he does not do this. Instead, the horse panics and he runs away. What is happening when a wolf wanders into a flock of sheep and kills twenty or thirty of these sheep?'

'That's greed for you. The wolf is a glutton. Eyes bigger than his belly.'

'No. That is not so. It is a failure on the part of the sheep to communicate. The wolf is initiating a sacred ritual and is meeting with ignorance.'

'I don't understand.'

'Mr Lane, we are dealing with a different kind of death from the one men know. When the wolf ask for the life of another animal he is responding to something in that animal. This thing say my life is strong. It is worth asking for. This death is not tragic. This death has dignity. I have lived a full life, says the animal. I am ready to die. I die so that my brothers live. I am ready to die because my leg is broken. My time here is finished. This meat has power. This meat is consecrated. Do you understand?'

Lemuel had no idea what this man was talking about. He wondered for the first time about the sanity of Hellström. He'd heard about wild men in the woods who had taken themselves away from the society of others. He had heard how their isolation had marred their senses, making them eccentric, and even lunatic, and he wondered if Hellström was perhaps one of these men. But he took a sup from his goblet, the wine sweet and strong.

'I understand.'

'Good. We must know that the wolf earns his meat. He does not keep his prey in pens and sties. He does not keep this prey captive behind walls and fences. He does not tether this prey to a post. His prey is free. I try and be like the wolf. The difference between wild meat and tame meet is profound. You know this? Dying is as sacred as living. You understand, Mr Lane, yes?'

Again, without really comprehending, Lemuel nodded.

The man from Gothenburg nodded too. He kept on nodding. Then he pulled his face and gurned. He stood up and spun around on the ball of his heel. He burst into a manic laugh.

'Mr Lane. What is it you say? I pull your leg.'

He gave Lemuel a look that curdled his blood. He no longer knew whether what this man said was one thing or another. It was like the man from Gothenburg was possessed.

'Dying is sacred, yes? And I love death. Do you love death, Mr Lane?'

Lemuel tried to join in with the man's levity, attempting to shed whatever strange joke the man kept. But the man did not laugh. His face went stiff and serious. His eyes burned like hot coals.

'I am talking about the death of others. We must enjoy this death.'

He held Lemuel's gaze again. Lemuel tried not to look away but the man's eyes burned into him. He tried to steer the conversation back to business.

'So, how do you propose catching my wolf?'

'You have heard of King Edgar the Peaceful, yes?'

'Yes.'

'And do you know that he is allowing his men to pay their taxes in wolf heads? And their fines in wolves' tongues?'

'No, I haven't heard that.'

'This is why there are hardly any wolves left in your country.'

'Good.'

'Yes, good, you say. It is good. You are free of the wolf. My sheep are safe, you say. My veal is safe, you say. But you must be careful what it is you wish for.'

Lemuel was becoming impatient with this man now. 'But you're a wolf killer!'

'Oh yes, kill, kill, kill. I kill hundreds of wolves. I am wolf hunter. I kill the wolf. And yet I rely on the wolf. If there are no more wolves, I am out of job. Do you see?' The man laughed heartily at his own joke.

'I get what you are saying, Mr Hellström. But I am hiring you to kill a wolf that is roaming this land. At great expense to me. A wolf that has killed my only son. A son I was to leave everything I have earned. My son and heir. A son who was to keep my name alive.'

In his mind's eye he saw his son in the last moments of his life.

He saw himself pleading with Stoker, the physician. Stoker shaking his head with such solemnity. He could feel himself approaching the black spot and he glugged back the claret to quell the sensation.

'I will kill your wolf for you, Mr Lane. All I say is that there is a price to pay above your bounty, above my fee. And we will all have to pay this price.'

Hellström sat back in his chair and nodded sagely. He bit into a heathen cake.

'I ask for two hundred pounds, plus fifty pounds for expenses, and unfettered access to the land. I also require two of your best men to assist me.'

'Two hundred and fifty pounds! You must think I was born yesterday!'

'For this I take your wolf back to Hell. I do the devil's work. Then we can dance.'

Lemuel met the man's eyes. They were deep-set and icy. Older than the Earth. He felt a serpent writhe across his spine. Could he find this money? He would have to. He had no choice.

'I'll arrange everything.'

Feasting on Venison

As Elizabeth carried plates and pots into the kitchen where the cook was washing up, she was thinking about the previous night. She had stayed up late waiting for Lemuel to come to bed, listening to the men's muffled voices beneath the bedchamber, unable to make out anything that was said. She'd strained to catch the conversation, hearing laughter and taking this as a good sign. Sleep must have taken her before their business was over, because her next memory was waking up in the morning, with Lemuel, still fully dressed, lying on top of the bed, next to her, smelling of claret and tobacco. He hadn't smoked since he was garrisoned.

She remembered him joining the campaign. Thoughts of him going off to fight had troubled her. Lemuel was a man of principle. Like her father. Lemuel had fought for a just cause, and the war had allowed him to rise in rank, to become so much more the man than she had married.

She went back into the dining room. Both girls had excused themselves and left the table. Lemuel was finishing the leftovers, mopping up bacon fat with a hunk of bread.

'So, how was the business conducted last night?' she said.

Lemuel explained the deal he'd struck with Hellström.

'That's an awful lot of money. Are you sure we can afford it, Lemuel?'

'It's our son, Elizabeth. Our only son. Our boy. How can we not afford him?'

She observed his forehead furrow in concern. 'I suppose we can sell the Cotes' place. We'll find the money somehow. Who are you going to ask to assist him?'

'Gad and Ezekiel. Who else?'

Elizabeth weighed this up. She didn't share her husband's fondness for these men. They were half-competent, but she often wondered if her husband elevated Ezekiel in his mind, due to a sentimental attachment. She had heard many times how Ezekiel had pushed him out of the way of the cannon ball that would have torn him to pieces. And how that self-same cannon ball had ripped a hole through another man. What was left of the man after he bled to death on the field. Afterwards, the ground was too hard to bury him, and they left him for the kites and crows. But just because he'd saved her husband's life that didn't make Ezekiel a paladin. Surely any soldier in his position would have done the same?

'There's people round here won't like them wandering onto their land as if they owned it.'

'Let me deal with that, love. A fat purse quells tongues.'

Elizabeth stood up and started to wipe the table with the cloth the cook had left.

'What did you think of this Mr Hellström, Elizabeth?'

She considered this. She knew that Lemuel valued her opinion, that he knew her to be a better judge of character than himself.

'I hardly had any time with him.'

'But your first instincts? I mean, did you think he was a trustworthy fellow?'

She thought to herself that she would trust him as far as she trusted their tom cat with a vole. But as she wiped the crumbs from the table she observed his troubled brow, and said instead, 'Don't worry, I'm sure it will be fine. He's said to be the best.'

Seeing that he wasn't reassured by this, she bent down and kissed his cheek. She had seen how much pain he was in, watched him take to the bottle till he was insensible, staying up later than usual, long nocturnal walks clutching the whisky jar, screaming out in the middle of the night. He was drinking too much, not sleeping, and not eating properly. She had observed grief consume him so that he could barely concentrate on anything else. He'd always been so thorough in his conduct, discipline he'd learned in the army, but he no longer seemed to care about the farm, the estate, or his other properties. He hadn't even mentioned the shooting lodge he'd been so keen to invest in, or the racing horses.

She shared his pain, lived in the same shadow, woke every morning to find it squatting on her chest. She too lay on her back at night with her eyes closed, staring deep into hell's gaping hole. And yet to see this man, the man she loved with all her heart be so crippled by sorrow, was unbearable. If she could, she would lift this pain from him and put it with hers. She would gladly combine their grief if it meant alleviating her husband's suffering. Perhaps, if he caught this wolf, they could be happy again. It would not bring Thomas back, but it would bring something to a close. It would offer a paltry solace. They had to find a way out of this, to live again. They had two daughters, two beautiful daughters. They had to get over this somehow, for the sake of their girls.

After Elizabeth had gone, Lemuel put his boots on and went to find Jacob, who was in the stables tending to the horses. The stableboy had taken sick. There was something wrong with the lad. He was forever sickening. He asked Jacob to bring Gad and Ezekiel to see him and met with them within the hour, in the main barn.

'Mr Hellström is lodging in a room above The Moorcock. I have told him you will help him in any way he requires.'

'Sir. Beg pardon, sir. But what happens to us?' Ezekiel wanted to know.

'What do you mean?'

'Well, that's to say, we were after the bounty for ourselves, sir. Kate's due to give birth soon. And I need money to pay this outstanding physic.'

'Don't worry. You work with Hellström from now on. Follow his orders. You do as he says, do you understand? When I get my wolf, Hellström gets his fee, and you get your money.'

'Beg pardon, sir. Is the reward still a hundred pound?'

'Yes. Split two ways. Fifty each. Now take those two geldings. Jacob's already saddled them for you. No need to bring them back, keep them until all this is over.'

'But sir, we've no stables.'

'They'll be all right in your shed for now. Look after them. They're two of my best.'

Ezekiel smiled. He looked over at Gad and nodded. Surely, this was the most favourable outcome. They were now working with the best in the business. If anyone could catch the wolf it was this man Hellström. All he and Gad had to do was assist him and the money was theirs. Not only that, they now also had their own horses.

'Is that settled then?'

Both men agreed.

'Good, now get yourselves over there.'

The men were walking over to the geldings when Lemuel called them back. 'One more thing. This Hellström, he's got a gammy hand.'

'I'm sorry, sir, what do you mean?'

'You'll know when you see it, but whatever you do, don't stare at it. Got that?'

'Yes, sir.'

'See that you don't.'

The men rode over to The Moorcock Tavern, first by the bridleway, then along the road that connected Lemuel's estate with the village, just over a mile away. For once it wasn't raining, and in fact, most of the sky above them was an even chalk blue shade. It was a cold and blustery morning in early December, but Ezekiel didn't mind the cold. As long as it was dry. He was intrigued to meet this Hellström, having heard so much about him. And he was also keen to tell Kate about the agreement. She'd be soothed by the news. It wouldn't be long now before he'd have the money for her physic, and he could settle his account with that robbing bastard, Stoker. Ezekiel turned to Gad as they rode further along the bridle path, across the potsherd to where it merged with Lowe Lane. He could see the spire of the village church pike the sky in the distance and the slate roofs of some of the houses.

'They say he's killed five hundred wolves,' he said.

'That's a lot of wolves.'

'They say that he was nearly killed by a wolf and that he only survived because the wolf had so much respect for him that he spared his life.'

'They do.'

'They say he killed a wolf with his bare hands.'

'They say lots of things.'

'Remember what Lemuel said, don't stare at his disfigurement. We don't want to get off on the wrong foot.'

'Or wrong hand,' Gad said, smiling at his own joke.

'Ha! Good one.'

They rode on in a contented silence for some time, until they came to the main road of the village. It was still early, and the streets were quiet. A small brindled dog sniffed around a midden heap. An old woman chucked a bucket of filthy water in the gutter. There was another miscreant shackled in the stocks, covered in shit, piss and rotting vegetables. A pigeon strutted close by.

'How much do you think he's paying this Hellström then?'

'If he's set a bounty at a hundred, you can double that.'

'You reckon? Must be loaded then. Five hundred wolves, times two hundred pounds. That's ...'

Ezekiel tried to do the sum in his head. Ciphering had never been his strength.

'I make it one hundred thousand pounds,' Gad said.

'One hundred thousand! One hundred thousand! That's a princely sum.'

'It is,' Gad said. 'But what you've not taken into account is that's what he's worth now. Now he has his reputation. He wouldn't have charged that to begin with. He might have even done the first few for free. Takes years to build up a reputation like that.'

Ezekiel considered this. 'Yeah, you're right. But still. Bet he's loaded.'

They rode on in silence again until they approached The Moorcock. They dismounted and roped their horses to the tethering post.

'Let me do the talking,' Ezekiel said.

'I always do.'

It was too early for punters and the landlord was still clearing up from the previous evening, putting fresh straw on the floor, getting ready for opening. As they entered the main room of the tavern, they found the landlady sweeping up. They explained that they were here to see Hellström and she ushered them to a staircase round the back.

'Up them stairs. Second on your left.'

The two men climbed the stairs and approached Hellström's door. They paused for a moment. Ezekiel gave Gad a look before reaching up with his clenched fist and knocking on the door twice. They waited. Nothing.

'Perhaps he's still asleep?' Gad said.

Ezekiel shrugged. He knocked on the door again. This time they heard someone shifting on the other side. Then a voice. 'What you want?'

'It's us, Mr Hellström, sir. Our master said you'd be expecting us?'

They heard footsteps, then a key turn in the lock. The door opened. A giant man was standing in his nightshirt. He towered over them as he looked first at one then the other. The men seemed to shrink in his presence.

'Which is Gad and which is Ezekiel?'

Ezekiel explained and offered his hand to shake. Hellström offered his crab claw. Despite what Ezekiel had said to Gad about not staring, he found himself transfixed by the man's disfigurement. He shook the claw awkwardly, trying not to grip too hard. But also making a point of not gripping it too softly. He didn't think the man would appreciate being treated like a leper. Gad did the same. Hellström seemed to enjoy their discomfort. He grinned, flashing a row of pointy teeth. The man opened the door fully and invited them into the room. He closed the door behind them.

'I have only one chair. You sit on the bed.'

He pointed to the bed, which had been made impeccably. The blankets were folded neatly and the pillows plumped. The room was a reasonable size, and apart from the bed, there was a desk, a chair and a chest of drawers. There was a large rug on the floor and a tapestry of a white horse on the wall above the bed. The desk was positioned beneath the only window in the room, which faced east, so that the morning sun poured through the panes, brightly illuminating everything it touched. On the desk was a brass canstick, a lanthorn, a quill, an inkwell and some parchment. Hellström somehow looked too big for the room. He went to the chair which was tucked under the desk and pulled it out enough for him to be able to sit down. He pointed to the bed and the two men perched on the end of it, careful not to mess it up too much.

'So, Mr Lane tells me you are hunting this wolf for some time now.'

'Er, yeah. About a month, sir, I think,' Ezekiel said.

'But you have no luck?'

'The thing is, Mr Hellström, hunting wolves, it's not really our thing, sir. I'm a sawyer by trade. Gad here is a waller. We both mainly do walling and delving these days.'

'Mr Lane tells me you are a soldier. You serve under his command?'

'Well, sir, that was some years since now. But I'm no carpet knight, that's for sure.'

Hellström nodded. 'To hunt the wolf is not an easy task. So tell me, what are you doing to catch it?'

Ezekiel told Hellström about all the traps they had dug, and all the irons they'd had the smithy make for them. He didn't tell him about the man pit or the false trails they'd laid with the dummy paw prints.

'So, you use the sledgehammer to break the nut.'

'Eh?'

'Traps do not always work. Neither do irons. If the wolf knows he is being hunted, he proceeds very cautiously. We must be clever and patient.'

'What's your plan then?'

'We will get onto this. But before we do, I want you both to know that I hunt by a code. It is very important, if you work for me, that you agree to follow this code.'

Ezekiel gave Gad a somewhat bemused look. They were hunting a wolf, not jousting with a duke.

'And what code is that, Mr Hellström?'

'Men round here, they say the wolf is a coward. They say the wolf is stupid. Some say that the wolf is a minion of Satan. But we will not catch our wolf if we think like other men. In Sweden, I once saw three men on horseback ride down a she-wolf. They throw a noose over her neck. When she grips the rope with her teeth to keep the rope from closing, they drag her around the farm until they are breaking her teeth out. Then, while two of them stretch the animal between their horses with ropes, the third man is beating her to death with a hammer. They take the wolf round to their neighbours' houses, before throwing her in a ditch.' Hellström paused allowing his words to sink in. He looked first at Ezekiel, then at Gad. 'This is not how we treat the wolf. Do you understand? We kill this wolf. Yes. But we kill this wolf with dignity. It is an honourable thing. Yes? We must live and die with honour. You agree?'

Ezekiel nodded. So did Gad.

'I was only saying to Gad a few weeks ago that we always work with dignity. Wasn't I, Gad?' Ezekiel lied. Gad agreed, going along with the fib.

Hellström nodded sagely. 'Good. With dignity. Good. Wolves, they are like us. This is how we proceed.'

Ezekiel smiled. He didn't really know what this one-handed freak was banging on about, but he wasn't going to let on. Hellström stood up and pulled off his nightshirt so that he was now standing in front of them completely naked. He folded the shirt neatly and placed it on the desk. He was as lean as a whippet. His body was ripped with small, tight muscles. There was no flab on his bones, only flesh and sinew. There were several marks and scars on his skin, including a line straight above his navel that looked like a knife gash. Around his neck was a silver chain and hanging from the chain was a silver pentacle.

Hellström paced the room, stroking his chest. Ezekiel tried not to look at the long fleshy appendage dangling between his legs.

'I want you to take me, first of all, where you see the wolf. Then, where this wolf is attacking your master's boy. Then I want you to take me to each of the places you have put traps and irons. Yes?'

Ezekiel nodded. He told the man where they'd first encountered the wolf, and subsequently, where they'd found the wolf's tracks. As he spoke, Ezekiel was relieved to see Hellström get dressed.

'One last thing.'

Ezekiel nodded for the man to continue. 'What I say you do. You carry out my orders. Any arguments and I will feed you to the wolf. Do you understand?'

Ezekiel looked to see if Hellström was joking but his face was set and his silver eyes blazed with malevolence. He nodded, as did Gad.

'Do you know what is inside the wolf's tongue?'

Both men shook their heads.

'Inside the wolf's tongue is the doe's tears. Come then. Let us go and see.'

They rode out of the village, over field and meadow, to the copse above Eddie's farm. They dismounted. Ezekiel and Gad led the way to the first trap they had laid. When they approached it they saw that it had been disturbed. They peered into the hole that had been uncovered. Impaled on the wooden pikes was a young roe deer. Its eyes were open but it was dead. Ezekiel reached in and with Gad's help they freed its corpse.

'What are you doing?'

'Good meat, that. I'm going to take it back, butcher it.'

'But you know that this is a fining offence, no?'

'Normal rules don't apply.'

Hellström shook his head. 'You will do this in your own time, not in mine.' He peered into the pit then shook his head and laughed.

'What's the matter?'

'In my land we build pits. It is the law. There is no exception. We dig holes. We line the holes with wood or dry stone. Three and four yards diameter. We dig three yards deep. What is this little thing you have made?' He laughed again.

'Well, like I say, it's not really our area of expertise.'

Hellström paced around the pit and examined the area carefully. He unsheathed his sword and used it to sift through the forest detritus. He picked up a lump of dried shit and pulled it apart with his crab pincers. He sniffed it.

'Wolf excrement. A week old. Female. We are looking for a she-wolf.'

'And you can tell that from sniffing it?' Ezekiel was impressed.

'A wolf's excrement is like a print of the finger. It is unique to the wolf. You put this in a line of one hundred wolf stools, and I will pick it out. She knows you are hunting her. This is why your traps and your irons are bootless.'

They rode over to the neighbouring wood and showed Hellström where they had set iron traps there. Hellström stooped down to examine them. He shook his head and tutted.

'In my land we have a row of pits thirty to fifty metres apart. We have fencing system to force the wolf towards the pit. What you have done is no good.'

Ezekiel went to say something but thought better of it. He watched Hellström as he patrolled the surrounding area. He found something dead in the undergrowth and bent down to pick it up. It was the corpse of a raptor, but Ezekiel couldn't make out whether it was a puttock or a glede.

'See this. A healthy red kite. How do you think this bird die?'

Ezekiel looked at Gad. Both men shrugged.

'Poison. This bird lives on the kills of others. It is eating poisoned flesh. See, there is no mark.'

He turned the bird over for them to see. Then he spread each of its wings.

'Good, young, healthy. Very good plumage.'

Hellström laid the bird on the ground close to where he'd discovered it and searched round some more. Soon enough he found what he was looking for, a rabbit corpse. He picked it up and examined it. He showed the men the part of the rabbit's flesh that had been pecked at, near its breastbone. He sniffed at the meat.

'See here?' He pointed to the rabbit's fur – a patch of white powder next to where the flesh had been pecked. 'Arsenic. In the hunt for the wolf, they kill everything in their wake. In their hunt for the wolf they make the world a barren place. This is not good. They do not kill with dignity.'

Ezekiel didn't let on that they had been laying down meat laced with arsenic and other poisons for days now, although this rabbit wasn't one of theirs. The arsenic powder they'd been using had more of a yellow hue. They'd killed fox, fitchew, weasel, raven, magpie and glede. He didn't like such blunt methods, but the other men were doing the same, and he had to get that reward money. Kate had made a full recovery now, thanks to the physic, but the bairn was due any day, another mouth to feed. He also had to counter with the doctor, who was becoming more strident in his pursuit of his fee, threatening him with the magistrate.

The men rode out further, examining more poisoned corpses.

Their final reconnaissance was Lowe Dene. They traversed fallen trees as they walked to the beck. It had rained so hard that there was no strength in the soil, and where the slope was steep and the trees reached for the sky, they were vulnerable. Ezekiel had never seen so many fallen. At the beck the water gathered in pleats of froth. White foam drifted. The wet rocks glistened. He saw a small stout bird with a striking white breast perched on a flat-topped rock, bobbing and cocking its tail. A dipper. He led Hellström to the patch of woodland where they'd found first Thomas's tackle, then Thomas himself, mortally wounded.

'The wolf is biting the boy's neck. But she is not eating the boy. Why is this, do you think?'

'Dunno.'

'She uses her energy. She is hungry. She is starving. But she does not feed on his young flesh.'

'I never thought about that. Maybe Thomas scared her off?' Ezekiel said.

'This is what you think?'

'Like I say, I don't know.'

Hellström stroked his beard. He ran his pincer claw through his hair. He examined the spot in more detail, kneeling down and taking a handful of mulch in his good hand. He held it up to his nose and sniffed. Then he stuck out is tongue and licked the mulch tentatively.

'I think this wolf is being disturbed.'

'By what?'

'You say this farmer, close by, he has two dogs?'

'Two bloody big lurchers.'

'Two dogs of any size are no match for one wolf in full strength. So our wolf, she is not in full strength.'

They rode back to The Moorcock and ordered ales. Hellström had to stoop to avoid low beams. Leaning against the bar was a bedraggled old man, clearly in his cups. Hellström pushed the man out of the way. The man fell over and groaned. They found a table near the fire. Hellström looked around at the walls and the ceiling.

'This is good place. Is new?'

'There's been a tavern here before my father's time. This was rebuilt three years ago. The old tavern burnt down,' Ezekiel explained.

'These beams are so big,' Hellström said, pointing to the ceiling timbers.

'That's the wood from a ship that fought against the Spanish Armada.'

Hellström nodded. He seemed impressed. He drank some of his beer then expanded on his theme.

'In south Russia, I have seen men use eagles to kill wolves for sport.'

'How does that work then?' Ezekiel asked.

'The birds they are trained to slam into a wolf's back and bind its spine. They do this with such force that the wolf is almost paralysed. The bird is binding the spine with one foot and as the wolf turns its head to bite, it is binding its nose with the other foot, suffocating the beast. These birds are very strong. A ton of binding force in each foot and a blow from a wing can break a man's arm. But the eagle, it will never attack an adult wolf in the wild. Wolf hunting is something they are being trained to do. They are training these birds first by turning them lose on their children.'

'You're jesting us?'

'It is no joke. They dress the children in leather armour and cover them with wolf skin. Then they strap raw meat to their backs. Once the birds are used to knocking down children for meat, they put them in an enclosure with wolves. It is many weeks to train them.'

'Is that what we are going to do?'

'No. Absolutely not. We will try different ways. We will start tomorrow.'

The man who Hellström had knocked over had got to his feet. He was making his way over to Hellström, who watched him as he approached and smiled. He jumped to his feet like a jack-in-the-box and turning to the other drinkers at the bar, said, 'This man, I see him last night. I see him with a goat. He is naked with the beast. He is in the beast. Copulating.'

Hellström looked around at all the drinking men. 'Why do you wait? Place this man in the stocks.'

A man put his pot down and stood up.

'Come on, all of you. Take him away.'

There were four or five men now who had got to their feet and were shouting and swearing. The largest of the men grabbed the accused by his collar and started to drag him outside. He was aided by another who grabbed his ankles. The accused man was screaming out, protesting his innocence. The men carried him outside. Hellström watched all this with a big grin on his face.

'Did you see him do this?' Ezekiel asked.

Hellström laughed. 'In life we must have fun, yes? This is why we live. I will leave you now, gentlemen. I am attending to some other business. Catching a wolf. There is a lot to do.' He drained his tankard and pointed to the ceiling timbers. 'Is harder than beating the Spanish Armada.' He laughed again, with another flash of pointy yellow teeth. He grabbed each man by the collar. First Ezekiel, then Gad. He took his tankard back to the bar and went to the door at the rear still chuckling to himself, opened it and disappeared.

'What do you think of that?' Gad said, shaking his head.

'That man is the devil,' Ezekiel replied. 'But he's our devil. I think our luck has changed.' He nudged Gad and grinned. 'Come on, let's have another drink to celebrate.'

After their celebratory skinful, the two men returned to the deer carcass. They carried it back to Ezekiel's and butchered it. Ezekiel bagged up some chops and steaks for Gad, keeping the lion's share for himself. Tonight he and Kate would eat like King and queen. And where they would have been too scared to dare to eat venison, now they could eat it with impunity.

'And you're sure we won't have to pay a fine?' Kate said when she served them venison steaks and claret later that night.

'The master said we could. Here, have a bigger piece. You're eating for two don't forget.'

He used his fork to pick up another slice from the serving dish in the middle of the table and piled the meat onto Kate's plate.

'You'll have to get used to this. When we get that money we can feast like king and queen of the dene every night.' He grinned at Kate.

He looked over to their daughter, who was sleeping in her cot close to the table. It will be good for her to have a playmate, he thought. Two years was a good age gap. He saw his wife wince.

'What's the matter, love?'

'It's nothing. It's just the bairn kicking.'

She smiled. Ezekiel got up and went round to where Kate was sitting. He knelt down and placed his hand on her rounded belly.

'Can you feel?'

He held his hand there, but he felt nothing. He spread his fingers across the mound of tight skin. Then he felt it. One, two, three kicks. It was a heel he could feel. How weird it must be to carry another life inside you.

'Must be a boy.'

'How do you know?'

'Girls don't kick like that.'

'You've got a short memory.' Kate nodded over to where their daughter slept. She had a point. He now recalled how Rose had kicked inside her mother's womb like she were belting a football. He went back to his place and sat down again. He sliced into the venison as he told her more about Hellström, about their first encounter, and his nakedness. Kate laughed.

'He wore a silver pentacle around his neck. They say it wards off evil spirits.'

'They do say that. I've also heard it can be used to invite them.'

Ezekiel shrugged. He'd never come across this idea before.

'What did you make of him?'

'He's very tall and lean.' He stopped to think. He really didn't know how to describe him to Kate, so different was he from anyone he'd met before. 'He's like some weird sinister emperor of an underworld kingdom.'

He told her about the drunken man in the pub that Hellström had accused of copulating with a goat.

'Well, he sounds like trouble, that one,' Kate said. 'Let's just hope he's the right kind of trouble.'

The next day the two men rode over to The Moorcock where the drunk was still fastened in the stocks outside. It had rained heavily overnight and the man was soaked to the skin. When he heard their horses approach he looked up and pleaded with them. Ezekiel thought about offering some of the food he had with him but was worried Hellström might see him. Instead, he shrugged and gave the man an apologetic look, then went inside. Hellström was sitting downstairs in the bar area, finishing his porridge.

'This English food. I am never getting used to. It is no good.' He scraped the remnants with his spoon and swallowed the last of the bowl with a look of distaste. 'In my land we feed goats with this food.' He stood up and put on his sea-gown and wide-brimmed bandless hat.

'I have spoken to your master. We go there first.'

They rode out to the largest mistal, where Lemuel had already arranged for Jacob to meet them, poniard in hand. Hellström explained the plan and the men gripped one of Lemuel's milch cows that was coming to the end of her productive life, while Hellström bled the beast with the poniard. They winched the beast by its back legs and caught the blood in a milk pail. The cook would curdle it later and make it into black pudding. They wrapped the animal in cloths and carried it onto a cart, then attached the cart to two of Lemuel's strongest geldings and the three of them rode off to a spot that Hellström had already chosen. They dragged the bloody corpse of the milch cow through Dale Edge Woods, to leave a trail ending at a spot that Hellström had carefully considered. Hellström took out a length of rope from his saddlebag and they helped him hang the animal up a tree by its back leg. Hellström tied the rope tight around the trunk.

'What now, sir?'

'We wait.'

The three men concealed themselves and waited with crossbows loaded. As Ezekiel crouched next to Hellström and Gad he could already feel his bones begin to stiffen.

'Sir. How long for?' Ezekiel whispered.

'Hush! We do not speak,' Hellström answered.

An hour went by. Then two. The men did not stir. Ezekiel could feel the cold creep into his marrow. The seat of his slops was damp, absorbing moisture from the foliage he leant against. He looked at Gad who was crouching with his head bent low and his eyes closed. Was he asleep? How could he sleep in that position? It was like being strung up on the rack. He nudged him and Gad opened his eyes, giving a startled look before realising it was Ezekiel who had woken him. He shook his head.

'I'm hungry,' Ezekiel whispered.

'Hush!' Hellström put his finger to his lips.

Another hour went by. A jackdaw showed some interest in the corpse. As the cow was hanging by only one of its back legs and the jackdaw hopped onto the free leg, which jutted out like a perch. The bird pecked at the meat half-heartedly before flying off again. They waited in silence. Ezekiel tried to wiggle his toes but couldn't feel his feet any more. He wiggled his fingers to stop them seizing up. They were stiff and sore, and it took some effort to move them. He tried to wiggle his toes again, but they were completely numb. This was so boring. Was this really the great plan that this legendary hunter had come up with? Surely there had to be a better way? But then again, this man had killed five hundred wolves, and Ezekiel had killed a grand sum of none, so what the hell did he know?

He thought back to the previous eve, feasting on venison with Kate like they were royalty. Feeling his child inside his wife's belly. He didn't care if it was a girl or a boy. As long as it was healthy. It was his child. The child that he and Kate had made together.

His mind wandered back to the wolf and to this man his master had hired. He'd imagined the man would have specialist equipment, new-fangled contraptions, not just lumps of meat. He imagined at the very least that he'd have a clean shirt. And yet this man seemed so much more than a man. What manner of creature was he? As he cogitated, he saw a large dark bird landing on a branch close by. It was a raven. The bird stared first at the corpse, then over at the bush where the men were concealed. It peered into the bush as though it knew they were hidden there. It held that position for a time, so that

Ezekiel became convinced it was cognisant of their whereabouts. Nonchalantly, the bird began to groom its long black flight feathers, while all the time, staring into the bush where the men were secreted. Eventually the raven bowed its head, opened its beak wide and made a hoarse croak. It spread out its shoulders until its wings crossed over at the back. It fluffed up its head feathers. Then it spread its massive wings and majestically took flight. As it did, Ezekiel saw something else move, no more than ten yards' distance. A large grey dog. No, it was their wolf. He leapt up, brandishing his crossbow, and as he did Hellström leaped too, drawing his bow and firing the bolt. Ezekiel's bolt quickly followed. Then Gad's. But the wolf scarpered. Each of the three arrows fell short of the wolf as it ran off. Ezekiel threw down his bow in frustration. Hellström muttered something under his breath.

'There she goes. We were so close.'

'I didn't even see it. I was watching that raven.'

'I watch this too.'

Hellström muttered something in Swedish.

'So what now?'

'We can no longer use this place or this bait. We must start again. But first we will do a full reconnaissance. I have map.'

He reached into his bag and pulled out a rolled-up parchment. He spread it out over the forest floor, using four stones on each corner to keep it flat.

'You show me.'

Ezekiel pointed out Sheep Brink, Lowe Dene, Bluebell Woods, Dale Edge, Hazel Hirst, Long Royd and Hanging Fall Woods.

'And this?'

Hellström pointed to the top right-hand corner of the map.

'That's Black Clough Woods, sir.'

'It is a very big forest, yes?'

'Biggest in the Ridings.'

'And you have baited this forest?'

'No, sir.'

'Why is this?'

'It's mostly fens.'

'What is fens?'

'Water. A lot of the forest is underwater. Wolves don't like water, right?'

'Ah, so now you are the expert on the wolf?'

Ezekiel shrugged. 'Not saying that.'

'Then what are you saying?'

Ezekiel shrugged again.

'You say nothing. You let me decide these things. We must not underestimate this wolf, do you understand?'

'Sir, I can take you there. It's about nine or ten miles north-east.'

Hellström removed the stones and rolled up the parchment. He secreted it in his satchel.

'We have no time today. And I must think. We go back.'

'Sir. What about the cow, sir?'

'As I have said, we cannot use.'

'But we're not going to leave it are we? I mean that's good meat is that.'

Hellström shook his head wearily. 'You want to eat this saggy old beast? No wonder you are so weak. You do not eat with dignity. You eat like a filthy rat.'

Out of nowhere Ezekiel felt the back of the man's good hand across his face. His cheek stung and his ear rang. That was one hell of a slap. He rubbed where the flesh was hot. There was no need for that. Hadn't they done everything this wolf hunter had told them to do? Why shouldn't he eat this cow? It was past its prime, that was true, but it would tenderise eventually in the stew pot. He wasn't proud. Hadn't he eaten worms at one time?

Hellström laughed manically. 'I joke. You eat this piece of filth.' He watched Ezekiel hesitate. 'Go on. It is yours now.'

Ezekiel, still a little unsure, went over to the carcass, took out his knife and cut the rope.

As Ezekiel rode back his thoughts were conflicted. He was still sore about the slap. He hadn't deserved that, even if it had been a joke. But also, he couldn't wait to tell Kate about their day. They had been so close, practically felt the wolf's breath. The closest they had ever been to the beast. Mr Hellström's bolt had reached the furthest, just a few inches short. A month they had been tracking it and hardly a sighting. Now, the very first day of proper hunting work with Mr Hellström and they had come within a few feet. It had taken them just a few hours to draw the wolf into their lair. He could see the prize in sight. Soon he and his family would be rich.

A Puttock's Leftovers

The wolf had given up on finding her mate. Although she had not seen or heard or smelled anything to prove it either way, she sensed now that she was on her own in these woods and indeed in this land that she roamed. She had to stay alive for the sake of the life that was growing, day by day, inside her. Every day getting bigger, slowing her down. She could feel the little ones kicking. It wouldn't be long now. A week, maybe two. She was looking for food. As the life inside her grew, so did her appetite. She was ravenous. She craved meat. Warm, succulent flesh. She made her way along a marten path, sniffing at the marten's droppings as she did, knowing that she no longer had the agility to hunt a marten, or even a rabbit. Like a kite, she would have to rely on the remnants of another beast's feast. She sniffed for a puttock's leftovers.

She had found a rat two days ago, which a raptor or a raven must have got started on, because its guts had been ripped out. The bird must have been disturbed as it fed. She hadn't bothered to pick for the meat, instead she had gripped the dead rat between her jaws, chewed it up and swallowed it in one gulp. It was an unsavoury supper. But it was sustenance.

She wandered along the banks of a shallow stream where the water flowed fast over rocks and sand. It was crystal clear water. She stooped where a rivulet plummeted from between jagged rocks to a pool below and she drank the ice-cold water, lapping it up in the ladle of her tongue. She approached the edge of the pool and slowly waded in, letting the water lap over her fur. She lay down so that her body was fully submerged. She paddled about, pawing the surface of the water, splashing it, taking gulps into her mouth. It felt good, this cold sensation on her skin, soothing. She ducked up and down, letting the water flow over her back. She climbed out and shook her coat, sending a myriad of droplets cascading. They glistened in the dappled sunlight like pearls of mistletoe. She found a clear flat space and rested for a while before the hunger in her gut spurred her on once more.

As she walked further into the woods she caught a scent of fresh meat. It was the meaty iron smell of fresh blood. It lingered on the browning ferns and bracken. She sniffed at the blood-touched fronds. She followed the trail of scent, quickening her pace as the aroma grew stronger. The smell of meat was overpowering. She came to a path where she found the blood of a cow smeared on the forest floor. The blood clung to the leaves and stalks of the wood anemone that grew near the base of the trees and across the long blades of yellow flag. She followed the trail as it meandered through the wood, until it led to a clearing where she could see the beast the blood belonged to, dangling by its hind leg, from a rope attached to a tree branch. The scent was mingled with another. What was it?

Her instincts told her that this was not right and that she should tread carefully, but her ravenous hunger drove her on. The smell was so strong now that her mouth watered and drool dripped from her jaws. She was about to walk further towards it when she was stopped in her tracks, first by a loud hoarse cronking sound, then the sight of a massive black bird. It was the raven who had guided her to the sheep a month or so ago. It perched on a low branch, its iridescent feathers flashing green and purple before turning back to coal black. The raven bowed low and nodded. She knew that this was a sign now, and she lowered her head too, mimicking the raven's actions. Then the bird used its enormous bill to point towards a thicket of holly and gorse.

She wondered what the bird was trying to communicate. Months before she would have dismissed the bird, but she had learned from experience to take note of these signals. So instead of creeping any closer to the meat, she studied the thicket, and as she did, she picked up the scent of men. She focused on the thicket and could just make out the russet of a man's gabardine, and she realised there was one, possibly more men, hiding in the bush. The raven was not leading her to food this time, it was warning her off it.

She scurried back the way she came and as she did she heard the men leap up. She didn't turn to see them. No time. Instead, with what little strength she had, she ran deep into the woods. Arrows flew towards her, falling short. She kept on running. Only when she could run no more, did she stop and look around to make sure she was safe. She stood beneath the cover of a spruce, panting. She thought about the raven. Grateful to the bird once more. Once again, this bird had saved her from danger. Why the bird would do this was not clear to her. The first time she had thought that she was entering a pact. The bird had needed her to finish the sheep off, then open it up so that it could feast on its innards. But now … what possible gain was there for this bird?

What she did know was that these woods were no longer safe. She would wait until nightfall and then break her cover. Then she would travel north along the river, across the barren moor, to the woods north-east, where the forest was more extensive, and where the fens offered protection from the men who came to hunt and kill.

Hair Like Writhing Worms

The first snow had fallen – a light flurry whose flakes did not stick. It was cold enough to form a hard crust of frost on the forest loam, which made it tough work digging. We were delving for wild parsnips to the east of the camp. Jenny called them cow-cakes. I'd learned that it was best to concentrate on the late flowerers and wait until the first frost before digging up the roots. That way they were soft and sweet. If you picked them too early they were thin and wiry.

'You'll get them at their best when the leaves have turned brown. That's what Alice taught us,' Jenny said, as she placed another root in the basket.

She told me how they ate them, peeling them first and boiling them. Then mashing and sieving, patting them into cakes and frying them with flour. I'd been with Alice and her forest family now for nearly a month, but I was still learning new things every day. As my knowledge of the forest grew, so did my ability to find food. How to find burdock roots when the leaves had diminished. Where to find clumps of Oak Moss. I'd learned that although the scarlet waxcap, with its livid red colour, looked poisonous, it was very good to eat. And how the snowy waxcap, that looked neither edible nor remotely tasty, was full of flavour. I'd learned how to make fruit leather from the winter sloes, haws and rosehips. Where to find wood blewits growing in abundance. I could now easily identify bittercress, jew's-ear, yarrow, velvet shank and crow garlic.

I had come to know all the group as sisters. They were my family now and although we quarrelled from time to time, we usually resolved whatever our issues were. Just over a week since, there had been a big altercation. There were sometimes tensions in the evening when there was uncertainty about who would be chosen to spend the night with Alice, but I wasn't party to these tensions. Jenny was now my constant companion and we would often retire earlier than the others and climb under the sheets together, so we didn't always witness how these tensions played out either.

'I need to talk to you about something,' Jenny said. She'd been unusually quiet most of the morning.

'What is it?'

She put down her basket and came closer, speaking in a lower tone as though the trees were spies and might hear us. 'Holly is thinking of leaving.'

'What? Why would she do that?'

'Things here. They're not exactly what they seem.'

'I don't understand. I thought we were a family?'

'I think we should go with her.'

'What?'

'That place you mentioned. The one your father told you about.'

Some weeks now I had spoken to Jenny about the plans my parents had made to create a better life for me and for them. She had been fascinated by the story and had wanted to know more, but I could only tell her what I knew, which was hardly anything at all.

'I don't really know where it is.'

The image of Da on the floor in a pool of his own blood filled my mind. The image that had haunted me for weeks hadn't entered my head of late. And its intrusion now was a shock.

'Holly travelled all over the country when she was with Carlow. She knows this place your father spoke of. She told me how they all shared the labour and the profits of the labour. How there were no laws or punishments, people were free to do and say what they liked. There were no leaders and they lived off the land like we do and do not go hungry. Not like—'

She stopped talking and I saw Alice approach, wearing a worried countenance. She halted close to where we were standing.

'He's hired a wolf killer.'

'Who has?'

'Lemuel Lane. I've just heard. He's hired Johan Hellström.'

'Who's he?'

'He's a bounty hunter from Sweden. A legend across North Europa. Killed over five hundred wolves. Some say more like a thousand.'

'Do you know him?'

'I've heard the stories. He's not just an amateur opportunist like the rest of them. This man is lethal. He must be stopped. We've got to stop him.'

'So what do we do?'

'I don't know. I need to think.'

We collected our tools and the basket full of roots and returned to camp with Alice. She went back to her hut, leaving me and Jenny by the fire with our sisters. There was a lot of talk of this Hellström, but no one really had any idea who he was. When Alice returned an hour later, she called a meeting. She smoked her pipe and told us more about the wolf killer.

'If Lemuel Lane has hired this man he must have lost faith in the other bounty hunters.'

She pointed to Jenny.

'I want you and Rowan to go into town. Find out where he's lodged and get as close to him as you can. Find out as much as you are able to.'

'We don't even know what he looks like.'

'You won't mistake him for anyone else.'

Alice described the man's physical appearance, his Goliath height, his insect limbs, and his disfigured hand. It was now too late in the day for our journey, so we rested and the next day we got dressed in more conventional attire, fixing our hair beneath bonnets and booting our feet. We didn't want to be conspicuous in any way. We clambered over moss-covered boulders, and through mire, the suck of the mud pulling at my feet. Everything was sloped and slanted, dark and dank. Twisted oaks that wound like pigs' tales. Past the trees that do not shed their leaves: pine, yew and spruce.

'Why do you want us to leave?'

'It's not like it was when we first came here.'

'How so?'

'It's just not.'

I tried to coax more from her, but she changed the subject. We made our way through the fens, out of Black Clough Woods, beyond an old wall. The path meandered through a brooding bower, and to the edge of the lumb. It was the first time we'd left the cover of the woods in nearly a month and the world beyond felt foreign.

As we dropped down to a drover's road we came across a wooden gibbet.

'Anyone found stealing more than thirteen pennies' worth gets executed here,' Jenny said. She knelt at the gibbet and I stood waiting for her. We took a track along the beck, which fed into the main river that flowed below Broadhead Moor, past High Cragg and Dale Edge. Jenny hadn't said a word since kneeling at the gibbet. I sensed that she was holding something back, but I respected her silence. Eventually she said, 'My father was brought there.' We walked in silence for a few minutes before she added, 'He was a good man. We had nothing. If there had been another way he would have taken it. We had no food. My poor mother. What do you do when there are five hungry mouths to feed? I'm glad in a way that I left. At least that's one stomach that doesn't need filling.'

I thought about my own father who had done everything he could to provide for me and Ma. I felt the familiar sadness that recollections of my parents always brought, but I also felt closer to Jenny. We had both lost our fathers. Though her mother was still alive.

The mist had lifted and the trees were no longer netted in a milky shroud.

'What will Alice say?' I said.

Jenny gave me a quizzical look.

'If we tell her we're leaving?'

'We won't tell her. She doesn't need to know.'

When we got to Mickle Beck we followed it for three miles before heading south, until we came to the village close to Lemuel Lane's estate. We'd walked about nine miles and it had taken us the best part of four hours. There were plenty of people going about their business, but we had no idea how we would find this Hellström man. We sat on a bench by the village green. It wasn't a village I had been to before as I'd never travelled this far south.

'So what now?'

'I suppose we just wait for him.'

'He's probably lodging at The Moorcock Tavern. The Lamb doesn't do rooms,' Jenny said. She had been to the village before. It was a reasonable assumption. With nothing else to go off it was our only idea. The Moorcock was positioned at the opposite side of the green. We could see from where we were sitting when and if Hellström left the tavern. The ground was iron-hard with frost. The boughs of the trees were floured with white powder. Swords of silver ice clung to the underside. We sat watching village life, while all the time keeping an eye on the door of The Moorcock. As we did the cold began to creep into our bones. There were two men close by playing nine men's morris. They'd marked the squares out on the ground and we observed them move their pieces around, each trying to be the first to get three in a row. I took my time from the church clock. An hour had gone by. We saw men enter and leave The Moorcock, but no one fitting the description of Hellström.

'Maybe we should go inside,' I said.

Alice had given us a groat to cover any eventualities.

'I don't think that's a good idea,' Jenny said.

'I'm getting cold.'

'Me too.'

'I bet there's a fire inside.'

Jenny nodded. I tucked my hands under my shawl and wriggled my toes to stop them going numb.

'I still don't understand. Why you want to leave.'

'Alice has changed.'

'It can't be just that, can it?'

'I overheard her talking. She's willing to go to war with the wolf hunters – it won't end well for anyone.'

I'd run from one war, like Jenny, and I was in no mood to run from another. We would do as we had been instructed and find as much out as we could, but then we would travel to a place where men and women lived in peace. Somewhere we could be safe and free from fear. We talked about the cottage we would build with our own hands from woodland timber, as I had seen Da do and had helped to construct. We'd decorate our home with forest flowers.

'My mother loved us all,' Jenny said. 'But she told me in private that I was her favourite, on account of me being the oldest. I think about her every day. It must kill her not knowing where I am, or even if I'm still alive. Once we're settled I'd like to get word to her.'

'We'll do that,' I said. 'Maybe you could arrange to meet her. Somewhere that wouldn't put either of you in danger.'

I was shivering. I'd lost feeling in my face now. My lips were numb and it was an effort to talk. I rubbed my hands together and stamped my feet. We watched a man stumble out of The Moorcock Tavern. He was tall but not unusually so. I glanced at his hands just in case. He was not our man. I watched smoke rise from the chimney and I thought about the fire burning inside and imagined Hellström sitting close by.

'I can't stand out here much longer,' I said.

Jenny nodded.

'I don't care, you know.'

I shrugged. I had no idea what she was talking about.

'About Alice or the rest of them. As long as we're together. We don't need anyone else.'

I held her close to me. We were going to make a life together and it was going to be beautiful.

'We don't have to go back if you don't want to,' Jenny said.

'But what about Holly? We can't leave her. You said we'd leave together.'

'All right. We'll talk to her when we get back. We'll leave as soon as we can.'

'Come on, let's go inside,' I said. 'We'll catch our death out here.'

We walked past the two men playing the game across the green then stopped outside. The last time I'd been in a tavern, my family had been attacked. I tried to calm my beating heart by telling myself that no danger could come to us here. We were entering a public arena.

'If anyone asks, we'll say we're waiting for someone,' Jenny said as she opened the door and we both went inside.

It seemed as dark as night at first but our eyes soon adjusted. It wasn't busy, maybe a dozen customers were scattered about the main bar area. I was relieved to see a large fire burning logs and peat bricks. Beneath large black ceiling beams, a group of four was huddled round the skittles, and another three by the ring-a-bull. Two men by the bar were playing tray-tip. The noise and chatter stopped and the men ceased their play and turned round to us. It was obvious they were not used to seeing girls enter their alehouse. I eyed them all furtively, making sure there was no one here who would recognise me. We went and stood by the bar and the drawer approached us. He was suspicious but seemed more reassured when we explained that we were waiting for our father. We ordered two ales and paid him and found a table near the fire. We could see clearly anyone coming in. I glanced about the room, surreptitiously examining each man, checking for the disfigured hand. None of these men was the man we had come to spy on. The heat from the fire was soothing. As it thawed my flesh I felt my skin itch. I was so glad to be sitting by that fire that for a moment I forgot the reason for our visit.

Close to where we were sitting two labourers were in deep conversation and their loud voices made it easy for us to overhear.

'He's dead,' one of them said.

'Sorry, pal,' said the other, and tapped his friend's hand reassuringly.

'Last night. Took ill the day before. Was drinking water like it was going out of fashion but wouldn't touch his food. He was panting awful. When I got up this morning and went into the barn, there he was. Dead as a doornail.'

'And you're sure it's poison?'

The man nodded. 'He wasn't even four year old. Fit as a fiddle.

Don't get me wrong, I want rid of this wolf as much as the next man. But the way some of them are going about it, it's carnage. I'm not bothered about crows or gledes, or foxes for that matter. But farm dogs. I mean, it's not on is it? That dog was one in a million. Took me ages to train him.'

'Sooner we catch it and kill it, the sooner this place can go back to how it was. Did I tell you the wife had an encounter day or two ago? Some lads whistling at her. Offcumdens. Saying they wanted to do this to her then do that to her. My blood were boiling. I told her to tell me who they were, but she wouldn't say. Said I'd only make it worse.'

We sat in silence, sipping our beers, trying to stay as inconspicuous as a shadow. I noticed a thick-necked man with a purple face standing at the bar kept turning away from his mate and towards us. He nudged his mate and nodded in our direction. The two men laughed. I saw that Jenny had noticed too. She looked worried. The men were talking but I couldn't hear what they were saying. Next, the purple-faced man approached us. He stood above where we were sitting and leant into us. In a low voice he said, 'How much?'

At first I didn't know what he meant, but I saw the indignation on Jenny's face and I realised what the man was intimating.

'I think there has been a misunderstanding,' I said, also in a low voice.

'Think yer too good, do yer?' he said in a louder voice. A few heads turned to look at us.

'Really, you've got this wrong. We're here to meet our father,' I said.

The man was shouting now. 'Yer nothing but ha'penny whores done up like tuppeny whores!'

Spittle flew from his lips. We put our heads down and tried to ignore the man, but he continued his invective.

'My money is as good as any man's here!'

His mate had come over and he grabbed his friend by the arm.

'Come on, John. Don't upset yersen. They're not worth it. Come on. Yer beer is getting flat.'

The purple-faced man shook his head but returned to the bar with his friend and carried on drinking. Those who had turned their heads to look turned back. I looked at Jenny. Her face was drained of colour.

'Told you this was a bad idea,' she whispered.

Two men entered. One was about twenty, the other was probably in his mid-twenties. The younger was tall and lean. The older, stockily built with a ginger beard. They looked familiar. They didn't order a drink. Instead, they sat down next to each other and said nothing. Which seemed odd behaviour. It was clear the men had come to meet someone and that it wasn't a social visit. Shortly after, a tall wiry man with hair and beard like gold, entered from the rear. He was somewhat ill-attired and so tall that he had to stoop to avoid nutting the ceiling beams. The men who were stood in his way quickly made a path for him, doffing their caps. He looked around the room, spotted the two men, then approached them. He nodded without smiling and sat opposite them. He seemed to suck the air out of the room. His presence somehow made the room darker and colder. As he pushed up the sleeve of his sea-gown I could see that his right hand was disfigured, with just his thumb and index finger remaining and more than half his hand missing. Here was our man. I nudged Jenny, but she'd already eyed him.

'Don't stare at him,' I whispered.

'I'm not,' she whispered back.

Hellström was doing the talking, but it was hard to hear exactly what he was saying over the din of the other conversations in the room. I had to concentrate really hard to block them out and focus on Hellström's voice. He spoke with a strong accent and was talking

253

about the work they'd done yesterday. They had spotted the wolf and had fired at her with arrows, but they'd missed and she'd run away. He took out a rolled-up parchment – a map – and unfurled it across the table, then pointed to the top right-hand corner. The three men were talking in low voices and I couldn't catch much of what they were saying. 'We'll do it in two hours with decent horses', 'crossbows', 'Lemuel Lane says', 'along Black Clough Beck', was all I caught. Hellström rolled up the map again and secreted it inside his sea-gown. He stood up and the other men stood too. The pair made their way to the front entrance, passing very close to where we were sitting. The two men were about to leave, when Hellström approached them. All three were now just a few feet from where we were benched.

'Listen,' Hellström said. 'What I have to tell you. It is not safe in here. Meet me behind the church in half an hour and I will give you more instructions. There is a wooden tool shed by the back transept chapel.' The men nodded and left. Hellström disappeared through the same door he'd entered at the rear.

I waited until all three men had gone and then turned to Jenny. 'We need to be there.'

'Too dangerous.'

'Not if we get there in plenty of time and find a good place to hide.'

'They were talking about Black Clough Woods.'

'I know.'

We finished our drinks and left the alehouse. We walked across the village green and over the bridge that crossed the beck. We approached the church, opened the gate, and made our way past the porch and the side chapel, past a row of tombstones, to the transept. There we found a wooden tool shed that looked like it had seen better days.

The door was missing and there were no tools inside. The wood was quite badly rotted and it was clear that it was past the point of repair. We had a look around.

'Here,' Jenny said, pointing to a place behind it.

Between the stone wall of the church and the back of the shed there was a pile of old roofing material and past this, a space where we could cram ourselves where we wouldn't be spotted. We clambered over the pile of wood and slate and nestled into the gap. There was just enough room for both of us and we could even see into the shed through some gaps in the wood. It was a perfect place to spy from. Whatever the men were coming here to discuss, we had a stage-side seat. We hunkered down and waited.

My knees were drawn up to my chin and a pain in the back of my legs was shooting up my spine. I had made a note of the time when we had first arrived at the church, just past the half hour, so when the church bells rang on the hour, I knew that we only had five minutes or so to wait. I started counting down from sixty in my head. I looked around and made sure that we were sufficiently concealed, crouched in such a way that the pile of wood was above us. Unless you were looking for us you would not know we were here. Just to make sure, I took hold of a paling and pulled it across. We waited.

As we crouched silently in our hiding space, I thought back to the men, to the two I'd recognised. They were the men who had been with Mr Lane in my kitchen. I saw the seven men. Da lay across the flags. Ma gagged and tied to a chair. Sudden panic. First in my gut, then my blood, then it was beating in my head. I wanted to run. To get as far away as I could. If I ran now I would have a chance.

I nudged Jenny and whispered, 'I've got to go'. She didn't even have time to react. I heard a man laughing. I looked up and I saw peering at us from over the woodpile three faces: Hellström and the other two men. When we both looked up, all three of the men burst out laughing.

'Well, what do we have here? Two little chicklings in their nest. How cosy!' Hellström said.

The blood in my veins turned to ice, my heart clambering to the back of my throat.

'So, you fell for our little trick did you? Do you think I will not see two girls spying on us in a tavern full of men?'

I was too scared to say anything, but I heard Jenny say, 'No, mister, you've got it wrong. It wasn't us. We weren't there.'

Hellström and the other two men laughed again.

'Well now, this is nice windfall. We do not catch the wolf, but we catch two little witches. This is good.'

'What do you want us to do with them?'

'You will gag them and tie them up. I will fetch the cart.'

The man with the ginger beard tried to grab hold of Jenny, but she fought back. He caught her punch, then dragged her by her arm over the woodpile. She started screaming. He punched her in the face. Once, twice. I was trapped. Boxed in. There was no way out. They gagged Jenny and tied her wrists and ankles. They threw a hessian sack over her head, then they reached for me. I lashed out, kicking and punching. The men caught hold of my limbs and pulled me over the woodpile and gagged me. I felt the rope catch the skin on my wrists as they tied me up. The world went dark as they placed a sack over my head. I swallowed dust. I felt their rough hands on me as I was hitched over one of the men's shoulders and carried across the churchyard. My heart was pounding like a hammer. I was thrown into the cart, wincing in pain as my body hit the wooden floor hard.

The cart travelled down an uneven path, and I was thrown around like a sack of potatoes. The path became smoother and we rode along this for maybe a mile or so before we came to a halt. I could hear one of them, I assumed Hellström, dismount the buggy and the sound of a heavy gate latch. The gates swung open. I heard Hellström take position again and felt the cart move forward over a yard. Shortly after, it came to a halt again and I heard Hellström dismount once more. Then nothing. Silence. About five minutes went by before I heard footsteps approach.

'Over here.'

'Let's have a look then.'

Someone was pulling the sack off me. It was the man with the ginger beard. Close by was his lanky companion. Standing next to him was Hellström. There was another man with them, a great big bear of a man, with a broken nose. It was Lemuel Lane. The man who had murdered my ma and da. My mind flipped back to that day, fetching the eggs and hearing the gunshot. I was walking into the house, the seven men stood in our kitchen. It was this man who had held the gun to my mother's head and pulled the trigger. Now I was gagged and bound and at the mercy of this man again.

'You know who this is don't you?' the man said to his companions. The one with the ginger beard shrugged.

'This is the O'Fealins' daughter: Caragh.'

The man with the ginger beard nodded, as did the lanky man who was standing next to him.

'Let's have a look at the other one.'

Ginger beard removed Jenny's sack. The men scrutinised her closely.

'No, don't recognise her.'

'Bring them to the main mistal.'

Jenny was grabbed by the younger man. I was grabbed by ginger beard, thrown over his shoulder and carried out of the barn and across a yard, past some stables, to buildings further on. Inside were two chairs and Jenny and I were tied to them.

'Take the gags off them. They can make as much noise as they like here.'

Ginger beard ungagged us and I gasped for air.

'Wait here. I'm going to fetch my stuff.'

Lemuel Lane left the other three to watch over us.

'I hear it's hard to get a witch to talk,' said ginger beard.

'It's nothing that rack, strap or screw won't fix,' the lanky man said.

'Lucky you spotted them, sir.'

'I see them even before this. I look out of my window as I wash and I dress. It is east and I like to watch the village green as the sun is rising. I see these two girls sit on the bench and they are looking over at this Moorcock. Why do they do this, I think.'

'But, sir, how did you know?'

'A thing is bothering me. When I leave you yesterday, I cannot stop thinking about the wolf and the raven. Something is not right. How did this wolf know we are there? We are so well hidden. So I go back to the place where we hide. I follow the direction that the raven flies. It flies north-east and I look at my map and I see this is where Black Clough Wood is. And I think about what you say about this fen. It is a good place to hide, is it not?'

'I don't get it, sir. How did you know all this just from that one thing?'

'I have this before. You know that a witch has a familiar. Always one, sometimes two, or even three. This is where the witch is getting her power. Without her animal companion she has no force. The familiar is the intermediary that links the witch to the one she serves: the Prince of Darkness, the Lord of the Flies. In Sweden I have a curse. The only way I can lift this curse is to sprinkle the walls with the blood of a black dog. It is good that I know this. This is why I wear a charm.'

He reached for the pendant beneath his shirt. It was a silver pentacle that flashed as it caught the light.

'I still don't fathom.'

'So then I ride over this Broadhead Moor. So bleak. And I keep on riding till I get to this Black Clough. And I follow a beck that goes deep into this forest, through fens. I almost die trying to make my way through this fen. I think I will turn back. All the time I am slipping and sliding. But I see this raven, and it is flying north-east, and I go on. It is hard work. I slip but I grab branch. I tread very careful. So careful. And I get through this fen. And do you know what I see?'

Ginger beard and wiry man shrugged.

'There is a camp, north of this fen. And there are these wild women living there. They are witches dancing around a fire. And now I understand.'

'I'm glad you do, sir, cos I haven't got a clue what you're banging on about.'

'Ezekiel, you are not stupid,' he said to ginger beard. 'You never think, why is it so hard to catch this wolf?'

'Er ... yeah. But, I mean, sir, it's like I said. Me and Gad, we don't have specialist knowledge in that area. We're wallers and delvers.'

'You build walls. You dig holes. But you have eyes. You have brains. You know there are many men trying and trying. This wolf, it is so hard to catch because it is protected. Do you see?'

Ezekiel and Gad shrugged.

'It is protected by magic. The magic of a witch and her demonic familiar. We must break this hocus-pocus.'

'Sir, how do you know this wolf isn't one of these familiars?'

'No. A wolf is never a familiar. A wolf is always a wolf. Always. It does not work for anyone else. It does not serve another. The wolf is a sovereign beast. And this one has a spell that we must break.'

'And how do we do that, sir?'

'Leave this to me. I have done this before.'

As he was speaking, I saw my parents' killer return with a leather box. He placed the box on a table close to where we were tied to chairs and opened it. I could see metal implements catch the light. He took out a black object with two metal plates that were fastened by protruding studs. There was a wing nut threaded along the middle stud. He spoke to Jenny.

'Do you know who I am?'

Jenny shook her head, her eyes bulging with fear.

'I am Lemuel Lane. Have you heard of me?'

Jenny shook her head again.

'I own this estate and most of the land hereabouts. Just over a month ago, in a little copse called Lowe Dene, my son Thomas, my only son, was so badly mauled by a wolf that he died in my arms. My son and heir bled to death through the savage attack of a baneful beast. The same wolf you and your friends have been protecting. Do you know how that makes me feel?'

Jenny didn't react.

'I don't suppose you do. I'll ask you another question. Do you know what this is?'

He held up the black object and moved towards her so she could get a proper look.

'Well?'

She shook her head.

'This lovely little thing here is called a pilliwinks.'

He waited for her to respond. When she didn't he held it even closer so she could see it at mite's-eye.

'You might know it by another name. Some prefer to call it by its more functional moniker, the thumbscrew.'

He watched her flinch and took this as an answer. He smiled and nodded.

'So, now you know what it is. Good. The beauty of this device is its simplicity. It's really just a tiny little vice. Your thumbs go in there.' He pointed to the space between the metal plates. 'Then, by turning this wing nut here, I can slowly crush your thumbs. Works a treat. I got this made specially for me by a smithy in Wetherby, back in forty-three. Cost me half a crown. Best half a crown I've ever spent. Never fails.'

'This is not good,' Hellström said. 'This is not how we work.'

Lemuel turned to Hellström and said, 'Please, Johan, I hired you to catch my wolf. This little business is between me and these two lasses. This other lass, here –' he pointed to me '– is Caragh O'Fealin. She burned down my house. Destroyed my property. Her kin killed my family over in Ireland. So, you see, I've got a bit of business with both of them. And if you don't mind, I'd like to settle that business in my own way. There's no need for any of yous to take up your time with this matter. Now, if you'd be so good, I'd like you and my two men here to do as we arranged last night, namely, ride over to Black Clough where the wolf is likely to be. The sooner we catch it, the sooner you get your money, and you can be back on that carrack to Norway or Denmark or Sweden, or wherever the bleedin' hell it is you're from.'

'No, Mr Lane. You listen to me. You follow my orders. I say dance and you do a jig. I know of these things. In Gothenburg we have witch. We have a woman who is giving blood to the devil and taking his seed inside her. And we cure the problem of the witch.'

'Mr Hellström, with all due respect, you have your ways, and I have my ways. I'm not saying the way you do things is wrong. We're not laikin' about here. But it's not how we do things, is all I'm saying.'

'No. This is not ways. This is not things. You must be careful. You can make trouble. I have seen this. Now, you do as I say.'

Lemuel Lane was visibly shaken. This bear of a man seemed to shrink three inches beneath Hellström's shadow. He went over to the table and put the pilliwinks down.

'Right. Tell me how you think we should proceed.'

'First of all, we must know they are witch.'

'But you told me that they are. You said you saw them round a cauldron, with that familiar close by.'

'Mr Lane, be quiet. Let me finish.' Lemuel held his hands out and shrugged. Hellström continued. 'The devil baptises the witch with blood from the mark he makes when he bites her flesh. We must look for this mark, teeth-shaped scars about her body. Once we have this we must then notify the magistrate. We must have papers. We must have permission. Once we have paper and permission we can proceed. We must make these witches lift the spell they have cast that protects your wolf, Mr Lane.'

'And how do we do that?'

'We keep them here. We guard them. And we wait.'

'What are we waiting for?'

'If we wait we will see.'

'What are you talking about?'

'If we wait, these witches will have visit. Their familiar beast will come to their aid.'

'And then what?'

'We capture these beasts. Then they have no power. We threaten to kill these beasts, and the witches will lift the spell. And we can catch the wolf.'

Lemuel shook his head. He went over to his box, he started to fiddle with it. Then he smacked the side. He began to pace the room. The other three men watched him apprehensively.

'Right. Right. Have it your way. Get them stripped. Find the mark.'

'Very well, Mr Lane. But we must do this by the book. How will this look when we go to the magistrate if we do not follow procedure?'

'I don't follow.'

'These women must be examined by a woman, and there must be a witness to this examination. Another woman.'

Lemuel nodded. 'I'll fetch Elizabeth and one of my girls.'

'The witness must not be family.'

Lemuel nodded again. 'Ezekiel, how about Kate?'

'Sir, as you know, sir, my wife is with child, my second bairn. She's due to give birth soon. With all due respect, sir, I don't think that it's a good idea to drag her across here in her condition.'

'Gad? How about your sister?'

'Sir, I'm afraid she will not comply. She will play no part in this. Please, sir, I know her well.'

'Then, Ezekiel, it's going to have to be Kate.'

'But, sir—'

'Look, I know it's not ideal. But these are strange times, and we all have to make adjustments. I've lost my son. My flesh and blood. Who's to say the wolf doesn't kill your daughter next? Then there's your unborn. Due in a day or two? You really want this wolf around when your wife is giving suck? Don't you know that a human baby is a wolf's favourite food? Think about that. We've got to stop this. It can't go on. It just can't. Am I the only one here with any sense?' He looked at the others and held up his hands in frustration.

Ezekiel shrugged.

'Look, Ezekiel, we've all got to make sacrifices. I wouldn't ask you if there was any other way.'

'But, sir, can't we get some wench from the village? Pay one of the strumpet maids that work in the bawdy house? They'll do anything for bunce.'

'Come on. You don't think I'd trust a job like this to a strumpet do you? Besides, the witness has to be credible in the eyes of the magistrate. He won't take a whore's word.'

Ezekiel shrugged. 'I'll see what I can do, sir.'

He seemed very reluctant to go, but he grabbed his gabardine and left the mistal, closing the huge door behind him.

'Right, here's what we do. I'll go and have a word with Elizabeth. I want you and Gad to watch over these two while we wait for Ezekiel to return with Kate.' He pointed to Hellström. 'Come and get me when they're here. I'll be in my study.'

And then he left, leaving us with this wolf hunter and his mate. They sat on bales of hay and we all waited. I looked over to Jenny, trying to reassure her that we were going to be all right, even though it was hopeless. There was no good outcome to this. They were going to strip us and search our bodies. We both had marks on us — who didn't? We had birthmarks and freckles and moles. I was fair-skinned as was Jenny, and it was common for fair-skinned people to carry marks on their skin. Would these be classed as evidence? Would these be seen as marks made by the devil that branded us witches? If so, we would be kept until our familiars came to our rescue. And if our familiars didn't come — and how could they, as we didn't have any? — they would deem us too cunning or they would falsify the evidence, I was sure of that. Then we would be hanged, for that was the punishment for witchcraft in these parts. And if they didn't find a mark that they deemed to be made from the devil, what then? Then we would be no threat to them, and they would go after the other girls, and hunt them, strip them, search them. Eventually we would all be hanged or killed in some other way.

Hellström turned to the other men. 'We must make the sign that will protect us.'

'What sign?'

Hellström reached under his shirt and lifted out the necklace again. He held up the pentacle attached.

'We must carve this sign at the door of the barn.'

Hellström took a knife from his pocket and carved a pentacle into the wooden doorway.

'Hearths, windows, doors. These are places we must protect.'

But it wasn't these men that needed protecting. We were the only ones in danger. Apart from anything else, I had burned down Lemuel Lane's property, as he saw it, and I couldn't see any way that he would let that go unpunished. There was no way to escape. We were bound and fixed to our chairs. We had two jailers watching over us. Our view was bleak in one direction and grim in the other. I tried the only thing that was left to us.

'Please, good sirs. Me and my friend, we are not witches. We are just runaways. We mean you no harm. We have no magic powers. We have no familiars. Please, can you not find it in your heart to free us? What you do goes against God. If you free us now, God will not punish you, but if you continue to support this campaign of persecution against us, you will go to hell for what you have done, don't you see that?'

Hellström shook his head sternly. 'You think you can threaten us? You have some nerve. I will give you this. Now, enough. I do not want to hear another word from either of you. Do you hear me?'

I nodded, and so did Jenny. I gave her a look. We were already dead.

A Black Cat Called Jill

Outside, Ezekiel fastened up his gabardine and mounted his horse. Kate was in no condition to be a witness to some witch inspection, but he knew better than to deny his master. He didn't understand why Lemuel had been so insistent. Surely any woman from the village would do? He supposed it was a question of trust. Lemuel knew Kate. He trusted Kate. As he rode along the bridle path back into the village, he started to question the whole operation. What was the point of going through the rigmarole of proving that this girl was a witch? They wanted to catch the wolf, that was all. And if this girl was a witch, and her companion, who was to say that the other women in the woods were not also witches, and had not also protected this wolf with their spells? They would have to capture them too. Hadn't they nearly caught this wolf the day before, using their ingenuity, despite a protective spell? They had been seconds away from killing it with their arrows. Inches from their prize. They just needed one more chance to get that close, and they would succeed. A witch's spell could not compete with their ingenuity as hunters, or at least Hellström's ingenuity. He was well aware of his own failings in that office.

He pulled up outside his cottage, dismounted and tethered his horse. Inside his wife was up to her elbows in a buck full of dirty washing. His daughter, Rose, had a miniature buck and was washing her doll's frocks and bonnets.

'Is everything all right?' Kate asked.

His daughter looked up too and said 'Dada'. She'd been walking now for six months and could already say mama and dada and a score of other words. But it still thrilled him when he heard her address him.

'I've come to fetch you.'

'What for?'

He explained everything that had happened. 'I'm sorry, I tried to reason with him. But he trusts you. He values your opinion.'

'I see.'

'I'm sorry.'

'It's fine.'

Ezekiel could tell from her tone that it was not fine.

'Let me finish this washing and I'll ride out with you.'

'There's no time. Get ready and I'll take Rose next door, see if they can look after her.'

He lifted up his daughter, dried her hands on a cloth, took her doll and handed it to her. Then he lifted her into his arms and walked round to the neighbours' house, making up an excuse. When he returned, his wife was now in her cloak and fastening her bonnet. They went out to the horse.

'I'll give you a hutch up. You ride on the horse, and I'll walk beside you.'

He crouched down and entwined his hands with his fingers, offering this as a mount. He helped Kate onto the back of the beast and took the reins, leading them through the village, along Lowe Lane, and towards the bridle path that led to the estate.

'You know the magistrate won't accept the mark on its own.'

'How do you mean?'

'There needs to be further evidence.'

'Hellström said we should watch them till their familiar comes.'

'They will probably accept this as some form of evidence. But if their familiar doesn't show, I don't see as how you can proceed.'

'Can't you swim them? I've heard of that being done.'

'Not round here. At least, I had word from the beadle that this magistrate doesn't set any store by swimming. Of course, there are other ways and means.'

'What like?'

'Some people believe that a witch has the power of taciturnity.'

'What's that?'

'It's the ability to withstand torture without confession. These people say that a witch sheds no tears. That's what some folk think.'

'So what then?'

'If the familiar doesn't appear, Lemuel will need to get confessions.'

'But you said that they can withstand torture.'

'Aye, there's the rub.'

They travelled some time in silence until Kate said, 'Have you ever wondered why witches are nearly always women, and usually poor ones at that?'

Ezekiel shrugged.

'The beadle was telling me about Mother Dutten. They said that she had a black cat called Jill and that she fed daily from a third teat she had between her breasts. And that she had a rat called Jethro she fed from blood issuing from her right-hand wrist. They say she gave her right side to the devil.'

'And did she confess?'

'She was hanged for it, yes. But the thing is, her accuser had ulterior motives.'

'What were those?'

'A long-standing disagreement between them. Started when she spurned his advances. Then there was a dispute about some land that he claimed was his by rights, but that she refuted.'

'And what's that got to do with her being a witch?'

'Then there was Widow Ludlow. Remember me telling you about her? Over in Lancashire. A man named Fortune said he saw her familiar. A rat that climbed up the chimney wall where it turned into a toad. Said this paddock held him in its gaze for two hours, during which time he couldn't move a muscle. Then he said it turned into a bat and flew out of the window.'

'So what happened?'

'They hanged her too. The thing is, Fortune's wife was jealous of the widow. Another long-standing enmity. Filled her husband's head with poison.'

Ezekiel thought about this. He nodded.

'What I'm saying is that it's very easy to tell tales. Muck sticks.'

Ezekiel nodded again. He steered the reins so that the horse avoided a pothole in the road.

The return journey took longer, due to Ezekiel being on foot. They were quiet for a while as they made their way across the potsherd and along the bridle path. Ezekiel thought about his wife's words. He wasn't sure whether he really believed all these tales of witches either. Kate was right. Seemed a lot of it was just vindictive people taking out their grievances on the weakest. That wasn't to say that the two women they held captive weren't witches. Witches were as real as cansticks. Maybe something was preventing the wolf's capture? Maybe it was protected somehow? All he really cared about was his fifty pound. If they could get this matter settled and catch this wolf, they could make a better life for themselves. Perhaps somewhere else.

After half an hour or so they arrived back at Lemuel's estate. Ezekiel helped Kate dismount, and the two of them went to the back door. Ezekiel knocked. Jacob answered, led them into the hallway, and went to inform his master that they had arrived. They waited in the hallway. A few minutes later, Lemuel appeared with Elizabeth.

'Thanks for agreeing to this Kate, I'm really most obliged, given your condition.'

'We all want to resolve this matter, don't we?'

'Well, yes. It shouldn't take too long. If you can just be witness to my wife's inspection, so that we can do everything by the book. You know what a stickler the magistrate is.'

'I do, sir.'

'Right. Let's get started. It's through this way.'

All the Creeping Things

I don't know how long we waited but it seemed like hours, with the hessian rope cutting into my wrists and ankles. I tried to wriggle free of the ropes, but they were tied with very tight knots, and the more I struggled against the binds, the more they cut into my flesh. Besides, what was the point of wriggling free of them? We would still be prisoners. Our predicament really was dire. The only comfort I could muster was that if we did hang for this, I would soon be reunited with my ma and da. And maybe that was no bad thing. Did I really want to live in this world of hunters and hunted, killers and killed? But then I thought of Jenny and the life we could live together. There was a place for us where we would not be persecuted. But how to get there? This Hellström and Gad were playing cards, but they kept looking over to make sure we were still fixed to the chairs. I pleaded with them once more.

'Please, good sirs. I know deep in your hearts you are gentle men.'

'I tell you once. You do not speak. Enough.'

'But we have money. If you let us go, I can get you some.'

'I do not take pleasure in beating women. But if you persist, I will strike you. Do you hear me?'

'I can get your wolf for you.'

Hellström smiled then nodded slowly as he got to his feet. He placed his deck on the table and walked over to where I was bound.

'She's right,' Jenny said. 'We can bring you the wolf.'

'Now you say something interesting. But tell me, girls, how will you do this?'

I was wracking my brains. In truth I had spoken foolishly, for I had no way of getting them what they wanted.

'We're not witches. Like Caragh says, we're just runaways. But the woman we live with, she is a witch and she has put a spell on this wolf. We can get you Alice, and if you have Alice, then you get your wolf.'

I looked over to Jenny. Why had she said this? Putting Alice in jeopardy and risking the lives of all the other girls too. But we didn't have anything else to bargain with, I supposed.

'You bring me Alice. I see.' He shook his head solemnly then burst out laughing. 'Why do I need you to bring me Alice? Do you not think I know where you live? Do you not think I know the whereabouts of this Alice? I have been to your camp. I have seen where you live. I have seen your leader in her fancy hut. We get you then we get your leader.'

'You'll never get her without our help.'

Hellström laughed again. 'This is good. You try for your life. I understand. Now, I will not say one more time. No more speaking. Or I will beat you.'

I looked at Jenny. She had tried but it was no use. What did we have that we could bargain with? We had nothing that these men wanted.

An hour passed, maybe more. Then I saw Lemuel lead Ezekiel and two women through to where we were being kept.

'Thou shalt not suffer a witch to live. Isn't that what the good book sayeth, my love?'

The woman closest to Lemuel nodded and I assumed that this was his wife.

'But the thing is, for me the book of Exodus doesn't go far enough.'

'How do you mean?'

'I'd like to extend the commandment: thou shalt not suffer a wolf to live and thou shalt not suffer a fucking papist to live. Witches, wolves, papists, they're all the same in my book. Pope stink is as rank as witch stink is as rank as wolf stink. Rack, strap and screw are too good for them.'

They walked across to where we were being held captive.

'This one here is called Caragh. You remember the O'Fealins, don't you, love?'

'I do.'

'And that one there, they call Jenny.'

'Very well, you can leave us to do our work.'

'And you're sure you know what to do?'

'Of course. Now go. Give us some privacy.'

She smiled at her husband and Lemuel nodded before turning to his men. 'Gentlemen, if you'd like to come with me.'

The other three men walked to where Lemuel was standing by the mistal entrance.

'We'll just be waiting outside, love. Give me a shout if you need me.'

He opened the door and the four men disappeared, leaving me and Jenny with Lemuel's wife and ginger-beard's wife.

'My name is Elizabeth, and this here is Kate. We're not going to hurt you as long as you do as you're told. In a minute we're going to untie you, then we'll ask you to undress, search your bodies thoroughly, and as long as you've no witch's mark, you've nothing to worry about. Is that understood?'

We both nodded.

'Good.'

Kate began working on the knots that bound me. Elizabeth was doing the same for Jenny. Would they say that the marks on our bodies were done by the devil? Kate had nimble fingers and quickly untied the ropes on my wrists and arms. As she did, I saw that Elizabeth was struggling with Jenny's knots, her fingers being less dexterous. As Kate undid the last knot, she bent down and whispered in my ear 'window'. I was confused. I wanted to ask her what she meant, but I understood that this was a message for my ears only. She looked over to the back of the barn. Kate saw that Elizabeth was struggling with Jenny's ropes and she went over to help her, but as she did, I saw something dripping from between Kate's legs, forming a pool on the floor.

'Oh, no. It's my waters. They've gone and broke.'

Elizabeth stopped what she was doing. I was now untied and I rubbed at my wrists to soothe them. Elizabeth looked at Kate and at the pool of water between her legs.

'Fetch the grace-wife,' Kate said to Elizabeth. 'Hurry, I can feel my baby coming.'

'We need to get you to a bed.'

Kate held on to Elizabeth and both women left the room. As Kate passed me, she nodded to the back wall. When they had gone I looked at the back window of the mistal. It was about six foot in height and four foot wide. I thought about the word that Kate whispered in my ear. The window was boarded with thin slats, so I had no idea what was through the other side. Could I do it? Could I jump? Would I break the slats if I ran hard enough? I knew it was the only chance I had. Could I trust this Kate? Perhaps it was a trap. There could be a huge drop. I could break my legs or my back. Why would Kate help me? She didn't know me and was on the other side. I had no choice. If I stayed I would die. If I jumped I might die. I might live. If I jumped and died I would die quickly. If I stayed, I would be tortured and then I would die. Ice ran in my veins as I realised what I had to do. Cold sweat. There were probably a few seconds, that was all.

I looked at Jenny, still bound, and I ran across to her but as I did Gad entered the room, saw what I was doing and shouted for the other men. He was running towards me as Jenny shouted, 'GO!'

Don't. Think. Jump.

I ran as fast as I could, straight at the slats, using my legs to kick them as I jumped up towards it. My feet slammed the flimsy wood. Splinters. Flying through the air. Then I was falling. A shower of splintered slats. Daylight. Falling. Sky. Land. The outside blurred. Falling. Heart pounding.

I collapsed in a heap on the grass outside, toppling, rolling, splinters strewn all around me. I was winded. Wounded. A shooting pain up my spine. I got to my feet. Without looking back, I ran across the field, not daring to turn until I'd cleared the field and made it to the hedgerow. That's when I saw the lanky one running towards me, his arms pumping, hands balled into fists. I began running again. Faster. Blind panic. My lungs on fire. Heart burning. I ran a mile, maybe two, before turning around again. I couldn't see anyone following me. I stopped briefly to get my breath back, and tried to think what was the best thing to do?

I had left Jenny at their mercy, had tried to untie her, but there hadn't been time. Maybe she had managed to free herself. Should I wait here for her? But what if Jenny hadn't got free? How could she have? I had to go back for her. But it was too late now. All that would achieve would be my own recapture. The only thing I could do was to find my way back to camp and talk to the others. I would ask them to come back with me tonight. Together we would find Jenny and free her.

I was still afraid that I was being followed even though there was no sign of anyone, so I took to running again, across fields, across meadows, alongside hedgerows, through a copse of trees, over a beck,

275

looking over my shoulder frequently, until I came to the river. I walked with the river to my left. I was travelling north, and I figured that this must be the main river that flowed close by Black Clough Woods. I came to a moor which I recognised from when I'd run away all those weeks before, and as I did I heard horses' hooves clatter on the stony path. I looked behind me. Three men on horseback. Quickly, I darted through a gap in the rocks and curled up as small as I could. The men whoa'd their horses. I could see the leg of a horse through a space in the stones.

'Thought I saw something move.'

'We can get off and have a look if you like.'

The men dismounted. I could hear them walking about. I saw a flash of a man's coat, then another. They were looking around the rocks where I was concealed. I tensed every muscle to keep myself still and held my breath. I hoped they couldn't hear my heart knocking against my chest. I felt a vein in my neck throb.

'Nah. Nothing. Come on. Let's carry on this way.'

I heard the men get back onto their horses. They rode off. I waited until I could be sure they were far enough away, then I took a deep breath and crawled from my hole. I looked around. They had gone north. I could just make them out on the horizon. I had seen them disappear over the edge, headed east.

This was Broadhead Moor and I knew that the safety of the woods was close by. I couldn't run any further and I walked as fast as I could muster over the uneven ground, past peat bog and tussock grass, until I got to the edges of the forest. I found the beck that led to the fens and followed its winding path through the cover of the trees. I looked around to make sure the men hadn't followed me.

As I walked all I could think about was Lemuel Lane, his voice in my head. His hideous face. Every step I took, Lemuel Lane, Lemuel

Lane, Lemuel Lane. He'd killed my kinfolk. Now he had Jenny and I had to get her back. Rescuing her was all I could think about.

I tried to remember the way through that was the least hazardous. I crept very carefully, watching every step. Placing it down first to test, before putting my weight on it. At the steepest part my foot slipped on a loose stone. The stone rolled and ricocheted down to the beck. I fell and grabbed a tree branch, clambering back up. I used roots and branches to steady myself as I traversed the worst part of the ravine. Eventually I got to the fens. In another half hour I had made my way through to the other side and arrived at the camp.

Alice and the rest of the girls were gathered around the fire.

'What happened?'

'Where's Jenny?'

'You're bleeding!'

The girls rushed around me. I had cuts and scratches all over from the splinters: on my arms and on my face and neck. I told them about everything that had happened.

'They'll keep her there until she confesses.'

'We've got to go back for her,' I said.

'You shouldn't have left her,' Alice said.

I couldn't look Alice in the eye. I told them about the mistal. And as much about the layout of the estate as I could recall.

'She won't be in the mistal now. If the window is broken, it's not secure. They will move her somewhere else.'

'They could have boarded it up again.'

'More likely to move her to another building.'

'So what do we do?'

'I'm going to work on a spell to bring the wolf to us, here in these woods, to be near us where we can protect her. And where we can use her power to protect us.'

I thought that this was the last thing we should do, if the wolf had a chance it needed to get further away from the men – they would come here and would hunt us all down. I wanted to go back for Jenny and together we could go to the place Da had instructed.

Alice had the others collect and prepare the ingredients for her potion. I wanted to say otherwise, that we needed to all get away from here as the men would come, if they were not already on their way. I saw Holly watching me. When the others were distracted, she approached.

'Did Jenny speak to you?' Holly whispered.

I nodded.

'The two of us, we'll find Jenny.'

I nodded. 'First dawn. We'll go first dawn.'

'We've got to try. She'd do the same for us,' Holly said.

That night Alice prepared a special concoction of henbane, fenny mandrake and liberty cap. She said that the potion would protect us and also protect the wolf. We would call on the power of the forest spirits. I said at first that I didn't want any, but Alice was insistent.

'We all have to take it, you silly girl, or it won't work. Don't you know that?'

I saw that Holly was also reluctant, but we were outnumbered. The others watched as Alice gave out the cups and made sure we drank every drop.

I felt the effects of the potion gradually, feeling light-headed to begin with, then the acuity of my senses sharpen. I could hear more precisely and see more vividly and I felt a sense of dread. As I started to feel the full effects of the witch potion, the first thing I noticed were the trees. Their form became more vivid, more real and alive somehow. The bark rippled. The branches wriggled. They had no fixed shape.

They had no rigidity. They were like clouds. The flames of the fire glowed gold, indigo and green, growing in height, seeming to envelop everything around them. There was a low-level humming. I wasn't sure if it was coming from the trees or from the earth.

Something moved behind a tree. I looked and saw a figure dancing about thirty yards away. I looked again. I couldn't make out what sort of creature it was. About three foot in height. Was it a boy? But he wasn't human. He kept changing shape. Becoming something different. The creature came closer and I could see he had a brown suit on. As he came closer still I realised that he was naked, but covered in brown hair. Then he wasn't. It was green scales. He danced around another tree, moving his arms about, then he stopped and stared at me. He grinned and his chin reached the floor. His tongue crawled from his mouth like a snake. I felt vague and unsteady. Like I was coming down with fever.

I looked around and saw there were more of his kind, either dancing around the trees, or standing and watching us. Some sat cross-legged. As they did they changed shape. I noticed other creatures, some much smaller than the boy, only six inches in height, and some much taller than humans. They grinned and gurned. Their arms and legs shrinking and growing. Black eyes spinning. Green things creeping from trees. Hobbled and hunched. Mouths stretched open. Claw-like fingers undulating. I looked at my own hands. They were glistening like fish, the flesh creeping and bubbling. Nothing was fixed.

I suddenly became aware that Alice was talking. Had she been talking before? Perhaps she had been talking for a long time. She too was changing. Shape, colour, height, form. Her hair like writhing worms. Her eyes were black wells. Everything that lived was listening attentively. But what she said didn't make any sense.

'Weca ly ou heprts o tse wds toproct inu hrfd anto roct olf mubing twol fohese oosher e shew ilbsf gid erto uuus.'

The moss mounds and lichen groves that dotted the forest floor were luminous green in the bright silver light of the full moon. The pools of water gathered in their crevices were shining like diamonds and undulating. The strands of ivy that covered every trunk and branch were like lanthorns, radiating an inner light. Clusters of pearl-white mistletoe berries, that clung to the branches of poplar, lime, oak and apple trees, glowed like a harvest moon.

I stood rooted to the spot, everything moving and changing. Alice grew still taller. Her eyes somehow even darker, cavorting, grinning, grimacing, smiling, leering. Long spindly fingers, wrapped around trees trunks and branches, writhed and stretched. Sinewy bodies vibrating, and a chorus of humming emanating from every creature that moved.

Alice had changed. She was no longer Alice. She seemed to be made of the forest, of the moss and lichen, holly, ivy and mistletoe. Her eyes were the verdant pools that surrounded us.

'Wkll ny udeep grer rrgrgrsg reesrgs plngerlkg dflsgmr reg eod snp r frrlgr ofor sr fgmfglmdfgl ersaopwea.'

She was talking but her lips were not moving. The sound of her voice was coming out of the trunks of the trees, out of the waters, and out of the earth. As she spoke, her familiar flew down and perched on her shoulder. It opened its massive bill and croaked. Its bill was as big as a scythe. And Alice was croaking, as were the other women and all the creeping things. The whole forest was croaking. I closed my eyes and also began to croak.

A Witch's Curse

Lemuel was watching Gad and Ezekiel board up the broken window. How did these witches know? He had heard that some could look into a man's eyes and see his soul. Others could peer into the hole of a hag stone and see into the future. He had sent three of his men to capture Caragh. They were on horseback and would easily catch up with her and bring her back here, then he would find a better place to contain the two cunning girls. She was a lot pluckier than he'd given her credit for, this O'Fealin lass. Would he have had the balls to jump? He doubted it. Despite everything, he had a sneaking admiration. Perhaps she had changed into a bat or a bird and simply flown away. He had heard that some witches could do that.

He went back inside and to the bedchamber where his wife and Gad's sister, the village grace-wife, were attending to Kate's labour. He knew better than to interrupt, so he stood outside the door and waited. An hour went by before he heard the first sounds of new life. The baby was crying. Got a pair of lungs on it, he thought. We come into the world with our eyes closed, bawling and skriking. Some of us leave this world in the same manner. He'd seen men on the battlefield, blinded by gunpowder, screaming for God's mercy. It was no way to make your exit.

Then there were the runaways. Men with soft hearts and no guts. There were so many on both sides. Breathless and speechless, and so full of fear that Lemuel had not taken them for men.

After that final battle Lemuel had coasted the country meeting with a shoal of Scots crying out 'weys us, we are all undone'. Men so full of mourning and lamentation, as if their day of doom had overtaken them. He had met with a ragged troop reduced to four and a cornet, with a foot officer without hat, band, sword, or indeed anything but feet and enough tongue to enquire the way to the next garrison.

But then had come his horse and foot and they had cleared the field of all enemies, recovered their ordinance and carriages, taken all their enemies' ordnance and ammunition, and followed that chase of them within a mile of York, cutting them down so that their dead bodies lay three miles in length. He, Lemuel Lane, had done that, and felt no pity for those on either side whose hap it was to be beaten down upon the ground. He had gored the troopers' horses and piked those who could not rise from their wounds. On those fields he had seen the best and worst of men. He would not leave this world screaming. He would die fighting.

The door opened. It was Elizabeth.

'Go tell Ezekiel she's had a boy.'

He went back inside the mistal where Jenny was still tied to a chair, where Ezekiel, Gad and Hellström were playing cards. Lemuel looked at Ezekiel and nodded, and together they went back to the chamber. Lemuel spoke to his wife. 'Will you be able to carry out the inspection still?'

'Yes, move her to the largest cellar. I'll do the examination there.'

'But what about a witness?'

'To hell with that.'

Lemuel and Hellström carried Jenny, still tied to the chair, down the steps that led to the main cellar. It was cold and dark below and Lemuel lit two lanthorns. Further on was another cellar where Lemuel kept his beer, wine and spirits, further still a room of powder kegs, but this room was sufficient for their purposes. Why had he allowed himself to be persuaded to play this by the book, when he could just put money in the magistrate's purse as usual? He supposed the money he would save would help in his campaign against the wolf, which was becoming costlier by the day. If he wasn't careful, he'd run out of funds before they'd captured the fiend.

'We'll be waiting outside,' he said to Elizabeth.

When the men had gone, Elizabeth unfastened the bindings that tied Jenny to the chair, then the ropes that bound her arms and legs.

'Don't worry, like I said before, I won't hurt you. Now, can you take off your clothes?'

Jenny did as she was told. She was shaking as she removed her shawl, frock, underskirts, and other garments, until she stood before Elizabeth as naked as a newborn. Elizabeth held up the brightest lanthorn as she searched her body. She started at her toes, moving round her feet, lifting them up one at a time and examining the soles. She worked up the calves, knees, thighs, hucklebones, belly and chest.

'Lift up your arms.'

Jenny complied. Elizabeth examined her fingers, one by one, her hands, turning them over so she could see both back and palms, the wrists, forearms, elbows, and so on. There were no marks.

'Turn around.'

Jenny did as she was told. Elizabeth held the lanthorn close, so that she could examine her. As she did, she saw, just below her left shoulder bone, a distinctive blemish.

She examined it, prodding it with her finger. Elizabeth couldn't be sure but it did look like a teeth-shaped scar. Was this where the devil had bit into her flesh and baptised her with her own blood? Her own flesh turned cold as she contemplated the idea that she was now in the presence of a revolting witch. She grimaced in disgust. She took the steps two at a time as she called for the men. They came down into the cellar and Elizabeth showed them the mark.

'Looks like it to me,' Lemuel said, backing off and screwing up his face in revulsion.

'I agree. This is the mark,' Hellström said. He clutched at the pentacle beneath his shirt.

'Well, there you go then. That's all the proof we need,' Lemuel said, shaking his head. He spat on the floor, as though losing a bad taste in his mouth.

'As you say, Mr Lane, this magistrate is a "stickler". We must now tread careful. We have found the mark, but we also need confession. Or evidence of the familiar beast.'

'Very well. We'll keep her here under constant watch.'

'Yes. This you must do. Until we meet her familiar or until she is confessing to being a witch. Have Gad and Ezekiel watch her day and night.'

Lemuel fetched Gad and Ezekiel and explained that they were not to let her out of their sight at any point. The men allowed her to dress and tied her to a chair again. Lemuel left them to it and went outside to where Hellström was smoking his pipe.

'Tell me exactly what you saw, Mr Hellström.'

'As I have said. I know of witches. In Gothenburg we have problem. The familiar is only one type of evidence. There is something I thought. How can this wolf evade capture? There are thirty or forty men hunting her. Maybe fifty. Who can know? There are poison trails, iron traps, wolf pits. And then I see this bird. This raven. It is a fine familiar. A witch with a raven is a powerful sorceress. It is the raven that works for Odin. He has two birds. Both Huginn and Muninn bring him information. They work with Odin's wolves, Geri and Freki. The birds perch on Odin's shoulders. The wolves lie at his feet. They are always together. It is Odin that gives the raven the gift of speech. I see this bird with your wolf. And I follow where it flies. I look at the map and I see this Black Clough. I ride over Broadhead Moor.'

'A man died in those woods, three year since. Fell into a swamp. He wasn't the first. Folk round here avoid that bloody place like the plague.'

He didn't tell him that it was the wood's reputation that had allowed Lemuel to purchase it for a song. He intended to drain those fens and fell the timber. After months of haggling over the contract, the ink from his signature was still wet. He did not want to let this man into his business affairs.

'Yes, and this is why this is good place for both wolf and witch. Do you see? I go through these woods. It is very dark. My journey is hard. I come to the place you call the fens. The journey is now harder. Is like a maze is it not?'

'I've never been. But that's what I'm told,' he lied.

'Well, I get to the other side and I find this camp where the witches live. And there is the bird also. There is a woman with black hair and dark skin and she is talking to this bird. This is the leader of the coven. I cannot hear what she says. But I see the others. Six witches are standing round a big fire. One is Caragh and the other is Jenny.'

'We need to capture all of them.'

'Yes, we do. But do you not see? They will come here. They will try and rescue their friend.'

'They won't all come. Maybe one or two. I want you to take us to this coven in the woods.'

Hellström took a drag of his pipe. 'Remember that we are here to catch the wolf. This is what we do. And if this means that we catch the witch then we catch the witch.'

Another Night in Bedlam

That night I dreamt that there was nothing left to eat. All there was for miles around was a child. A baby. My hunger was so strong. I bent down and picked up the baby by its foot and bit into its supple thigh.

Then Holly was shaking me. It was the time before dawn, of first light.

'Come on,' she whispered. 'We've got to go.'

I was already dressed, save for my boots and shawl. I felt heavy and strange from the night before, like some of the potion was still in me. Holly was already shawled, shoed and bonneted. We crawled out of the hut, making sure not to cause a sound. We crept through the camp, past the firepit and Alice's hut, and set off back through Black Clough. We got to the edge of the glade and to the first covering of yew and spruce. What had happened last night? I wanted to ask Holly, but we were too close to camp for conversation. I would talk to her about it later.

'Where do you two think you're going?'

I jumped out of my skin. It was Alice. She was standing under an ancient yew, with a pistol in her hand, pointed at us.

'Nowhere,' I said.

Holly nodded. 'We couldn't sleep,' she said. 'We were just going for a stroll.'

'I know where you were going. And I won't have it. We stay together. No one leaves. Do you not understand that? Haven't I taught you anything? How can you be so ungrateful?' She shook her head. 'Come on, you're going back where you came.' She pointed the pistol again and we turned back.

She made us sit by the fire and she woke the others. We gathered round the pit and poked the embers until the flames grew. Heather was still half-asleep, yawning and rubbing her eyes.

'The men are going to come here and we need to be ready. We are going to take all the iron traps we've amassed over the last five weeks or so and surround the camp with them. As many full circles as we have traps to complete.'

We each started to work on the first circle, moving clockwise around the camp, digging shallow pits and setting traps close to each other along paths, deer, boar and rabbit runs, and other points of access, concealing them with twigs and fallen leaves. The ground was frost-hardened and the trees hoarfrosted. Digging even a few inches was hard work. As I panted my breath turned to steam. When the first circle was complete, we started another one about six yards further on. When we had finished we looked at what was left. There were nearly enough traps for a further circle and we started work on that. If all of Lemuel's men were to attack, we had a good chance of disabling most if not all of them. I waited for a chance to talk to Holly without anyone else hearing.

'We can try again tonight. When everyone has gone to bed,' I said.

Holly nodded.

As we finished setting the last traps, I wondered about the wolf. How would she be protected from the traps? Could Alice communicate with her? Perhaps through her familiar?

There was nothing for us to do except wait. So we huddled round the fire, trying to stay warm. The leaves of the ivy were sugared with frost.

'What if men get through rings? Me scared,' Heather said.

Alice went into her hut and brought out the matchlock pistol she'd pointed at us.

'But I thought that we rejected the world of violence?' Ivy said.

'Can me have gun?' Heather said. 'Me want gun.'

'I have always preached non-violence, but this violence is not violence, if it is self-defence.' She issued us all with knives.

'Should any man make it through our defences, then we will have no choice. We will kill them in order to defend ourselves. Are you all ready to kill?'

I nodded. I knew that Holly and I would be gone before the men were here. I didn't want to stay another night in this bedlam. We would rescue Jenny, then we would find the place that Da said, a world free of dogma and tyranny. I looked around at the others. I felt bad about leaving them to their fate, but I knew that it was too dangerous to talk to them about our plans. Perhaps one of them wanted to be free of Alice too. Maybe they all did. There was no way to tell and I could not wait to find out.

The Potions and Hexes of Witches

Ezekiel was thinking about Kate and their new child. Their boy had a thick crop of black hair and a red face. Like Rose when she was born. He'd held him in his arms and looked into his pale blue eyes. He didn't want to be here with Gad, watching over this witch, he wanted to be with his wife and his little daughter – wanted to be with his newborn. They had spent most of the day watching over this girl, waiting for her familiar, but they had seen nothing. Not even as much as an itch mite. He got to thinking about what Kate had said, about wrong accusations. He thought about the girl who had been hanged as a witch, when all she had done was tell a farmer she hoped he dropped dead when he refused her alms. He knew that the farmer was old and frail. He'd been ill for some time. On death's door by any account. Reaper-bound. What was to say that the old man wouldn't have died anyway? It was too easy to blast someone's reputation. Mud stuck, as Kate said. And there was a difference between a gripe and confirmation of guilt. He questioned once again whether in fact he should be partaking in this dubious process.

If this girl was a witch then there should follow due legal suit. Why hadn't the magistrate been informed already? Surely they must seek his permission? And not carry on handy-bandy? Ever since the war it seemed the whole country had descended into anarchy. Sanity had lost its hold. At least when the King was on the throne there was some semblance of order. Things were done by the book even if the book was corrupt. Charles had introduced ship money on every county in England, without the permission of Parliament. The sheriff of this Riding had refused the request. And good on him. But other places had not been so lucky. It was a sign even then that the King was determined to dispense altogether with parliamentary government. The seeds of discord were sown in the field the King furrowed.

He thought also about what Lemuel had told him, of his family over in Ireland, and what they'd had to endure. It was dire. It was vile. What had happened to his sister and her husband. With her eight months pregnant. He thought about Kate suckling his young 'un, his son. How would he feel if Kate had been the victim of that kind of retribution? He would be sickened, naturally, and want the perpetrators to pay the price. With interest. But weren't the Catholics in Ireland retaliating to the wrongs that had been visited on them by the Protestants? He understood the depths of his master's feelings, but it wasn't Ezekiel's battle. Hadn't the curate said in church that only he who was without sin should go casting stones? He had done things just as bad, maybe even worse. He knew that the Bible taught an eye for an eye and a tooth for a tooth, but Kate always said that violence begat violence. There was no end to it. The fire would forever burn if the way to put out the fire was to make more flame. And didn't it also say in the Bible to bless those who curse you? How was a God-fearing man to know which way to turn?

It was Kate who had made him doubt. Kate was well-schooled in scripture. Her father had been a lay preacher and she could read and write. In truth, Ezekiel only knew the bits of the Bible that he'd heard the curate quote on Sunday. And for every statement that he could give Kate was always able to countenance it. As soon as all this business with wolves and witches was over he'd look for another job. Whatever debt Lemuel thought he had to pay him he had now paid it. What did he want to tie himself up in this world of rancour and reprisal for? It wasn't his world and he had no place in it. All he cared about now was Kate and his two bairns. They had called their son Matthew, after Kate's favourite gospel. Once they had got settled in their new home Ezekiel would ask Kate to teach him letters and words. He wanted to read the good book for himself. He was sick of being at the mercy of another's instruction. He wished to read God's words, not have someone interpret them.

His thoughts were disturbed by Lemuel who had climbed down the stairs to see what was going on. He saw Gad sitting on a barrel fast asleep, his head propped up with a sack of flour. Lemuel kicked him in the shin. Gad gave a start.

'Wake up!'

Gad muttered something. He opened his eyes, looking surprised at first, then embarrassed as he realised that his boss had caught him having a nap.

'Well, any sign?'

'Nothing, sir. Not even a cockroach.'

'I need you otherwise. Both of you. We're going to attack the camp tonight.'

Outside the men saddled up. Lemuel ordered them to check their muskets and pistols. After mounting their horses, they made their way across the estate and towards Mickle Beck. There were seven of them: Lemuel and Hellström, Gad and Ezekiel, and the only three other men he had come to trust – the twins and Gibbs. The moon was full and high, although partly obscured by clouds. They called the full moon at this time of year a Cold Moon. Some called it the Wolf Moon, though others insisted that was the full moon in January. Who cared what it was called? It was a good night to attack. The cunning lasses would be asleep, and they would be able to find their way through the fens with Hellström's help. But didn't witches hold their mass at midnight? Or so he had been told. Hellström had explained that this was only at the witches' sabbat.

They made their way along Black Clough Beck and tethered their horses near the foot of the woods. The path followed the beck, which now flowed about forty feet beneath them. To their right was a virtually vertical descent of scree and fallen trees. The path was thin and anyone who slipped would be a goner, smashing their bones to smithereens on the rocks that jutted out from the water. Further on, the path crossed the beck where it was shallow, and they had to cross using the stepping stones that had been placed there before men were too cowed to venture through. The ground was frozen in places, iced puddles like black glass.

Eventually they reached the fens. Hellström took the lead, carefully navigating the dark pools of water. There was just a thin crust of ice, not enough to support boot. The men followed in single file, each watching exactly where the other had gone. It was slow work in the darkness of the woods and Lemuel had to strain his eyes to see each footfall. He kept the gap between him and Hellström only what was sufficient. He'd heard the stories of the men who had ventured in and never returned and he did not want to be one of them. The bank was claggy and as the crusts of ice broke, mud covered his boots. The earth lacked firmness.

As they ventured slowly through, Lemuel heard someone gasp behind him. He heard ice crack, and turning, saw Neb slipping. He tried to grab hold of him but it was too late. The man had fallen into the swamp to the left of the path and was waist-deep in mud, shards of ice surrounding him.

'Hang on,' said Lemuel, as he looked for a branch to wedge across.

But the man was sinking further. Holding on to a tree with one hand and reaching across to Neb with his other, Lemuel tried to get a grip.

'Come on, you can do it.'

Neb stretched as far as he could and just managed to clasp hands. Hellström, seeing what had happened, grabbed Lemuel by the waist. Lemuel pulled with all his strength, but the man's hand was slippery, covered in mud, and he lost Neb's grip. He lurched deeper into the swamp. Neb was now up to his chest in mud.

'Grab hold of that.' Lemuel pointed to a fallen branch close to where Hellström stood. The two of them managed to carry it to the swamp where Neb was now up to his neck. They threw the branch across so that Neb could take hold of it and use it to pull himself out. He grabbed it with both hands and clung on.

His brother, Meth, was trying to get closer. 'Let me past,' he said to Gibbs.

Seeing how precariously Meth was placed, Lemuel shouted to him, 'Stay where you are. You'll make it worse if you come any closer.'

Meth watched on, helpless. Neb tried to lift himself up. But as he pulled, the swamp pulled back harder, taking hold of him, and sucking him under. He gripped the log tighter. He was now up to his chin. Lemuel looked around to see if there was anything he could do to help. But what could he do? He leaned across the branch and tried to grab the man's wrist. But Neb lost his grip and the swamp swallowed the rest of him. The last they saw of him was his right arm held up, as though he were waving or asking permission. Then there was nothing. A bubble of mud rose up where Neb had stood. Then it popped and was gone. The man had been eaten by the swamp.

'No! No! No! No!' Meth was on his knees, crying for his brother. Lemuel had a grim thought: he would not mistake the men now. Then he thought about Neb's wife and child waiting for him at home. He would have to break the news in person as soon as they had finished this business.

Hellström was shaking his head. 'You men, you think you know best. You do not listen. And now look! This is a serious business.'

Lemuel held up his hand. 'Just give him a minute,' he said, nodding over to Meth, who was staring at the spot where his brother had been, as though waiting for him to reappear. They all stood and waited for Meth respectfully. At last Meth looked up, his face a mask of grief.

'Do you want to stay here?' Lemuel asked.

The man shook his head.

'You must stay close and you must watch where I stand,' Hellström repeated. 'Do as me.'

Neb was gone. There was nothing they could do. Lemuel wanted to say some words to comfort his brother but no words formed. Perhaps they should turn back? But they had gone so far now that to return was no safer than to continue. He had no time to grieve the man. There would be time tomorrow for their grief. They must carry on through the woods. He'd known Neb for several years, a brave man, a good loyal man. When he and Elizabeth took the estate from the Royalist scum who had previously lived there, Lord Whatisface and Lady Gobshite, they had called on Neb and his brother's services. Casual labour at first, helping Lemuel and his family bring in the harvest, but he'd kept him on, as he had Meth and Gibbs. Neb was still a young man. Over the years, he had got to know his family. His mother had become friendly with Elizabeth. Now he would have to go to his family home and tell the man's parents, as well as his wife, that their son was dead. And he knew how that felt. The wound of it was still raw and fresh.

They were walking very slowly. For each footfall, the ground first crunched then yielded. Lemuel was careful to place his foot in the exact place he saw Hellström place his. And Ezekiel, who was directly behind Lemuel, did the same as did Meth, who was behind Ezekiel, and Gad who was behind Meth. They used the trees as banisters to help steady their progress. These witches had found an almost impenetrable place to make their home and despite his detestation for everything they stood for, he couldn't help but admire their canny good sense in finding the location. Lemuel thought again about witches, wolves and Catholics all being cut from the same cloth. They were enemies of God. Minions of Beelzebub. The vilest witches and sorcerers of the Earth were the priests that consecrated crosses and ashes, boughs and bones, stocks and stones. Confirmation was plain sorcery. The bishop mumbled a few Latin words over the child, charmed him, crossed him, smeared him with stinking Pope oil, then tied bonds round his neck and sent him home. Wasn't the act of transubstantiation an act of witchcraft? And wasn't the Agnus Dei worn by so many Catholics, a sorcerer's trinket? They had killed the King. That dribbling, bulbous-eyed, bandy-legged closet sodomite was also a closet Catholic. For wasn't his wife, Henrietta-Maria, a practising papist? The war had split father and son, brother and brother. He had tended to a Roundhead soldier at Hillsdean, who confirmed, as he lay dying from his wounds, that it was his own Royalist brother who had fired the fatal shot. That was the battle of Marston Moor, a turning point for their campaign and the rise of Cromwell. The war had been a purge. And this camp was a remnant of that purge.

Truly England and the Church of God had a great favour from the Lord in the victory he had given them that day. Their absolute victory was evidence of the Lord's blessing upon his Godly party. Lemuel had commanded the left wing, saving a few Scots for the rear. And they had beaten all the Prince's horses. God made them as stubble to their swords. The Prince had marched twenty thousand and had not four thousand left. His man had tried to save the life of his commer, who was cannon-shot. The shot had broken his leg, and his man had held the man down while Lemuel sawed through the bone. But the man had died shortly after, despite their efforts to save him. That man reminded him of Neb. Good true men. And now, in turn, Neb was dead. A fine man. Loins of iron. Guts of granite. Lemuel hoped God would now give him comfort.

He looked around at the phalanx of trees that surrounded them. Good thick trunks. Soft wood and hard wood. The work of felling would not be easy. He would have to empty most of the village of men, but the money the timber would bring would clear their debts, pay Hellström's bill and give them succour. As soon as this business was completed, he would commission the labour.

They were now clear of the worst of the fens and Hellström's pace quickened. Lemuel was still walking directly behind him. But as they wended through bramble, bracken, root and puddle, somehow they lost the party at the back. Lemuel turned to look. Behind him was Ezekiel, but there was no one behind Ezekiel. He motioned for Hellström to stop.

'Where are the others?'

'They were behind us a minute ago.'

'We wait for them.'

The three men waited in the dark for the stragglers. The night air was thinning, crisping, getting colder. When a few minutes had passed and there was still no sign of them, Lemuel said, 'Perhaps we should double back. Go and look for them.'

'We wait. They will catch up.'

But when a few minutes more had passed and still no sign Lemuel said that he would go and find them himself. He held up one of the lanthorns and taking Ezekiel with him, they turned around and went back the way they had come.

They heard a scream. Lemuel turned to Ezekiel and the two of them ran. A few hundred yards back they found Meth leaning over another man, who was lying on the ground. As they got closer, Lemuel could see that the man on the ground was Gad. He and Ezekiel quickened their step.

'What's happened?'

'We got split up somehow. We took a wrong turn. He fell into a trap.'

The first man pointed to a hole in the ground, which had been disturbed.

'I managed to pull him out of it. But he's bleeding really bad.'

Lemuel and Ezekiel examined the wounds. Gad had been impaled half a dozen times. One of the spikes had pierced his chest, and from this hole he was bleeding profusely. Ezekiel tried to plug the hole with his kerchief. The cloth was soon soaked with the man's blood.

'We're going to have to take him back. He's in a bad way,' Ezekiel said as he bent down low so he could get closer to Gad's ear. He didn't want to raise his voice.

'Did you hear that? We're going to take you back. Me and Meth here. We'll get you physic.'

There was no answer.

'Gad? Did you hear me? You're bleeding like a stuck pig.'

He bent low again and received a low groan as answer. He took hold of his cousin and gripped him under his arms, clasping his hands over the man's chest. As he did, Ezekiel could feel the hot sticky substance of his cousin's heart spill over his hands and run down his sleeve. The liquid oiled his grip and he could feel his fingers slipping.

'Hang on.'

Ezekiel and Meth stopped. The two men placed him back down again.

'We need to staunch the wounds. He's pissing blood.'

The men searched around for something to sop the wounds.

'Hold in there, cuz.'

This time when he didn't receive an answer he shook his cousin gently. When still no answer, he bent down and felt for his pulse. First Gad's wrist, then his neck. Then he noticed the silence. The cracked tap of his heart had stopped.

'He's dead.'

'What?'

Lemuel bent down and felt for Gad's pulse as well. 'No!' He shook his head. Another man! Another dead. Surely the witches had cursed these woods. He looked at Ezekiel, at the shock on his face. He gave him some time to compose a semblance of dignity before asking, 'What do you want to do?'

The men stood in silence. Somewhere a corncrake cried, like a human fingernail drawn down the teeth of a comb. Lemuel gave Ezekiel more time to collect his thoughts and quash his grief.

'I'm so sorry,' he said, and placed his hand on Ezekiel's shoulder.

'He should have kept up. Stupid fucker.'

'Listen, we'll get him a decent burial. You can stay here with him if you want? We'll come back for you, once we've cuffed these witches.'

Ezekiel stared at Gad, unable to believe his friend and cousin had gone. He shook his head.

'Look, we'll manage without you. Stay here. It shouldn't take us long.'

'No point. He's dead.'

Ezekiel stood up. He looked down on the corpse. The moon shifted from behind a cloud and briefly, the scene was illuminated. The trees looked like hobgoblins, and unnaturally hued, as though a malign force emanated from them. Ezekiel shivered. Hadn't Gad said not to venture this far in? Hadn't he also said the woods were witch-hexed? He had not listened to him.

Lemuel patted him on the back. 'Come on then, we'll come and fetch him on the return.'

The two men walked on to where the party was waiting for them and explained what had happened. Hellström stamped his foot in fury.

'This is why I say stay together. It is easy to get lost in this wood. It is easy to die in this wood. We lose two men. Two men! When we start we are seven, now we are five. Now the witch outnumber us. From now on, we stay close by and you do as I say,' Hellström said.

He led the way again, first through dense forest, then through sparser woodland that opened out again to a series of large, irregular pools that shone silver in the moonlight.

'We must be careful here. Follow where I go. Where I put my foot, this is where you put your foot.'

Lemuel walked even more cautiously than before while they navigated the narrow isthmus of land between the waters. It was slow-going. Eventually the waters became less frequent and the path opened out again, so they could walk two or three abreast.

Something snatched Lemuel's leg. Sharp claws. Cold. Hard. A hot searing pain at his ankle. He looked down. His leg was caught in an iron trap. The metal teeth of the trap bit through his skin and muscle, gripping the bone beneath. He bit his fist to stop himself from shouting out in pain. Ezekiel saw what had happened and ran to his master's aid. As he did, he also stepped on an iron trap and felt the red-hot pain of the metal teeth bite into his flesh. The two men were pinioned to their spots. Hellström and Gibbs went to Lemuel's aid and Meth to Ezekiel's. The traps were difficult to open. Their jaws gripped bone and chewed into marrow. Hellström managed to free Lemuel first, then went to Meth's aid, and the two of them freed

Ezekiel. Meth and Hellström bandaged the two men's wounds with strips they tore from their own garments.

Hellström was shaking his head. 'We go back. We cannot now go on.'

Lemuel was in agony and could hardly walk. Hellström found two branches and fashioned them into Y-shaped crutches. As much as it hurt Lemuel to admit defeat, there was no way he could attack the witches in this condition. The five of them turned around and made their way back even more cautiously than they had made their way forward, a sorry party. For every step Lemuel took, he winced. The wound was throbbing.

It took them nearly two hours to hobble through the woods back to where they had tethered their horses. The journey had been a disaster. Lemuel had lost two good men. Two of his best. He would make those witches pay. Seeing them hanged was not enough, he wanted them to suffer hell's torment first, have them racked, make them the most wretched creatures on Earth. Death would come, but it would not be quick.

Hellström and Meth helped Lemuel and Ezekiel mount their steeds. They rode back over the moors, along the river, past Dale Edge, until at last they arrived at Lemuel's estate. Ezekiel said goodbye to the men and made his way to the village and to his house. Kate was waiting for him to return. Seeing his condition, she ran over to him and took the reins. He explained what had happened and she helped him dismount, putting her arm around his shoulders and leading him through the house, to their bedchamber. He collapsed on top of the blankets and she unravelled the makeshift bandages and examined the wound.

'It's bad. Cut to the bone. I need to bathe it so it doesn't get infected.'

She washed the wound carefully, cleaning it until the water turned rose-coloured, then dried it as best she could. She concocted a healing salve that would also keep the wound clean. The remedy was something her mother had taught her to prepare and it consisted of chickweed, comfrey root, elm bark and woundwort. She found some freshly laundered cloth and made a bandage from it. She redressed the wound.

'If we keep it clean, it shouldn't spoil.'

She gave him a cup of kill-priest and when he'd drunk the draught down she brought him a healing posset of milk and ale, then hot broth. She held the spoon to his mouth.

'Once you've had this, you need to sleep.'

She was interrupted from her nursing by the sound of their son crying. The child was only a day old and already he knew how to summon his mother.

'I best go and feed him. You get some rest.'

Just over a mile away, in Lemuel's bedchamber, Elizabeth was tending to her husband's wound in a similar way to that of Kate. Both women trusted their own remedies to those of the physician or the apothecary. Lemuel watched his wife fuss over him, hardly able to move. He saw the door open and first Catherine and then Olivia came to perch on the bed, either side, holding his hands. He smiled at them to reassure them that he would be fine. But he felt weak. Battle-scarred. An old pike badged with sores. He needed to sleep. He asked them if they would leave him now and his wife kissed his brow.

When they had left the room, he lay back and stared at the ceiling. What a disastrous campaign. He'd fought Royalists, outnumbered five to one, and come out better than this. He wondered again whether the witches had cursed the woods. Surely they must have done. It wasn't just bad luck that had seen them lose two men and injure two more. To lose one, to injure one, would not be unthinkable, but so much tragedy had befallen them in such a short space of time. If the witches were that powerful, if their magic were that strong, then how would they capture them and bring them to justice? If they could get a confession from Jenny it would be easier to persuade the magistrate to provide enforcements. But would more men solve the problem of a witch's curse? He didn't know enough about these matters. Give him an army of Royalists, armed with sakers, culverins, muskets and swords, any day over these unarmed witches, with their potions and their hexes, their curses and familiar beasts. These bloody Black Clough witches, Black Wood hags, bloody Black Wood women. He tried to think of how best to proceed, turning the problem over and over again in his head, until sleep came, and he thought no more.

The Jaws of the Trap

The wolf dug out an abandoned fox den and curled up as much as she could in the dark damp hollow to trap heat. The wind howled through the trees and the rain pelted the ground. She slept in fits, waking with the shivers, drifting off to sleep, waking again with the wind or the cold. In the morning there was frost in her fur. She tried to stretch. Muscles stiff and chilled.

Snow was falling in patches, the flakes freezing where the ground was dry and melting where it was muddy. Hunger drove her on. There was no food. She broke the film of ice over a pond and drank the stagnant water.

She was walking where she had no cover. Hunger had taken her out of the shadows of wooded cloughs. At this season the does were already carrying calves and often aborted the one least favoured. In the grass she found a pale still-warm unborn. It was a milky blue colour and lay blind and dying in the frost. She ate everything, bones and all.

As she slunk through the undergrowth she heard voices. Men. Hunters. She took cover by a holly bush as she gathered her strength. They were coming this way and she could smell their sweat in the air. And something else. Horses. The men were riders. There was nowhere to hide except for the bush where she crouched. She heard dogs too. They would soon sniff her out. There was nothing else to do. She made a run for it and as soon as she did, she heard the men holler and shout. The dogs barking. She ran across a meadow and leaped over a stone wall. The dogs were gaining on her. Close to them the men on horseback. She ran faster, across a field. There was a wood further on. If she could get to that, and over the river, she might stand a chance. She peered over a ravine. No time to think. She leapt. Falling. She landed on her front legs. Buckled, rolled down, scrambling to her feet, she slid ten yards or so. Disturbed debris rolled behind her. Stumbling, she plunged into the ice cold water and let the current carry her.

Over the other side of the river she dragged herself onto the bank. Somehow, she had outrun them. She stood panting, her breath like steam. How much longer could she keep ahead? More of them each day. Men with dogs. Men on horses. With guns. With traps.

As she made her way through the wood, she felt something bite and she cried out in pain. She looked down. Her leg was caught in an iron trap. She tried to pull it out but the teeth of the trap dug in harder and she howled again. Through fur, skin, flesh. Blood oozed from the wounds where the metal had cut. She tried to twist it out. The pain seared through her. She panted with the effort. She leant down and tried to bite the trap to open it, but it wouldn't budge. She stood frozen to the spot.

What now? If she stayed here the men would come. She tried again but the pain was even worse. It fixed her to the spot. Then she could hear the men again, far off, but their voices were getting louder – they were heading in her direction. The teeth of the trap had bitten down to the bone. She could see the white through the puncture wounds. No time. She twisted and twisted, then with one final twist, the bone snapped in two. Flesh and muscle ripping. The pain seared and she tore through the skin, leaving her paw in the jaws of the trap. She looked down at it as though she might be able to stick it back on again. She looked at her back leg, a ragged stump. Blood pumping. As the voices got louder still, she limped on, half running, half limping, until she had evaded them again. She took cover in a ditch and licked the gaping wound. She found a frozen puddle and plunged the stump through the ice.

Supping from the Whisky Jar

We were gathered round an extinguished fire, Alice pacing around the pit, pistol in hand. I thought about Jenny. I had escaped one prison and now I had found another. I thought about how we were going to escape and I was filled with dread. I wasn't even sure that Alice was capable of sleep in this state: she had guarded all night, standing over us with a loaded pistol, a demented jailer. How was I, or how were we, going to free Jenny if we couldn't free ourselves? The men had muskets and pistols, crossbows and sabres. We had two primitive knives.

'Thorn and I have done a ring-walk this morning and we found this.'

Alice held up the green gabardine that I'd seen Gad wearing.

'We then found the body it belonged to. A man who worked for Lemuel, who was mortally wounded by multiple pike wounds. We also discovered that two of the irons have been triggered. And there was blood on the teeth. What I have said has come to pass: Lemuel and his men attempted to attack us last night. And they failed. The magic held strong.'

Alice laughed like a maniac, her eyes dancing in their sockets. Some of the other girls joined in, as though they didn't know how else to react. Holly gave me a look and shook her head discreetly.

'Me like magic,' Heather said.

'We cannot be complacent. The men will come back. They will return for the body of their friend. They will want to bury him on consecrated ground. But I think they will be back to attack us too. I can't be sure when this will happen. It could be tonight, it could be tomorrow. But it will be soon, I'm sure of that, and they will bring reinforcements.'

'What do we do?' Ivy said.

'How can we stop them?' Thorn said.

'We can't. We can't stop them. All we can do is be prepared for when they come.'

'How do we do that?'

'We have to move.'

'Where?'

'Deeper into the woods. Thorn and I have found a place two miles north. It is surrounded by water on one side and a steep-sided clough on the other. It will be very hard for anyone to attack us from that vantage point. And if they do, they will be weakened.'

'And what about the wolf?'

'She's safe. My raven feeds her. That's all you need to know.'

'What about all our stuff?'

'Bring what you can, but travel light. What you cannot carry on your back, you do not need.'

Alice threw Gad's gabardine into the firepit. We started on the move after we'd eaten. First we collected up all the iron traps, then our possessions. It took several trips through the woods to move all the things we needed. The first task was to fortify the camp. This was much easier than the original camp as there were only two ways in. One by the clough, and another way in along the beck. We were able to re-use the irons and dig traps along these routes. The next task was to provide a roof over our heads and we cleared space beneath the holly trees, so that the base of the trees and the leaves and branches above became our floor and roof. The foliage was dense enough to protect us from raindrops. All this took most of the day.

I asked Alice about Jenny. When were we going to mount a rescue campaign? I was shocked by her answer.

'We won't be doing that. It's too late. If she's not dead already then they have taken her to the jail. It's only a matter of time before they extract a confession and then they'll hang her. If we try and rescue her, we'll only risk getting caught ourselves.'

'But she's one of us. We have to do everything we can.'

'I know it's hard, but I've been here before. I know what I'm talking about. Men can make you say anything. I'll never go there again, to that place those men took me. You have to trust me, Rowan, and do as I say.'

But I didn't trust her and I couldn't accept what Alice said.

I spoke to Holly when the others were distracted.

'How are we going to get out of here?'

Holly shook her head. 'She has to sleep at some point.'

That afternoon Alice was agitated. She paced round the fire, smoking her pipe.

'I am not afraid of dying. I have died once before. They hanged me – placed the noose around my neck. I was standing on the stool. A crowd had gathered to watch me drop. They kicked the stool away and the crowd cheered. I was dangling, choking, saw my life rush before me – all the lies I'd been told. I was dying, couldn't breathe. I kicked my legs, grabbed at the rope that was strangling me. I tried to suck air into my lungs. I felt light-headed and knew that this was the end. I was close to the edge. I was dead. Then the rope snapped and I fell to the ground. The curate said, and the magistrate said, that it was God's will. And they would not go against God's will. I could live. I was free. And they let me go. I walked from that town and I never went back. From that moment I would speak the truth. I would no longer live in a world made of lies.'

I looked at the scar tissue below Alice's jaw. Let her talk and talk,

I thought. I wanted her to tire herself out so she would sleep soundly tonight.

Alice relit her pipe from the fire and drew the smoke into her lungs. I noticed that her hand was shaking. She and Thorn had returned earlier to where the corpse lay. It had been removed. The men had been back to collect it and I could see that she was rattled by this. She wouldn't sit still and kept pacing, smoking from her pipe constantly. We were set to work on further fortifications. Alice wasn't satisfied with our work. She had identified a number of weak places and her solution was to dig deep pits at both entrances that we would cover.

I worked with Ivy and Holly on the beck hole, and Alice worked with Thorn and Heather on the clough hole. It was hard work as the ground was frozen and when we managed to break through the crust of it with our simple tools, underneath was stony. Huge rocks that needed digging out, and this back-breaking work returned my thoughts to that day over a month ago, when I had dug my parents' grave.

We worked in pairs, taking it in turns to rest so that there were always two people working and one resting. When we'd finished we used hazel branches to make pikes and we hammered them into the base of the pit before sharpening their ends to a point. All the while Alice stood close by clutching the gun. We stood back. We took branches and covered the hole, then concealed this with dead leaves. I looked at the trap from different angles. There was no way to tell there was a pit underneath. Alice came over and did the same, nodding and saying we'd done good work. But she wasn't satisfied. She had identified some gaps in the gorse and brambles further up the beck that she thought the men might be able to crawl through. She ordered us to plug the gaps with gorse and brambles from nearer the camp.

It was difficult to collect the branches in the half-dark. We didn't have gloves so we used rags that we wrapped around our hands, grasping the thorny branches and cutting them at the base with our knives. The wrappings were inadequate and soon our hands and arms were full of cuts – slim rivulets of blood stained our skin. When we had gathered sufficient to plug the gaps we pushed a good amount through the holes so that there was no way a man could crawl in.

Alice was by the fire cleaning her pistol. The mood around the camp was pensive. The other girls were either sitting listlessly or had taken to their beds and no one seemed to be in the right frame of mind for conversation. I looked at Alice, at the grey streaks in her black hair. There seemed to be more grey than when I had first seen her and somehow her face had aged. I looked to see if there were any more wrinkles, but it wasn't that, it was more a weariness in her expression, like the muscles in her face had given up. I noticed for the first time how sad her eyes were.

Heather was rubbing her feet.

'Me cold. Me cold. Me freezing,' she was repeating as she rubbed and Alice watched.

'Wear shoes if you like, you stupid girl. I've tried to teach you how to connect with the Earth. I've tried to teach all of you.' She reached for a bag and delved in. She took out some shoes and threw them at Heather. 'There. Have them. Have these stupid shoes. See if I care, you ungrateful brat! It's men who made shoes. Don't you see. Men.'

Heather looked shocked by Alice's tirade but put the shoes on anyway, muttering to herself about something. I watched Alice pace, clutching the pistol. I wondered about that gun. One gun between six of us would do no good. The men would be more than adequately provisioned with pistols and muskets. Even if Alice managed to shoot one of them, there wouldn't be time to reload before one of the men shot her. There didn't really seem much point in having it, but then I thought back to her words about not letting the men have her. She had said that she would never put herself in that position again, where she was at the mercy of those men.

That night Alice gave us all something that she said would help us sleep. I tried to throw mine away, but Alice watched carefully, making sure we drank every drop. So just before I went to bed, I stuck my fingers down my throat and made myself cast out the potion. Holly did the same. We lay in bed listening for Alice. I thought about Jenny again, but I pushed the thought out of my head. Alice was right, there was no way she could have survived their torture without confessing. The rack, the strap, the screw, the pilliwinks – she would have been able to take each one of those tortures for some time, but eventually she would have told them anything they wanted to hear. Everyone had their breaking point. I only hoped that Jenny had already been hanged, and that the magistrate hadn't asked for further proof. They had swimmed her once, her right thumb tied to her left toe, her left thumb tied to her right toe. They had attached a rope about her middle, so long as it reached from one side of the dam to the other, where on each side a man stood, so that if she sank they could pull her up. To swim her again before hanging her would be unthinkably cruel.

I thought about my ma and da, and the plans they had for their future. For my future. Da had been saving money from his fights. Money that Lemuel had stolen from them. My da had endured punches, kicks, biting. He'd sweated and bled for that money, had bones broken, wrists stamped on, ribs kicked, knuckles cracked, skin cut, eyes blackened and his nose smashed. My ma had stayed up on many a night poking the fire and supping from the whisky jar, waiting for Da to come through the door, not knowing if she'd ever see him again. And now they were both in the ground, with worms crawling over their bones.

'Wait here,' I whispered.

'Be careful.'

Very slowly, so as not to make any noise, I slid from under my blankets and on all fours I crept like a cat over to the bush, which I hoped Alice was now sleeping beneath, then paused to calm my breath and let my heartbeat slow and quieten. When I was sufficiently calm I placed my head through the gap in the bush, very gently. I stayed like that for several minutes, letting my eyes get used to the dark, so that I could make out Alice, lying down with a blanket over her, eyes closed. She was fast asleep. On her chest was the pistol, its steel glinting ever so slightly in what little light remained, her left hand clutching the handle.

I watched her chest rise and fall, and with it, the gun also. I studied her for several minutes to make sure she was sound asleep, then I crept further into the hole, stopped and listened. Her breathing was still regular. I waited for my heart to return to its quiet beat, then very carefully I took another step inside. I proceeded in this way, taking one step, then waiting, watching, listening, before taking another, until I was fully inside her sleeping chamber. I was now crouched beside her and could easily reach for the gun from where I squatted. Very slowly and ever so carefully, I wrapped my fingers around the barrel. I made sure that my hand and arm took the weight of the machine, so that none of the weight was on Alice, as I carefully moved it towards me. I watched as the grip slid from her fingers.

It must have taken me half an hour to get the weapon, but now, as I left her hovel and rose to my feet, I was clutching Alice's pistol. My mind went back to that day again, to Lemuel clutching his flintlock, and in that moment we were linked. I shrugged off the thought and made my way back to where Holly lay. I nudged her and showed her the gun, and together we made our way through the maze of fenland and out along the ravine above the beck. I tucked the gun into my bag and tied this over my shoulders as we moved south-west over the moor.

No Man's Land

Lemuel had slept all day and night and it was late afternoon when he eventually stirred. Elizabeth was waiting by his bed.

'Lem? Are you awake?' she said softly.

He opened his eyes and looked around the room, then made eye contact with his wife and smiled weakly. His ankle was still throbbing. The pain was intense.

'How are you feeling?'

Lemuel winced. 'Help me up.'

'You need to rest. You've had a nasty injury.'

'I've got stuff to do.'

He tried to get himself out of bed, but the wounds seared. It felt like each sore was being poked with a red-hot rod and he cried out in agony, almost passing out with the pain. He leant back on the pillows again.

'What did I tell you?'

'Very well, I'll rest. How's Ezekiel?'

'Same as you. Bed-bound.'

'Can you get Jacob to fetch Mr Hellström?'

'Are you sure that's a good idea, love?'

'Please, Elizabeth. If we don't act now, it will be too late.'

Elizabeth tried to persuade him to rest, but eventually he managed to convince her to carry out his wishes. She returned within the hour with Johan.

'You are awake. This is good. You need to keep this wound clean. If it is infecting it is bad. You may be losing this leg.'

'I know all that. Look, I need you to do two things for me.'

Hellström nodded.

'First, I need you to check on Gibbs. Then come back here.'

'Mr Lane, I am not your minion. What is the second thing?'

'I'll explain when you return.'

Hellström made his way to the cellar where Gibbs was taking it in turns with Meth to guard Jenny. When he got there he saw what state the girl was in. She had a black eye and a cut mouth and her dress was torn in two places: at the neck and at the hem. When she saw Hellström she sat up straight in her chair, to which she was still tied. He looked at Gibbs who was sitting nearby clutching his musket. Hellström noticed that the girl had been tied up with a different type of knot to the one they'd used before.

'What is happening to this girl?'

'He did it,' she said wearily, nodding to Gibbs.

'I had to. Her familiar came. I had to fight it off. Nearly killed me.'

'Her familiar is coming here, you say?'

'Yes, this morning, just when we changed shifts. At first it was a rat. Big greasy thing. Walked straight up to her. Then it changed into a black dog, turned on me, started snarling. I held my musket to its head and it changed again into a bird. Flew at me and tried to peck my eyes. It flapped around her, attacking the ropes. The next thing, she was unbound. Somehow her creature had untied her. I tried to grab her, to tie her up again, but the bird kept on at me. I whacked it with my musket. Then she tried to gouge my eyes out. She was like a thing possessed. I had to slap her about. And I gave her bird a right good clout. Sent it packing. I knocked her the other side of the room. Tell,

314

you, the pair of them, they could have killed me. Good job I acted when I did.'

'He's lying,' Jenny said.

'If this is true then we have proof. Are you willing to give a statement to the magistrate?'

'Course I will. I'll tell him exactly what I told you.'

'But this is not good. This bruise. This cut. It will go against us. If the magistrate thinks we have not treated her fairly he may not believe your statement.'

'But I'm telling you the truth.'

'He's a liar and a bastard. Do you know what he did to me?'

'Hush, hush. I cannot hear myself think. I have no time. I must tell Mr Lane. You must stay here and guard her. I will not be long.'

'Please, sir, don't leave me with him. He's a brute.'

Lemuel asked Elizabeth to prop up his pillows so he could sit up straight in bed. He was thinking about the wolf and the witches, knew that he would have to act swiftly and decisively, no time now to follow the letter of the law. Legal process was a luxury and in these times of necessity, they would have to dispense with it. He'd had times before, commanding an army, when he had acted without due authority, and he had reasoned then that if he had the good will of the Lord, then this surpassed any legal jurisdiction. He would have to strike with a hammer blow that would end all his strife. The land to the south and west around Black Clough was once owned by the Sunderland estate, but he now had the deeds in his safe. The land on the north and east had been owned by the Radcliffe estate, but again, the deeds were now behind lock and key. Radcliffe estate still owned Willow Garth to the north and this was the place where willow was grown for basket making. The Sunderland estate retained the common turbary where folk cut turf and peat for fuel. Technically and legally the heart of the woods was owned by no one. Not so much a glitch in the law, but a desired consequence. He'd learned that many years ago both the Sunderland and Radcliffe estates had hired lawyers and other legal persons to renegotiate their deeds to exclude this dark stretch of ravine, tree and fen. No one wanted to own Black Clough Woods because no one wanted the responsibility for it. It was a no man's land, a cursed cesspit, and now he could use this to his advantage.

There was a single knock at the door, then Hellström entered. He conveyed what he'd seen and ascertained from the girl and from Gibbs.

'Well, like you say, it could go either way. If he's prepared to give a statement that's one thing. But if the magistrate looks unfavourably on her injuries, then he might want further proof.'

'He'll want a clean confession,' Elizabeth said. 'And if that's not forthcoming, they'll swim her.'

'They will not swim. Not in this parish.'

'So be it. It's out of our hands now. I want Gibbs and Meth to take her into town and hand her over to the magistrate. Gibbs can write his statement. That's all we can do. It's in the hands of the magistrate now.'

'Very well.'

'Besides, I've got more pressing issues.'

'And what are these pressing issues, may I ask?'

'That thing you mentioned when we first met, where your people form a chain of men?'

'*Rovdjursskall?*'

'Yeah, whatever it's called. Where you get hundreds of men and form a chain and walk through the forest driving out the wolf.'

'What of it?'

'I want you to do this for me. For the wolf and for the witches. Drive them all out.'

'And then what?'

'When my men return, I want you to employ at my expense and on my behalf, as many of the labouring men in town and village as are willing. We will raise an army and take Black Clough Woods.'

'Why is this?'

'I need you to surround that wood on all sides and drive out that wolf and every witch with it. You take them well clear of those woods and you burn the lot of them.'

Hellström looked at Lemuel as though he were staring at something he had stepped in. He shook his head slowly then smiled.

'I have better idea. I take those barrels of gunpowder from your cellar. I load up a cart with kindling and wood.'

'What for?'

'I will take your men. I will employ all the *allmogen* from the village as you say. We will surround the wood with gunpowder, oil, kindling and logs. We will set fire to that wood, so that it burns from the outside in. We burn the wolf and we burn the witches, along with everything else that lives.'

'No, you mustn't burn the trees, do you hear me?'

'Ha! We will burn every tree and everything else in that wood. The wolf will burn and every witch. Every deer, marten and wildcat in flames.'

'NO! you mustn't harm the trees.'

'Mr Lane, you sound like one of these crazy witches.'

'You don't understand. I own those trees now. They're mine. I intend to make a great deal of money from the timber. You want paying don't you?'

'I will get what is owed.'

'Then you will do as I say. When you have, come back here and I'll pay you what we agreed. And I'll pay every man who takes part in this work a handsome fee. Let that be known.'

'But there are things worth more than money, Mr Lane.'

'Oh aye? Such as what? Gold? Diamonds?'

'I am not talking gold or diamonds.'

'Good. Then that's settled. Two hundred pounds plus fifty pounds expenses.'

'I come for the dance, Mr Lane.'

'What dance?'

'I have come for my massacre.'

'You'll get your massacre as long as I keep my trees.'

'Well, we will see. Good day, Mr Lane.'

'Is that it? Come here. I've not finished yet.'

Hellström didn't answer. He had already left the room. Lemuel was flabbergasted. He looked at his wife but didn't know what to say. He'd trusted this man to get the job done. He knew that Elizabeth had always had reservations about his suitability, but he was supposed to be a professional wolf hunter. The best in North Europa. Surely he would do as instructed? He turned to Elizabeth.

'What just happened there?'

Elizabeth said nothing. She was staring at the door as though she expected Hellström to burst back in and tell them it had been one of his jokes.

'He wouldn't. Would he?'

'I don't know. I just don't know.'

It was true that no rational human being would set fire to the entire forest. But this man was completely insane. The Lord, Lemuel's God, had given him this land and the Lord would help him defeat anyone who tried to take it from him. He would do as Joshua, son of Nun, had done. The Lord had commanded Joshua to set the city on fire not the forests. Like Joshua he would smite and slay them and hang them from five trees. He pulled the blankets away and swung his good leg off the bed.

'What are you doing?'

'I can't take the risk. That timber's already sold. If he burns it we're ruined.'

'Don't be stupid, love. You're in no fit state.'

'I can manage. Fetch me that brandy will you, and my crutch.'

Lemuel took a few good slugs of the brandy and used the crutch to hobble across the room to where his clothes were draped over a chair.

'Give me a hand with these, will you, love.'

Elizabeth helped him get dressed and he hobbled to the door. She opened it for him and he stumbled across the landing and down the staircase, taking it step by agonising step. He stopped halfway for another slug of brandy. He explained his plan to Jacob. Jacob was to take Jenny to the magistrates first thing in the morning and he was to bring the stableboy with him so he had an extra pair of hands. He, Meth and Gibbs, were going to put a stop to this Hellström, even if it meant shooting him. Rather see the man dead than his trees burn. Then they would go into town and rally an army who would surround Black Clough. They were going to drive out every witch and wolf and put them in the same hole as Hellström.

The Missing Kitling

The wolf was heavy with the life inside her. She sensed that it was time and needed to find somewhere to lie down, where she could birth her young. She made her way through this strange new place that the raven had led her, hobbling on three legs. The air was rank. The earth was stale. She watched the bird hop and nod in front of her, understanding now the raven's language. It flew from the branch in front of her to one about twenty feet away. She knew to follow. She was slow, taking care not to put her severed leg down, but the bird was patient, and she managed to navigate the maze of sour black waters the bird took her through until she came to a secluded spot that was well guarded by rock and water, gorse and bramble. She would be safe here.

The raven had brought her to this place just in time. The life inside her was pushing to be born and she crouched in position as she gave birth to three pups. One dog and two bitches. She licked them clean. She could taste blood and bile on their skin. Their eyes were closed. She positioned herself so that they could each reach for a teat and watched as each in turn took one into its mouth and made suck. She felt them nibble her flesh. Hot sweet milk seeped from her as she lay back and rested while the kitlings fed.

She must have fallen asleep like this with the blind whelps suckling. When she woke up her three pups were curled in the hollow space between her feet. They were fast asleep. She was ravenously hungry. Something caught her attention, it was the smell of fresh meat, and she saw now, almost under her nose, the corpse of a leveret. Good meat. Careful not to wake her kitlings, she leaned across and took the beast into her mouth, chewing first its back legs, then opening up its stomach and feasting on its guts. She licked and slurped at the soups and juices of the animal's innards. Then she ate the remaining meat, leaving only the animal's head. She noticed in a nearby beech tree, perched quite high up, her raven watching over her.

She was so weak from giving birth, months of near starvation and the injury that was still fresh and raw, that she could hardly move at all. She spent the next three days like this, her young feeding on her milk, sleeping in the warm hollow between her legs. She licked the red flesh of the wound. Every day the raven brought her good fresh meat: fitchew, rabbit, otter.

It was on the fourth day, when she woke, that she saw that there were only two pups curled about her. She looked around. Where was the third? It must have wandered off. But why would a pup so young wander from its mother? She tried to get up, but despite three days of rest, she was still too weak to stand. She tried again. It was no use. Her legs would not support her. She tried to reassure herself. Her pup could not have wandered far. The young were sometimes too curious for their own good, but it would come back soon, once it had explored. She sat looking all around her, alert to any movement. Her pup was so small that she wondered whether she would be able to see it move in the undergrowth. She sniffed the air for its scent. There was a movement – just a woodcock furtling through dead leaves. She stayed there, patiently watching for anything that moved, but her pup did not return.

She must have fallen asleep again, because the next thing, when she opened her eyes, it was dark. She checked that all her pups were with her, but there were still only two. The third pup was missing. By her feet was the fresh corpse of a pheasant. She plucked the feathers with her teeth and gorged on the meat. She tried to stand, and this time she managed to get to her feet. Her legs were shaking, she felt light-headed and unsteady, but she was standing. One of her pups was awake now, and it began to whine softly. Ignoring it, she walked away from both pups, looking for the missing kitling. Hobbling on three legs, she searched the immediate area, sniffing the ground, trying to pick up her scent. She sniffed the earth beneath her feet until she identified her third pup's distinctive smell and followed it towards the beck. She sniffed again and followed the trail as it led to the bed of the beck, where it stopped. Her pup must have fallen into the water. It would have been taken downstream. The flow of water was fast hereabouts, albeit shallow. It was a mistake to give birth so close to water. Perhaps it had been washed up further along the bed.

She started to paddle through the shallow water, but as she did, she picked up another smell, that of burning wood. As she paddled further, the smell of burning became stronger. Then she saw a low patch of thick black smoke, and it was coming towards her. The forest was on fire. She must get back – move her pups. She leapt out of the water and ran as best she could towards them, taking the first into her mouth and carrying it further into the woods, away from the smoke, returning for the second and doing the same. But the smoke was getting thicker and it was still heading towards her. She took the first pup in her mouth again, and this time carried it much further, returning for the second and doing the same with this pup. Still the smoke thickened and came closer. She did not know what to do. Where could she go that was safe? She looked around for a better route, scanning every bough and branch, looking for her bird. The raven would know a way out. Surely her bird would come and rescue her. But the bird was nowhere to be seen.

Alice's Eyes

As we made our way out of the woods and onto Broadhead Moor, I could feel my legs weaken, until a heavy fatigue overtook me. I looked at Holly – she was struggling too. Her brow glistened with sweat.

'I don't feel right,' I said.

Holly nodded weakly. 'Feel like I'm dying.'

'We're not dying,' I said. 'We'll be all right.'

As we traipsed over peat bog my legs seemed to turn into lead. I was aching all over. Every gland and every muscle throbbed with a dull pain. Although it was night-time and the air was cold, I felt like I was on fire. My garments were wet with sweat. I placed the palm of my hand on my forehead. I was burning up. I tried to ignore the fever and carry on walking, but I could hardly keep myself upright. I looked at Holly and could see she was staggering behind me.

'Come on,' I said. 'Need to walk it off.'

For a time my fear fuelled me, cutting through the fever, but as I walked on, my legs felt like they were manacled to the earth. I looked round. Holly had collapsed. I went back for her. Tried to stir her. No use. We would have to sit out the fever. I found a hollow under some rocks and dragged Holly inside.

'You have to fight it,' I said, but she didn't respond. Her eyes were closed now and her body was limp. I shook her gently. 'Don't fall asleep,' I said. I propped her against a rock and loosened her shawl. 'We can rest here for a bit, until the poison has worn off.' I shook her again. 'Holly, say something!' I lifted one of her eyelids. 'Open your eyes. Don't sleep. Whatever Alice gave us, we got rid of most of it.' There was no response and I had no strength to nurse her any longer. I lay there, aching and sweating and burning up. The effects of the poison were getting stronger.

I pushed my fingers down my throat again, but I had nothing inside to cast. I suffered agonizing cramps, crouching on all fours like a dog, clutching my stomach. Please God, protect us. I fell back on the ground ... couldn't breathe ... or swallow. I was dying. I punched my chest as hard as I could, trying to get my lungs to work, struggling to suck in any air at all. It was like my throat had been sewn up, and there was just a tiny gap. I tried to swallow again. My tongue cleaved to the roof of my mouth. Trying not to panic, I sucked in more air. I lay in the dark, choking and gasping for breath.

Eventually the muscles in my chest loosened, and I began to breathe more easily. I was still burning up and now I was overcome with a heavy, sinking feeling. It was all I could do to keep my eyes open. I must have lost the battle because the next thing, it was light. I was still curled in my hollow place, burning up with fever. I lay there unable to move. Every fibre of my body ached. In my delirium, I saw Ma standing over me.

'Ma, is that you?'

'I'm so sorry, my lovely daughter. So, so sorry.'

I tried to get up but I was frozen to the spot.

'Rest, child.'

'But I don't know what to do. Or where to go. I don't have anyone.'

'Sure you do. You've got yourself, and me and your da are watching over you, and the Lord God, and Jesus his son, and Mary his mother. We're all here. You'll have a lovely life, Caragh. We'll come and get you when you're ready. Live your life without hate. And don't forget to say your Hail Marys.'

'How do I carry on, Ma?'

'Sure, you'll figure it out, child. Do you want me to sing you a song?'

'No, Ma, you know I don't like you singing to me.'

'I know nothing of the sort. Didn't I always sing to you in your cot?'

'You did.'

'And didn't you like it?'

'No, Ma, you've a voice like a strangled cat.'

'Now, there's no need to be insulting me, Caragh.'

'Sorry, Ma. I do love you. I just can't stand it when you sing.'

'Well, I must say, you've left it awful late in the day to be telling me.'

'Can I see Da?'

'You know he's not one for talking, Caragh.'

'Just for a minute.'

'Maybe later. Get some rest now.'

'But I've so much to tell you, Ma. I've done things, seen things, and I don't really know where to start.'

'Don't you think your da and me are watching you?'

'And I had this dream—'

'Now, don't be telling me your daft dreams, Caragh. If you've got something to say, there'll be plenty of time in eternity to tell me and your da.'

I started to protest, but she'd gone. I lay back and closed my eyes. I must have fallen asleep again, because this time, when I opened my eyes, it was night once more. The fever had lifted. I felt weak still but the aching pains had diminished. I crawled over to where Holly lay and shook her, 'Wake up, Holly. The poison has gone. The fever's over.' But she was stiff and cold. I collapsed on top of her and wept. Hot tears stung my eyes and I cursed God. What kind of creature was he? Some sort of sadistic lunatic? He'd built this whole world, this whole stinking world, and every stinking thing in it, and for what? Was his creation just a divine act of vanity? Strike me down for my blasphemy, oh Lord. I don't care. I don't love you, God. I waited for my Maker to blast me into hell. But no damnation came.

I lay on top of Holly's body weeping until no more tears would come. Then I noticed a strange smell in the air. At first I didn't recognise it, but as I came round more, I realised what I was smelling was burning. Something nearby was on fire. I managed to crawl out of my hole, and as I did, I could see a glowing red shape to the east.

At first I thought it was the dawn rising, but as I got to my feet and stood upright, I saw that the rest of the sky was pitch black. Maybe my eyes were playing tricks on me on account of the fever – but the fever had lifted, so what else could this light be? If this were not the sunrise, then what?

It wasn't until I got closer that I saw the source of this light – flames. The forest of Black Clough was a conflagration. The fire rose up high above the horizon and mingled with thick smoke. From this angle it looked like the whole skyline was ablaze. I stood and watched the spectacle, listening to the roar of the flames as they consumed the trees. I thought about Alice and the girls. Had they died before the fire, or were they now being burnt alive?

I walked further and could see that there was no way through the fire. Now I felt the heat. The flames roared. I thought that there must be another way through and I circumnavigated the woods, travelling clockwise. The fire was as advanced elsewhere as I had seen it from the moor. I travelled north, still further, until I reached the most northern peak of the forest. The flames formed a wall of fire.

It was then that I spotted the men in the distance. And with them, a very tall woman in a red dress. Except, as I looked harder, I realised it wasn't a woman. The tall figure was Hellström, standing closer to the fire than the others, his face lit up by the flames. The red dress he was wearing was too small for him and the effect was to accentuate his arms and legs. He held his arms aloft, as though summoning some spirit from the flames. He looked like a demon. Then I saw Lemuel, twenty paces behind, being held back by four men. He was roaring like a bear, trying to free himself from his captors. I could hear Hellström cackle. Then I saw a figure, a burning effigy, run out of the forest screaming, running towards Hellström, wearing a suit of flames. It was Alice. Her hair had been burnt off and her head was black like coal. As she ran the flames danced all around her. The sound of her screaming was awful, a primal wail that cut through the night. She got to about six feet from Hellström and collapsed, first kneeling in front of him like some demented supplicant, then falling face first into the peat. Hellström was clapping his hands together and laughing.

I felt sick at the horror of the scene. I could not bear to watch any more and I returned to my cave on the moor. I hid from the men and shut my ears to Alice's death screams. I closed my eyes but still saw in my mind Alice as a burning effigy. When I could hear no more outside I got up and placed rocks over Holly's body. I said a bitter prayer and crossed myself. I lay close by in a heap, my shawl pulled tight around me, and wept. I slept and woke in the dark. I got to my feet and went to the edge of the copse where I could see that Black Clough Wood was still in flame but the men had gone. I stood leaning against a tree and watched. For hours I stood there, rooted to the spot, unable to turn away from the macabre spectacle in front of me. I thought about all of the animals that would also be trapped and either burned by flames or suffocated: the ounce, the otter, the fox, rabbit, deer, badger. Only the birds would escape.

Surely the other women, in the deepest part of the wood, would not survive such a vicious conflagration? Almost certainly everything including the wolf had perished. Once again, I felt the deep weight of knowing I had no one and nothing.

The fires burned all night, and I sat vigil, watching on. Unable to turn away. Paralyzed by the sight. Where else could I go now? What future could there now be? I had no idea how to find the safe place Da had described. All was lost. I sat leaning against the tree, as numb as its trunk. It was raining now and ice-cold drops fell on my head and on every part of me, soaking me to the bone.

By midnoon the following day the flames had abated, the persistent rain finally dampening the fires. I walked over to the edge of the forest and saw that everything was black and charred. I walked along the path that went above the ravine, traipsing now over cold cinders. The forest foliage was burned to the ground and the trees were just blackened stumps. I made my way to the fens, and navigated the maze of black waters until I came to the original camp. The huts were blackened remnants of what they had been, the roofs burned away and hardly a wall left. The cauldron still hung from the hook above the firepit, swinging like a clock's pendulum.

I travelled further north until I came to our new camp. The holly trees were reduced to charred stumps. Nothing of our new cover remained. I saw blackened cadavers, not knowing which was who. They lay on the ground in different postures of horror, clawed hands grasping, mouths grimacing. Had the fire killed them or Alice's poison? What did it matter? They were just as dead. I came across the bones of a different animal, and I realised this was what was left of the wolf. Close by were the remains of two pups. The wolf had given birth.

I found the burnt remains of other animals, that I could only guess at. In the end the fens had not been able to offer sanctuary. The men had succeeded in killing both the women they accused of witchcraft and the wolf they branded a murderer. And pretty much everything else that lived.

I sat by the charred corpses of the women and the wolves and felt nothing. Every emotion I once had was spent. I was hollowed out. A shell. Everything that had once been lush and green was withered and black. There was no point to any of it. Life had lost all meaning. I would sit among these black bones until I withered away. Until I was one of them. I did not want to be of this earth. I yearned to be black dust.

A day passed, then another, maybe a third? I lost all track of time. But something compelled me to stand up and turn my back on this gruesome funeral. Whether it was thirst or hunger or madness, I had to go on. I found myself making my way back through the woods, drinking from the beck and finding burnt leaves to eat. I dug up roots and ate them raw. They were hard and bitter.

I thought about the only person I knew who would not try to kill me or reject me and the only name I could conjure was Kate, Ezekiel's wife. I hardly knew her. Had spent less than an hour with her, and yet, when I pictured her face it was a kind expression that carried no malice. She had whispered a word in my ear that had saved my life, and in so doing, had risked her own. Perhaps she would help me again.

At the edge of the woods I crossed over that which was black and entered again a world that was green. I rose up from the ravine and crossed the meadow between moor and clough. As I did I heard a sound. Something was crying – whining. I looked around but I could see nothing. I took another step and heard it again. A faint whining sound. Searching the area, I saw at the edge of the meadow, close to the beck, curled in some long grass, grey fur among the green. I stooped to examine. A wolf pup. Barely a week old. The wolf had given birth to at least three pups. Were there any others? I searched but found none. I picked up the tiny mewling infant. How had it survived all this time without its mother? I gave it water to drink and wrapped it up in my shawl. It desperately needed to eat and that made two of us. I didn't think I would manage to keep it alive – it was barely even breathing – but I would try. I dug up a worm and cut it into small pieces. I attempted to feed the pup the worm morsels but it was too weak to eat. I wrapped it warm in my shawl and placed the bundle in my bag. I took the gun and buried it under some stones. Ma was right. Hate would only destroy me. No good could come of it.

I made my way back over the moor, weak with hunger. I waited for night to fall so I wouldn't be seen, before approaching the village. I had no idea how I would find Kate and I wandered round aimlessly, traipsing around the green and the church, the alehouses and shops. I wandered round the streets where houses and cottages were placed, careful not to be noticed. I peered into every window, both back and front. Eventually I peered into one window and I saw a woman giving suck to her infant. It was Kate. I went to the window and tapped gently. I startled her and she looked up, puzzled at first. Then she saw who I was and still clutching her infant, came to the door. She checked that no one had seen me and ushered me into her home.

'You look half-starved lass.'

I sat down at the table and she brought me small beer and victuals. I ate bread and pease pudding.

'I heard about the fire,' she said. 'I want you to know, Ezekiel was nothing to do with it. He's still in bed. He got caught in one of the leg irons. Got infected. The physician came this morning with the barber surgeon. Stoker held him down while the barber sawed it off at the knee.'

'I'm sorry,' I said. I wasn't sorry in the least. I was glad that man had tasted a morsel of suffering. A small sacrifice.

'Well, at least he's alive. He never should have taken part in the first place. The carpenter says he'll make him a wooden leg. He'll be able to go back to work. But not walling or delving or sawyer work. It was

Hellström who started the fire. Lemuel tried to stop him. Apparently, he'd bought the forest and already sold the timber. Lost a lot of money. I've heard he's in big trouble. Although he paid Hellström every penny. Had to borrow it from another landowner. Better than that, Lemuel has paid us out! We've got fifty pounds, Caragh. Fifty pounds! We're going to find a bigger place. We're going to use the money to set up a business. I don't know what yet, but I don't want him to go back working for Lemuel. That has to stop.'

I nodded. I was trying to take all this in.

'And his friend? What's he called? Gad?'

I pictured the green gabardine.

'He's dead.' She shook her head. 'Mr Lane has given his money to his sister. The grace-wife who delivered this little 'un.'

I didn't know what to say. I knew of his death already and I didn't want to keep saying sorry. I looked down at my plate and used the last of the bread to mop up the remnants of pease pudding.

'What about Jenny? Where is she?'

'They took her into town. She's in the jail.'

At least she was still alive. Where there was life there was hope.

'What will you do?' Kate said.

I shook my head. 'I've no idea, Kate. I don't have any family or friends. All my kin are dead. I don't have any money, or anywhere to live.'

I thought about my parents' home in Ballina. I had kinfolk there it was true, but none that I'd ever acquainted with.

Kate got up. She crossed the room and opened the drawer of a cabinet. She took out a box full of money and handed me a note.

'Here. Take this.'

'But, I can't take that. It's your money.'

'I want you to have it. Please.'

'But, it's such a lot of money, I—'

She opened my hand and folded the note into it, curled my fingers around it.

'No arguments. You're having it and that's that. I want you to stay here tonight.'

And then I was holding her, clinging on to her, weeping into her sleeve.

She made up a bed for me. I asked her for some hot milk and when she had gone to join her husband in their bedchamber, I took the wolf pup out of my bag and spooned warm milk into its mouth. The wolf was barely alive, and it was slow work, just a few drops at a time. But after an hour it had managed to drink most of the milk. Exhausted by the effort, the pup fell asleep in my arms, and I swaddled it once more in my shawl and returned it to my bag. I slept in the makeshift bed Kate had made up for me.

In the morning, Kate insisted that I ate breakfast with her and afterwards she persuaded me to discard my filthy dress for a clean one of hers. Seeing I was without a shawl, for it was concealed in the bag, she gave me her winter cape. She wrapped up a penny loaf for me and corked a flask of milk. She put her arms round me and I sank into her. I held her tight, feeling her warmth and softness. I thanked her again and left.

As I trudged aimlessly through the village I came across a rowdy crowd. On the village green men, women and children had gathered. A man with crutches grimaced. A beshawled woman held her baby close to her chest. Men in fine tugs and hats were smoking clay pipes. Others supped from tankards. There were vendors selling food and ale. There was music from a fiddle player. Some danced a jig.

Amongst the merrymakers a tall man stood out. He was wearing a beautiful brown suit that looked newly tailored. He wore shiny black boots with gold buckles. His beard was trimmed and his golden hair was combed back high over his head so that it shone like a halo around his face. The man was Hellström and he was dancing with one of the young maids of the village. He held her tight, then spun her around as though she were as light as a feather. They were both grinning from ear to ear. I could see that she was basking in his attention.

I looked about to see what they had gathered for. Then I saw a makeshift stage and a gallows, its stark black frame made starker by the bright grey sky. It looked like the torched skeleton of some mythical beast. Two men were holding up a girl and lifting her onto a stool above a noose. It was Jenny. Her hands tied behind her back. She was still wearing the ripped dress and I noticed that it was also torn at the shoulder now, so bad that one of her sleeves was hanging off. Her flesh was badged with scabs and bruises.

I covered my face with the hood of the cloak and watched as they put a sack over her head and placed the noose around her neck. They tightened the noose as a man addressed the crowd, but I couldn't make out what he was saying, and I didn't want to get any closer. I thought about Alice and what had happened to her. The only way that Jenny could survive this was if the rope snapped and the curate and the magistrate agreed that it was an act of God. Under my breath I prayed for Jenny. This was the chance now that God had to show me his mercy. He was a loving god. He would intervene in the same way he had intervened with Alice.

A man kicked the stool from beneath Jenny's feet and she fell, then dangled from the rope. The rope did not snap. The crowd cheered. I felt the shock ripple through my bones. Her legs kicking at first, but then gradually slowing to a stop. Her lifeless body swung in the winter wind. The crowd were still cheering. Already the crows and kites were gathering. I stood and watched, desperately hoping for a miracle, for her limp corpse to reanimate.

At last I turned away from the hideous spectacle in front of me and walked out of the village. I was in danger – if I were to be spotted by this mob they would brand me a witch.

I traipsed north, stopping only when I was a good three or four miles from the village and sat down, unfurling the pup from my shawl. It was whining now and I gave it some of the milk. Then soaked a piece of bread in the milk and fed it this also. It fed with more strength this time. Perhaps it would live after all. I wondered again how it had survived all this time without its mother's teat. Perhaps Alice really had cast a protective spell.

Its little pink lips nibbled at the moistened bread and its eyes opened for the first time. They stared directly into mine, and for a moment I wasn't staring into the eyes of a wolf, I was staring into Alice's eyes. The moment passed and the eyes I peered into were those of the wolf pup once more. Perhaps I was going mad? In a world full of mad men and crazy women, would anyone notice one more?

If I could keep this wolf alive I would take it somewhere it could be with its own kind. I thought about what Alice said. In Scotland wolves were still in number. I would travel north to another country. I would go to Scotland and find a place where wolves roamed free of persecution and find a family for this wolf. I let the wolf finish the bread and milk then I swaddled it once more in my shawl, placing the shawl in the bag, standing and straightening my dress. I carried the bag over my shoulders and fastened the top button on my cloak. The wind was whistling through bare boughs as I began again to walk north. I was taking the last wolf in England to a better world.

Acknowledgements

All writing at some point becomes a collaborative act. I am extremely grateful to friends and writers who have been kind enough to offer comments, critical feedback and encouragement at various stages of the book's development. These are: Claire O'Callaghan, Simon Crump, Steve Ely, Jim Greenhalf, Sara Read and Lisa Singleton. Thanks to Anna Viberg for her help with Swedish language and terminology, and the historic detail around wolf hunting.

A special thanks goes to everyone at HQ, HarperCollins, and in particular my editor, Cat Camacho, whose feedback and suggestions have been invaluable, my copy editor, Cari Rosen, whose meticulous attention to details is much appreciated and my fantastic cover and map designer, Caroline Lakeman.

Bibliography

On Witches:

Witches: James I and the English Witch Hunts by Tracy Borman

Witches: The History of a Persecution by Nigel Cawthorne

Daemonologie by James I

The Dark World of Witches by Eric Maple

A History of Witchcraft in England by Wallace Notestein

The Lancashire Witches: Histories and Stories by Robert Poole

Yorkshire Witches by Eileen Rennison

Witchcraft in England 1558–1616 by Barbara Rosen

The Discovery of Witchcraft by Reginald Scot

Malleus Maleficarum by Sprenger and Kraemer

Religion and the Decline of Magic by Keith Thomas

Miscellaneous:

The Holy Bible

Gerrard Winstanley by David Boulton

Being a Beast by Charles Foster

Cromwell: Our Chief of Men by Antonia Fraser

The Shadow of a Year: The 1641 Rebellion in Irish History and Memory by John Gibney

The West Yorkshire Moors by Christopher Goddard

The West Yorkshire Woods by Christopher Goddard

Slang Down the Ages by Jonathan Green

The World Turned Upside Down by Christopher Hill

Thorson's Guide to Medical Herbalism by David Hoffman

The English Civil War by Tristram Hunt

Magic in the Middle Ages by Richard Kieckhefer

Of Wolves and Men by Barry Lopez

Into Another Mould by Ivan Rooks

Yorkshire's Forgotten Fenland by Ian D Rotherham

The Ravenmaster by Christopher Skalfe

The Family, Sex and Marriage in England 1500–1800 by Lawrence Stone

Wilding by Isabella Tree

The Forager's Calendar by John Wright

A History of Medical Psychology by Grefore Zilboorg

Trees – Octopus

Food for Free – Peerage Books

ONE PLACE. MANY STORIES

Bold, innovative and
empowering publishing.

FOLLOW US ON:

@HQStories